SOFT TARGET II

Tank

CONRAD JONES

GerriCon Books Ltd

CHANDLER
BOOK DESIGN

First published in Great Britain in 2009
by
GerriCon Books Ltd
Orford Green
Suite 1
Warrington
Cheshire
WA2 8PA
www.gerriconbooks.co.uk

Copyright © 2009 Conrad Jones

Names, characters and related indicia are copyright and trademark
Copyright © 2009 Conrad Jones

Conrad Jones has asserted his moral rights
to be identified as the author

A CIP Catalogue of this book is available from
the British Library

ISBN: 978-0-9561034-1-3

First published by GerriCon Books Ltd. 02/2009

Cover Photo: ©istockphoto.com/Arne Thaysen

Cover designed and typeset in Meridien 11pt
by Chandler Book Design, King's Lynn, Norfolk
www.chandlerbookdesign.co.uk

Printed in Great Britain by the
MPG Books Group, Bodmin King's Lynn

CHAPTER 1
Chester

The Vessel Princess Dianna was tied to its moorings, and swayed gently as the muddy waters of the River Dee flowed lazily around her. The beautiful white riverboat had been hosting floating parties on the River Dee for over twenty years. A crowd of impatient revellers stood on the promenade waiting to board the Dianna, many of the crowd were already inebriated and the volume grew louder as the safety rails were removed to allow boarding to begin. The partygoers were predominantly students from the local Chester University, celebrating the end of their second year. Chester was founded as a fortress town by the Romans in AD 79 and was the scene of battles between warring Welsh armies and the Anglo-Saxons for centuries. It boasts the best-preserved Roman walls in the United Kingdom, which follow the course of the river. The city's university was a magnet for students from all over the world. The banks of the River Dee and its' Roman ruins are a favourite tourist destination. The banks of the river are lined with wide tree covered areas, which are terraced so that people can sit and picnic close to the flowing water. At the centre of the tourist area high above the water a white suspension bridge carries a footpath from one bank to the other. Swans and ducks inhabit the area in large numbers fascinating young children and adults alike. Small cafe bars and restaurants, which are situated beneath the forty-foot Roman walls, are packed all year round.

The men that were invited to the end of term function were dressed in black tie attire, and the women wore ball gowns of every colour and description. Four waiters dressed in white formal naval suits adorned with gold buttons and braid stood on the afterdeck holding trays of champagne for the giddy guests to take as they arrived on board. The pilot of 'The Princess Dianna' revved the propellers in anticipation of departure, the water at the stern of the boat turned to white foam as the huge engines growled. The drunken students cheered and clapped as the water splashed and foamed; the Captain sounded the foghorn and the students cheered again, excited by the ships preparations to sail.

Ivan Coley and Matt Halt sat at a table watching the students board the riverboat. They were drinking pints of lager in the beer garden of a bar called the Boathouse, as they waited for their target to arrive. The riverside bars were always busy, especially on long warm summer evenings like this one. The two men sat unnoticed by the crowds of chattering tourists that surrounded them, until they stood up. Both men stood over six feet tall and were unusually heavily muscled; they both had shaved heads and a menacing aura. They belonged to a secretive fascist organisation known as the 18th Brigade, a splinter group of a more mainstream white nationalist political party that boasted over fifty councillors in local government. They were committed to stemming and reversing the tide of non-white immigration, by both legal and violent means. America and Europe had experienced the rise and fall of hundreds of small neo-Nazi groups since the demise of Adolph Hitler. In recent times, however the Internet and other technological advances had fuelled and moulded such groups into organised political parties and crime syndicates. Eastern Europe and the Russian satellite countries had experienced an explosion of organised crime, involving drugs trafficking and the sex trade. The majority of the successful crime organisations hold fascist ideals, and attract members of smaller Nazi groups into their employ. Ivan and Matt were two such affiliates. They were not fully aware of who was pulling their strings today, but they didn't really care. To be trusted to complete a mission of such political significance as this was a real macho ego boost. It would put the 18th Brigade on the worldwide map; people would have to take their organisation far more seriously from now on. The political muscle gained would increase their share of the drugs business, and that meant that a significant amount of money could be made.

A black Mercedes pulled slowly to a halt close to the Dianna's birth. A man of Middle Eastern appearance opened the front passenger door and stepped from the vehicle; he was wearing a red and white headdress, which identified him as a Saudi Arabian national. He scanned the area through dark sunglasses. The Saudi bodyguard reached for the handle of the rear door and opened it. A young woman exited the backseat and stood on the busy promenade. She was dark skinned with long jet-black hair and her eyes were a deep brown, almost liquid looking. Her hair blew gently in the breeze and looked like black satin. She wore a sparkling silver gown and appeared every inch to be a princess. Her name was Jeannie Kellesh and she was the youngest daughter of a Saudi Arabian diplomat, and the target of a politically motivated kidnap plot.

"That is her. The target has been dropped at the promenade. Wait until the driver and the bodyguard have left," Matt Halt said into a small transmitter that was fitted to his jacket lapel. Ivan Coley walked slowly toward the Mercedes and put on a pair of dark sunglasses. His size and demeanour made him look like a bouncer. No one in the waiting crowd paid any attention to him. The Saudi bodyguard climbed back into the black car and it drove away. Their instructions were to wait for the return of Jeannie Kellesh in an allocated parking zone two hundred yards away. As the Mercedes pulled off Matt took a small spray bottle from his jacket pocket and walked toward the Saudi Princess. She was standing alone at the rear of the waiting guests; everyone's attention was focused on the boat as boarding had begun. He squirted a fine mist into her face as he passed and she collapsed onto the floor immediately. The spray contained a concentrated chemical that was derived from chloroform and could drop a gorilla in seconds.

"Stand back, she has fainted. Give her some room please," Ivan said to the concerned onlookers as he pretended to attend to the fallen woman. He spoke into a walkie-talkie and called for medical backup increasing the creditability of their pretence as security guards. Few people in the crowd paid any attention to the incident, which seemed to be under control. An ambulance appeared almost immediately and two shaven headed paramedics exited the vehicle. The medics wore lime green jump suits as they went about their business with a concerned professional manner. They placed the Saudi woman on a stretcher. A guest who was already aboard the vessel thought he had seen a Swastika tattooed on the wrist of one of the paramedics, which he thought was a little odd. Within seconds Jeannie was put into the back of the ambulance and whisked away.

Ivan Coley and Matt Halt walked away from the promenade toward a car park that was a short distance away from the riverboat's birth, behind the Boathouse pub. Matt seemed extremely anxious to get away from the boat but Ivan just put it down to him being nervous. They had just orchestrated the kidnapping of a foreign diplomat's daughter after all. Excited students were still boarding The Princess Dianna gossiping about the poor girl that had fainted on the promenade. Shore crewmen started to unfasten the huge ropes that attached the riverboat to its rusted metal mooring rings, and the foghorn blasted again as the boat prepared to depart. The propellers roared again and a tall plume of frothy water erupted at the stern of the boat.

Suddenly an explosion from deep within the lower decks of The Princess Dianna shattered the vessel into a million pieces of flying debris. The bodies of those revelling on board the boat were torn into red confetti, and blasted over a large area of the River Dee. Only the lower section of the boats hull remained in a recognisable piece, still attached to its moorings. Ivan Coley was blown off his feet by the force of the shockwave, and he was still stunned as Matt Halt stooped to pull his huge frame up of the floor.

"What the fuck just happened then Matt? Please tell me that was nothing to do with what we have just done," Ivan said in a hurried mumble. He looked back at the ruined hull of the riverboat, and the unrecognisable scene of carnage that surrounded it. Panic was starting to cloud his mind as the realisation of what he had become involved in hit him. He looked at Matt for some kind reaction but Matt just ignored the question and pulled him toward their van. They had arrived at the river in a white Ford Transit an hour before, and had parked the vehicle behind the Boathouse. Ivan had noticed that the storage compartment of the van was packed with five litre drums of gasoline. Matt had told him that the fuel was required for a project later that week and Ivan had no reason not to believe him; they had torched two mosques and a synagogue only the week before, as inciting racial tensions was high on the Brigade agenda.

"Matt, tell me what just happened was nothing to do with us

grabbing that girl," Ivan spoke slowly and tried to hide the panic that was in his voice. They had agreed to kidnap and hold the girl for a couple of days, but no one had mentioned blowing up two hundred students. Ivan knew that the explosion must be linked to what they had done; it could not be a coincidence. They had reached the van and Matt was still pushing him forward and ignoring his questions. Frightened tourists were running for safety away from the river. Many had been seriously injured and screamed as they ran through the car park away from the carnage. Ivan noticed a young man carrying what looked like his own severed hand trying to open the door of his car; he placed the severed appendage on the roof of the vehicle whilst he opened the door and climbed in as if he were carrying his shopping.

Matt opened the door of the Transit van and jumped into the passenger seat, and then shouted at Ivan to do the same on the driver's side. Ivan opened the door and flopped into the driver's seat. He felt hot tears stinging his eyes and rolling down his cheeks. He felt like he was going to vomit as he watched a middle aged woman crawling away from her severed leg. Ivan began to rage inside as he assessed the hellish scene around him. He had not agreed to this. He was not averse to using violence but not against his own kind. Not innocent bystanders. He turned toward Matt and opened his mouth to speak. Matt sprayed the concentrated chloroform into Ivan's open mouth and he passed out before he could say a word. Matt grabbed a canister of petrol and poured it all over the unconscious skinhead. He placed a short black-haired wig onto Ivan's baldhead and then doused the rest of the vehicle. The vehicle was registered to a Blackburn man named Abdul Aziz; the hair would just muddy the water further, making identification near impossible. The discovery of a burnt out van belonging to a Muslim gentleman this close to the explosion, would send the police looking for Islamic extremists. Ivan's charred remains would give them a suspect. The fact that he was dead would make them think that this was a suicide mission and they would hopefully look no further. Matt grabbed another full container and covered Ivan with the contents. Ivan stirred a little as the liquid entered his mouth and nostrils; he coughed as the stinging liquid ran down his throat. Matt opened the passenger door and collided with an old man and his wife as they tried to escape across the car park. The old man stopped next to the van and asked Matt if he would help them.

"Fuck off granddad or I will give you something to moan about," Matt snarled at the elderly couple as they staggered away from the van toward safety. Matt struck a match and with it he lit a twisted piece of newspaper. He tossed the burning paper into Ivan's lap and turned him into a human inferno. The flames from the van shattered the windows of the vehicle with their intensity. A huge orange fireball spiralled fifty feet upward as the fuel canisters in the back of the transit exploded.

CHAPTER 2
Terrorist Task Force

John Tankersley was the lead officer of the Terrorist Task Force, a mixed group of civilian and military personnel that specialised in counter-terrorism operations. He stood over six feet tall and carried seventeen stones of solid muscle on his huge frame, his friends and colleagues called him 'Tank'. He walked slowly around the police cordon, which surrounded the scene of the riverboat bomb. Uniformed officers from the Cheshire Constabulary had sealed the area off from the press and the public. There had been over two hundred students on the vessel Princess Dianna when it had been torn apart by an explosion. Distraught family members and the press were encamped around the scene awaiting information.

Tank watched as a dozen, Scene of Crime Officers (SOCO) painstakingly searched through the debris of the bombing. There was an ever-increasing line of plastic body bags being formed on the car park of the Boathouse pub. The shapes beneath the plastic liners had no resemblance to a human form; they were merely remnants to be identified at a later date. A further two SOCO were busy analysing the remains of a burnt out van which was also on the car park. One of the officers noticed Tank's approach and removed a white paper suit from his field kit.

"Good afternoon sir, could you put this on please," the officer said passing the protective clothing to Tank. Tank wrestled his huge frame into the paper suit and walked to where the two men were working.

"What are your first impressions of the situation?" Tank asked as he ran his huge hand over his shaved head. He always did this when he was thinking.

"We are ruling out an accidental explosion. We have found fragments of explosive caps stuck into the boat's hull which would suggest a sophisticated explosive device was place below decks. The fire crews originally thought that this van might have caught fire as a result of burning debris, however upon further inspection it's obvious that an accelerant has been used. There is virtually nothing left of whoever this body belonged to and the way the vans sub-frame has melted suggests a large amount of flammable material was inside it," the SOCO explained.

"Could have been suicide attack then?" Tank pushed the scientist for his opinion. The next few hours of the investigation would prove crucial, but it was very easy to make assumptions and follow a wild goose chase. Tank wanted to be absolutely sure that they would at least start the investigation in the correct place.

"If you are thinking that it could be an Islamic extremist attack then I would be very careful," the investigator warned, "the type of device that use explosive caps similar to the ones that we have found, are far more sophisticated than we are used to seeing in this country."

Tank had to agree with the SOCO. Most attacks on British soil had been carried out using various homemade devices, which combined hydrogen peroxide with flour. It was an extremely effective explosive when manufactured correctly. The deaths of fifty two people and the injuries caused to seven hundred more were the result of such an explosive device on Thursday, July 7th 2005. British Muslim extremists carried out a direct attack on London's overcrowded public transport network using such homemade explosives with catastrophic results. The evidence from the riverboat scene was pointing to the fact that, the explosion that had destroyed the vessel Princess Dianna, had been caused by a plastic explosive substance such as Semtex. This fact made the involvement of extremists unlikely; it indicated the involvement of a military nature.

Tank had spent much of his military career in Special Forces operations. He had trained the counter-terrorist forces of a dozen different countries in the use of plastic explosives and covert operations, especially members of the Soviet Union. In 1991 when the huge Russian Empire started to collapse, so did the intelligence agencies of its satellite countries. This made thousands of expertly trained covert agents literally unemployed. Many became mercenaries for sale to the highest bidder, others used their talents to their own ends and crime organisations appeared all over Eastern Europe. Their military talents, which included the use of explosives, struck fear into the hearts of their enemies and law-enforcement agencies alike. Tank knew that whoever had manufactured this bomb had the knowledge that could only be acquired from Special Forces personnel. Furthermore, this type of explosive chemical was strictly weapons grade and difficult to acquire. Semtex and explosives in general have two grades, commercial grade for mining or demolition, and weapons grade for munitions.

"We won't be able to be more specific until everything is analysed at the lab, but we can confirm that the explosion on the boat and the explosion in this van were not accidental," the scientist said without committing any further speculative opinions. Tank nodded his thanks and walked through the car park toward the River Dee. A big yellow crane that was mounted on the back of truck was in the process of lifting the riverboat's shattered hull from the water. A four-foot brass propeller hung precariously from the wreckage, as it was swung toward a waiting low-loader. Tank noticed a dark scorch mark about three foot long in the centre of the hull. He waved to the crane operator to stop the lifting. The man crunched a gear stick and the boat hull swayed back and too from the chains which supported it. Tank pointed to a SOCO that was tasked with capturing photographic evidence and indicated that he wanted him to photograph the deep burn.

"What do you think caused that John?" asked Major Stanley Timms as he approached Tank. The Major was the head of the Terrorist Task Force and had just arrived on the scene. He was a Major in the Royal Marines for thirty years before his secondment to the TTF, a Green Beret with a war record that would make Rambo blush. He was the only member of the Task Force that called Tank by his first name.

"Hello Major," Tank greeted, "can you see the triangular shape of the burn?"

The Major stared at the scorch and could make out a triangular shape about three feet wide; he nodded to Tank in confirmation.

"It looks like the residual burn mark of IFD," Tank said, "An

'Improvised Formed Device' or shaped charge. They were first used by the Iranians to penetrate Iraqi tank armour. Now the technology has advanced and they are standard special operations tactics. The force of the blast is directed by an armour shield on one side of the device, forcing the blast in this case upwards through the upper decks. This is no amateur Major, it is Black Operations technology. This bomb was planted with the sole purpose of leaving nothing above it alive."

Major Stanley Timms nodded slowly and walked closer to Tank linking his hand into the crook of his elbow, he led him away from the crane. The Major looked toward a guard tower on the Roman walls. The walls ran beside the River Dee for about two-miles and offered a raised vantage point to the press and curious onlookers. At this point of the river the walls were set back one hundred yards from the water and towered forty foot above ground level. Some of the best viewing points in the City of Chester were from the great grey stonewalls. Tank followed his gaze, assessed the sight then quickly looked away so as not to attract attention. Tank could see that high up on the Roman walls, stood three men wearing dark sunglasses. They were wearing dark suits and Arabian Ghutra headwear; two of the men were looking at the scene through binoculars. There were hundreds of ghoulish sightseers lining the Roman edifice but these Arabian men were very distinctive and were definitely not tourists.

"I've had a call from Whitehall, John. One of the passengers on that boat was the daughter of a leading Saudi diplomat. They're anxious for whatever information they can get their hands on. We need to make sure that we do not allow any information or speculation to leave our team. The last thing we need now is the Saudi Secret Service orchestrating some half arsed retaliation," the Major whispered using the noise of the crane to hamper any listening devices that may be pointed in their direction. Intelligence departments all over the world now had equipment that could pick up a conversation from five hundred-yards away. Tank waved to the SOCO chief who was stood on the opposite side of the boat hull fifty-yards away. He placed his right index finger into his right ear and the chief copied his action. Tank nodded. The gesture meant that the crime scene could be under surveillance from undesirables. Without any undue activity the officers made the scene covert. Covers and canvas screens were used to cover anything that hadn't already been assessed, and all conversation about the evidence was stopped immediately. The general public on the Roman walls would never have noticed that anything had changed. All the forensic scientists were now aware that they were being watched by agencies unknown.

Two hundred young people had lost their lives to an act of terrorism, and it appeared that foreign militia were involved. Tank would take the culprits to task, and he wasn't afraid of anyone who stood in his way.

CHAPTER 3
The 18ᵗʰ Brigade

The 18ᵗʰ Brigade had been formed when a breakaway group became dissatisfied with the political wing of The British National Front. The political party boasted fascist ideals, which were intended to appeal to the growing number of people who were becoming concerned about mass immigration. The merging of European borders in the early twenty first century had allowed a tidal wave of foreign nationals to head to the British Isles looking for work. The appeal of high wages and a better standard of living was irresistible to poor Eastern Europeans. Many indigenous people were concerned with the crime wave that arrived simultaneously, and right wing political parties benefited from this demographic shift in opinion. Whilst contesting local elections were the British National Front's main objective, the more extreme right wing members wanted affirmative action. Their idea of solving the issues of Islamic extremism was to meet violence with violence. Their solution to the fact that the National Health Service and the education department were collapsing beneath the weight of immigration could be solved by quite simply sending everyone back to where they came from. The cost to the taxpayers for the running of maternity wards had spiralled upward by two hundred and fifty million pounds in a five-year period, with one in four births belonging to immigrant mothers. Forced repatriation was the panacea to all Britain's issues according to their racist opinion.

The extreme views of the Nazi element within the right wing political parties caused massive rifts between the opposing factions. Small breakaway groups were formed as satellite associations to the British National Front. Groups such as Combat 18, Column

88 and the 18th Brigade used the numerals 18 and 88 in their names as a reference to their Nazi ideals. The number 18 is often used to represent the first and eighth letters of the alphabet, A+H, Adolph Hitler. The same rule applies to the numerals 88, H+H, Heil Hitler. These small extremist groups were intent on violent action against people of Asian, Black or Jewish backgrounds. Homosexual communities were also often attacked. The predominantly Afro-Caribbean communities of Brixton in London were attacked with nail bombs several times in the 90's, and the perpetrators were found to be members of white extremist groups. A neo-Nazi also attacked two pubs in the Brick Lane area of Soho in 1999 because of its homosexual clientele.

The softening of Europe's borders brought a whole new swathe of extremism with it. The incidents of organised crime, drug trafficking and forced prostitution exploded across Western Europe. The once small, politically motivated groups now affiliated with massive crime families. The Russian Mafia was especially successful as they were staffed by ex-military personnel. Their profits were in the millions because their discipline was brutal. Mistakes or descent were not tolerated and the only way to leave such organisations was in a wooden box.

The 18th Brigade was a local organisation that dabbled on the fringes of foreign crime syndicates. In comparison to its Russian affiliates it was like the boy scouts versus Predator. They had been formed by Pete Dodge in 1998. Dodge was the landlord of a pub called the Orford Arms, which had first opened its doors to thirsty customers in 1856. The building was a huge grey-stone Victorian monolith. It had twelve chimneystacks along its black slate roof and it was three storeys high. At the rear of the pub was a large courtyard that was surrounded by outbuildings that once would have serviced a stables and coach-horses. The old stables that were once servants' quarters and the home of the stable-lads and grooms had become a fully equipped gymnasium. Pete Dodge used the pub as the headquarters of the 18th Brigade. Its' members frequented the bars and used the gym to learn martial arts and lift weights. The Brigade members operated a door security firm servicing the local cities of Liverpool and Manchester with over three hundred bouncers. Door security contracts, and the opportunities that came hand in hand, were big business. The standard charge to a brewery for a door supervisor was eighty pounds per man, per night; when all three-hundred men were employed that equates to twenty-four thousand pounds per night, seven nights a week, three hundred and sixty-five nights a year. The 18th Brigade was turning over nine million pounds per annum legitimately.

"Not a bad business for a bunch of Nazi thugs," Pete Dodge said frequently. When the profits from the sale of drugs within the licensed premises they guarded were added to it, then the sale of muscle and brute force was a very lucrative business. Providing door supervisors gave the 18th Brigade control of the drugs trade in the north of England and Wales. Cocaine and cheap ecstasy tablets were imported and supplied to the Brigade by the Russian Mafia. The 18th Brigade's network of club doormen provided contact with an endless supply of customers, and also gave them the authority to stamp on any opposition drug dealers that tried to operate on their patch. This gave them the complete monopoly. Steroid abuse amongst the doormen was an essential part of maintaining the Brigade members' size and fuelled the aggression that enhanced the Brigade's reputation. Gang wars between rival crime families were commonplace, but were often played down by the government and law enforcement agencies as isolated events. When the amount of money that is involved in the business is looked at in detail, then there is little wonder that rival gangs fought to control territory.

It was during a drug deal with Russian importers that Dodge had been offered the opportunity to be involved in the kidnapping of a young female student from Chester College. The job seemed to be simple enough for an outfit like the 18th Brigade, and it could only increase their credibility within the crime world. Dodge had over three hundred soldiers on the payroll and most of them were very bad men. Kidnapping a young girl should be a piece of cake, he thought. The Russian Mafia man offered Dodge seventy thousand pounds to deliver the girl to them.

Pete Dodge was only five feet three inches tall but had been a Judo champion in his twenties and he was no pushover. He had a stocky build, thick black curly hair and a drooping Mexican moustache, like an extra from a spaghetti western. He looked completely out of place amongst the huge skinheads he employed. The contract to kidnap the Saudi girl was discussed in detail, and the Russian was insistent that the snatch had to be carried out at the riverboat party, despite Pete's concerns about the number of witness's. The Russian had guaranteed that there would be a diversion set in place that would distract attention. Dodge had no inkling that the diversion was going to be a huge bomb. Now he had a major dilemma, the Saudi girl was unconscious and bound up on the third floor of his building, and every law enforcement officer in the country was looking for the bombers. The national news was saturated with the terrible events that had taken place on the River Dee. Fortunately there had been no mention yet of any kidnapping. The Russians had made sure there was no one left alive to mention the Arabian girl that had been taken away in an ambulance minutes before the explosion. Pete Dodge felt that he had been disrespected by his Russian colleagues but he didn't want a war, it would be bad for business.

Pete Dodge sat in small anti-room at the rear of the Orford Arms playing cards with four Brigade members. The men in the bar were all skinheads, large men, most of them pumped up on nandrelone injections and dianabol tablets. Four more skinheads were playing pool in the main room when the front door opened and two men walked in wearing dark overcoats. They approached the bar and asked to speak to Mr Dodge.

"Tell him Alexis sent us," said one of the men in an Eastern European accent.

The barmaid opened a serving hatch that opened into the back rooms of the pub.

"There are two blokes here that say Alexis sent them, and could they speak to Mr Dodge. Mr Dodge, that's a laugh," said the peroxide blond, she had at least two-dozen piercings in her face.

"Shut the fuck up Charlie and send them through here," Pete replied. He was balancing a fat cigar between his discoloured teeth, "be on your guard lads this could be the ruskies or it could be the police, either way it is trouble."

The two Russian men walked into the rear barroom, their hands deep inside their overcoat pockets. They looked around the group of bald men one at a time. The silence was deafening. The skinheads stared hard at the intruders, testosterone reaching dangerous levels. The atmosphere felt like the public house was about to explode.

"How can I help you gentlemen? Your boss Alexis said that he would telephone me about our business," Dodge spoke first.

"We have come to pickup our package; there has been a change of plan. I am afraid we need to move our goods immediately," the older of the two Soviets said, referring to the kidnapped girl, his accent was thick and guttural.

"I bet you do after the stunt you pulled. I would imagine that your property, as you put it, is too hot to handle at the moment," Dodge wanted the girl taken off his hands quickly, but he wanted them to squirm first, " I am afraid that the price has increased due to the extra risk that your little diversion has attracted. I also need cash on delivery."

"It would not be wise to anger Alexis, Mr Dodge, you should hand over our goods and then discuss your issues with him tomorrow," the Russian said, his jaw muscle tightened and twitched as he tried to keep control of his anger. The skinheads that were surrounding Dodge were big angry looking men; the Soviets had also counted at least another half dozen in the front barroom drinking and playing pool.

"Fuck off Trotsky and you can tell your boss to do the same. The girl will be kept safely until I receive one hundred and fifty thousand pounds. Pounds, Dollars or Euros are all acceptable as long as they are used notes. You can call it a bonus for all the trouble you have caused. Now leave my bar, you are interrupting our card game," Dodge took the cigar from his mouth and stubbed it out in the overflowing ashtray. He never took his eyes away from the Russians stare. The Soviet's jaw twitched again while he deciphered what the English man had said, the vein in his right temple throbbed visibly as he decided what the next step would be.

Terry Nick was the biggest Brigade member in the room. He was also the Brigade's Lieutenant and its' main enforcer. He stood over 6 feet tall and weighed nearly twenty stone. He was injecting nandrelone twice a day to maintain his huge muscle mass, and he held a third Dan Judo belt. Hand to hand combat was like second nature to Terry, so he wasn't scared of the Soviets, but he knew that the Russians were packing guns. They would never have walked into the Orford Arms unarmed, this was 18th Brigade's turf. Guns or no guns, he needed to call their bluff. Terry Nick walked up to the Russian that had been doing all the talking and pressed his nose against his face.

"Mr Dodge has just told you to fuck off. I suggest that you do just that," Terry snarled in to the Russians face. The Russian moved back slightly, the big skinhead's fetid cigarette breath repulsed him; he turned toward the barroom door as if he were about to back down and leave the room. Terry Nick turned toward his bald friends and started laughing at the Russians. The skinheads at the card table joined in the jeering but they stopped laughing when the Russian stopped.

The Russian looked set to leave with his tail between his legs, instead he picked up a square topped bar table and jammed it between the door handles, stopping anyone from the adjacent room from opening the door. He turned round in one fluid movement drawing his Berretta 9mm automatic simultaneously. The Russian fired two shots into Terry Nick's right foot causing a fountain of blood to splatter the ceiling with red dots. The monstrous skinhead toppled backward over the card table screaming in pain as his shattered foot burned in pain. The second Russian drew a .44 calibre Bulldog and fired it into the nearest Brigade member's thigh. He was a huge fat skinhead covered in Nazi insignia tattoos. The bullet smashed through his thigh muscle and splintered his femur into pieces. The fat skinhead grasped his hands over the massive rent in his leg in a vain attempt to stop the bleeding but the wound sprayed a red jet of fluid between his fingers. The Mafia man closed the gap to the table quickly and brought the heavy Bulldog revolver down in a clubbing motion into the screaming Nazi's face. His cheekbone imploded beneath the devastating force and his face collapsed on one side resembling a deflated football.

Pete Dodge and the remaining two Brigade members held up their hands in surrender while their two colleagues screamed in agony on the floor. The hatch burst open and the peroxide barmaid, Charlie poked her head through, an expression of shock spread across her pierced features as she took in the bloody scene. The big Russian punched her hard in the mouth splintering her front teeth and driving her incisors through her top lip. She was thrust backward from the small wooden opening and dropped out of sight. He slammed the wooden serving hatch closed and jammed a stool between the handles. The thudding noise of the 18ᵗʰ Brigade members from the front bar trying to gain access was reaching a splintering crescendo.

"Tell your people to remain calm and there will be no more violence Mr Dodge, we just want the girl," said the Soviet, "you will still get the money that was agreed if you hand her over and you and your men will live. If not Mr Dodge you will all die."

"Bring your vehicle into the courtyard and I will bring her to you," Pete nodded to the two frightened skinheads, "go up and bring down the girl. It's all right lads stay where you are," he shouted to the Brigade members that were still hammering on the barroom door.

The Russians ushered Pete Dodge to the rear fire escape and waited for the unconscious Arabian girl to be carried down the old wooden stairs. The girl was placed into the back of a black Ford Navigator and the two Russians kept their guns pointed at the brigade leader until the wheels were spinning and the vehicle lurched forward out of the courtyard and away.

Pete Dodge stood in silence for a long moment wondering what the next move should be. He had the men and the muscle to destroy and burn every Russian Mafia owned brothel and casino in Britain, but his drug supply would stop if he went to war. The British police did not take kindly to gun battles in the streets either, which made his men vulnerable. They could not carry guns when they were going about their legitimate security business, so they would be sitting ducks. The Russians had taken the piss out of him twice in two days. There would not be a third time; he would make sure of that.

CHAPTER 4

Terrorist Task Force/
Liverpool

The headquarters of the Merseyside Police Force was situated on the banks of the River Mersey in the city centre of Liverpool. The building serviced two thousand six hundred uniformed officers, a plainclothes force of detectives that numbered one hundred and fifty, and occupying the top floor was the Terrorist Task Force. The TTF was a mixed counter-terrorist force that worked independently of MI5 and MI6. They were tasked with dealing with counter-intelligence information that could not be dealt with by more legitimate law enforcement agencies. They were based at the huge red brick building, which resembles a fortress on the River Mersey. The police station had been built in the seventies when civil unrest was commonplace, so police stations were designed with a siege mentality top of mind. Trade unions were powerful associations that commanded the loyalty and respect of millions of nationalised-industry employees. Strikes were often used as a tool for negotiation frequently ending in violence on the country's streets. The race riots in the late seventies, which started in Brixton, London but soon spread to every major town and city in the country further influenced the architectural design of government buildings. The headquarters in Liverpool looked like a concrete castle with tall narrow windows like arrow slits, in the event of public unrest the building would be easy to defend by armed officers. Across the road were the River Mersey and the Albert Docks. The port of Liverpool is hundreds of years old and was for centuries the most important docklands in the world. The port was a key stopping point for boats, which serviced the slave trade. Now the Albert Docks were a tourist hub transformed from derelict five storey dark brick warehouses, into art galleries and restaurants. The buildings formed a large rectangular promontory, which protruded out into the river. The interior of the rectangle was a marina once used by slave galleys and cotton trade ships to resupply on their long voyages across the Atlantic Ocean. Now the marina was home to beautiful tall wooden sailing ships, which were modern replicas of ancient vessels. The Terrorist Task Force offices were situated on the top floor of the Canning Place building, which afforded a stunning view across the docks and the river to the opposite banks, two miles away.

Tank sat in a leather chair opposite Major Stanley Timms; their conversation had just been interrupted by the arrival of two senior task force agents, Grace Farrington, Faz to her colleagues and Chen. Chen was of Chinese origin and was fluent in English and Cantonese as well as several other Chinese dialects. He was slightly built but was a Kung-fu exponent of some considerable talent. His father had been a restaurant owner by day and a Wing-Chun teacher by night. Chen had been brought up learning the finer skills of both cooking and Kung Fu. He had joined the Merseyside police force immediately after graduating from Liverpool University, and had progressed quickly from a uniformed position into the intelligence-gathering unit. He was a natural selection for the new Terrorist Task Force when it was formed. Now he stood next to Grace Farrington with a computer disk in his hand ready to start the team briefing about the riverboat bomb.

Grace Farrington pulled up the chair next to Tank and nudged him purposely as she sat down. She didn't think the Major had noticed but he had, and he eyed her coolly. Faz was a stunning black woman who looked more like a pop star than a counter-terrorism agent. She was tall and lean, muscular around the thighs and arms but slim around the waist and hips. Faz kept her body hard and toned training in the gym with Tank and Chen. Her two male colleagues were mixed martial art experts and she loved to spar with them. Tank had handpicked her for her position from a group of prospective Task Force applicants that represented regiments from all three armed services, and the police force. Competition to be selected was fierce and only the best had even a slim chance of being a successful candidate. Faz had scored higher on the fitness test and combat shooting sections than every other female applicant. She had also beaten all bar four of the men. Faz was born to Jamaican parents in a suburb of Liverpool called Toxteth. The area was infamous because of its large black community, poverty and high unemployment. Tensions in the community had simmered for years and finally exploded during the national race riots of the late seventies. Grace Farrington's father had joined the army in his mid twenties in an attempt to seek out a long term career, and to escape the desperation that was felt by many of his friends, who were the same age. Unemployment was the highest it had been for decades, and gaining useful employment was difficult enough for white people. It was almost impossible for the black population. He had made a success of his army career becoming one of the first black Regimental Sergeant Majors in his regiment's illustrious history. Faz knew she would follow in her father's footsteps by joining the military, but she had surpassed all her wildest ambitions by being selected for the elite Terrorist Task Force.

When the Task Force had been created Tank had been offered the job of heading up the agency, reporting directly to Major Timms. They had worked together briefly during their military service. Tank and the Major were sent to Afghanistan to complete a Special Forces raid on a compound in the Hellman Province. Tank was the commander of a force, which combined American Delta Force members, and British SAS men. The mission was to extract or assassinate a Taliban warlord that was known to be operating from a heavily defended compound in the area. Major Timms had a gut feeling from the start of the mission, on which he was just an observer, that Tank had no intention of extracting anybody. He had been correct in his assumption. The warlord and his men were terminated without the loss of a single allied soldier. During the mission a Taliban soldier took aim at the Major, but Tank killed him with single punch to the throat, which shattered his larynx. Timms had noticed the expression on Tank's face had barley registered the incident. The Major knew that the leader of the new Terrorist Task Force would need to be able to command the respect of Special Forces and Intelligence agents on a domestic and international level. He would also need to operate outside of the usual rules of engagement that applied to high profile government agencies. The first name he thought of for the job was 'Tank'.

"What have intelligence got for us Chen?" Tank asked starting the meeting off.

"You all have the list of casualties from the explosion. There is nothing of great interest to note, apart from the Saudi girl Jeannie Kellesh. The list is a normal mixture of the different races, creeds and colours that we would expect at any British University. The Saudi girl is the daughter of a senior member of their Royal Family. He has been positioned as a diplomat here for three years, working from the Saudi embassy in London. His daughter was two years into a three-year course in English law. He has apparently been earmarked for the job of Interior Minister back at home, which he planned to start on his return to Saudi next year," Chen placed the computer disk into the digital projector and a series of photographs of the Saudi minister appeared on the digital screen.

"Now these two men are the dead girl's body guards, they are members of Saudi Secret Service. They have been making a lot of noise trying to gather information about who we think is responsible for the explosion. Counter-intelligence is telling us that the Saudis believe it was an extremist act carried out by Shia's Muslim followers, probably sanctioned by our friend Yasser Ahmed, the leader of the Axe group," Chen paused. It was only twelve months since the team had tracked Yasser Ahmed from America to the UK. He had attempted to carry out a number of suicide bombings using his affiliates across Britain. The team had foiled several attacks but Ahmed had succeeded in the bombing of York Minster, and the giant Liverpool Anglican Cathedral. Tank had nearly lost his life in a bomb blast planned by Ahmed and the mention of his name made pulses race.

"Our intelligence teams are telling us that the Saudis are preparing an airstrike against an alleged Ahmed sponsored training camp. The camp is situated across the Syrian border, which will antagonise the Syrian military. We have not confirmed or denied our findings as of today," Chen pointed to a digital map that had appeared on the screen. He tapped the screen and the satellite picture zoomed in closer. A group of brick built buildings appeared next to what looked like a small runway, which was carved out of the desert sand. Two civilian private aircraft were stood idle next to the largest building. Groups of armed men could clearly be made out moving around the isolated camp. There was nothing else close to it for one hundred miles.

"While we can't see anyone losing sleep if one of Yasser Ahmed's terror camps is bombed, the fact that the camp is situated in Syrian territory could destabilise the whole region." Chen sat down and turned off the screen.

Tank had a dilemma. He could use the disinformation that the Saudis were acting upon to eradicate Yasser Ahmed's training camp, but that could result in an armed response from Syria. His natural instinct was to let the Saudis blow off steam and take out the Ahmed sponsored terror camp. Tank still suffered from severe headaches as a result of the head injuries, which he had sustained thanks to Yasser Ahmed, during the 'Soft Target' campaign the year before. The surgeons had drilled a hole in his skull to release the pressure on his brain, which was caused by the shock wave of the blast. He also still suffered the recurring nightmares of seeing Yasser Ahmed's innocent younger brother dead in an autopsy photograph. He had been mistakenly tortured to death by a foreign government at the request of an unknown western intelligence agency, using rendition to ascertain information from extremists. They had incorrectly assumed that the innocent sibling was Yasser Ahmed. Tank had promised that he would keep Mustapha safe but he had failed, and he lived with the images, which still haunted him.

"Forget the Saudis for a minute and think about whom else could have planted a device as sophisticated as the riverboat bomb. It cannot have been a local cell, no matter how determined, they couldn't have acquired this type of explosive technology," Tank said trying to lighten his thoughts and think objectively for a minute. Thinking about Yasser Ahmed brought on his headaches, and seriously affected his ability to think rationally.

"Shaped devices are a special operations tactical weapon; therefore it could be any intelligence agency, or mercenary force from numerous countries. The burnt out transit van was registered to an Asian Muslim from the Bradford area, but he reported it stolen a month ago. The body in the van is proving to be unidentifiable because it is so badly burned," Faz explained. She was in constant touch with the pathologist department as they identified the victims using DNA and dental records. It was always a very tedious heartbreaking process. The parents of missing students had to surrender their children's possessions to aid the identification process, hairbrushes were the scientists first choice vehicle for recovering matching tissue samples.

"We have our intelligence teams cross checking eyewitness statements as they come in. Uniform division is trying to track down every tourist that was in the area at the time. Someone must have photographs or video footage of the River Dee prior to the explosion. An appeal for information is scheduled for the Crime-Watch programme on TV tonight. We still haven't read all the statements from the people that were in or around the Boathouse pub yet, because everyone ran away from the scene. It's impossible to trace everyone because the majority of people were day-trippers," Faz continued, "until we have collated all the information from uniformed division then we are speculating."

"I agree with Faz," Tank said, "Let the Saudis do what they feel is best for now. We can't influence their thoughts one-way or the other, they could be right about Ahmed's involvement. We should give it twenty four-hours before we inform anyone about our conclusions."

Tank's eyes met the Majors and a knowing look passed between them. The Major had his suspicions as to why Tank wanted to let the Saudis think that Yasser Ahmed was involved. Tank would grasp any opportunity to strike at Ahmed no matter what the consequences could be.

CHAPTER 5
Syria/Saudi Arabia

The Eurofighter Typhoon is a twin-engine, multi-role, strike fighter-aircraft. The Saudi Air Force had ordered and received seventy-two Typhoons in 2006. The aircraft is capable of sustained supersonic cruising at fifty thousand feet, which makes it difficult to track by radar. It reaches this height from take off, in under a minute. It is an air superiority fighter, which other Middle Eastern countries do not possess. The Saudi Minister for Defence, Abdul Kellesh, was extremely proud of this lethal addition to his air force. The news that his niece had been killed in an explosion in England, possibly sponsored by Yasser Ahmed, would give him the opportunity to demonstrate the awesome power of their air force to its' troublesome Arab neighbours. The countries of the Middle East were constantly flexing muscle as a deterrent against the threat of military force. The introduction of the Typhoon strike aircraft into the region meant that the Saudi government was now holding all the aces from a military capability point of view. Abdul Kellesh had persuaded the Saudi Royal Family, who held all the true political power and ultimately made important decisions, that the chance to show its neighbours the tactical capability of its' new air force should not be missed. The Saudi leaders had agreed that an airstrike was a just response for the death of Jeannie Kellesh. The Saudis were wary that the airstrike was to encroach on Syrian land; however the Syrians denied the existence of such terror training camps within its borders.

Previous attacks on Islamic terror training camps had never attracted international condemnation no matter what the scale of the attack. On August 20th1998, the Americans launched

Operation Infinite Reach, in retaliation for al-Qaeda attacks on the US embassies in Kenya and Tanzania. The embassy bombs planted by al-Qaeda operatives killed two hundred and twenty four people and wounded five thousand others. In response seventy eight Tomahawk Cruise missiles were launched from US warships in the Red Sea; several destroyed a suspect pharmaceutical factory in the Sudan, which was linked to the production of chemical weapons. In addition seventy five Cruise missiles landed on four insurgent training camps around Khost and Jalalabad, Afghanistan, leaving nothing but smouldering craters. In retaliation a Muslim organisation bombed a Planet Hollywood restaurant in Cape Town, South Africa killing twenty five and injuring twenty six. Protests were held across the Islamic world but international condemnation never materialised. The Saudis were banking on a similar response this time round.

The Ishmael terror training camp was positioned between the borders of Syria and Jordan. The camp had between two hundred and three hundred men there at any one time, learning the basics of how to shoot and maintain a weapon, and the manufacture of roadside bombs. Yasser Ahmed did not force any of the young men that attended the camp to stay there. Any one that wished to leave could do so. Neither did the religious teachers brainwash any one. The young men that flocked to the camp in Sudan and those similar in Afghanistan and Somalia did so of their own volition. Most of the volunteers were dedicated to Yasser Ahmed and his Islamic Jihad long before they arrived in the camps. Many of them had overcome huge hurdles and great hardship to reach the camps. Yasser Ahmed was receiving requests from all over the Islamic world for finance and logistical help with planned bomb attacks and assassinations on a horrific scale. These requests and the recruits that carried them, originated from the increasing number of disaffected young Muslims that were motivated enough to devote substantial parts of their lives to Islamic extremism. The Ishmael camp was isolated from the outside world and conditions were harsh. There was no running water hence the sanitation facilities for two hundred men gave the camp a permanent lingering odour of human sewage. Supplies of food and water were flown in daily in two small aircraft from Damascus. Financial donations from Islamic sympathisers kept the recruits fed and watered. Arms and munitions were delivered monthly on the back of Syrian military vehicles even though the government constantly denied the existence of training camps. The majority of training was carried out at sunrise after morning prayers before the desert sun became too hot. It was still early and the men were resting when the Saudi jets taxied to their runway takeoff positions. The insurgents were drinking mint tea or sleeping.

Six Eurofighter Typhoons took off from their base near Rhiad, Saudi Arabia. In under a minute they had climbed to their cruising altitude of fifty thousand feet. They were beyond the radar capabilities of Iraq or Iran as they headed over Jordanian air space into Syria. Two of the strike aircraft were armed with MBDA Meteor air to ground missiles, which had bunker busting warheads attached. The missiles would be aimed at the larger hangers next to the runway. The weapons were designed to pierce reinforced concrete structures before detonating massive incendiary devices, which carried napalm like chemicals. The devastating effects of incendiary explosions within the confined environment of a bunker would annihilate any human life within.

The second wave of Typhoon fighters were armed with AGM-84 Sidewinder missiles and Storm Shadow cluster bombs. The Sidewinders were designed to explode one hundred feet above the target showering the area with shaped metal charges, which could penetrate armoured vehicles and brick buildings. This devastating weapon was capable of destroying troops and armoured personnel carriers over a wide target area. The Storm Shadow cluster bombs were a very controversial choice of weapon. They were contained within a hollow rocket, which was filled with a mixture of airborne incendiary bombs and fragmentation anti-personnel grenades. They were designed to wipe out any enemy troops that had somehow managed to survive the initial airstrikes. The controversial part was that they also showered a wide area with anti-personnel mines. The ordinance was designed from a non-corroding plastic material, which left the mined area inaccessible for decades. The idea was stop the enemy from ever returning to the site again. The truth was that innocent civilians would become casualties for generations to come.

The first Typhoon unleashed hell in the form of four, MBDA Meteor missiles. The insurgents that were working or resting in the hanger areas never even heard the aircraft before they were incinerated by the burning liquid. The intense fires stripped flesh from bone in seconds, few men had chance to scream before their lungs seared as they inhaled the scorching air. When the young terrorists, whom were in their dormitories, heard the initial explosions they picked up the nearest weapons to them, and rushed outside. It was the worst place to be. They were shredded and burned to cinders in minutes by the shaped metal charges and incendiary devices that were descending to earth slowly on tiny little parachutes. The charges were set to detonate at different times to maximise the killing zones of the bombs to devastating effect. The two small aircraft that were used to ferry supplies to the camp, were turned into pieces of tin foil confetti blowing across the desert in the second wave of the attack. The final Typhoon approached the smoking devastation at Mach speed. Using the heat from the fires on the ground as the target it launched a five hundred pound Brimstone bomb. The shockwave was felt three hundred miles away in Damascus. There were no bodies to count and no DNA to identify. No one could confirm or deny that that the camp ever existed or if it was sponsored by Yasser Ahmed. No one could say that it was training a new generation of terrorists. There was simply nothing left.

CHAPTER 6
The Russian Embassy/ London

Roman Kordinski was born in Poland to Jewish parents in 1968. Jews were in the minority in both Poland and the Soviet Union, so his father drifted from one dead end job to another. His mother had died from pneumonia when he was four years old, soon after his alcoholic father left him with his grandparents and disappeared. The rumour mill said that he had been the victim of Muslim gangsters when he couldn't afford the repayments to a loan shark. His grandparents spent their meagre savings on what education they could afford for Roman. It soon became obvious that the young Kordinski was incredibly bright. He was selected for state sponsored grammar school and was taken to Moscow to complete his studies. Even at school his skills as an entrepreneur began to surface. He would split packets of cigarettes into smaller more affordable bundles, and sell them to his fellow students at a huge profit. Roman also ventured into the money lending business, loaning small amounts of cash at extortionate rates. One semester an older boy borrowed money from Roman but reneged on his repayments, embarrassing him in front of a group of his closest friends in the process. Roman had walked away very calmly from the boy and then doubled back on him. The older boy was discovered a short time later with his hands pinned to his wooden desk by his geometry compass. He had refused to identify his attacker stating only that he was a stranger with a beard and glasses. No one believed the boy, but there was no proof against the young Kordinski. The incident was brushed under the carpet and there were no late payments ever made again.

At nineteen he started a degree in business studies before

graduating from the Russian Law School three years later. Roman Kordinski and five of his university colleagues started a small company, which bought and sold crude oil and petroleum products from Iran and the USSR state run oil companies. By 1991 after a bumper year, and the collapse of the Soviet Union, they were in a position to float their company on the stock markets worldwide. The company was massively undervalued at just over 1-million dollars and the five friends bought their own stock at a huge discount between them. Roman and his best friend Yuki owned fifty percent of the stock. Roman had threatened a local bank manager to loan them the funds to facilitate the deal, however the bank manager refused to co-operate. Roman followed the banker's wife to the local school where she was taking her son the next morning. As they crossed the road to the school gates Roman mowed the mother and child down in his grey Lada. The wife suffered multiple fractures, which kept her in hospital for six months. She was too ill to attend her son's funeral. The bank manager had four other children to consider, and the next day the funds were made available for Roman to purchase the lion's share of his own stock.

Seventeen years on he was riding in the back of a bulletproof limousine accompanied by nine armed bodyguards, on his way to the Russian embassy in Admiralty Square, London. Roman had been summoned by the Russian Ambassador to a crisis meeting regarding his Russian businesses. The Russian government had always known that Roman had grossly undervalued the stock when it was floated. They also knew that he was responsible for the suspicious deaths and disappearances of the five other major shareholders. His close friend Yuki had died in a fire at his home four years ago. Despite the fact that the post mortem discovered the presence of cyanide in his charred remains a verdict of accidental death was recorded. Two other shareholders died together in an assassination attack, which was made to look as if it was conducted by Chechen Mafia men. The Chechen Mafia had denied all knowledge of any such operation and the finger of suspicion pointed back to Roman Kordinski. The last of the five oil pioneers had received a short prison sentence for tax evasion in Russia. The offence was minor but the Russian courts were making an example of a rich businessman flouting the tax laws. He was found in his cell beaten to death with his tongue cut out. The removal of the tongue is a traditional mafia tactic to identify a snitch. This unfortunate series of events left Roman Kordinski in the fortunate position of being one of the world's richest oil tycoons.

Roman had embraced the opening up of the Soviet Union in 1991. He had used his wealth and influence to build one of the most ruthless, diverse criminal organisations ever known. Legitimate multi-million pound companies masked the more profitable drugs and people trafficking trade. He specifically advertised for, sourced and recruited ex-KGB and Spetsnaz (Russian Special Forces) personnel to operate his illegal operations. Between 1991 and 1998 the Russian Mafia gangs targeted commercially strong businesses for their protection and extortion rackets. The fragile Russian banking system was initially used to launder vast sums of dirty money. The natural next step was to control the banks themselves. 1993 saw the kidnap and murder of ten local Russian bankers, 1993 to 1998 saw a total of ninety-five more bank employees killed for refusing to co-operate with the Mafia gangs. Gang warfare was commonplace as battles for territory and lucrative protection contracts raged across Moscow and the fragmented Soviet satellite countries. Religion split the gangs further as Roman hired only Jewish personnel and the Chechen gangs were predominantly Muslims.

In November 1996 Paul Tatum was assassinated. He was an American millionaire hotel owner. He purchased the Radisson-Slavanskaya Hotel in Moscow with a Chechen business partner. Several threats to the American's life were made when he refused to sell his half share in the hotel. He tightened his security, took to wearing a bulletproof vest beneath his business suit and surrounded himself with armed bodyguards. When his assassin struck his bodyguards did nothing to protect him as he was shot eleven times in the head and neck, the shooter obviously knew he was wearing a vest. Roman Kordinski was now a multi-billionaire. The problem was that the Chechen Mafia was now stronger in Moscow than his Russian organisation. The Chechen gangs were pouring their profits into buying arms and munitions to supply the Chechen rebels in their fight for independence against Russia. To them the business was part of a Jihad, a religious war against Russian invaders. It made them more determined and brutal than Kordinski's men, making Moscow a dangerous place for him to live. He had survived several assassination attempts and managed to avoid lengthy prison sentences by a mixture of bribery and intimidation.

Roman moved his operational base to the UK in an attempt to raise his profile as an international celebrity. It would be far more difficult for him to be assassinated in the West if he were in the public eye. In 2002 he purchased an ailing football club, and with his millions he attracted the brightest young talent available to play for them. He became a household name quickly across Europe and the West by donating publicly to popular charities. He made himself untouchable but he still maintained a heavy security presence wherever he went. Now he was arriving at the Russian embassy for a meeting he had been anticipating since the day he moved west. The Russian President had bullied the Kremlin into constitutional changes, which outlawed the ownership or control of Russian assets from outside of Russia itself. Roman Kordinski was Polish by birth and could not return to Russia without fearing for his life or his liberty. The Kremlin had served him with a termination notice, which effectively returned all his stock options to the state. His business interests in Russia, which were worth billions, would not be worth a penny. He had ninety days to comply and handover the running of the companies to the Russian government. His oil company pumped twenty-five thousand barrels of crude oil per day, with ninety days left that equalled 2250000 barrels. He had to force OPEC (Organisation of the Petroleum Exporting Countries) to increase the cost of a barrel of crude oil significantly, to enable him to maximise his profits over the ninety days that he had left. That is the reason why he had arranged for the kidnapping of Jeannie Kellesh. The Saudis thought that she was dead, although no body had been found. They would soon find out that she was in fact alive, however if they didn't cooperate with Roman Kordinski then she wouldn't live much longer.

CHAPTER 7
Matt Halt/Bradford

Matt Halt sat in the driver's seat of a stolen Mitsibushi Shogun, and considered his decision to defect from the 18th Brigade. He had the window open half way so that he could blow his cigarette smoke out of the vehicle. Matt was waiting for his new Russian boss Alexis, who hated the smell of stale smoke and always made a fuss about it. He was sweating and felt incredibly nervous as if he wanted to cry or laugh aloud like a lunatic. Matt Halt had joined the 18th Brigade after a short spell in Strangeway Prison for football hooliganism. He had been just nineteen years old when he became involved in the culture of football violence, being tall and lean for his age he appeared older than his years. Most of the violence, which occurs at football, is arranged by rival gangs or 'firms' contacting each other and arranging a battle at a designated venue away from the prying eyes of the police and genuine football fans. The adrenalin rush Matt experienced every time he went into battle was unlike anything he had ever experienced before; it also gave him a sense of belonging, a family. He had been unhappy as a young boy and eventually given into the care of his grandmother for safekeeping. Matt didn't really fit in anywhere until he joined the 18th Brigade. He met two brigade members inside prison who also enjoyed football violence. They took him under their wing and protected him from older inmates, then upon release introduced him to their leader Pete Dodge. Six years on Matt had climbed the ranks of the Brigade and grown into a steroid mass. He worked as head doorman for several of the Brigade's biggest clients, his intimidating size and penchant for violence had given him a fearful reputation. Matt's problems had started when his ego became as large as his reputation was. His position in the Brigade brought him into contact with their Russian drug suppliers. During one meeting he was acting as a minder for Dodge when dealings became a little heated. No weapons were allowed into such meetings for obvious reasons; however a Russian bodyguard who was protecting Alexis produced a box cutter blade, which had been hidden inside a fake credit card. Matt had been impressed by the covert weapon, but he had no fear. He had snapped the Russians forearm like a twig, stepped on his head and carved the numerals 18 into the Soviet's forehead with the man's own blade. Matt always carried a hidden weapon after that day, usually in the form of a neck knife, which looked like an innocent pendant but concealed a blade within. Once the situation had been controlled Alexis had taken Matt to one side and complemented him on his skills. Alexis told him that a man of his talents should be much further up the organisation than he currently was, earning a lot more money too. Matt had succumbed to his ego being stroked and started feeding Alexis with vital information from within the Brigade, culminating in the kidnapping of the Saudi girl, being party to the bombing of two hundred students, and murdering his friend and colleague.

Matt felt physically sick as he sat waiting for Alexis. His stomach was churning with nervous tension because he knew that he had crossed the point of no return. He had betrayed his friends in the 18th Brigade for the promise of power and money. There was no way back for him and he knew that when the Brigade realised that he had known about the bomb they would look for him. Dodge had told them to disappear for a couple of days after the kidnapping, but he would soon realise that they were not going to return. He had betrayed them and killed Ivan in the process; they wouldn't rest until he was found. Now only Alexis and his Organizatsiya (organisation) could protect him from prosecution and the 18th Brigade. He lit another cigarette and inhaled deeply trying to gain some comfort from the warm smoke in his lungs, none came.

Matt sat up quickly when he saw a small Asian man leaving a terraced house opposite him. He recognised the man as Imran Patel, his target. Patel was a Pakistani immigrant who had entered the UK two years previously to marry a British Asian woman in an arranged marriage. He had become disillusioned with life in the West and started to travel around Britain to attend meetings with extremist Muslim groups. Some Mosques were more militant than others, but his activities had brought him to the attention of MI5. He was now on a watch list of 2000 possible terrorists. Alexis had informers within Britain's intelligence services so acquiring the name and address of someone on the watch list had been no problem. It was Imran Patel's transit van that Matt had stolen one month before, the same van that Ivan had burned to death in. Alexis wanted the security services to assume the riverboat bomb was an act of Islamic extremism. Local uniformed police divisions had spoken to Patel regarding his stolen van, but they were not aware that he was on any MI5 watch lists, because the different agencies rarely swapped information effectively. Now it was time to cement the theory that Patel was indeed responsible for the bombing of the riverboat on the River Dee.

Matt jumped in fright when Alexis knocked loudly on the passenger window. He leaned over and unlocked the door allowing the Russian to climb in beside him. Alexis said nothing and nodded toward the Asian man waving with a gloved hand. Matt started the engine of the Shogun and slowly followed Patel along the road. Patel walked to the end of the street and turned left, a man stepped out of a doorway as he passed and followed at a distance. Imran Patel stepped from the pavement and crossed the road heading toward a newsagent. Alexis banged on the dashboard with his leather gloves, making Matt jump again.

"Now quickly hit him with the car, quickly," Alexis growled his instructions to Matt, and Matt stepped on the accelerator. Patel heard the screeching of tyres but by the time he had realised they were heading in his direction it was too late. The Shogun hit Patel with enough force to knock him over the bonnet. The Russian that was tailing him moved quickly and grabbed Imran off the road. Alexis jumped out of the vehicle and assisted in shoving him into the back seat of the Mitsibushi.

"What are you doing? Let go of me," Imran moaned confused. He had been shaken by the impact but he was not seriously hurt. He looked around him and could not fathom what was going on, two men were sat either side of him in the back seat of a strange vehicle. Alexis had sat to the Asian man's right hand side and he punched him hard in the stomach knocking the breath from his lungs. Matt watched in the rear view mirror as the colour drained from Imran's face. He looked small and very frightened. Alexi punched him again this time in the side of his head. The sickening blow made a dull slapping noise and the Asian man tried to curl up in a ball to protect his head from further blows.

"Who are you, why are you hitting me? What have I done?" Imran whined, starting to cry. He thought that these men were either racists carrying out a random attack or government agents trying to intimidate him because of his attendance at certain mosques. He had heard that MI5 were watching certain groups of Muslims, but he had never imagined that they would just snatch him off the street and assault him.

"Well my little Pakistani friend I have been told that you would like to become more politically active to help your oppressed Muslim brothers. I am going to give you that opportunity. You are going to become a famous martyr in the Islamic struggle just as you have always wanted," Alexis sneered. He lifted his elbow above the Asians skull and drove it down with brutal force, Imran's body went limp as he lost consciousness. Matt glanced in the mirror and saw the look of glee on his new employers face, he was not sure that he wanted to be on Alexis' team anymore, but he was sure that he had no option. He had an idea what Alexis was planning to do with Imran Patel; it would make the riverboat bomb pale into insignificance.

CHAPTER 8

Terrorist Task Force/
Liverpool

Grace Farrington hung up the telephone and clapped her hands together. The final pieces of the jigsaw were still missing but she had made progress. Faz had just spoken to Graham Libby at the coroner's office and he had confirmed her suspicions. She looked across the street from her office window and saw the huge Liverbird statues perched high on top of the Liver Buildings. The giant birds were the symbol of the Port of Liverpool and were a welcoming landmark for mariners arriving home from the sea. Urban legend states that the giant bird statues will remain perched, protecting the city, until a virgin walks beneath them. Grace thought that they would remain there for some time yet. She picked up her file and headed to the progress meeting.

Grace walked into the room where the rest of the team were gathered waiting for her. She placed a disc into the digital screen and it lit up. An aerial picture of the River Dee appeared on the screen.

"Forensics has finished compiling the information that they have so far. This is the where the boat was moored," Faz said pointing to a charred section of the riverbank. "Three hundred yards down river is a tidal weir. The weir traps anything of substantial size, which has enabled us to recover boat debris and bodies that would otherwise have been washed away."

Grace changed the digital image from the river to the picture of a severed limb. The arm, which had been severed at the elbow, still, had the hand attached to it. Attached to the wrist by a black strap was a digital camera covered in pondweed.

"The arm belonged to a mature student called Peter Mcraenor. He was a member of the Metropolitan Police Force for ten years until he took study leave to complete a degree course at Chester University. His camera was water resistant so the integrity of the pictures was maintained," Faz handed out copies of the digital stills that had been recovered prior to the explosion. The images showed students boarding the vessel, and half a dozen group pictures of smiling happy young people enjoying the party atmosphere. In the background was a crowd of guests waiting to board the boat.

"Watch the area to the rear of the crowd, specifically the two security guards to the right hand side," Faz focused the image to enhance a small section of the larger picture. A black limousine appeared on one of the stills, and the two security men seemed to move toward the passenger as she joined the queue.

"This is where it gets interesting. Peter Mcraenor must have seen something that made him become suspicious. It could be his police training, we will never know, however he switches to video mode here," Faz started the video sequence. The two security men were stood over the female passenger that had alighted from the limousine. An ambulance arrived and two shaven headed paramedics placed the prone woman into the rear of the vehicle. As they picked the girl from the floor Peter Mcraenor had focused in on the paramedic's wrist, it revealed the bottom half of a Swastika tattoo. As the vehicle left the two security men could be seen in the background walking quickly away from the scene then the screen went black.

Grace looked at the confused faces that stared at her and she smiled. Her eyes sparkled mischievously as she started to explain her theory.

"We have checked with all the function's organisers and there was no security company engaged to work at the party. These two men are not genuine security guards, however their uniform patches match those worn by a company called Brigade Security," Faz pointed to the company logo that she had acquired.

"Brigade Security are the business wing of the 18th Brigade," Tank interrupted, "they are a serious organised crime family with an extreme right wing political agenda. They run the door security and drugs trafficking across Liverpool and Manchester."

"Correct. That also fits in with the Nazi tattoo on the paramedic's wrist. There was no emergency medical team deployed to the River Dee area that day, before the bomb exploded. The ambulance is a fake just like the security guards. All of the men involved resemble 18th Brigade members. We are scanning their profiles through police files to see if we can get concrete identification," Faz cleared the image and Jeanie Kellesh appeared on the digital screen.

"Jeannie Kellesh is the daughter of the next Saudi Interior Minister and a relation of the Arabian Royal Family. She was two years into her degree course and was always shadowed by Saudi Secret Service, which we believe brought her into conflict with her family and bodyguards. The security men had dropped her off at the boat and then retired to a car park in close vicinity to the dock. It was literally minutes between her arriving and being kidnapped. The good news is that everyone thought she had died in the explosion, obviously she didn't," Faz shrugged her shoulders to gauge the reaction from her fellow agents.

"If we are to believe that a bunch of Neanderthals like the 18th Brigade have masterminded the kidnapping of a Saudi Princess then we must also assume that they have had help," Tank said, "they don't have the technology to build and detonate a bomb as sophisticated as this one."

"They certainly didn't have before this incident however, drug squad detectives that I have spoken to are convinced that the 18th Brigade are selling drugs brought in by Eastern European crime families," Faz continued, "the Russian Mafia are predominantly of Jewish extraction but the Chechens are Islamic. We know that both these crime syndicates use ex-military and Special Forces personnel that have this type of explosive capability. The van that was burnt out in the car park was stolen a month earlier from the Bradford area which has a large Muslim community. Uniformed division interviewed the owner of the vehicle, who is a Pakistani man called Imran Patel, briefly and released him. It has since come to light that Imran Patel was, unbeknown to uniform, on an MI5 watch list. He was frequenting several extremist mosques and placed on a casual observation list twelve months ago. We have two agents on the way to his house to pick him up and bring him in. There could be an Islamic link to the explosion on the boat if the Chechens were involved."

"It's possible. The 18th Brigade is a bunch of fascist bigots but they are also mercenaries so they would get involved in anything for the right price. Why blow up a boat in a violent gesture of

Islamic Jihad and then kidnap a Muslim Princess? It doesn't make sense," Tank said, "it's more likely that the bomb was a massive diversion to make everyone think that Kellesh was dead."

"Have we identified the body that was recovered from the burnt out van yet?" Chen asked. He took of his suit jacket, as he felt uncomfortable. This meeting was going to be longer than he anticipated. There did not appear to be any clear suspect.

"No, we haven't been able to recover enough usable DNA from the cinders but Graham Libby did find synthetic fibres welded to the skull of the victim," Faz answered, "It seems that someone wanted us to think that the victim had black hair."

"Why would anyone want us to think that? I am not following your drift," said the Major confused.

"The forensic lab is certain that the charred remains from the van had been wearing a black synthetic wig when it was set alight. They are also sure that the subject was alive when the fire was set. There is extensive damage to the lungs and stomach indicating that accelerant was poured down their throat. The only reason I can think of to put a wig on a dead body is if you were trying to hinder identification," Faz said, "especially if the victim had no hair of their own."

Grace Farrington walked over to where Tank was sitting and she rubbed his shaved head with both her hands.

"You could put a wig onto a corpse and set fire to it if you did not want anyone to think that the body belonged to a skinhead," Tank said rubbing his bald head to demonstrate his point, "let's prepare a raid on the 18th Brigade headquarters. We need to bring them in and question them immediately to find out if they are working with the Russians or the Chechens."

CHAPTER 9

18ᵗʰ Brigade/Liverpool/ Manchester

Pete Dodge had called a war council meeting. The council sat in a meeting suite that occupied the third floor of the Orford Arms. The council was made up of six Brigade Lieutenants and Pete Dodge. Any decisions made by the council were filtered down through the ranks of the18th Brigade and then out to other affiliated organisations that orbited the Brigade. Business with the Russians had always been risqué but in general it was a lucrative arrangement. Few disputes had resulted in violent confrontation because both parties considered money more important than petty feuds. Any friction was usually between rival gang members flexing muscle, and was quickly resolved via one-on-one violence. Fighting a rival soldier and defeating him publicly could rocket a gang members reputation sky high, visa versa, reputations could be destroyed just as quick. Racial tension always burned below the surface because of the Brigades Nazi ideals, and the Russian Organizatsiya being of Jewish decent. The bulk of the Brigade men had no idea that their superiors actually did business with the Jewish gangs. The kidnap plot had been a diversion from usual business relations, which had gone badly wrong. The Brigade now had two key men in hospital suffering from gunshot wounds and two more missing. Ivan Coley and Matt Halt had never returned from the kidnapping, and both of their mobile phones were diverting to voice mail. Dodge was concerned that they had died in the blast or worse, turned traitor and become involved with the Russians. He had received his money from Alexis in payment for the kidnap, but it made no difference. A line had been crossed and word had got out that the

Russians had turned the Brigade over in their own headquarters. There had to be consequences and they needed to be severe.

"Do you have all the information that I asked for?" Dodge asked the skinhead sitting to his right hand side.

"Yes boss. I have the address of thirty-two Russian owned brass houses, twelve in Liverpool, and fourteen in Manchester, and six around the Oldham area," the skinhead answered.

The brass houses were operated in the guise of massage parlours but were actually brothels staffed by Eastern European sex slaves. Forced prostitution is wide spread across the western world and is usually the result of people trafficking. Traffickers use coercive tactics to deceive their victims into believing that they will be freed on arrival in their chosen country. Fraud, intimidation, isolation and physical force are used to control and enslave female victims that believe they are headed for a better life. Women are typically recruited by the promise of good legal jobs that never materialise. The traffickers arrange the travel and job placements then escort the victims to their destinations where their passports are confiscated. The women then learn that they have been deceived about the nature of their new jobs and that they have been lied to about the financial arrangements. Most are told that they now owe huge sums of money to the traffickers, which they have to repay before their passports are returned. They then find themselves in abusive situations where they are kept in a form of debt bondage from which escape is difficult and dangerous. Forced prostitution is huge business and the Russian Mafia controlled a large piece of the market. They relied on the cash rich business to provide them with a constant income.

"We are going to hit them all at the same time. I want the women roughed up and the properties torched," Pete Dodge snarled, "We are going to cripple the Russian bastards. Synchronise the attacks for nine o'clock tomorrow night. Three men at each address, make sure the tarts are bruised around the face. I don't want them to be working for a while. If there are any punters in there then give them a good kicking as well. That should deter any regular customers from ever returning. Douse everything in petrol take any money that's on site and burn them."

Dodge made sure that the message would reach all his men that would be working security positions across the two cities that night. Retaliation from the Russians would be swift and brutal but they would be ready for it when it came.

"Make sure everyone has access to weapons, open the gunroom in the cellar and distribute the body armour," Dodge said. The priority now was to strike first and strike hard.

CHAPTER 10

Imran Patel/
Manchester

Imran Patel opened his eyes and winced at the pain that throbbed in his head. He tried to swallow but couldn't because of the gag that was tied tightly around his head. He could feel motion around him and he assumed that he was in the rear of a lorry cab or something similar. He couldn't move because he was bound with plastic bag ties. He heard the crunching of gears coming from the front of the cab, it sounded as if someone was unfamiliar with driving the vehicle. Imran heard the pulsating beep of a reversing alarm and then he felt the vehicle moving slowly backward before coming to a standstill. He turned his head to try and get a better look at who was driving the vehicle but he couldn't see them. His face touched the bulkhead of the lorry and he flinched away from the hot metal surface. Imran thought it was very odd that the rear metal wall of the drivers cab should be so hot. The engine was nowhere near this part of the vehicle. The truth of the matter was that there was a large thermo-chemical reaction-taking place in the rear of the refuse collection lorry.

Matt Halt turned the engine of the bin wagon off, and turned to speak to his Russian passenger.

"What do we do next Yuri? I am not happy about this at all. Alexis has done nothing but fuck me about since day one. He told me I was going to be placed in a senior position but here I am arsing about in a bin wagon with a Paki in the back. What's the score?" Matt was losing his temper but he knew it was because he was out of his depth. The Russians were too cold and too calculating for him to fathom them out. When he was working in the 18th Brigade everyone was informed about what was going on. Now he was always kept in the dark. The Russians used their own language when he was around excluding him from the conversation. Alexis told him to drive the stolen refuse truck to Manchester's Piccadilly railway station but nothing further.

"We need to fasten him into the driver's seat," Yuri said without looking at Matt. He checked his watch nervously as if he was concerned about the time.

Matt reached around the driver's seat and grabbed Imran by the hair, pulling him roughly into the front cab. The two men fixed Imran's hands to the steering wheel with more cable ties around his wrist. The Russian man smothered Loc-tight super glue to the Asian man's hands and pressed them to the steering wheel. The adhesive grips in seconds and Imran could not move them at all. He was starting to panic. Tears ran down his face into the gag and he sobbed uncontrollably. Matt placed three thick elastic bungee cords around Imran's waist and fastened them behind the driver's seat. Two more bungees were attached roughly around the weeping man's legs and then fastened to the metal frame beneath the seat. Imran wanted to plead with the men but he couldn't make himself understood. He squeezed his eyes closed tightly in a futile attempt to escape this horrific situation. He opened his eyes wide when he smelled petrol fumes and heard liquid being poured around him. Matt Halt doused the cab with petrol and then doused Imran Patel with the remaining liquid.

"This is twice in one week I have done this so, don't you worry. I know what I'm doing," Matt said to the struggling man. Matt was working on autopilot as he covered Imran with fuel. It was his way of disassociation. Imran was no longer a human and this was just another job. "Right. We are ready to rock and roll. What's next?"

"Wait at the back of the truck," Yuri said as he opened the passenger door and jumped down onto the pavement. The truck was parked at the top of a steep slope facing toward the main entrance of the busy rail terminal, which was situated at the bottom of the hill. The front of the terminus was built in crescent shape and was made of glass from ceiling to floor. Above the station entrance hall was six floors of expensive office space. Matt thought the idea was to roll the burning truck into the station with Imran Patel at the wheel, which would link him to the riverboat bomb and deflect attention from the Russian Organizatsiya. There was however more to the plot than he realised. Matt reached the back of the wagon and strong fumes greeted him. The smell was pungent and urine like. Yuri walked to the back of the bin wagon and looked Matt Halt in the eyes.

"It's a real pity that you are such a fat fuck," Yuri said smiling at the huge skinhead.

"You said what?" Matt replied reaching for the blade that he wore around his neck. He knew that the Russians carried weapons all the time but he couldn't understand why Yuri had chosen this moment to start an altercation. Yuri pulled out a 9mm Beretta with a silencer attached. Matt froze in fear when he saw the dull metal gun pointed at him. He thought that a brutal justice was coming to greet him. This was payback for becoming a murdering traitor. The gun spat three times and high velocity bullets smashed into Matt's huge chest. He collapsed to the floor clutching his ruined body and the light started to fade from his eyes.

"Like I was saying it's a pity that you are such a fat fuck because now I have to pick you up," Yuri said grabbing Matt's dying body from the pavement. He lifted him over the edge of the bin wagon and into the crushing well of the refuse truck. Yuri pressed the start button and the metal crushing plate descended on Matt Halt squashing his massive body to a bloody pulp, and then it dragged him into the refuse hold alongside three tons of ammonium nitrate.

Ammonium nitrate is a chemical used as fertiliser. It decomposes into highly flammable gases including oxygen when it's heated or compressed. It has been used many times as an explosive by terrorist organisations. The explosion can be triggered by compressing the ammonium nitrate then, either igniting it with a flame, or initiating the blast with an explosive charge in the mixture. In 2004 a North Korean freight train carrying ammonium nitrate exploded near the Chinese border killing one hundred and sixty two people, and injuring over three thousand others. An important railway station was destroyed along with nearly eight thousand homes. A crater five hundred meters long and ten meters deep was left at the seat of the explosion. The secretive Korean government blamed human error for the explosion, however it was in fact an attempt to assassinate the Korean leader Kim Jong-II, who was scheduled to be passing through the station at the time of the explosion, but had changed his itinerary at the last minute.

Yuri pressed the red button again and the press crushed the Ammonium Nitrate to a highly unstable explosive mass. He pulled the pin from a phosphor grenade and tossed it into the back of the truck. The truck weighed nine tons and was filled with three tons of compressed explosive. It had in effect been transformed from a bin wagon into a twelve-ton fragmentation grenade. Yuri opened the driver's door and released the handbrake. Imran Patel tried to scream beneath his chocking gag when Yuri tossed a burning box of matches into the cab igniting the petrol that covered him. The huge refuse collection truck rumbled forward down the steep slope toward the busy rail terminus. It gained speed as it approached the station and flames roared from the windows of the driver's cab as they exploded from the scorching heat inside the vehicle. The truck bounced over the kerbstones and ploughed into the glass frontage of the station showering rail passengers with broken glass and twisted metal frames. The bin wagon seemed to lumber to a standstill inside the main passenger hall when the grenade in the back exploded. The truck's thick metal walls contained the explosion from the grenade, but the intense heat of the phosphor grenade ignited the decomposing gasses from the Ammonium Nitrate. The huge metal truck disintegrated into a deadly spray of twisted shrapnel. Everyone within a hundred yards of the blast was shredded.

CHAPTER 11

Task Force V's
18th Brigade

Tank exited the side door of a black Mercedes Vito van and checked all the fastenings on his battle vest; Grace Farrington was close behind him checking hers. Uniformed officers, led by Chen, were taking up positions at the rear of the Orford Arms; its' towering chimney pots and tall arched windows resembled a scene from a history book. Two police vans parked at the side of the building to stop anyone exiting the courtyard gates. There were six Terrorist Task Force agents plus Tank, Faz and Chen, supported by an Armed Response Unit which consisted of twenty men that were dressed like Robo-cop. Local law enforcement units had shared detailed knowledge with the Task Force about the layout of the building. It was like a rabbit warren inside. The building had four storeys above ground level, a courtyard and annexe buildings to the rear. In addition there was a cavernous beer cellar below ground. There were rumours of a hidden arm cache, which previous raids had failed to uncover, but none of the undercover agents could confirm or deny its existence. The 18th Brigade had been under covert investigation for several years. The Merseyside Police Force and the Greater Manchester divisions had undercover officers planted in the ranks of the Brigade, and their positions were well established within the organisation. They were in the process of building cast iron cases against Pete Dodge and his Lieutenants for offences including drug trafficking, racketeering, extortion and incitement to racial violence. The offences that the traditional enforcement agencies were investigating were beyond the jurisdiction of the Terrorist Task Force. The riverboat bomb changed that forever. The full attention of International Secret Service Agencies was now firmly focused on the Eastern European, Russian and Chechen operations of a dozen gangs. That included their affiliate organisations such as the 18th Brigade. The apparent kidnap of Jeannie Kellesh was linked to one or all of them, and had the potential to throw the Middle East into chaos.

Tank flicked the safety catch of his 9mm Glock 19, and replaced it in his shoulder holster. Faz did likewise and then she entered the front doors, which led into the main barroom. Four skinheads were playing pool at the right hand side of the room, three more were leaning on the bar holding pint pots of beer. The room descended into complete silence when the door opened and an Afro-Caribbean woman walked in armed to the teeth. The barmaid on duty was peroxide blond with at least an inch of dark black roots showing, and a dozen facial piercings. She was cleaning a glass when Faz walked through the front doors, and as she looked up to greet the new arrival Faz noticed heavy bruising beneath the woman's eyes. It was as if time had stood still for a moment. The man taking a shot on the pool table completely missed the ball, his friend almost choked on a mouthful of beer. The barmaid dropped the glass she was cleaning as the shock of a black woman entering the Orford Arms sunk in. Tank followed her closely and he laughed as he saw the confused expressions on the faces of the Orford's Nazi clientele. Tank's appearance confused them further still because he looked like he belonged in the 18th Brigade. He flashed a badge at the barmaid and asked to speak to Pete Dodge. Faz made her way over to the doorway next to the pool table, where she could see four men playing cards at a table in the small back room. One of the men fitted the description of Pete Dodge; the men stared in silence at the dark skinned woman, venom in their eyes.

"Who's asking?" said one of the men at the bar. He was wearing a green United States Air Force, bomber jacket; bleached jeans and high cut Doc Martin boots. The big skinhead was the epitome of white power skins. He stepped closer to Tank as he spoke, which unfortunately for him was a huge mistake.

Tank's hand speed was incredible for such a big man. His right hand shot toward the advancing skinhead and smashed into his larynx with his fingers extended into what martial artists call a knife hand. When the fingers are straightened tightly together they become a lethal weapon if they are used in a stabbing motion against the softer areas of an opponent's body, such as the throat or eyes. Tank drove his extended fingers hard into the windpipe area. The skinhead folded from the knees and he dropped onto the barroom floor gasping for breath. A second Brigade man swung a clumsy punch toward Tank, who stepped inside the blow and drove a powerful head butt into the skinhead's face, crushing his nose and fracturing his cheekbone simultaneously. The unconscious Brigade man rocked back violently against the wooden bar cracking his skull, and then joined his colleague on the floor.

Faz watched the men in the back room. They stopped playing cards when they heard the altercation in the front bar. She sensed movement behind her. A pool cue whistled through the air aimed for her head, she ducked beneath the blow and the cue shattered against the wall. Faz kicked hard at her attacker's knee joint. The heel of her foot connected with the skinhead's kneecap snapping the joint backward with an audible crack. He screamed and fell beneath the pool table clutching his shattered limb. Faz stamped her foot hard into his temple and he fell silent. She pulled her 9mm Glock to discourage any further attacks and the advancing skinheads stopped in their tracks.

"Pete Dodge is in the back room Tank," Faz said covering the remaining Brigade members with her weapon.

Uniformed officers entered and started to handcuff the Brigade men in the front bar. One of the card players launched a pint glass at Faz and it smashed against the wooden doorframe close to her head, causing her to turn away for a moment. When she looked back Pete Dodge and his affiliates were disappearing down the cellar steps.

"I'll go first, you cover my back," Tank said as he reached the top of the basement stairs. He flicked the light switch but nothing happened. He tried it again but the cellar stayed in darkness. Faz reached into a small black belt pouch and retrieved two mag-lights. They clicked them on top of their gun barrels to illuminate the staircase and the cellar beyond. Tank advanced down the steps into the darkness, his mag-light gave him a limited field of vision. The smell of stale beer became stronger as reached the cellar floor; the staircase creaked loudly behind him as Faz descended. The cellar seemed to stretch forever in both directions.

"I'll take left, you go right," Faz said sticking to the contours of the cellar wall as she disappeared out of sight. Tank nodded a silent confirmation and crouched low as he headed in the opposite direction. He stopped suddenly as he heard the clattering of an aluminium beer barrel ahead of him somewhere in the gloom. He shone his mag-light in a wide arc around the huge basement trying to locate the fugitives. A barrel clanged against the concrete floor and the silhouette of a large Brigade man loomed behind it. The deafening noise of a 12-bore Mossberg shotgun being discharged echoed through the darkness. The blast showered sparks as it slammed against the stonewall narrowly missing Tank. Tank fired three times in the direction of the gun-flash. A muffled shriek and the sound of barrels clattering indicated that he had struck his target, the clatter of the shotgun falling on the concrete floor echoed through the cellar.

Faz froze when she heard the gunfire coming from the direction that Tank had taken. She pressed herself flat against the cellar wall and listened intently, the sound of breathing was coming from a dark corner of the basement that she couldn't see clearly. The breathing sounded laboured, the gunfire had obviously made someone nervous. Suddenly a Brigade man broke cover and ran toward Faz's position. He held a Scorpion machine pistol in his hands and he fired it's deadly high velocity bullets in a random arc. The Scorpion can release one hundred high velocity bullets a minute and the brigade man unleashed a lethal barrage. Bullets ricocheted in all directions and Faz knelt behind a metal beer barrel for cover. The skinhead was twenty-yards away when Faz aimed the 9mm Glock and pumped five bullets into the man's chest and midriff. He staggered and fell knocking over a shelf containing spirit bottles. The bottles shattered on the concrete floor, their contents spilling across a wide area of the basement. The wounded man tried desperately to stand and raise his weapon. Faz fired again and the bullet left a ragged bloody hole in his forehead as it entered his skull and turned his brains to grey mush. The high velocity bullet exited his brain taking a large chunk of bone with it; the bullet struck the cellar wall and sparks sprayed the air. The hot metal fragments landed in the pool of alcohol and a huge wall of flame erupted from the basement floor.

Tank heard the unmistakable noise of an automatic machine gun behind him, and then saw the flickering glow of flame spreading from the far end of the basement, where Grace had headed. Tank knew Grace was the best agent he had worked with, but their sexual relationship had developed into something much more. He had become worried for her safety in a way he would never be about other agents. There could be no room for emotions in a firefight. He couldn't remain down there for much longer or the basement would become a tomb. A square of light appeared in the basement ceiling about sixty-yards ahead of him. Tank realised that a delivery hatch had been opened as an escape route. He raised his weapon and aimed at the open hatch, waiting for a target to immerge into the light. For what felt like an age nothing happened. Someone was waiting for him to disclose his position. There was a sudden flash of light from below the hatch, and a deafening roar as another Mossberg 12-gauge shotgun unleashed its deadly load. Tank ducked behind a barrel for cover and watched dismayed as the silhouette of a man sprinted up the delivery hatch stairs to freedom. The shotgun blast had been covering fire for one man to escape, and the chances of them repeating the process were good. Tank steadied the Glock on top of the barrel he was using for cover, and he felt sweat trickling down his back as he tensed for the shot. The Mossberg roared again and again, both loads of shot crashing into the low ceiling, shattering fluorescent light tubes into a thousand pieces, forcing Tank to cover his eyes for precious seconds.

At the other end of the cellar Faz moved quickly away from the spreading inferno and headed toward Tank's position. She navigated between the cellar's paraphernalia silently, keeping the Glock aimed in front of her. She saw the delivery hatch opening and spotted Tank's muscular frame taking cover from a shotgun blast. He looked as if were about to fire when another shadowy figure appeared behind him. Tank was caught cold; he had not heard the assailant creeping up on him in the dark. Faz fired twice at the figure knocking the man off his feet as the bullets slammed into his back. A second later the shape of a man appeared on the delivery hatch stairs and Tank fired. The figure seemed to continue unaffected for a moment, then he span off the staircase completing a bizarre cartwheel as he crashed to the cellar floor.

"Thanks, I owe you one," Tank said to Grace as she caught up. She nodded her affirmation and took up a covering position next to him. He shone his mag-light along the cellar wall. A large wine rack had been pushed aside revealing a small room hidden behind it that was fitted with gun racks. The racks were nearly empty. Tank looked at Faz and they silently acknowledged that empty gun racks were a very bad omen. They headed toward the safety of the delivery hatch away from the spreading flames.

The courtyard was like a scene from a Second World War movie. Tank counted over a dozen men lined up against the walls with their hands cuffed behind them. Uniformed policemen were bundling them into the back of prison vans. Chen approached Tank shaking his head.

"There is no sign of Pete Dodge. He must be still be in the cellar," Chen said.

"Did you see anyone coming out of that delivery hatch before we did?" Tank said, knowing that he saw someone escape from the cellar.

"We were busy rounding up this bunch of Storm Troopers! I didn't notice anyone," Chen said, alluding to the numerous Nazi tattoos that the Brigade men displayed.

Tank knew that the 18th Brigade leader had escaped capture. He was concerned that Dodge was at liberty. Tank had no idea what was planned for nine o'clock that evening. The 18th Brigade was fully armed and set to strike back at their Russian partners in retaliation for the Kellesh incident. Tank turned to watch the advancing flames as they spread up the building from the cellar threatening to devour it. They could hear small explosions from the cellar as bottles of spirits were engulfed by the flames.

"Do you think we should call the fire department?" Chen asked sarcastically.

"I can't see any fire, let it burn" Tank said walking away.

CHAPTER 12

Saūdi Arabian Embassy/ London

Omar Kellesh had been relieved of his duties as a diplomatic ambassador on compassionate grounds. He had insisted on waiting for the British government to complete their investigations into the riverboat bomb before he would consider returning to Saudi. Muslim tradition prefers that the burial of a loved one should be performed within twenty four hours of the death. Omar still did not have a body to bury which compounded his grief. Jeannie was his youngest daughter and had been the most troublesome; she was incredibly bright and determined to be educated in a Western university. Women in Saudi Arabia are forbidden to drive motorcars and are used in marital chess games to bolster political standing. Jeannie was determined to choose her own destiny, aspiring to become a female barrister of law in her homeland. She could wrap her father around her little finger and he conspired with his daughter to help her achieve her ambitions. Such was his love for his daughter he was prepared to compromise tradition, to make her happy. Now he was haunted by his decision, and guilt had become his permanent companion.

There was a knock on his door, which released him from his tortured thoughts. He opened the door and his minder stepped into his living quarters.

"There is a telegram for you Sheik," the Arabian bodyguard said handing Omar a small padded envelope, "I have taken the liberty of scanning the contents so that we know it is safe. The Saudis were at full alert in case of violent retaliation from the sympathisers of the Axe terrorist organisation, following the bombing of their training camp in Syria. Threats had been forthcoming that Saudi interests would be sanctioned as legitimate targets; any threats from Yasser Ahmed had to be taken seriously. The Saudi Royal Family had become pariah amongst the more extreme factions of Islam. Their country is the biggest oil-producing nation on the planet yet the wealth of the average man on the street had not increased in the last twenty years. Educational standards had soared in recent years with the introduction of universities, however young disaffected Muslims with university degrees still could not find well paid employment in their own country. The Royal Family became more decadent, owning huge ornamental palaces and racehorses while the poor stayed poor.

In 1990 at the end of the Soviet-Afghan conflict thousands of Arab Mujahideen returned to their homes in the Middle East. One of them was a Muslim war hero called Osama bin Laden. In September 1990 in the city of Riyadh he had requested an audience with Crown Prince Sultan, who was then the Minister for Defence. Bin Laden attended the meeting accompanied by a group of senior Afghan Mujahideen leaders. They were all well respected as soldiers of Islam, and prominent veterans from the war in Afghanistan. Osama bin Laden submitted a five-page proposal to the Crown Prince, which described his plan to gather an Islamic army, which could respond to any Christian or Jewish aggressors. He proposed to convince the Saudi Royal Family that he could raise an army of Islamic militants, and war veterans who could protect the kingdom of Saud under bin Laden's command. The fact that the kingdom needed to be protected was not in doubt, and bin Laden was playing on the political uncertainty in the region to sway favour. On August the 2nd of the same year Saddam Hussein had invaded Kuwait and now appeared to be threatening Saudi Arabia itself. The Saudi Royal Family were terrified at the thought of a fully armed extremist force that could number two hundred and fifty thousand based outside their palaces. It would threaten their regime from within and would be a formidable enemy within its own borders. Osama bin Laden's proposal was rejected and a week later the Saudis' Government accepted the offer of American military assistance. Within days US forces arrived in the land known to Muslims as 'the land of two holy places'. The fact that the Saudis had refused bin Laden's offer of an international Islamic army came as a profound shock to the entire area. Iraqi tanks moved into

Kuwait City with the same seismic shock as the Soviet invasion of Afghanistan, and it was the despised American government that was asked for help. The Saudi Royal Family always justified its position of power by visually displaying its' religious credentials. They had funded bin Laden and his Mujahideen in their war against Russia, and they protected and maintained the crucial holy cities of Mecca and Medina; but they did not trust him and the hard liners to build an Islamic army on their own doorstep. The willingness to accept thousands of American soldiers to be stationed in their country stunned many Saudi Arabians. The Saudi government had adhered to the teachings of Islam, which insists that there should never be two religions in the Holy Land. The building of churches and synagogues were banned, but now the defence of the kingdom itself was in the hands of the US military. Osama bin Laden and his followers such as Yasser Ahmed took umbrage with the Saudis and they had to be on their guard against militants at all times.

In the embassy Omar opened the envelope and looked inside. His troubled mind could make no sense of its contents. He tipped the envelope upside down and emptied the contents into his left palm. There was a small electronic chip and a decorated synthetic thumbnail. He stared at the nail and the clouds of confusion started to clear. He recognised the fine artwork and a small diamante jewel that sparkled from the corner of the nail. He picked it up and held it close to his face, as his eyes widened in shock. Was this all that remained of Jeannie? He looked at the back of the envelope for a return address or a government stamp. There was nothing there to indicate who sent the package. It couldn't possibly be from the British authorities; even they would not send the remains of his daughter in an envelope. He turned the nail over to look at the back. Bile started to rise is his throat and he gagged when he saw the blackened scab attached to the nail, small withered slivers of skin hung from the sides. The nail had been removed from its' thumb by force. Omar staggered backward, his legs weakened from the shock and his bodyguard grasped his arm and guided him to a chair. He mouthed soundless words to his minder and held out the bloodied nail. The big Arab took the nail and studied it carefully; then he opened Omar's fist and removed the small chip from his sweaty grasp. He studied both sides.

"It's a SIM card from a mobile phone Sheik," the bodyguard

said removing his own cell phone from his pocket. He removed the back from his mobile and slid his SIM card from its fastening. He placed the chip into his phone and replaced the back. A polyphonic tune announced the phone being switched on. Omar seemed to be getting a grip of the situation and he pushed himself up from the chair.

"What does this mean Yusuf?" Omar said squeezing his bodyguards forearm tightly. He still couldn't comprehend what was happening. His mind raced through the different scenarios. Yusuf's mobile rang.

"We are about to find out Sheik," Yusuf replied to his panic stricken boss. He placed the phone firmly into Omar's hand and placed it near his ear switching the speakerphone mode on. Omar pressed answer. A thick guttural accent spoke.

"Omar Kellesh?"

"Yes this is Omar Kellesh speaking," he answered; his voice almost a whisper, as sweat stared to run down his forehead. He felt the trickle of cold sweat run down his back.

"The SIM card you have received has some pictures stored on it that may be of interest to you. Your daughter is alive however, she will not be if you do not follow my instructions," the voice sounded Soviet to Omar and Yusuf, and they both stared at the handset.

"I want to talk to her. Let me talk to her please. Please don't hurt my daughter. I will pay you as much as you want, please don't hurt her," Omar babbled into the phone as any frightened father would.

"We don't want your money Mr Kellesh. There is a bank of telephones at Euston station next to the flower stall. You need to be next to the second phone from the left in exactly one hour, or you will never see your daughter again. We have your telephones tapped, if you tell the police she dies. If you contact your embassy she dies. If you bring anyone except your driver she dies," the soviet voice tailed off and static noise replaced it for a second before the line went dead.

Omar collapsed back into his chair emotionally exhausted. His hands were shaking visibly. His daughter was alive but her life was in mortal danger. He stared at his bodyguard Yusuf as he calmly started to look at the photographs that were stored on the SIM card. Jeannie's image was captured holding yesterdays newspaper. Yusuf started to dismantle the cell phone.

"The SIM card goes to our Secret Service for analysis. I am sure from the static noise on the line that the call was international. The accent was Soviet but I can't pinpoint which country. We need to get to Euston station Omar. I will be your driver. Let's go and find out who has Jeannie my Sheik," Yusuf said as he checked that the magazine of his Uzi machine pistol was full. He strapped the weapon inside his leather jacket and placed two spare magazines into his inside pocket.

CHAPTER 13

Jeannie Kellesh/ Chechnya

Jeannie Kellesh opened her eyes and the world was white. The ceiling was white as were the lights that illuminated it. The walls were tiled in shiny white squares, and the floor was finished to match. It smelled of antiseptic like a hospital. Jeannie felt like she had been in a long dark dream. She could remember being in the queue for the boat trip but after that it was a haze. She had dreamed of being carried and moved several times, and remembered hearing strange foreign voices around her, some English and some she didn't recognise. Jeannie could recall sharp scratching pains in her upper arm, and then comforting warmth that spread through her body afterward. She winced in pain when she tried to move her right hand. A throbbing pain radiated from her thumb but she didn't recall hurting it. Jeannie tried to sit up but she was restrained by something, so she could not. She noticed a drip feed attached to her left hand and followed the line up to a medical bag containing clear liquid. The bag had the word methadone, printed on it. A small mechanical intravenous driver whirred and Jeannie watched helplessly as the methadone flowed along the drip toward her veins. She didn't feel fear, because she didn't feel anything at all, just the comforting warmth of the drug spreading through her body.

Jeannie was in a secure ward in a hospital in Dagestan, Russia. The town was called Kizlyar. In 1996 the hospital had been the target of Chechen rebels, who, in order to draw attention to their claims for a separate state, independent from Russian rule, attacked the building. In one of the most daring and brutal attacks of its kind, Chechen rebel warlord Salman Raduyev held three thousand people hostage. Russian forces surrounded the hospital to contain the rebels but did not attack in case the rebels killed the large number of hostages. Spetsnaz (Russian Special Forces) troops were brought in but even they could make no headway against the rebel barricades. There was a military standoff for nine days, which was highly embarrassing for the Russian government. The Russian government suddenly announced on national TV that the hostages in the hospital had been killed by the Chechens; it was a complete lie constructed so that they could launch an eight-day rocket barrage on the town, without condemnation from a watching world. The hospital was attacked and taken by Russian Special Forces resulting in the death of many hostages. The Russians refused to confirm the number of fatalities but estimates run into the hundreds.

The conflict between Russia and Chechnya had raged since the 15th Century when the area was dominated by the Muslim Turkish Ottoman Empire. Following its collapse in the 18th Century the Russians took over trying to secure buffer states around Mother Russia that could repel any future invasions. With the advent of World War 2, the Chechen people threatened to take arms against Russia in league with Nazi Germany. Concerned by the threat of a rogue state in his empire Stalin ordered the deportation of Russian based Chechens to Kazakhstan and Siberia, causing thousands of deaths in the process. The forced exile was swift and brutal. It is now believed a quarter of the indigenous Chechen population was decimated. There was no surprise when the Soviet Union began to collapse in 1990 that the Chechens rebelled again. The country was economically deprived, and was ruled by renegade warlords with different political agendas. Some genuinely fought for independence from Russia and a free Islamic state, while others fought to line their own pockets. The situation remains the same today.

Following her kidnap Roman Kordinski had arranged for the Saudi Princess to be smuggled out of the UK, across Europe to Dagestan. She was far enough from Moscow for the authorities not to become aware of her presence, and close enough to the Chechen border to be extracted quickly in an emergency. The hospital was used by several different Organizatsiya for the same reason. Plastic surgery was a speciality and often used by Mafia members who needed to disappear. Mafia soldiers on both sides were treated here for gunshot wounds, away from the prying eyes of the Soviet government. The hospital had become a medical fortress since the hostage crisis. The Russian Spetsnaz had attacked the hospital with anti-personnel, mine dispersing, cluster bombs, which would remain in place and functional for decades. Access through the surrounding grounds was now impossible because of the remaining ordinance. Pathways had been cleared to certain entrances but they were top-secret. Entry could only be gained at nighttime, under escort by troops that knew the secret paths through the minefields.

Chechen rebels controlled the hospital and its access. They charged the warring Mafias huge fees to use the heavily defended medical facility. Even an archenemy like Roman Kordinski was welcome to use its facilities for the right price. Roman Kordinski planned to force the Saudis to increase the price of a barrel of crude oil, by threatening the life of his hostage. He would increase the price of his own crude produce simultaneously forcing the price worldwide through the roof. He could skim millions in profit before he had to return his interests to the Russian government. The Chechens were aware that he was a fading star in the Soviet Union, but they were willing to assist him with his plan by holding Jeannie Kellesh at their facility in Dagestan. Roman Kordinski was planning to return the Saudi Princess to her family if they cooperated with his demands. He had no reason to keep her in captivity. The new celebrity image that he had built carefully in the West was still fragile. His football team was prospering and it lifted his profile into the public eye on a daily basis. The longer Jeannie Kellesh was held the more chances of a mistake being made increased, jeopardising his public image.

The Chechens however had a different plan. Once Roman Kordinski had returned his Russian business interests to the Soviet government he would have no further use for the Saudi Princess. The Chechens were planning to renege on the deal, and extract a huge ransom from the Saudi Royal Family for her safe return.

CHAPTER 14
Terrorist Task Force

Major Stanley Timms stood at the window of his office, looking at the River Mersey flowing past. A tall four-mast, wooden sailing ship was docking next to the historic Albert Dock buildings. The port of Liverpool played host to the fleets of tall ships that constantly circumnavigated the globe when they visited British shores. As he watched the sailboat the Major recalled the last voyage he had made aboard a sailing vessel. It was as part of the Marine Task Force that was sent to fight Argentine military forces, which had invaded the Falkland Islands, in the South Pacific, 1982. The naval task force that had publically left English waters watched by the worlds television networks had been spearheaded by the Royal Navy's nuclear submarine the Water Sprite. As the fleet sailed from the port the submarine dived beneath the surface in full view of the cameras. The Argentine military Junta feared the presence of a Polaris nuclear submarine in their waters more than anything else, so they kept most of their fleet harboured safely in port. The truth was that the Water Sprite never actually left Liverpool harbour. When it dived beneath the waves at the head of the Royal Navy fleet it stayed on the ocean floor for the whole period of the conflict. It had suffered a major fire in one of its reactors several weeks earlier, which virtually rendered it useless. The mere suggestion that Britain had sent a nuclear submarine to the Falklands had been enough to neutralise the entire Argentine Navy. The Major had received a citation for his service in the Falklands where the regiments of The Royal Marines and the Parachute Regiment had dismantled the invading Argentine army in a matter of days. He had followed his distinguished career in the Royal Marine Commandos by heading up the formation of the Terrorist Task Force. Military life seemed far simpler in comparison to the world of espionage that he now worked in. Using hindsight he realised that conventional war was straightforward. The enemy wore different uniforms, waved different flags and drove different vehicles, which in theory made them easier to identify and eliminate. The world of counter terrorism was far more cynical. The hidden enemy were masters of disguise and deception, avoiding close quarter battle was an art form. Tank and his team had raided a crucial target earlier that day arresting nineteen suspects. While this was a serious blow to organised crime in the region, they had made little impact on a potentially critical political disaster, which still faced the Middle East.

"Sorry to disturb your thoughts Major but the team are ready," Tank said poking his big baldhead round the doorframe.

"Come in for a moment John," the Major, said waving his hand. He was the only Terrorist Task Force member that called Tank by his first name, and when he did it usually meant that he was troubled by something. Tank stepped into the glass walled office that was called the goldfish bowl, and closed the door behind him.

"MI5 have requested a full update on the Jeannie Kellesh situation. They are concerned that the Saudis will discover that we were aware that she didn't die in the riverboat bomb from the start. The political fallout would be disastrous," Major Timms said shaking his head, "so, I have confirmed that they can release the information that we have to the Saudis." Tank thought that the Major suddenly looked old and tired. The creases in his forehead seemed deeper when he frowned, and he frowned a lot these days.

"We have ordered our interrogation teams to concentrate their questions on the kidnapping, but we seem to have arrested only low level or prospective 18th Brigade members. No 'tier one' personnel were captured at the scene," Tank explained. 'Tier one' was the description applied to leaders or key individuals of a target organisation.

"No one is talking at the moment, or my guess is that they are all too far down the ranks to know about the kidnap," Tank said, thinking about the empty gun racks in the cellar, "It looks like all the Brigade's serious muscle were otherwise involved. Their armoury room was empty before we arrived, which is very concerning."

"Ask the team to join us in here John please; I need to

bring everyone up to speed. The international consequences are frightening," Major Timms said picking up a file and tapping it on the desk for effect. Tank thought about reinforcing the point that the key personnel from the 18th Brigade were at liberty and armed, here in the UK not in the deserts of the Middle East. That was a bigger priority to Tank than the ramifications that could potentially take place thousands of miles away. Major Timms was becoming increasingly concerned about political claptrap and less concerned about taking down terrorists in Tank's opinion. Tank's loyalty lay with the British public and he would ensure their safety at any cost. Westminster could worry about foreign diplomacy and political correctness, which was bullshit as far as Tank was concerned. He waved to the rest of the team and beckoned them into the goldfish bowl office.

"What is the latest from the interrogation rooms?" the Major asked Faz as she walked into the room. She shot Tank a glance that indicated there was little progress so far. The longer the interviews went on the more obvious it was becoming that the detainees didn't know anything of any value.

"The only new information that we have is that there was a shooting incident at the Orford Arms yesterday, which involved foreigners," Faz began. This was news to most of the team as the Brigade had refused to involve the police, even though two of its senior members had been shot. Organisations like the 18th Brigade dealt with their issues internally.

"According to the barmaid that we interviewed two Russian men walked into the Orford and asked to speak to Pete Dodge. There was an altercation in the back room and two Brigade Lieutenants were shot, one in the foot and one in the leg. Dodge's right hand man is called Terry Nick and he was shot twice in the right foot with a 9mm weapon. The second man is still a critical condition with a gunshot wound to the thigh and serious facial injuries. Apparently the Russians left through the back doors but no one seems to know what the altercation was about," Faz finished shrugging her shoulders and took a seat next to Chen.

"If that's true then we need to assume that the armoury room in the basement has been emptied for a reason. I think the Brigade has planned an attack against the Russians in retaliation for the shootings at the Orford. Chen you need to inform the uniformed divisions that we suspect an armed incident of major proportions is imminent. Order them to despatch every Armed Response Unit they have available, and to cancel all leave and rest days," Tank said pointing to the door to underline the urgency of his directive. Chen stood and left the meeting to carry out Tank's order. The gravity of the situation required immediate communication to the regional uniformed police divisions.

"We still cannot identify which crime organisation is behind the kidnap plot. The Brigade's involvement looks to be irrefutable so we must assume that the information we have collated from the Organised Crime Unit is correct. They are certain that the Brigade work directly with the Russian Mafia. They supply the Brigade with imported weapons and drugs. We need an up to date list of all suspected Russian business interests in Liverpool, Manchester and the surrounding towns," Tank pointed to a map of the region that was on the digital display board, "we are looking for casinos, night clubs and brothels that have any Eastern European connections." The Terrorist Task Force would have to rely on the information that the conventional law enforcement agencies had, but Tank had a hunch that any retaliation attacks would be imminent. Collating information from several departments would take up valuable time that they didn't have. The Major stood up from his desk and changed the map image on the digital screen. He flicked through several images of the Middle East until he found one that demonstrated his narrative.

"We have informed the Saudis today that we know Jeannie Kellesh was not a victim of the riverboat bomb. We know that there was definitely no Islamic extremist influence involved," The Major said looking directly at Tank. Tank knew what was coming but he didn't care, a terror training camp of any description was still a legitimate target for an airstrike no matter what the reasoning behind it. The destruction of the terror networks was the number one priority for his Task Force. The Major was concerned that they had withheld information from the Saudis, and he felt that Tank had influenced his decision to do so.

"We incorrectly allowed the Saudis to believe that Yasser Ahmed may have been involved in the bombing on the River Dee, which resulted in them launching an airstrike in Syrian territory. Syria, Iran and their allies are looking for a reason to attack Israel and the Arab states that support or trade with the West, including Saudi Arabia," the Major tried to emphasise the international ramifications. No one else in the room could see the urgency of the situation that he was outlining. Tank suddenly clicked, and the point became frighteningly clear.

"What the Major is saying is that if a Jewish Russian becomes implicated in the kidnapping of a Muslim Princess, extreme Islamic states such as Syria and Iran could call open season on the Jewish state of Israel in retaliation, which would in turn drag America into the conflict. We could be looking at the start of a third world war," Tank said out loud for his own benefit as well as for the benefit of others.

"Exactly," said Major Timms, "Syria has already mobilised its armoured divisions to defend its southern borders, if they discover that the airstrike by the Saudis was carried out without proper justification then the situation could deteriorate."

"Point taken Major," said Tank, "however we need to concentrate on the fact that the 18th Brigade has armed and mobilised its members in the last twelve hours. I want every available Task Force member suited and booted ready for whatever is going to happen. Put the bomb squad on standby and issue fully automatic weapons to every agent. Full body armour is compulsory even for uniformed officers, no heroes."

The goldfish bowl door opened and Chen returned into the room looking red faced. He crossed to the digital screen without saying a word and tuned it to a Greater Manchester Police Force channel that was being broadcasted from a surveillance helicopter. The image of what used to be Manchester Piccadilly Station appeared. It was a scene of total devastation, obviously the result of a huge explosion. Glass, twisted metal and human remains were scattered across the station's approach.

"This explosion happened two minutes ago. Early reports indicate a refuse truck was driven into the terminus and then exploded," Chen explained.

"Chen and Faz, you need to head to that station. Gather what information is relevant and call in when you are ready. I'll prepare the team here. Call a helicopter to pick you up on the roof," Tank ordered without taking his eyes off the screen. Tank knew that the explosion was probably unrelated to their current case, but he had a sneaking suspicion that somehow it was connected. He picked up the phone and speed dialled one of his agents.

"John Tankersley speaking, what happened in Bradford when you went to arrest Imran Patel in connection with the van we investigated at the River Dee?" Tank asked. He listened briefly and then replaced the handset gently as if it might break. "Imran Patel left his house this morning to buy a newspaper and never returned. Eyewitnesses report seeing an Asian man was being knocked over by a dark SUV in the vicinity of the newsagents. He was placed in the back of the vehicle. No one remembers the make or model and there is no registration number. I am laying odds that Imran Patel's disappearance is connected to that bomb," Tank said staring at the digital images of carnage being broadcast from the ruined Manchester train terminus.

CHAPTER 15

Omar Kellesh
and Yūsūf

Yusuf was forty-five years old and had worked as a personnel security advisor for the Saudi Royal Family for fifteen of those years. He had been directly responsible for the safety of the Kellesh family in England for the last five uneventful years. Yusuf had been educated and brought up as a moderate Sunni Muslim. After completing his education he joined the Saudi armed forces as a commissioned officer after university. He was selected for a unit that was spending time training with British Special Forces in Egypt. Following that he was selected for counter-terrorist security and placed on the payroll of the Royal Family. Yusuf's first assignment was as a close protection agent at a meeting of OPEC (Oil producing countries) in Geneva, which was being attended by high-ranking ministers from the richest nations on the planet. The meeting was targeted by a terrorist organisation from Venezuela. The terrorists stormed the meeting, which was being held on the first floor of a government building, killing two policemen in the process. The leader of the attack was the infamous terrorist known as Carlos the Jackal, and although a Muslim himself he had a tainted opinion of certain Islamic countries, which in his opinion were becoming servants to Western governments. His agenda was the annihilation of the Jewish state of Israel, the freedom of Palestine, and the removal of Western backed Arabian governments. Carlos separated the diplomats into three groups, which he categorised as the conservative countries, Algeria, Libya and Kuwait. The neutral countries of, Venezuela, Indonesia, Gabon, Ecuador and Nigeria; and finally the countries that he considered to be the enemies of Islam, Saudi Arabia, United Arab Emirates, Iran and Qatar.

His intention was to demand a huge ransom for the safe return of the Foreign ministers and to execute the representatives of the countries he called criminal. Carlos and his two affiliates separated the liberal ministers into different rooms and segregated the others. They then surrounded the 'criminal' diplomats with explosives. They had not identified Yusuf, who had remained calm throughout the incursion, and dressed in a business suit he had convinced the unsuspecting terrorists that he was a Foreign minister too. Throughout the hostage situation it became very clear that Carlos the Jackal had a violent temper, and Yusuf was convinced that he intended to execute everyone if necessary. The tension amongst the foreign diplomats was dreadful as negotiations with the authorities began for the release of the valuable hostages. A telephone call was received by the kidnappers from the security services that surrounded the building, who were trying to negotiate with Carlos for the release of the diplomats. In a moment of extreme anger Carlos emptied the magazine of his machinegun into the telephone switchboard. The switchboard was blown into a thousand pieces as the high velocity bullets struck. When the Terrorist's machinegun clicked empty Yusuf made his move. Within seconds Yusuf had shot and mortally wounded all three terrorists without them firing a shot. Yusuf reloaded his 16-bullet Glock 9mm and emptied the entire clip into Carlos's dying body. He then repeated the process with the two other terrorists to ensure that there was no chance of survival, sixteen bullets for each terrorist. Yusuf had been hailed a hero and moved into key Saudi close protection roles immediately afterward.

Now he was stood next to his charge, Omar Kellesh, in Euston station, London, waiting for a kidnapper to call. They had been instructed to wait for a call at a specific bank of public pay phones. He checked his chronograph watch and saw that it was exactly an hour since they had received the first contact from the kidnappers. Suddenly a phone rang. Omar snatched the receiver from its cradle and stammered into it.

"Hello, Hello. Is anyone there?" Omar took the phone from his ear and looked into it as if he could see the person at the other end if he stared hard enough. The ringing sound continued and Omar became confused. Yusuf reached past his boss and felt beneath the metal body of the phone. He removed a Nokia cell phone that had been taped to it, and it was still ringing.

"Hello," Yusuf said into the Nokia pretending to be his boss Omar.

"You are not Omar Kellesh. Put him on immediately," said the voice, a heavy guttural accent reinforced the Russian connection. Yusuf now knew that whoever was making the call could see them from wherever they were positioned. There is no way they could have known that he was not Omar, unless they were being watched. Yusuf passed the phone to Omar and stepped away from him scanning the floors above them as he moved. He expertly tried to identify where the caller could be stood. There were several people stood in the correct position to be observing them but no one was using a cell phone simultaneously. Yusuf left Omar and blended into the crowd frantically trying to find the kidnapper before they ended the call.

"This is Omar Kellesh," the Saudi minister said shaking uncontrollably. He looked toward Yusuf for support, but he was nowhere to be seen. Omar was suddenly very frightened, Yusuf's presence made him feel safe but he was gone.

"If you feel beneath the telephone you will find the key to a left luggage locker. Take it and make your way to the lockers," the Russian voice directed him. Omar felt underneath the metal box and grasped a piece of duct tape. A silver key was attached to it; there was also a metal disc with the number thirteen engraved on it. He looked around the crowded station area desperately trying to spot Yusuf. The station hall was five hundred yards square surrounded by restaurants and retail outlets. There were thousands of commuters in every direction he looked, it was hopeless to try and find Yusuf; he had to follow the instructions to save Jeannie by himself without his protection agent. It occurred to him that whoever was directing him could have taken Yusuf. If they could remove a man as skilled as Yusuf then they would have no problem killing him. He felt alone and exposed without his trusted bodyguard.

Two British Transport Police officers passed by him and eyed him coolly, because of the explosions at Piccadilly station officers were being extra vigilant. Omar realised that he must look like he was under immense stress, as sweat was running from his forehead down across his cheeks. He felt completely lost and frightened, so he started toward the police officers wondering if they could help him to recover his daughter, panic was beginning to set in. If he alerted the British police to Jeannie's kidnap the perpetrators would surely kill her, but he could see no alternative. Suddenly he was grasped tightly by the arm, strong fingers dug into the soft flesh inside his bicep. Omar felt himself being guided roughly away from the policemen.

"Your daughter is a very attractive young woman Mr Kellesh. I think that her guards would have fun with her before they killed her. You should not consider talking to the police," the Russian voice hissed into his ear. The grip on his arm tightened and pulled him toward the left luggage area.

"Who are you? Why are you holding my daughter? Please don't hurt my daughter," Omar whispered almost vomiting from the fear that overwhelmed him. The thought of his beautiful daughter spending the last hours of her precious life being brutalised by violent men made his knees weak. The grip on his arm was now bearing his weight as his legs refused to carry him. Fear gripped him and turned his heart to ice.

"I am called Yuri, and your daughter will be safely returned to you untouched if you cooperate. The lockers are fifty-yards in front of you. Inside you will find your instructions Mr Kellesh. If you fail to comply with the instructions then I will personally see that your daughter is visited by more men than a Babylon Hoar before we cut her up. Do you understand Mr Kellesh?" Yuri snarled the instructions into his ear so that passersby had no idea what was being said between the two men. Omar turned to face the Russian in an attempt to plead for his daughter's safety. The vice like grip on his arm had gone and so had the big Russian. All he could see was hundreds of commuters going about their business.

Omar started to cry as he approached the locker. His hand was shaking and he struggled to insert the key into the lock. A tear ran from the corner of his eye as he thought that it might have been better if Jeannie had died in the explosion. She would be in heaven now not lying somewhere at the mercy of bad men. His stomach twisted and he felt bile rising in his throat as he imagined his beautiful angelic daughter being scared and alone. A father's natural instinct would be to kill anything that threatened his children. Fear started to turn to pure rage as he opened the locker. Inside was a brown manila envelope, which he tore open with shaking hands. He read the instructions and then screwed the paper up and shoved it into his pocket. He had to get back to the embassy immediately.

Omar Kellesh ran as fast as his weakened legs would carry him toward the car park. Yusuf had driven the Mercedes SUV and parked it in the station multi-storey. Omar crashed into a middle-aged woman as he reached the escalators, knocking her headlong across the tiled station floor. He staggered up and continued down the metal stair without pausing to apologise or even to acknowledge that the collision was his fault. Omar ran from the escalator along a dirty corridor that smelt of urine until he reached a fire door that led into the concrete multi-storey car park. He paused briefly to catch his breath, but he had to get back to his embassy as quick as he could. He spotted the Mercedes and hurtled toward it like a mad man. He was panting for breath and soaked with sweat as he neared the vehicle, but he suddenly stopped at what he saw in front of him. Yusuf was stood waiting by the back of the Mercedes as if he were on a shopping trip. He held the keys in his hand and he smiled when Omar approached. Omar opened his mouth to speak but the combination of exhaustion and shock left him tongue-tied. He placed his hands on his knees trying to catch his breath, staring at his bodyguard all the time.

Had Yusuf betrayed him and left him to the Russians on purpose? Had he gone to the toilet at a crucial time like this? Yusuf was too professional to be so blasé, so what was going on? Omar thought in his jumbled mind.

Yusuf stepped away from the rear of the Mercedes and Omar saw that he was holding his UZI 9mm machinegun beneath his jacket. Yusuf reached toward Omar and guided him gently toward the rear of the vehicle. Omar thought that his time was up; Yusuf was going to assassinate him. Yusuf opened the rear door of the Mercedes and smiled at Omar again. Omar stared into the vehicle and a smile spread across his face, he broke into nervous laughter nodding his head as relief and understanding descended on him. In the back of the vehicle was the big Russian who had called himself Yuri. He had threatened Omar with the gang rape of his daughter. Now he was trussed up like a chicken in the boot of his car, and was gagged with silver duct tape. His nose was bleeding profusely which made Omar happy. The best part though was the look of terror that was in his eyes. That look of sheer unadulterated fear was priceless.

CHAPTER 16
18ᵗʰ Brigade Strike back

Dano leaned against a wall looking at a reinforced metal doorway across the street from where he stood. Dano had been with the 18th Brigade since he left school ten years ago, working as a door security man at first, before being promoted into the drug dealing area of the business. He looked every inch like a fascist skinhead. His hair was shaved with a razor to the scalp and he sported Swastika tattoos beneath both ears, along with SS insignia on both hands. Dano worked out using heavy weights at the brigade gym, and he enhanced his training with anabolic steroids. The steroids made his moods unpredictable and violent. The excess testosterone in his blood stream fuelled an unnatural sex drive, which compounded his mood swings. He held a short metal baton in his fist and he tapped it threateningly against his palm. He had two colleagues with him, who were known as Clarky and Pinn, one stood next to the reinforced door that he was watching, and the other approached it straight on. They all shared the same taste in haircuts and tattoos.

Clarky rang the doorbell, which was attached to a wooden doorframe. The frame itself was reinforced with a wrought iron grill that was shaped into metal flowers. The decorative shapes could not disguise the fact that someone was fortifying the premises behind it. An intercom crackled and a female voice spoke through it.

"Hello my love there's a ten-minute wait at the moment. Wait for the buzzer and then push the door, we're up the stairs on the left," the woman's voice clicked off and the door lock buzzed open. Clarky pushed the door open and turned toward Dano and Pinn gesturing them to follow him. The three skinheads ran up the

73

stairs, their Doc Martin boots thudded loudly as they ascended. They were greeted at the top of the stairs by a woman in her fifties; she was plastered in make-up, and was surprised by the sound of multiple footsteps coming up the stairs. She was obviously the madam of the operation; her years of being able to command money for sex were well behind her, but she could answer the telephone and account for the cash with no problems. Her years on the game had given her a no nonsense approach to dealing with punters, along with a matron like manner with the working girls, who she empathised with too much sometimes. She opened her mouth to object about the three men entering the building but was silenced by a vicious punch in the stomach. She collapsed against the wall gasping for breath.

A small waiting area was located on the left, similar to a small living room with two comfortable chairs. They were occupied by two scruffy looking men in their fifties, who were sat in an awkward silence trying to avoid eye contact with each other. They stood from their seats as the three huge skinheads entered the room, and froze like rabbits caught in the full beam of an oncoming juggernaut.

"Look mate I think there has been some kind of mistake, I was just about to leave when you came in," one of the men started to say, his eyes widened in fear.

"Oh I don't think there is any mistake you little pervert," Dano said grabbing the little man by the throat. He picked him off his feet and threw him against the window. The glass shattered and the man fell to the floor clutching his face, blood was flowing from between his fingers. Clarky looked at the broken window and laughed; he picked the man up from the floor and launched him toward the shattered pane. He smashed through the window into the cold night air and landed in a broken heap on the stone cobbles of the alley way behind the building. Dano looked out of the window and laughed insanely with the other two skinheads at the twitching body below. The second punter tried to make a break for freedom but he ran straight into Pinn. Pinn slashed a razor sharp carpet blade across the man's face almost splitting his nose into two pieces. He grabbed the bleeding man by the back of his neck and flung him toward the staircase. The man clattered down the narrow stairs breaking several wooden banister rails on his way down, and sprayed the walls with blood from his wound.

74

Two doors opened simultaneously down the hallway. Startled prostitutes and their half dressed customers headed toward the staircase. Dano, Clarky and Pinn positioned their massive frames across the hallway blocking any escape route. The two punters were grabbed and thrown to the floor. Three pairs of Doc Martins boots rained down on the two men inflicting a savage barrage of blows. Pinn held one of the men by the throat on the floor and slowly carved the numerals 18 into his cheek with his carpet knife. The man ran screaming down the stairs and out into the night bleeding from the knife wound. The second man had not managed to pull his trousers up over his exposed buttocks as he tried to escape in a panic. The three skinheads carved 18th brigade across his arse, laughing uncontrollably as they cut him.

The two prostitutes screamed as they watched the carnage unfold in the hallway, but they stopped screaming when the big skinheads let the punter go and turned toward them.

"Now then girls, let's have a little fun before we burn this place to the ground. What do you think about giving us a couple of freebies?" Dano sneered as he approached the two scantily clad women. One of them backed away but he grabbed her roughly by the back of her hair with his right hand and tore the skimpy thong that she wore away with the other.

"Go and get the petrol. This shouldn't take very long, then you can have a go when I've finished," Dano said as he and Clarky pushed the women into the room and closed the door behind him with his boot.

Pinn left Clarky and Dano to have their way while he fetched the petrol can from the van. He punched a telephone number into his cell phone and dialled the offices of the Organised Crime Unit at police head-quarters. Pinn had been undercover for two years. He had lived and breathed the 18th Brigade as he infiltrated into its ranks. Pinn knew that the retaliation attacks against the Russian Mafia were scheduled for 9pm but he had not been alone long enough to alert his commanding officers. He was connected and explained briefly that Russian interests were about to come under attack all over the North West of the country. Pinn informed his head office that following the attack at the brothel several Brigade units were heading to a Russian owned casino in Liverpool. Their mission was to rob it and then destroy the building.

With the Organised Crime Unit alerted he headed back into the brothel. At the top of the stairs Pinn stepped over the prone body of the old madam. She was still clutching her stomach and gasping for breath. Pinn stood over her, one big boot on either side of her chest.

"Where is the money you old slapper?" Pinn growled. The old woman curled up trying to protect herself, she had seen Pinn's carpet blade handy-work earlier and she was terrified. She stayed mute in a foolish attempt to protect her employer's business interests. Pinn lifted his right foot and whilst holding onto the banister rail he stamped his heel into her face. She screamed and scrambled away from the skinhead into the waiting area. She peeled back a section of carpet to reveal a floor safe, blood and saliva drooled from her swollen lips onto the safe dial. The madam opened the safe and then cowered in the corner of the room as far away from Pinn as she could get. Pinn took a large bundle of notes from the safe and counted it quickly.

"Eight-grand, that's not bad. Your tarts must have been very busy," Pinn said stuffing the money into his jacket pocket, "now this will have to be between me and you. Do you think I can trust you not to say anything?"

The frightened woman nodded silently. Her mascara had run down her cheeks in a cascade of tears. Her face was swelling along the jawbone as if she had a boiled egg beneath her skin and her chin was caked in blood.

Pinn took a Colt .45 from his waistband and pointed it at the brothel manager. She squeezed her eyes shut trying to escape the inevitable. The big undercover agent screwed a suppressor to the barrel of his Colt and then pressed the gun into a cushion to further silence the weapon.

"I can't trust an old slapper like you to keep your big gob shut," Pinn said in a whisper. He pulled the trigger four times and the woman's face disintegrated into a bloody inhuman mess. A red fan of blood and flesh dribbled down the wall behind her. Pinn closed the safe and covered it with the carpet then headed for the hallway and closed the waiting room door, hiding the dead woman from view. He doused the staircase and waiting area with fuel while the grunting and slapping noises continued from the bedroom down the hall.

Eventually the two prostitutes emerged from the bedroom looking like they had stepped from a car wreck. They staggered off on shaky legs down the stairs into the night, hiding their nudity with small towels. Dano stepped out of the room laughing as he fastened his trousers and he patted Clarky on the back in a twisted gesture of companionship.

"I think we should visit a casino for the rest of the evening gentlemen," Dano said as he tossed a light match onto the fuel soaked carpet; the corridor erupted into an inferno as they ran down the stairway toward their van.

The 18th Brigade executed similar missions across every Russian backed business in Manchester and Liverpool. The police switchboards were swamped. It took the British fire departments eighteen hours to bring the flames across the region under control.

CHAPTER 17

Yuri

Yuri was struggling to breathe. He was strapped to a chair in the basement of large building in London. He did not think it was the Saudi embassy, but the personnel that had removed him from the boot of the Mercedes were defiantly Arabs. His memory of how he had ended up in the trunk of a car was hazy. He had delivered the message to the Saudi diplomat and intervened when it looked like he was approaching the British police in the station. He had guided the crying Arab away from the police to the left luggage lockers and then used evasion tactics to disappear. He remembered entering a corridor on the way to his vehicle. He could also remember a shadow to his left and then a blinding pain in his nose. When he came round he was trussed up like a prize pig in the boot of a vehicle. His nasal passages were blocked with congealing blood and his mouth was covered with duct tape, so he was suffocating slowly. Yuri had lost count of the number of men and woman he had processed through interrogation over the years. He had watched his prisoners without the slightest prick to his conscience. Many of them tied to chairs and gagged just like he was now. The gravity of the situation was not lost on Yuri. The processing had not even begun yet and he was frightened. He had tortured enough people himself to know that few people resisted the pain of torture and even fewer actually survived.

Yuri had been a member of a Russian Special Forces Unit, Alpha Group, also known as Spetsgruppa A. They were a specialised counter-terrorism group of seven hundred agents, who had been selected from the cream of Russian elite units. The Spetsgruppa A primary function was to carry out urban counter-terrorism missions under direct control of the Russian government. They had no military commanders. By Russian standards Alpha Group were lavishly supported and funded to ensure they were armed with state of the art arms and munitions. Yuri was involved in several hostage situations where chemical agents were employed and they were required to operate in full NBC (nuclear, chemical, biological) equipment. In 1979 he had been part of a small group of Russian Special forces that captured the Amin's Palace in Afghanistan triggering the first Soviet Afghan war. Sixty members of Alpha Group seized the palace and killed two hundred elite Afghan troops, along with the Afghan president Hafizullah Amin. Yuri was promoted to Sergeant rank following the mission.

His introduction to interrogation came later in October 1985 when his unit was sent into Beirut where four Russian diplomats had been taken hostage by militant Sunni Muslims. The diplomats were the first Russian nationals to be targeted by Islamic extremists. By the time Alpha Group had been deployed and delivered to Beirut one of the hostages had already been murdered. Yuri and his team met with a KGB operative who had been active in the area for a substantial length of time. He had gathered information and identified the kidnappers. The next step was to identify the perpetrators' families, which didn't take very long. Yuri and his elite squad quickly captured twenty-five members of the kidnappers' families and held them captive. The Russian Alpha Group then severed the little fingers of every Arab person that they held captive and delivered them to the Sunnis with a warning that there would be no negotiations. If the Russians were not released immediately then the families of the Muslim kidnappers would be delivered to them in pieces. The Russian hostages were released immediately and no Soviet national was taken hostage in the Middle East for over twenty years.

After the collapse of the Soviet Union the armed forces were not paid their wages for months on end. Yuri realised that his years of loyalty and service were not being rewarded financially. As the Soviet Block approached bankruptcy their armed forces disintegrated. There was more money to be made for men of his calibre working for the rising Russian entrepreneurs as security and enforcement officers. He had started working for Roman Kordinski earning more money in a day than the army paid him in a month.

Working for Roman had involved capturing and processing many business rivals. Processing, usually involved long periods of torture and death. The bodies of rivals were dumped in public places as a warning to potential enemies.

Now he was strapped to a chair and the roles had been reversed. The screaming faces from years past of his victims flashed by in his mind. The mumbled pleading of men and women to end their lives quickly, rather than endure any more torture echoed in his thoughts. He had never heard them properly before, but now they seemed very clear. Yuri decided that he would tell the Saudis whatever they wanted to know in order to speed up his death. He had been a war hero for many years but this was a contest with only one winner. There was nothing to be gained from protecting Roman Kordinski now.

A bright light was switched on and Yuri heard people entering the room behind him. The Arabic tones of at least three men were close by. Yusuf took hold of the duct tape and ripped it from the Russian's face. Yuri breathed in cool fresh air in huge gasps, the feeling of suffocation passed quickly.

"My name is Yusuf and I am head of security for the Kellesh family. I am sure that a man of your experience realises that I need information from you. I do not care how long it takes or what we need to do to you to persuade you to part with it. Where is Jeannie being held?" Yusuf said taking the top off a cold bottle of water. He placed the bottle to the Russians lips and allowed him to drink from it. Yuri swallowed the cold water and tasted the copper flavour of his own blood at the back of his throat.

"She was taken from this country twenty-four hours after she was captured. She was flown via Marrakesh to Russia. Our people there have her under armed guard but I do not know where exactly." Yuri said telling the truth, he really didn't know where she was though he guessed that she might be at the hospital facility in Dagestan. It was too early to pass on speculative information.

"Who exactly do you work for?" Yusuf asked allowing the Russian another sip of water.

"Mosvar Barayev is the nephew of a Chechen warlord. He gives me my orders. I do not know who ordered the kidnap directly," Yuri lied, although he couldn't understand why he was lying exactly. Perhaps all his military training was taking over.

"Unfortunately that is your first lie. You are a Russian Jew, ex-Special Forces; you have spent most of your life killing Chechens, so I very much doubt that you are working for them now. One more time, who are you employed by?" Yusuf poured the rest of the water over the Russian's head making him blink as the liquid ran into his eyes.

"The Chechens moved into Moscow years ago. They pay better money than the Russian Mafia. I don't care if they are Muslims or not, their money is the same colour as yours," Yuri lied again, hoping that the Saudi's knowledge of the Soviet underworld was not in-depth enough to make his lies too obvious.

"I am disappointed that you think we are so stupid Yuri. I hoped that we could conclude our meeting quickly with the minimum of noise, however it seems that you are determined to hear yourself screaming," Yusuf said waving his hand to a colleague that was behind Yuri. The Saudi security man struggled to carry a large truck battery which he placed between Yuri's feet. There were leads attached to each terminal. At the end of each lead was a copper spring-loaded crocodile clip. The guard took out a switchblade and proceeded to cut the Russians pants and underwear from his body exposing his genitalia. The feeling of being naked made Yuri feel incredibly vulnerable and he squirmed uncomfortably against his restraints. It was a classic interrogation technique especially when processing female prisoners. The threat of rape was all the more ominous when the captive was naked. Being naked exposed a person to their true vulnerability. The security guard clipped one of the spring-loaded clamps to Yuri's exposed testicles causing him to cry out in pain. The copper clamp bit into the delicate skin drawing blood and crushed the soft organ beneath simultaneously. Tears filled Yuri's eyes as he anticipated the electric shock that was he knew was soon to follow.

"Who do you work for Yuri?" Yusuf asked lighting a cigarette. The guard attached the second spring-loaded clamp to the end of the Russian's penis. The copper teeth pierced the skin and Yuri gritted his teeth against the pain. Yusuf nodded to the guard and he switched the battery power on. Yuri twitched violently in the chair as the voltage entering his genitals was increased. He finally released a scream that came from the bottom of his soul and echoed through the basement of the building. The pain through the most sensitive parts of his being was indescribable.

"Stop! Stop the fucking thing. Please stop," Yuri pleaded gasping for breath as the power was turned off. The muscles in his throat constricted, and he felt like a hot knife had been stuck into his groin. "Roman Kordinski, I work for Roman Kordinski. The girl is probably at a hospital facility in Dagestan."

Yusuf remained silent waiting for the Russian to expand on the information he had given. He nodded to the Saudi guard and the voltage was switched on again. Yuri's body went taught as the electricity passed through his singeing testicles. The sweet acrid smell of burning flesh filled the room and Yuri screamed again. The veins in his face and neck pulsed beneath his sweat soaked skin.

"Fuck you, you bastard," Yuri snarled as the voltage mercifully subsided again, "the Chechens have a hospital in Dagestan. Kizlyar is the name of the town. They rent beds and surgeons to the Russian Mafia out of sight of the Russian authorities. It is heavily defended." Yuri lowered his head exhausted from the pain. He saw that the tip of his penis was blackening from the electric shocks. The pain in his abdomen was excruciating, and he knew that the way his heart was pounding signalled that he would not live through much more of this treatment.

"Why would a Russian celebrity like Roman Kordinski kidnap Jeannie Kellesh? He would hardly need ransom money," Yusuf mused out loud. The Russian stayed silent, barely conscious, his chin was resting on his chest.

"Get the others," Yusuf ordered, and a Saudi guard opened the door and summoned three more security staff into the room.

Yusuf poured more cold water over the Russian and he regained consciousness with a start. The pain that racked his body returned with a vengeance. He looked up at the Saudi security chief as he lowered his face towards his.

"Yuri, you unfortunately offended my employer Omar Kellesh at the station. You threatened to have his daughter raped which caused him great distress. We will investigate the validity of the information you have shared with us, and continue our conversation later on when you feel better. In the mean time Omar has ordered that you learn a little humility," Yusuf spoke softly into the Russian's ear.

Two of the Saudi guards grabbed Yuri by the arms and lifted

him from the chair. They dragged him to the desk and bent him over it. Yuri was confused at first; pain had clouded his perception of what was happening around him. It was only when the first guard started to bugger him brutally that he realised that the method of torture had changed. By the time the fifth guard had finished the abuse he could no longer stand up by himself and he looked forward to dying soon, very much.

CHAPTER 18

TTF/ Casino Liverpool

Tank, Faz and Chen exited their Mitsibushi Shogun in the car park of the Liverpool Casino. The casino was a relatively new building in comparison to the historic docklands in which it stood. Situated next to the Albert Docks it looked out of place next to its ancient neighbours. The walls were white and the building was almost triangular in shape. Thirty feet high glass windows surrounded the reception area, which revealed the interior of the casino and its first floor bar to entice passers-by in. The River Mersey ran past the rear of the casino, you could flick a poker chip into its murky waters from the casino's restaurant balcony. Tank walked to the trunk and opened it. Inside was a metal lock box and Chen opened it with a digital combination code. Tank reached inside and removed three battle vests, which he distributed between them. The battle vests were made from knitted Kevlar fibres, which made them light, but capable of stopping a high velocity bullet. Ounce for ounce the material was stronger than stainless steel. Faz removed three Mossberg 12 gauge pump action shot guns. Each gun had a magazine that held eight shells containing double o shot. Double o shot was comprised of the largest lead pieces available for ballistic use. It was designed with stopping power as the prime function, and could drop an elephant at a hundred yards. The three Task Force agents went through the motions of checking that the magazines were full and functioning. Tank removed his 9mm Glock pistol and repeated the checks on the smaller weapon, Faz and Chen followed suit.

A senior uniformed officer approached their vehicle, crouching behind it dramatically as he arrived. Tank recognised him as the chief officer of the Organised Crime Unit, and a major pain in the arse.

"I have an undercover agent inside the casino, with approximately six members of the 18th Brigade. My agent informed us that their objective is to rob the casino and burn it to the ground. I have the casino surrounded with Armed Response Unit officers, and when I get the word we will arrest everyone inside including my agent. We do not need Terrorist Task Force involved, it's my jurisdiction," the uniformed officer said agitated at the arrival of the Terrorist Task Force agents, "this is an Organised Crime Unit operation and I am ordering you to stand down."

"How does get stuffed and fuck off grab you?" Tank said in reply, "you have no authority over any of my agents, and the 18th Brigade became Terrorist Task Force jurisdiction when they decided to get involved in blowing things up. You can leave the Armed Response Unit in place. I have requested them as back up but you and your men aren't required here." Tank glared at the Police Chief. The domestic law and order agencies had no authority over the Terrorist Task Force, who answered directly to the British government. The police officer flushed a crimson colour in anger but he knew that Tank was right, and he had no authority.

"How dare you speak to a senior police officer like that, you Neanderthal? I will be making a complete report about this behaviour," the officer blustered.

"You are not my senior officer, and in case you hadn't noticed we are not members of the police force," Tank chambered a shell into the Mossberg loudly which made the policeman recoil adding further humiliation to the Police Chief's hopeless position, "now take your report and shove it where the sun doesn't shine, because we have some terrorists to catch." Tank pushed passed the policeman followed closely by Faz and Chen.

Faz noticed a marked police car parked in front of the main doors of the casino in full view of the armed men inside, two uniformed officers leaned against the vehicle chattering. Suddenly a burst of automatic machinegun fire pierced the night. The bullets were fired from an upper window inside the casino. The two uniformed officers dived for cover as their vehicle was peppered with high velocity bullets. Sparks and shattered glass filled the air. The tires exploded and the noise echoed across the dark waters of the River Mersey.

"So much for a low profile approach," Tank sneered, "uniform has screwed this up already. Faz, take charge of the Armed Response Unit, have them maintain the perimeter until we can work out what to do next. We have no idea if that's the Russians or Brigade men shooting at us, and we don't know who else is in there. Chen, you come with me I've got an idea."

Tank communicated with a special operations listening post that was situated in an old school building on the other side of the city. He requested an unmanned helicopter drone to survey the casino from above. Within a matter of minutes the miniature helicopter was above the building. The engines were capable of running in silent mode and the machine was almost impossible to detect at night. The unmanned drones had been used by American Delta Force operatives extensively in the mountains of Afghanistan, searching for Osama Bin Laden. On November 5, 2002 four senior al-Qaeda members who were travelling in a car through the Yemen, were killed by a missile launched from an American Predator drone. Their machines are described as 'medium altitude, remote controlled aircraft'. On May 15th 2005 Haitham al-Yemnini, a senior Pakistani extremist was also assassinated by a CIA controlled remote drone in the disputed territory of Kashmir. The unmanned drone passed information back to the listening post in the old school. Heat seeking equipment on board the drone showed the position of fifteen people, who were seated together in a group. Eight others were spread out around the building's perimeter. There were two other subjects giving off detectable heat, but not to the level a live human would radiate. Tank had to assume two people were already dead or dying.

The Armed Response Unit surrounded the casino alongside over a dozen Terrorist Task Force agents. Grace Farrington positioned the Task Force agents where they could get a clear shot at anyone trying to leave the building. The members of both elite forces resembled Robocop in their battle armour. They were equipped with state of the art night vision and motion sensors; nothing could enter or leave the casino undetected. The weapon of choice with British Special Forces was the new Brugger and Thomet Semi-Auto Tactical 9mm pistols, which are capable of firing over 900 armour piercing bullets a minute. They had the capacity to kill everyone inside the casino if the order was given, by simply shooting through the brick walls. The problem that the Terrorist Task Force agents had was that they couldn't identify the good guys from the bad guys, unless they breached the casino walls.

Major Stanley Timms spoke to Tank from the control room, via a micro-receiver which the TTF agents had inserted into their ears, "What's the situation Tank? Can we move in?"

"Negative Major, we have a group of fifteen subjects in the centre of the building, and eight others positioned around the interior perimeter, it looks like a hostage situation. Uniformed officers came under automatic gunfire a short time ago, so we have the building surrounded by Armed Response Units and our agents. The commanding officer from Organised Crime Unit has a bug up his arse because he has an undercover agent inside. The undercover officer has infiltrated the 18th Brigade ranks and apparently tipped of the OCU to the casino mission," Tank explained the situation.

"It would appear that the Brigade has taken issue with our Russian friends. We are getting reports of over thirty incidents in which buildings suspected as brothels have been attacked and burned. All have links to dubious Russian businesses. You need to get those hostages out of there in one piece Tank. Westminster is all over this following the River Dee and Manchester bombings," the Major sounded under pressure to get a result. The position was being compounded by the rising death toll. The British public were on the verge of panic fuelled by misinformation in the press. Islamic extremists were being blamed for the riverboat bombings. The responsibility for the bomb at Manchester Piccadilly station had landed at the same place. Dozens of buildings, reportedly being used for the sex trade were ablaze across the north west of the country, fuelling the flames of racial mistrust.

"We need to breach the building's perimeter Major," Tank said as he walked across the parking lot toward a building site. He could see a huge yellow JCB digger parked silently on the empty construction lot.

"I think I have an idea Major," Tank said.

CHAPTER 19

Pete Dodge and Terry Dick

Pete Dodge took off his mirrored sunglasses and opened the window of the Ford van that he was driving. He was looking at the smouldering embers of what was once the Orford Arms, his business, the base for the 18th Brigade, and his home. The buildings had been raised to the ground by the fire, which had started in the cellar and spread quickly. Two weeks ago he had a successful door security business and control of the lucrative drugs trade that came hand in hand. Now he was a fugitive from the law and his empire was crumbling before his eyes. Word had spread quickly that the Brigade's headquarters had been destroyed, and that its leader had gone to ground. Rival gangs were already moving in on his area trying to secure the security contracts that the Brigade held, in the event that Dodge didn't resurface. Whoever controlled the door security also controlled the drugs, which was a huge cash cow. He needed to regain his grip and enforce his authority immediately. The 18th Brigade had devastated the Russian Mafia's business interests overnight in retaliation for the deception surrounding the River Dee bomb, and the kidnap of Jeannie Kellesh. His troops had done well so far, but he had received a call from one of his lieutenants, Dano, alerting him to the situation at the Liverpool Casino. Dano had informed Dodge that he and his men were surrounded by armed police. The best option was to surrender and be charged for what could be construed as an armed robbery gone wrong. It would be difficult for the police to prove that it was anything other than that.

Dodge turned to his passenger and said, "We need to set up a new base immediately Terry. Use the offices above the Quarter-

Deck in Oakwood, and get word to all our people that we are very much still in business." The Quarterdeck was a two-storey pub building that the Brigade frequented. Terry Nick had just been released from hospital after being shot twice in the foot by a Russian enforcer. His wounded appendage still raged in pain but he needed to return to business immediately. Terry was Dodge's main enforcer and they needed to regain control. Nelson's Quarterdeck was a large pub which only traded on the ground floor. The void space above it was unused apart from a small office. It would suffice as a base for operations temporarily. Terry had already used his vast network of contacts both domestically and internationally, to apply pressure to the Russian Mafia to call a truce. Going to war was bad for business, especially against millionaire-backed mercenaries like the Organizatsiya.

Terry had spent six years in a Californian penitentiary following a foiled arms deal. The American courts looked dimly on foreigners breaking the law on American soil, and they placed him into the worst prison that an Englishman could enter, San Quentin. San Quentin was opened in1854 and is the oldest jail in its state. It is the equivalent of a human jungle where a lone white Englishman is at the mercy of the prison gangs. Terry Nick was a big man, pumped up by Nandrelone injections and a strict weight-training regime. His shaved head and Nazi tattoos made him an immediate target for the black inmates but a natural ally to the white Nazis. San Quentin was segregated into racial groups, The Black Guerrilla Family, Neustria Familia, Cripps, Bloods and Black P. Stones absorbed the majority of black and Italian inmates. The Mexican Mafia protected the Hispanic prisoners while the Aryan Brotherhood covered the white population. The Aryan Brotherhood took Terry Nick into their ranks and under their protection on day one of his sentence. The bulk of their memberships were white skinhead supremacists, most of them were marked with similar Nazi tattoos to those worn by Terry. The Brotherhood has a membership of over one- hundred and twenty thousand hard-core members involved in drug trafficking, racketeering and protection rackets. According to the FBI the Aryan Brotherhood makes up just one percent of the American prison population but is responsible for twenty six percent of the murders in the federal system. Their members were spread far and wide across the American continent making them a formidable crime organisation. The advances in technology now made controlling and the organisation of such gangs considerably easier. Mobile phones smuggled into prison extended the reach of the prison gangs, making them more dangerous. Prison guards and their families were identified and targeted. They were influenced or forced to turn a blind eye to contraband being smuggled into the prisons. Many warders had been assassinated for non-compliance or for giving gang members a hard time. Huge crime families could be operated from a prison cell, and multi million pound drug deals arranged from behind bars. It was just as easy to eliminate rival gang members and their business interests. Terry Nick had already contacted his affiliates within the Brotherhood to enlist their support against Russian Mafia aggression. The screw was already being tightened across the USA.

Dodge had made similar calls for assistance to groups sympathetic to the 18th Brigade worldwide. The alarm had spread around the globe overnight through fascist communication networks, the links normally used to arrange drugs and arms trafficking were now buzzing with a call to arms against Soviet Mafia interests worldwide. The Nazi website Stormfront.org was a hive of activity as word spread. A Nazi group known as the Hammerskins which has chapters in Canada, England, France, Germany, the Netherlands, Hungary, Portugal, Spain New Zealand and Australia has a membership which runs into the tens of thousands, and is just one of hundreds of similar groups. The specific policies of these neo-Nazi groups differ slightly from country to country, but they all include an allegiance to Adolf Hitler, anti-Semitism, racism, xenophobia and homophobia. They also use their large memberships to control the extortion, drug and sex trades. They actively seek to recruit disaffected violent youths into their ranks, some of whom would enjoy nothing more than going to war against a rival crime organisation for whatever reason at all.

"The ball is already rolling Dodge," Terry Nick said looking at the smoking ruins. His foot was throbbing with pain and he winced as he tried to move it to a more comfortable position. "If Alexis and his Russian friends want trouble then they are going to have their hands full."

"We have a problem now the government and the Terrorist Task Force are involved. Blowing up that boat was not the most subtle plan I have ever encountered. I think that we should arrange a meeting with the Task Force, we need them off our backs," Dodge said, "let's be honest we knew nothing about any bombs. We were tricked into this by the Russians."

"You can't be serious Dodge," Terry said, "you can't go to the police. They will string you up."

"Look what has happened since we became involved in this bloody mess," Dodge turned to Terry and looked him in the eye. Communication with the police was a taboo, problems were dealt with in-house. "Matt and Ivan are missing or dead. The arrival of the Task Force at the Orford means that the riverboat bomb is being linked to us. You got shot in the foot. Our boys are surrounded by armed police in a casino and we are ready to go to war. We will lose everything if we don't sort this out right now."

"Look what we achieved last night Dodge," Terry said angrily. The pain from his bullet wounds was increasing as his medication wore off. "We gave the Russians a good kick up the arse, they won't mess with us again in a hurry. Our contacts in America are ready to give them a good shoeing."

"Your Aryan Brotherhood friends will use it as an excuse to move in on Russian businesses. The same goes for all the rest of our affiliates, they all have their own agendas. The best we can hope for is that the Russians will see it as too much trouble to take us on. Be under no illusions Terry, if they want us gone then we are already dead." Terry remained silent as he mulled over what his leader was saying, it went against the grain.

"I tell the Task Force everything that we know and give them the fucking Russians on a plate. We can carry on as normal and pick up their prime sites," Dodge said slowly trying to coax Terry onto his side. "We didn't ask for any of this bullshit Terry, let's lay the blame where it belongs."

Terry nodded slowly as he saw the opportunities that would arise if the Russians' key players were arrested or shot by the Terrorist Task Force. The plan was brilliant and could definitely work. It looked like they would not have to wait very long to find out.

CHAPTER 20
The Saudi Embassy

The Saudi government knew that Jeannie Kellesh was still alive. They also knew that a Russian entrepreneur was behind her kidnap plot. Demands had been delivered to the Saudi Princess's father which instructed them to increase the price of crude oil by 10 dollars per barrel. The increase was to be maintained for a minimum of ninety days, after which she would be released. Any attempt to alert international security services to Jeannie's plight would result in her death. It appeared to the outside world that there was no tangible evidence that she was still alive. All the evidence pointed to her being a victim of the Islamic extremists that had bombed the riverboat at Chester, and the press were still all over the story causing domestic unrest.

The Saudis moved their crude oil price up and cut back production sharply, leading to diplomatic condemnation throughout the Western world. Since 1960 crude oil prices had been governed by the OPEC nations. Prices had historically been affected by conflict in the Middle East, but the unilateral price increase from the Saudis seemed to have no justification. The OPEC cartel is made up of Algeria, Angola, Ecuador, Indonesia, Iran, Iraq, Kuwait, Nigeria, Libya, Qatar, Venezuela, the United Arab Emirates and Saudi Arabia. The Saudis oil production counts for over thirty percent of the world's crude oil. If they increase the price then everyone else has to follow suit. OPEC's principle aim is to safeguard the collective interests of the oil producing nations, with a view to eliminate harmful and unnecessary fluctuations. This unilateral price rise had caused chaos to international business. Air travel and product transportation costs doubled overnight forcing many small businesses across the globe into bankruptcy.

The interrogation of the Russian Mafioso Yuri had delivered the name of the man behind the plot, and also the probable whereabouts of Jeannie. Even though they knew where she was being held the Saudis were reluctant to use their military forces to attempt to recover the Princess, because she was being held in Soviet territory. Tension between the southern Russian states and their Middle Eastern neighbours had been fraught for centuries. The Soviets had always supported and supplied Syria with arms and armour, which caused ill feeling amongst other Muslim countries. Military forces across the Middle East were on amber alert following the Saudi airstrike on Syrian land. An additional incursion into a Soviet satellite state would be seen as an act of aggression and political suicide.

The Saudis had decided to hand over both the perpetrators and the information that they had recovered to the British government. The bomb, which had killed so many young people on the River Dee, was an act of international terrorism on British soil. The fact that it had no political justification attached to it was irrelevant. If the British moved on the information that Roman Kordinski was involved, then the Saudis could not be blamed for outing the plot. British Special Forces were far better equipped to deal with a possible incursion and rescue attempt than the Saudi military. The decision was made; the Russian Yuri was to be handed to the British along with the recordings of his evidence under interrogation. The only way to carry out the plan without alerting the Russian Mafia was if Yuri was already dead.

CHAPTER 21

Newborough Preparatory School/ Woolton

The old school building stood on top of a hill overlooking Liverpool, in a part of the city called Woolton. The area was once the main provider of red sandstone in the country, and the school was made from the local rock. It towered above the other buildings on Quarry Street, looking more like Victorian lunatic asylum than a derelict prep school. The school was built from dark red-brown sandstone blocks each one at least three foot square. The black slate roof rose to a steep point four storeys above the overgrown playground, where children once played kiss and chase, and conker tournaments were as important as the World Cup final. It had been decades since the dark stone had echoed with the laughter of children playing, and the brass bell ringing to call an end to playtime. Huge rusted iron gates stood between the empty playground and the road, the old school crest hung from the metal bars at an odd angle, its fixings long since rusted away. To anyone passing it was just a derelict preparatory school. No one ever saw anyone entering or leaving the building.

Inside the broken facade the school was the most sophisticated surveillance facility in Europe. White tiled walls and polished marble floors were incorporated into this hi-tech listening post which was the nerve centre of Britain's security agencies. The old school descended deep beneath street level to a warren of corridors and facilities. Access to the bunker-like regions below ground was via an underground tunnel, which ran from the Canning Place police headquarters building next to the River Mersey. The construction companies that built the public road tunnels beneath the river were also contracted to build the secret subterranean structure under the city and the old school. It was a top-secret project sponsored by the government, so that they could hide the cost of the nation's secret spy centre in the building of the River Mersey tunnels.

Major Stanley Timms was holding a video conference with the directors of MI5, MI6, SL19 (Armed Response Unit), the Organised Crime Unit and the Minister of Defence. The Major was trying to explain that the evidence that had been recovered from the riverboat bomb did not support the theory, that an Islamic extremist cell was responsible for the explosion. It was much more likely that it had been a cover for a kidnap plot. The evidence recovered from the Manchester Piccadilly bomb pointed to the fact that an individual called Patel was linked to both scenes by a transit van that he owned, however the Task Force didn't feel extremists were to blame. The use of a fertiliser bomb at the station, which was much less sophisticated than the river bomb, supported the extremist theory, but the Major had serious concerns about it.

"I believe that Imran Patel has been used as a puppet," the Major explained, "a van owned by him was found burned out at the river, and there is no doubt that he was in the bin wagon that exploded at Piccadilly station. We have matched his DNA to human remains found in the driver's seat of the vehicle."

"That sounds conclusive to me. I don't understand why you are chasing shadows. This is obviously an Islamic extremist attack," said Agent Garden from MI6. Garden had been promoted to a level way above his capability by the old boy network. This meant that he frequently looked like a total asshole. He wanted the attacks to be laid at the feet of Islamic extremists to justify asking the government to increase his department budget. Politics were far more important to snakes like Garden.

"The opposite is true Agent Garden," the Major interrupted, "we recovered chemicals from the charred remains of the driver's seat that are consistent with superglue." Garden's face flushed red, and not for the first time he wished he had kept his mouth shut. He had no military or law enforcement training; he was essentially a civil servant, a pen pusher with important friends. He could pick up a grammatical error in a written report no problem, but if asked to provide a solution to procedural inadequacies he didn't have a clue. His mentors had realised that promoting him so far had been a huge mistake, but it was too late to alter the situation. MI6 were known as spooks, undercover spies, although their operatives had military backgrounds, their directors did not.

"There is also an elastic substance melted into some leg bone fragments, which would indicate that Mr Patel had been secured to the driver's seat by some type of bungee cord. Combined with the glue residue I have to conclude that Patel was forced into that seat under duress and he is a smoke screen. We aren't sure why yet, but we have some leads which are being followed," the Major explained.

"What is the link to the 18th Brigade?" asked the Minister of Defence.

"We know that they were at the riverboat and that there could be a kidnap incident which took place before the explosion. Until we can confirm the facts then I don't want to speculate," answered the Major dismissively. If the kidnap became the key issue then the Terrorist Task Force investigation would be hindered by the involvement of the other agencies. He needed to keep them at arm's length for now. The Major was not however aware of the depth of knowledge that MI6 possessed.

"I think that the Major is withholding information Minister," blurted Agent Garden seizing what he saw as a chink in the theory and relishing the opportunity to ruin someone's career to further his own. He had made backstabbing into an art form to speed his own progression up the ranks.

"We have information from our Middle Eastern agents that the alleged kidnap victim is part of the Saudi Royal family. If the situation remains static, and this is in fact an international kidnapping, then this investigation is MI6 jurisdiction and I must insist that Major Timms discloses all the information that the Task Force has."

"We are investigating that eventuality Agent Garden," the Major countered, "however I would not have disclosed such information about the Saudi connection during a routine update conference call, on an unsecured frequency, you bloody idiot." The Major raised his voice for the delivery of the last three words.

"Minister I must protest! I assumed that we were using a secure link," Garden protested stuttering, his face was a crimson colour. The Major picked up a telephone handset from the desk and dialled.

"Switch off the link to MI6," he said briskly and Agent Garden disappeared from the screen. Garden's expression looked like he was about to learn the hard way what it felt like to get shafted.

"There is an encrypted update of the situation being delivered to the Ministry as we speak Sir," the Major said, "once we have dealt with the 18th Brigade interrogations I will update you immediately."

The Minister of Defence disappeared from the screen looking flustered and embarrassed. One of his key security directors had made a schoolboy error, which was unforgivable. In the cynical world of espionage there was no room for mistakes, he was already thinking of the name of Agent Garden's replacement. The Major spoke briefly to the remaining directors from SL19 and MI5 to update them on the casino situation. The director of the Organised Crime Unit gave them all the details about his undercover officer who had infiltrated the Brigade ranks, and was now inside the casino. His undercover name was Simon Pinn, an excellent officer prior to being deployed as an infiltrator. There were some concerns that he had become too comfortable in his position as a Brigade member, and his recent Intel had been sketchy at best. The OCU director sent the officer's secure pager number. If the Terrorist Task Force could contact him inside the casino, then it would change the logistics of the hostage situation dramatically. The Major bid his goodbyes and took the pager details to the communications room.

"Pull up the building plans and the subterranean infrastructure details for the casino please," the Major ordered, "split the screen and show me the pictures from the remote drone too." The screen flickered and the aerial image from the unmanned helicopter appeared. Greenish human forms indicated body heat radiating from where the occupants of the building were currently. A plan of the casino and the land it was built on materialised on the opposite half of the screen.

"What are these lines here running through the casino?" the Major asked.

"They are service shafts built for the River Mersey tunnels. They run under the casino and the River Mersey to the ventilation towers on the far riverbank."

The Mersey tunnels were built in the late 1960's to accommodate road traffic crossing from the Wirral and North Wales into Liverpool city centre. There were three tunnels in total and a labyrinth of access and service shafts. Huge exhaust fans worked 24-hours a day to remove the toxic engine fumes from the tunnels.

"There is an access hatch to the shaft, which is at the rear of the casino in a utility room. It could be a cellar," the technician said.

"Page the undercover OCU officer and give him the details of that ventilation shaft. He can use it to get out, or we could possibly use it to gain entry, but we need to know if it's accessible," the Major said. The Major was aware that there were concerns about the OCU officer, but he had no idea just how far across the line Simon Pinn had gone.

CHAPTER 22
Tank and JCB

Tank leaned against the huge yellow JCB digging machine and listened to the Major in his earpiece. Chen was to his left observing the casino through night vision glasses, and listening to the Major on the open channel. Major Timms explained that the Organised Crime Unit actually did have an officer on the inside, and that there was a possible entry point through an access tunnel at the rear of the casino. He also explained that the OCU director had expressed concerns about the integrity of the covert agent who was called Pinn. The Major had passed on all the Intel available, including the positions of the casino's occupants. Tank considered the access tunnel but quickly ruled it out. They did not know if the shaft's hatch was accessible. It could be covered with carpet or laminate flooring. If it was a utility room or a kitchen back-up area it was probably tiled over. Then again if Pinn was untrustworthy there could now be half a dozen Brigade members pointing their machineguns at it, waiting for a head to pop up.

"It's your call Tank," said the Major, "what's your next step?"

"Kill the power in the casino Major and order Faz to follow me in with two units. Tell the remaining units to secure the perimeter and wait for my signal," Tank said.

"What do you mean follow you in? How are you going to get in? I think that you really should consider the tunnel as an entry point. Are you ruling it out?" the Major asked in a frustrated manner.

"If there is the slightest chance that the Organised Crime Unit's agent is bent, then the tunnel is out of bounds Major. I am not leading my agents into an ambush," Tank said tapping Chen on the shoulder to get his attention. He pointed to the big yellow machine and Chen's eyes lit up as he realised the nature of Tank's entry plan.

"Two snowmen stood in a field and one said to the other, 'can you smell carrots? '" Tank said climbing into the giant digger. Chen burst out laughing although he didn't get the joke, his English was excellent but he did not have the English sense of humour to match.

"What the bloody hell are you talking about Tank?" the Major spluttered. There was laughter on the airwaves as the other agents listened to the conversation.

"It's a joke Major, but sometimes the answer is right under your nose," said Tank as he pressed the huge diesel engine into life. The neon signs outside the casino blinked out and the interior went into darkness a second later as the power was switched off. Tank engaged drive and the yellow machine lurched forward toward the sidewall of the casino, there were no windows there, and the heat and motion trackers displayed the area was clear of humans. The giant digger bounced over the kerbstones into the casino car park picking up speed as it went. The sound of gravel crunching beneath the machine's wheels mingled with the roar of the diesel engine. Chen was still laughing to himself when he asked, "The snowmen were stood in a carrot field, right?"

"No my little friend they were not. It was just a regular field," Tank said wishing he had never started the subject in the first place. Chen frowned confused and held on tight as the JCB accelerated.

Grace Farrington signalled two units in readiness to attack. She indicated that infra-green vision was to be utilised inside the dark casino, and the agents snapped down night vision visors, which were mounted on their helmets. Faz smiled as she watched Tank hanging onto the controls of the giant machine as though his life depended on it, as it roared across the parking lot. It was now clear to all how they were going to breach the building and maintain the initiative. The element of surprise was essential in hostage situations. She could see Chen shifting levers that were to his left and the huge yellow bucket at the front of the digger lifted up twenty feet into the air. Its massive metal teeth gave the approaching digger the appearance of an animal as it roared across the car park toward the casino wall.

CHAPTER 23

Yŭri/ Yŭsŭf/ Saŭdi Embassy

Yuri woke with a start when he heard the cell door slam shut. He heard the sound of a metal cup scraping as it was placed on the floor close to him; a similar sound came as a tin plate was placed next to it. He tried to move his limbs but they were numb. Pins and needles racked his hands and feet as he encouraged them to function. His black hood was removed roughly by the Saudi guard, and his eyes closed tightly against the harsh light.

"What day is it?" Yuri asked hoarsely reaching for the metal cup of water. The guard ignored the question and left the small room closing the door behind him. Yuri had tried to keep a track of how long he had been held captive. It was a basic military tactic learned by Spetsnaz forces, learning escape and evasion techniques. They were taught to gather as much information as they could whilst being held captive. Who had captured them? ; How many the enemy numbered? ; What were the names he had heard used by his captures? ; How many days had been in captivity? ; The longer a soldier was in captivity the less likely he was to escape. Poor nutrition and the pain of interrogation would weaken even the elite special force operatives. Yuri estimated that he had been held for less than a week. He had been tortured for the first three days and deprived of food water and sleep. Yuri had witnessed enough torture sessions to realize that everyone breaks eventually, and that there is nothing to be gained from futile resistance except more pain. He had told the Saudis what they needed to know in the hope that they would kill him quickly or release him, but he had been subjected to a brutal male rape. Male rape is a tactic often used to destroy the self-esteem of an enemy captive especially in the Middle East. The rape had left

101

him with internal injuries and despite his best efforts he couldn't stop the bleeding. He had torn a strip of material from his bed sheet and plugged the wound but it only slowed the bleed. Yuri knew that if he didn't get medical attention soon he would die. The last two days had been a haze. He had slept fitfully for long periods at a time waking only when the pain from the electric shock treatment and his internal injuries reached a crescendo. The Saudis had brought him food and water and there had been no further torture. Yuri knew that this indicated that the information he had given them had been confirmed. He also knew that he was of no further use to them. Death or freedom would come to him soon. He had lost too much blood to put up much of a fight, and he realised escape was not an option.

Upstairs in the main body of the Saudi embassy, Yusuf placed the cell phone he was using into a towel and began wiping it, removing all the prints and DNA material. The phone belonged to Yuri. Yusuf had used the numbers stored in the phone to leave an electronic trail that would lead directly to Roman Kordinski. The security services would find text messages and calls made from Yuri to Kordinski all mentioning the kidnapping of Jeannie Kellesh. They could be discounted in a court of law, but the idea was to make the British agents look in that direction. The electronic trail would definitely achieve that. The recordings of the interrogations had been digitally cleaned to remove any screams of pain. Only the voice of the Russian admitting that his employer was responsible for the kidnapping and the riverboat bomb would remain. His indication of where she could be being held was the final part of the recording. A good defence lawyer could argue that the recordings were not to be submitted as evidence because they had been cleaned, but by then they would have served their purpose. All that remained was to put Yuri's DNA on the cell phone and deliver them both to the British security services. Yusuf picked up an intercom.

"Have the Russian dressed," Yusuf ordered. He opened a container, which was similar in size and shape to a cigar box. Inside were a silver coloured syringe and a glass vial of amber liquid. The liquid was a radioactive isotope called polonium 200, which is a bi-product that is created by nuclear fusion. The isotope is lethal to human beings even in small amounts. It is alleged that the Russian KGB have used the substance to assassinate critics of President Putin. One high profile case actually occurred on British soil in London where the lethal radioactive isotope was used to kill an exiled Russian dissident. On this occasion the substance was traced to a cup of tea, which had been poisoned. Once ingested the Polonium slowly killed the Russian exile, although he clung to life for over a week the fatal prognosis was never in doubt. Yusuf planned to inject Yuri with the isotope making it look like the Russians had killed their own man.

In his cell downstairs Yuri drained the final drop of water from his metal cup and started to sharpen the edge of it on the concrete floor when he heard footsteps outside of his cell. His heart quickened as he heard keys turning in the lock, he somehow knew that his end was close. The door opened and two guards entered the room. They remained silent as they handed a set of clean clothes to him and unlocked the chains that fastened him to an iron radiator. Yuri took the clothes and tried to stand up, but his legs were weak from blood loss and cramped from inactivity. He wobbled and steadied himself by holding onto the radiator. He placed the clothes on the small cot bed while he gathered his wits about him.

"Get dressed, you are being released today," the Saudi guard ordered.

Yuri heard him but he didn't believe him for one minute. He picked up a pair of khaki cargo trousers and slowly pulled them on. The numbness in his legs was fading and the proper use was returning to them. His hands were still restricted by handcuffs and chains.

"I can't put on the shirt with these cuffs still on," Yuri said holding out his hands to the guards. The guards looked from one to the other unsure of what to do. Two sets of footsteps could be heard coming down the corridor and Yusuf appeared at the doorway with another Saudi officer.

"I told you to have the prisoner dressed. Remove the cuffs while he dresses," Yusuf ordered. He removed a Browning 9mm revolver from his holster and pointed it at Yuri to discourage any escape attempts. The guard unlocked one of the cuffs and Yuri slipped the cotton shirt over his arms and began to fasten it. As the guard leaned close to him Yuri recognised the Saudi's body odour. It made Yuri recoil as he realised that the man was one of those that had raped him. The big Russian felt a surge of adrenalin and moved like lightening. Yuri wrapped the dangling handcuffs around the Saudi's throat. Yuri twisted his body away from the guard and bent his knees at the same time. The guard's neck snapped in a second. Yuri released the limp body and scooped up the metal cup in one smooth movement as the second guard approached. He struck the approaching guard with the sharpened edge of the metal cup across the bridge of the nose. The metal cut deep into his flesh and sliced clean through his nose bone. Yuri turned the injured guard around and placed the metal against his jugular vein.

"I will cut his throat if you move a muscle," Yuri said. Yusuf and the remaining guard stood side by side in the narrow cell completely blocking the entrance. Yusuf still had the Browning pointed at Yuri but now the target was significantly obscured by the incapacitated guard.

"You have nowhere to go Yuri. If you leave this place your employer will track you down. They will interrogate you to discover the depth of your betrayal," the Saudi talked very slowly, "I was going to make the end painless for you, but now the choice is yours." Yusuf took the revolver from his colleague's belt and opened the bullet wheel. He removed five of the six bullets and placed them in his pocket. The remaining bullet was thrown onto the bed. Yusuf pushed the remaining guard backward toward the door, and then he threw the empty revolver onto the bed next to the bullet and pulled the cell door closed. Yuri was left holding the injured guard in his cell. He struck the Saudi hard on top of the head with the metal cup and he crumpled in a heap next to the guard with the broken neck. There was no escape from his prison cell. The walls were thick and the door was reinforced metal. His captors would not return until they heard a gunshot. Then he would either be dead or unarmed, as he only had one bullet. The adrenalin in his system started to wear off and the pain in the lower regions of his torso began to burn again. His momentary burst of energy had passed and left him feeling weaker than ever. The violent struggle had made the wounds open and the blood was flowing freely down his thighs discolouring his khaki trousers. Yuri sat heavily on the cot bed and winced at the pain it caused him. He picked up the revolver in his right hand and the bullet with his left. Yuri placed the bullet into the wheel and snapped it into position. He had lived a violent life and he had always believed that he would suffer a violent death. He had not considered the option of death at his own hand. Yuri considered it for over an hour before he finally placed the barrel beneath his chin and pulled the trigger.

CHAPTER 24

Simon Pinn/
Inside the Casino

Simon Pinn joined the British Army at the tender age of seventeen. He had been an accomplished amateur boxer during his school days and passed the six-week physical induction with flying colours. He chose to join his home regiment, the Cheshires, and was soon selected for the regimental boxing team. Representing the regiment gave a soldier great kudos amongst his fellow soldiers and Pinn's career blossomed. He made the rank of Lance Corporal in record time. In the 80's he was stationed in Londonderry, Northern Ireland at the peak of the troubles. Regiments of the British Army were rotated on six-month postings in the province. It was during Pinn's second tour that his army career began to go wrong. He was stationed in an OP (observation post) one night , overlooking Derry when a known 'prime mover' was spotted completing an arms deal. Pinn's call sign was Zulu 1 and he called in the IRA activity to his chain of command requesting permission to shoot the target. Permission was not forthcoming so Pinn deployed a spotter to move closer to the target to identify which type of weapons were changing hands. The spotter called in that RPG 7 grenade launchers and AK47 rifles were being loaded into a tractor unit. Zulu 1 asked permission to fire again, and again permission was refused. Pinn heard two shots fired and watched helpless as the spotter he had deployed dropped to the ground. He had been shot between the eyes through his night vision glasses by an IRA sniper, who was providing cover for the deal. Northern Ireland was littered with such incidents where the army were defeated by politics rather than the enemy. Pinn decided that the next time he had the enemy in his sights he would shoot first and ask questions later. Several weeks down the line Pinn was on a routine street patrol of Londonderry when he spotted the same suspect arms dealer entering a pub in an area called the Cregan. He followed the suspect and waited ten minutes for the IRA man to get settled, and then entered the pub. When a British soldier entered a public house in uniform he was placing his life and the life of anyone he spoke to in grave danger. Anyone suspected of informing to, or even cooperating with the British forces was subject to brutal retribution from the Irish paramilitaries. Pinn was well aware of the situation as was every British soldier, but he chose to use it to his advantage in revenge for the death of his spotter. Pinn walked across the stunned pub with his gun chambered across his forearm, two of his colleagues stood guard in the doorway with their rifles covering the drinkers.

"Cheers for the information about the RPG's. It was very useful, I owe you a pint," Pinn said to the IRA man who was stood in the company of a dozen other locals. Pinn slung his Armalite rifle over his shoulder and left a five-pound note on the bar in front of the barman. All eyes in the crowded pub fell onto the IRA man and his face flushed purple with fear and embarrassment. The bar remained silent long after the British soldiers had left, and despite protesting his innocence, the shadow of suspicion had been cast over the arms dealer. Three days later he was found dead with his kneecaps blown off; he had died in incredible pain through blood loss, as the victim of a punishment shooting. Despite his cries for help no one dared to call for medical assistance to help an informer. Rumours of the incident reached the ears of Pinn's commanding officers and he was court marshalled two months later, and given a dishonourable discharge.

Despite being discharged he was given an excellent reference and he applied to work for the Merseyside Police Force. He was accepted and again his career seemed to be progressing well. Pinn reached the rank of Sergeant before applying for a vacancy in the Organised Crime Unit. He carried out several successful operations for his new unit and was selected for a covert mission infiltrating the 18th Brigade. The Brigade had been identified as major players in the drugs trade, using door security as an umbrella for their operations. Pinn was sent to the Orford Arms and was selected to work in the Brigades door security business. Within months his unarmed combat skills had catapulted him up the ranks of the organisation, overtaking dozens of long serving members in the process. Pinn was promoted to Lieutenant, which gave him the responsibility over six pubs and two nightclubs. Apart from his huge wage increase he was also given a substantial percentage of the drug money from each site. Pinn realised that the old adage 'crime doesn't pay' was absolute rubbish. It paid incredibly well and was great fun too. He continued to report snippets of useless information to his OCU department while his secret bank accounts were swelling beyond his wildest dreams. He had to declare and return his basic Brigade wage to the OCU, but he squirreled the rest away.

Now Pinn was sat in a leather chair in the strong room of the Liverpool casino. He had shot two Russian security guards in the process of acquiring the safe combination. They were both lying on the floor of the room bleeding to death. No one had heard the shots, not even his Brigade colleagues. They were securing the perimeter and guarding the hostages. Pinn used a suppressor on his pistol, which reduced the sound of a high velocity bullet being fired to a loud hiss. The Terrorist Task Force thermal scanners had shown two people dead or dying. Pinn was staring at three hundred and fifty thousand pounds which was the casinos playing float. It made the money he had stolen from the brothel look like small potatoes. This could be the last bent deal he would ever have to make. He could retire somewhere in the sun. He could take sick leave from the OCU and never return. None would ever know. Pinn had to hide the money or smuggle it out of the casino without the surrounding police forces finding it, or any of the Brigade seeing it. He was considering where to put the money when his Organised Crime Unit pager vibrated. Pinn read the message on the screen, which was informing him of the situation outside, and giving him the position of an access tunnel, which ran, beneath the casino. It was linked to the ventilation shafts of the Mersey tunnels. The message was from the Terrorist Task Force offices, according to the message data report on his pager. They were a serious heavy-duty outfit. The Brigade men inside the casino wouldn't last five minutes against the Terrorist Task Force. Pinn laughed out loud and clasped his hands together in a mock prayer, a gesture of thanks to a god of deliverance.

He moved quickly and stuffed the bundles of cash into cloth moneybags from the safe. Pinn needed to locate the access tunnel first and then deal with Dano, Clarky and the other Brigade members, before he made good his escape. He placed the suppressor barrel of his gun against the forehead of the prone Russian casino guard and shot him once through the head. He couldn't leave any witnesses to testify that he had taken any money from the safe. The second guard died the same way with a bullet through his left eye.

Pinn carried the loaded moneybags through the rear door of the strong room. It led to a long corridor, which headed toward the kitchen areas at the rear of the casino. He tiptoed silently down the corridor until he reached the open doorway, which opened into the service area. A young Brigade member was in the wash-up area standing on a stainless steel preparation sink, holding an Uzi 9mm machinegun. He was guarding a rear window and looked very scared. He nervously acknowledged Pinn as he entered the kitchen and nodded to him, he looked relieved to have some company. The window that he was guarding was fixed with exterior security bars to deter burglars, even the Terrorist Task Force agents couldn't break in without making a lot of noise.

"What are you doing up there soft lad?" Pinn scolded, "The window is barred, we'll hear someone breaking through there a mile away. Get in the main casino area with the others." The young Brigade man looked undecided but he didn't want to argue with a Lieutenant of Pinn's status. He jumped down from the sink and headed toward Pinn.

"Have you seen that lot out there Pinn? They look like Robocop. They have got some wicked machineguns out there," he said rambling, trying to make conversation with Pinn. He was still a teenager and the sight of armed officers surrounding the casino terrified him. He had only joined the Brigade for a laugh. He thought it was all about Paki bashing and beating up queers. The young skinhead was completely overwhelmed by the siege situation that he found himself in.

"The Uzi you're holding isn't exactly a pee shooter soft lad," Pinn replied sarcastically.

"Yes I know how to use it, but I didn't think it would be against the coppers Pinn," the young skinhead answered as he noticed the cloth bags that Pinn was carrying.

"What have you got in the bags Pinn? I hope it's a load of twenty pound notes!" the young skinhead joked innocently. Pinn smiled as he approached.

"It's funny you should say that," Pinn said as he fired point blank into the young Brigade man's face. The high velocity round tore his lower jaw from his ruined face and he lay on his back with his eyes wide open in shock, and his body twitching for several minutes before he was finally still.

Pinn opened a large steel door that sealed a walk-in fridge. The small cold room was filled with racks of salad and cooked meats. He scanned the floor space looking for anything that resembled an access hatch. The floor was neatly tiled with no breaks. Pinn returned to the young skinhead and dragged his body into the walk-in refrigerator. He left a bloody trail behind him but he couldn't deal with that just yet. The blood would have to remain there for now. He moved through the wash-up area and located a white plastic coated door. Pinn opened the door to reveal a short flight of narrow stone stairs leading to a beer cellar. He lurched down the stairs taking them two at a time and lost his footing on the last step. He fell heavily onto his elbows and jarred his skeleton to the core, but he maintained his grip on the moneybags. The cellar floor was tiled like the kitchen but he was certain that he was below water level. If there was a hatch in the casino it had to be on this level. Pinn stood up and walked away from the stairs staring intently at the floor but saw nothing. He scoured the entire room peering into every corner and beneath every shelf. He could see nothing that resembled an access cover. There were at least eight metal beer kegs in a group next to a noisy cooler. The metal fan was catching on the refrigeration fins making a clattering sound. The cooler motor was grinding out warm air as it struggled to cool the warm beer from the cellar. Pinn started to drag the barrels across the tiled floor like a man demented. The thought of loosing this much cash was driving him mad. The fact that he had killed three people already today seemed unimportant. He moved the last barrel and stared at the floor, nothing but neat square tiles. Pinn collapsed on the floor with his back against the cellar wall exhausted. He couldn't think of anywhere else to hide the cash. There was cool breeze blowing against the back of his head, which was more than welcome. Sweat was pouring down his face and back. The access tunnel must have been tiled over when the casino had been built. He would have to hide the cash here somewhere and come back for it another day. The thought of leaving the money turned his stomach, he felt nauseous. Pinn looked around trying to find inspiration, and again felt the cool breeze on his face. It was coming from behind him. He stood up quickly and looked at the wall he had been leaning against, there was small wooden door fastened with a metal latch. There was a red tin sign screwed to the middle of it, which said 'access only'. Pinn smashed the latch off with his boot and pulled the door open. A narrow tunnel six foot long and just high enough to walk through if you crouched, led into a larger ventilation shaft, which serviced the traffic tunnels. Pinn couldn't believe his luck, so he grabbed the bags and stooped into the tunnel. Once in the larger shaft Pinn walked around until he found an emergency cupboard. Fire fighting equipment was stored in the access tunnels in the event of a major traffic accident or fire in the traffic tunnels. He opened the door and removed two fire extinguishers and a folded fire blanket. He stuffed the moneybags into the closet and then replaced the fire equipment on top of them.

The money hidden, Pinn returned to the cellar. He climbed the stairs to the kitchen and recovered the dead skinhead's Uzi 9mm. He went to the wash sink and doused his face in cold water. He tried to slow his breathing and cool down but the thought of leaving the money was gut wrenching. Pinn needed to be convincing if the next part of his plan was to work. Pinn returned to the main body of the casino. You could cut the atmosphere with a knife. The Brigade men had come here to smash the place up and steal some money. They were now in the middle of a hostage situation surrounded by heavily armed police. Panic was setting in and there was no natural leader amongst them. Intelligence and common sense were not qualities that the Brigade's members had in abundance.

"Where the fuck have you been Pinn? We thought you had bottled it," Dano growled sitting on top of a slot machine, drinking a stolen bottle of vodka. He was actually pleased that he had arrived, because Pinn was very useful when there was trouble around. Dano out ranked Pinn, but often followed his instructions because they made sense.

"I was trying to get the safe open but there's no way. It is way too complex to break and there's no code, it's on a timer system," Pinn lied, "listen I've got an idea Dano. We're surrounded by serious firepower. We can't fight our way out and sooner or later they're going to come in. I have found a way out."

Pinn told Dano and Clarky about the ventilation shaft. He convinced them that Pete Dodge and the 18th Brigade needed them on the outside, and that Dodge would need all his key Lieutenants around him to withstand any retaliation from the Russians. Dano and Clarky glanced at each other, but they didn't really need much convincing. They were looking at armed robbery at best, which carried a ten-year sentence.

"You and Clarky take the lads down the tunnel. I will stay here and bullshit the dibbles (police) to give you a head start. I will let a couple of the hostages go one at a time. If I drag it out for an hour or so you and the lads will be miles away by the time they realise that there's only me left. I will tell the last few hostages to walk out, and that I'm watching them from the balcony. I will barricade the doors and then follow you down the tunnel. By the time they realise I have gone I can be down the tunnel and across the river," Pinn made the plan very convincing. It was plausible, especially to desperate men looking for a way to avoid a long jail sentence.

"That's fucking brilliant Pinn," Dano said excitedly and genuinely impressed with the idea. "We will leave Ken and Jono with you."

"No thanks. They're fucking idiots, I'll be better off on my own, besides the Brigade will need everyman we can keep out of jail. You lot go now and I'll be fine," Pinn didn't want any of them left when the police came. His plan was to wait until all the Brigade men had gone down the tunnel and then walk out with the hostages, and identify himself as an undercover agent. He would be in the clear and the money was safely hidden, where he could come back for it at a later date. The police would hunt down the Brigade men, but he was exonerated and his cover would still be intact. He didn't intend to ever need the Brigade or the Organised Crime Unit again, his money would see to that. Pinn knew that the Brigades contacts spread worldwide so he had to be very careful. He wanted to disappear, not become a fugitive from every neo-Nazi crime family on the planet.

"Go now, quickly," Pinn hissed. Dano gathered his men and

they sprinted for the rear of the building. Clarky stopped at the end of the corridor and looked back at Pinn. He couldn't understand how Pinn had just stumbled on an access tunnel. Something wasn't right. When he reached the door to the kitchen Clarky saw a blood trail across the kitchen floor as if someone had been dragged. He couldn't stop to question Pinn but he knew something wasn't right. They stared at each other down the length of the corridor, Pinn saw the glint of suspicion in Clarke's eyes but the thought of being incarcerated trumped any misgivings he had. Clarky turned and followed the others down the steps into the cellar. Pinn watched the Brigade men disappear into the cellar and then he froze. There was a loud rumble approaching the building and then suddenly the lights went out, plunging the casino into darkness.

CHAPTER 25

Roman Kordinski/Alexis

Roman sat in the boardroom of his Premiership football club. He had bought the club four years earlier as part of his profile raising strategy, but the project had failed miserably. His millions had attracted an array of talent but they were mostly Prima Donnas with no real skill. He bought the ailing club because the Russian government wanted him dead, as did his business rivals. It is far more difficult to assassinate celebrities without repercussions, than it would be if he were just another Russian exile. He kept the sharp end of his criminal business at a respectable distance from himself. Drug and sex slave trafficking did not fit hand in glove with his entrepreneur image. Rumours of his possible involvement with organised crime were rife in the British press but they added to his persona. His illegal activities were organised by his right hand man Alexis. Roman had no contact at all below his level. His soldiers were forbidden from contacting him directly unless it was an absolute emergency. Roman glared at the screen of his cell phone and he felt the anger rising in his throat. It was the third text message in six hours that he had received from one of his Lieutenants, Yuri. The direct contact alone was against procedure, but Yuri was enquiring as to how the Kellesh situation was being handled. Mentioning the name of anyone at all was a cardinal sin.

Roman was paying attention to his mobile and had stopped listening to the incessant whining of his overpaid football manager, who was making excuses for a four-nil defeat at the hands of Liverpool Football Club for the second time in the season. Roman was losing his temper and the people sat around the table were making him feel worse. He stood and left the table without a word, his chair scraped loudly. The surprised faces around the boardroom watched in surprise as he walked across the boardroom toward his office without so much as an excuse me. The shocked expressions at the table would have made a great picture as Roman stopped and kicked a tin wastepaper bin across the room angrily. It struck the wall with a tremendous clatter and then bounced onto a drinks tray. The tray contained a jug of water and a dozen glasses, which shattered into a hundred pieces in every direction. Silence fell as the metal bin rolled across the room. Roman entered his private office and slammed the door closed violently behind him. The senior members of the football club's staff were left stunned in the boardroom. They looked at each other in shocked amazement. The football team manager, who was a Portuguese character named Moanerio, started to cry for the second time that season.

Roman Kordinski opened the first drawer of his leather-topped desk and removed a blackberry phone. He entered the memory and selected a number. He slammed the drawer closed as he dialled.

"Hello Roman. What can I do for you?" asked Alexis in a cheerful voice. He was a little surprised by the call from his employer. Their calls were always scheduled, and on the few occasions when they did actually meet, it was always at a public event so that it never looked suspicious.

"You can begin by explaining why Yuri is texting me on my personal number, and you can also explain what the fucking hell he is doing mentioning names!" the volume of Romans voice rose to a scream. The men sat around the boardroom table in the next room could hear him shouting. One of them stood and indicated that they should all leave. They headed for the door like naughty schoolboys pushing each other to get away from their enraged teacher.

"Yuri is missing Roman. He was carrying out some work for me at Euston station but never returned. If he was still operational I would be very surprised if he would try to contact you directly," Alexis explained trying to calm his employer. He had worked for Roman for many years now and he was well aware of how quickly his mood could darken. He was a very dangerous man indeed when he lost his temper, almost uncontrollable. The charming smiling business man could disappear in seconds to be replaced by a screaming psychopath who thought nothing of killing anyone in his path.

"What do you mean he is missing? Is he dead?" asked Kordinski. He was starting to run the possible connotations through his mind. If Yuri was dead who was contacting his personal cell phone? If Yuri was dead then the fact that he was receiving messages was worse than he thought, much worse.

"I can only assume that he has resigned without notice or been incapacitated in some way," Alexis said trying to keep the conversation meaningless to anyone listening in. He had been aware of the British security service's desire to tap Roman's phone since his arrival in the UK. They constantly scanned his office for bugs. "We are currently experiencing some problems at our leisure facilities in Liverpool and Manchester. We incurred fire damage."

"Really, at which one," asked Roman angrily. The situation was going from bad to worse. He had to maintain his composure; he couldn't let the mask slip anymore than he already had today.

"All of them," replied Alexis nervously, "we lost over thirty sites, all the money and most of our staff have disappeared."

Roman Kordinski stayed silent. If he had a gun and Alexis was in the same room he would not stop firing until it was empty. His business had been severely damaged. He did not have to ask who was responsible because Alexis had warned of some kind of retaliation following the Kellesh episode. However he had not expected a bunch of skinhead thugs to be so audacious in their response. He was almost impressed, only almost.

"It appears that the fascists are flexing their muscle internationally. We have received threats from the Aryan Brotherhood against our interests in America. Several smaller European groups are also making noises," Alexis continued, "it could be more trouble than it's worth to respond immediately. I think we should conclude our current projects first then deal with the Nazis at a later date. Yuri's phone messages are a concern though. They are not being sent by Yuri. If he was still operational I would know it."

"We must meet immediately Alexis. I think someone is setting up a sting. If Yuri really is indisposed then his cell is being used to make a link with me. Meet me at the garage at six o'clock tonight," said Roman and the line went dead.

Alexis replaced the handset and stared silently at it for a long time. He had called many meetings at the garage over the years. If you were summoned to the garage it was usually a very bad thing. The garage was an empty ministry of defence vehicle testing station. Roman had bought the old army truck facility with a view to developing the land into apartments because of its proximity to the commuter belt. The structure was like an aircraft hangar in appearance. Inside was a wide-open area dissected by a huge inspection pit, which ran the length of the building. The inspection pit had been used to detain suspected informers, disobedient prostitutes and opposition agents. Once thrown into the inspection pit there was no way out unaided. The ladders had long since been removed. The poor unfortunates in the pit often became the sport for their captives above. They became target practice for their pistols or game for the Rottweiler dogs that guarded the site. On several occasions multiple victims in the pit had been armed with spanners or metal bars and left to fight to the death, a promise of freedom to the winner. No one ever left the inspection pit alive. The pit was frequently doused with concentrated sulphuric acid to dissolve any human remains and the slimy residue was then rinsed down a central grid into the sewers. The tiled walls of the pit were smeared with the bloody handprints of its victims. The grouting held several broken fingernails belonging to those desperate souls that refused to die quickly.

Alexis shivered slightly as he contemplated his meeting with Roman Kordinski. Alexis held the total loyalty of most of his men. He would handpick a group of his most trusted soldiers to protect him. If Roman had designs on placing him in the inspection pit, then Alexis would slit his throat and find a new employer.

CHAPTER 26
Tank / JCB

Tank pressed his foot to the floor forcing the accelerator as fast as it could go. Chen had raised the digger's huge steel bucket to eye level to act as a battering ram. Tank clung to the steering wheel as the machine careered across the car park toward the casino wall. He flicked on the JCB's lights and two powerful spotlights which were fixed to the roof of the yellow machine illuminated. The powerful beam cast the shadow of the digger's teeth onto the casino wall, and they grew larger as the machine approached. Tank took the safety switch off his Glock 9mm and chambered a round, and then he replaced it in its holster.

"Hold on tight Chen," shouted Tank over the noise of the diesel engine, "you break left on entry, I'll break right."

The huge yellow JCB weighed over 8 tonnes and it struck the casino wall at 40mph. The effect was devastating. The metal teeth on the bucket pierced the brick wall shattering brickwork over hundreds of yards. The casino wall collapsed beneath the gigantic force, and the machine crashed through the ruined brickwork as if it were matchwood. Chen covered his eyes, nose and mouth with his arms as the machine sprayed debris in all directions. The JCB screeched to a halt inside the main body of the casino. Slot machines and roulette tables were tossed in the air like balsa wood toys. Chen jumped from the slowing machine and rolled behind a bank of slot machines that were still standing. He identified a group of people in the centre of the building, some lying in shock on the floor, while others stood open mouthed. Chen was expecting heavy machinegun fire but none was forthcoming. The interior of the casino was bathed in the powerful beams of the spotlight. Deep long shadows were cast in the corners of the casino offering refuge to potential attackers.

Tank jumped left and took a covered firing position behind a slate dice table. He pointed the Glock toward the hostage position and then rotated the weapon looking for a target. Apart from the shocked civilians at the centre of the casino there appeared to be no other people present. Debris and broken wood crashed and rattled as Faz and the Armed Response Unit charged through the breached wall in support.

"Where are they Tank?" Grace Farrington asked on the open channel. The Armed Response Unit members secured the main area and then headed upstairs to clear the first floor.

"First floor area is clear," said the voice of an Armed Response Unit officer.

"Raised platform area is clear," said the voice of another.

Tank waved the unit to progress into the anti-rooms that surrounded the casino body. The gents and the ladies toilets were empty, as was the cloakroom.

"We have two men down in the strong room, multiple gunshot wounds," said Chen from the back office.

Tank organised the removal of the hostages and then regrouped with the Task Force at the entrance of the back-up corridor, which led to the kitchen service areas. The power was turned back on illuminating the back-up corridor. It looked completely empty.

"There was an undercover Organised Crime Unit agent with the Brigade. He was informed about a ventilation shaft, which leads to the Mersey traffic tunnels. We know it's located to the rear of the building. I think the agent has turned bad and the Brigade has used it as a getaway. If they have then they know that we will follow. There could be booby traps placed to hinder us so we do this by the book," explained Tank, "first things first, let's clear the building, and then we can find the shaft." He pointed his hand toward the corridor and Chen entered it crawling on his stomach. Chen flashed a laser pen from floor to ceiling looking for trip wires. He signalled an ok with his hand indicating that he had found nothing. Chen took a cylindrical aluminium stun grenade from his battle vest. He twisted the cap, which activated it, and threw it down the corridor toward the kitchen. The grenade exploded in a blinding flash of phosphor light. The concussion wave from the device shook pots and pans free from their resting places and they clanged across the kitchen tiles. There was no enemy response.

"Corridor is clear," Chen's voice crackled on the open channel. The Terrorist Task Force agents poured down the corridor hugging the walls as they advanced. An Armed Response Unit officer reached the corner of the wash-up area when suddenly a volley of 9mm machine gunfire smashed into the tiles near his head. He recoiled quickly back into the kitchen area diving for cover.

"Shots fired from the rear service area, 9mm bullets from one machinegun," said the agent from the kitchen floor.

Chen removed another stun grenade from his vest and signalled to Faz to do the same. Faz activated her thunder-flash device and rolled it into the wash-up area, seconds later Chen followed suit. The first grenade exploded with a huge flash of light and a deafening bang. Before the first concussion wave had finished the second grenade roared. The sound wave smashed tiles from the walls and the kitchen windows shattered. The whole purpose of concussion grenades was to completely immobilise enemy personnel without causing fatal injuries. They were especially effective in enclosed areas such as buildings or subways. Areas with strong acoustics such as concrete rooms or tiled areas amplified the devastating effects of the devices. Long seconds went by as the Terrorist Task Force waited for a response, and their patience was rewarded with a loud random burst of 9mm bullets, which ripped into the kitchen ceiling. Plaster fragments were blasted across a wide area, and the fluorescent light strip disintegrated into a thousand pieces.

"He is firing from a protected position," Faz guessed. There was no way anyone could still be functional if they had been caught in the open when the thunder-flashes exploded. She broke cover and sprinted across the kitchen area. She stopped by the metal door to the walk-in fridge and opened it so that it acted as a barrier. The chilled body of the young skinhead Pinn had killed earlier lay glassy eyed on the floor. His upper teeth were exposed in a macabre grin, which gave him a zombie like appearance. The exposed tongue, which lolled to one side, was already starting to blacken.

"Kitchen area clear, one man down in the cold room, gunshot wounds to the face," she reported.

"Can you see their current position Grace?" Tank asked. Faz looked through the hinged edge of the doorframe and she could see the snub noised barrel of an Uzi 9mm machinegun leaning against the tiled floor at the bottom of an open door.

"I can see their position. It looks like they are at the top of a flight of stairs, which descend into a lower level. I'm going to bounce a grenade off the wall in front of him and try to deflect it down the stairs behind him," Faz said twisting the cap of another concussion grenade. She tossed it across the wash-up area aiming just below the ceiling. The cylinder struck the white tiles and bounced across the room toward the open doorway. Grace heard the sound of footsteps running down the stairs and the clatter of the grenade striking the tiled floor of the cellar. There was an ear splitting explosion and a blinding flash followed by the sound of metal beer barrels clanging across the floor. Tank and his agents passed Faz's position and moved with military precision to the top of the cellar stairs. The cellar ceiling obscured the view of the lower level and there was only a small area around the bottom of the steps visible. Tank gestured to one of his agents and he removed a thin carbon fibre rod from his utility belt. He twisted the rod and a rectangular mirror fanned out from the end. He then extended the rod to its full length and scanned the cellar area with it.

"One man down in the centre of the floor space, looks to be incapacitated, Uzi 9mm machinegun in close proximity to his right hand side," said the officer. Tank waved his team down the stairs were they secured the small cellar and covered the ventilation shaft entrance. The man on the floor unconscious was Organised Crime Unit officer Simon Pinn, although they wouldn't know that until he regained consciousness. The effects of the concussion grenade had been amplified tenfold in the confined concrete area of the cellar, rendering Pinn senseless. There was a small trickle of blood running from his left ear indicating some internal damage. He was trussed up with plasticuffs and dragged up the stairs to a waiting prison van, which would be taking him directly to the Terrorist Task Force custody suite.

"Major, can you check the scanners for body heat? We only have one man in here," Tank asked over the communication channel.

"It appears they moved to the rear of the building seconds before you breached the building," the Major replied, "they're off the radar now so we can only assume they are in the tunnel network. There is too much water and concrete above them for the scanners to work. They can only be minutes ahead of you."

"Is there any indication which way they have taken?" Tank asked entering the access tunnel. He paused as it joined the main ventilation shaft and scanned the tunnel in both directions.

"Negative Tank," replied the Major.

Tank returned to the cellar and organised the Task Force into two groups. One group was to follow Chen and head west, further under the River Mersey; the second group was to follow Tank and Faz east, heading away from the river toward the tunnel entrance. The entrance was situated a half a mile away in a purpose built service building. The building housed huge ventilation fans that removed exhaust fumes from the traffic tunnels. Both units entered the tunnel and prepared to follow the Brigade men. Faz noticed that the thick layer of dust coating an emergency cupboard had been disturbed, and fresh finger marks were clearly visible. She nudged Tank and he covered the door with his Glock while Faz flung the door wide open. Apart from two rusty fire extinguishers and a fire blanket the cupboard was empty.

"Are you going to shoot the naughty fire extinguisher?" Tank teased.

Faz punched him on the arm and shut the cupboard door. Simon Pinn's hidden money was still safe for now.

CHAPTER 27

Yŭri/Yŭsŭf

Yusuf waited half an hour after he had heard the gunshot coming from the Russian's cell. He knew what type of man Yuri had been, and he knew that he had taken his own life with a single bullet. Despite one being Jewish and the other Muslim, they had a lot in common. Both were warriors of the highest degree. Their masters were essentially the same entity despite their cultural differences; they were powerful men who used violence to protect their empires. They paid the best wages to recruit the elite ex-military personnel for their private armies. Yusuf opened the door and ushered three guards into the cell. They picked up and removed two fellow Saudi guards, one was dead the other seriously injured but still breathing. Yuri was in a sitting position on the small cot bed. His chin was resting on his chest and the top of his head was splattered up the wall in a red slimy fan pattern. Grey globules of brain matter were running very slowly down the paintwork. Yusuf ordered a black plastic body bag to be brought from the nurses' quarters and they placed the big Russian into it. They left the gun in his dead hand and zipped up the fastener. The Saudis placed Yuri's body into the boot of a black Mercedes SUV. It was scarily similar to the one he had been brought to the Saudi embassy in.

Yuri had been seconded to Russia's elite Counter Terrorist Unit, Spetsgruppa Alpha in 1991. During an attempted coup in late 1991, the Alpha group had been led by Major General Viktor Karpukhin. The General had ambitions to storm the Kremlin using Special Forces and to wrestle power from the politicians. His plan was to attack and kill Boris Yeltsin and his leaders. Yuri and his platoon refused point blank to follow the General's orders, and wiped out a division of rebel Russian paratroopers in the process. The ensuing firefight lasted three and a half hours during which the Spetsgruppa Alpha killed every member of the rogue unit, without losing a single man themselves. Yuri was interviewed by the Soviet leadership about the plot and its possible connotations. Yuri had estimated that the Spetsgruppa Alpha would have stormed the Kremlin and killed the entire Russian parliament in under twenty-five minutes, had it chosen to follow the General's orders. As the Russian Empire crumbled Yuri had found employment with the notorious Mafia, the Organizatsiya. Now the once great warrior was being transported in a plastic bag in the trunk a family saloon.

Yuri's body was driven a short distance across London to Paddington police station. They pulled the body from the vehicle and placed it in a covered bus stop. The dumpsite had been chosen carefully because it was not covered by CCTV cameras, but was less than two hundred yards from the police station. Yusuf saluted the body bag and placed a leather holdall containing the mobile phone and audiotapes next to the body. As the Mercedes pulled away Yusuf made an anonymous call on a prepaid cell phone informing the police that a man connected to the River Dee bombings was in the bus stop.

CHAPTER 28

Pete Dodge/Terry Nick

Pete Dodge sat in a small interview room at the main police station in Warrington. The station had been built in Victorian times, which gave the building historic listed building status. The down side was that the cells and interview rooms were prehistoric and stank of urine. Facilities were basic to say the least. The table Dodge was sat at was fixed to the floor with metal brackets to deter angry prisoners from throwing it. He had been given a plastic cup containing a warm liquid, which vaguely resembled tea over two hours ago. Since then three different detectives had been into the room to question him briefly but they had all concurred that the information Dodge was giving was beyond the jurisdiction of the Cheshire Police Force.

The door opened and David Bell entered. Bell was an information analyst from the Terrorist Task Force. The Warrington police had contacted them, and asked them to send an agent down to interview Dodge. Bell had been involved in cracking a terrorist plot to bomb a football match at Anfield in Liverpool the year before. The nefarious terrorist leader Yasser Ahmed had wreaked havoc across American tourist destinations before attempting the same in the UK. David Bell placed two blank cassettes into an archaic recording machine and pressed record.

"Agent David Bell is present interviewing Peter Dodge at Warrington police station. The date is 8th January 2008, and the time is six pm," the agent said starting the interview. He had a feeling that this was going to be a waste of time but he had to go through the motions. There was no doubt that two members of the 18th Brigade had been present at the River Dee incident, but Pete

Dodge had walked into a police station announcing that he knew who was responsible for planting the bomb. The information may be genuine, it may be claptrap, but it couldn't be ignored.

"Can you repeat for the tape what you told my colleagues earlier regarding the bomb on the River Dee," Bell asked with a big sigh trying to give Dodge the impression that he didn't believe his claims.

"I was approached by a Russian business man by the name of Alexis to abduct a young girl from a party, which was being held onboard the Princess Diana, on the River Dee" Dodge began, "It was a straightforward business transaction."

"So you personally became involved in a conspiracy to commit kidnap for financial reward," Bell droned on thinking that Dodge was going to walk into an uncontested kidnap charge.

"No, I certainly did not. I declined the offer however I think that several of my ex-employees were approached at a later date," Dodge lied, "I now believe that they were involved in the alleged abduction."

"Really Mr Dodge, so you had nothing to do with the organisation or planning?" the Task Force man probed, "can you explain how one of your ex-employees ended up burned to death at the scene of the bombing?"

"I can only assume that my ex-employees had some kind of disagreement with the Russians or each other," Dodge shrugged his shoulders and he knew that no one could prove his involvement. The only corroborating evidence was destroyed when the Orford Arms burnt to the ground.

David Bell grasped what was happening. The 18th Brigade was washing its hands of the incident and offering evidence of who the culprits really were.

"We think that you were involved and that Jeannie Kellesh was taken to your headquarters," Bell pressed for a reaction, "we also think you're responsible for a series of arson attacks the following week."

"Prove it Agent Bell, as my business premises was burned down by your officers you'll find it difficult to support your accusations. Likewise with any alleged arson attacks. I am an honest businessman. I run a door security company, which brings me into contact with all kinds of dishonest characters. I can show you my telephone records, which will demonstrate calls made to me by Alexis Radev. He asked me to abduct a young girl, which I refused to do. The boat was blown up by terrorists and I think we both know who is responsible," Dodge thumped his clenched fist on the table as he made each point.

"What is your relationship with Mr Radev?" Bell asked sarcastically.

"He sometimes provides me with door personnel when we have absenteeism, he is involved in import, export business," Dodge answered equally sarcastically.

"He is involved with the import and export of drugs and prostitutes Mr Dodge," Bell said taking his spectacles off, "let's not fuck about, he supplies you with drugs to sell inside the venues that your bouncers police. You kidnapped the Saudi girl, and then things went sour with the Russians so you burnt down their brothels."

"You have an incredibly vivid imagination Agent Bell. I have come here out of my own sense of public duty and offered valuable information about a horrific crime," Dodge adopted a hurt expression as he rambled on, "if you're going to continue making such allegations then I think I'll leave and come back with a lawyer."

"That's your prerogative Mr Dodge," said the agent, frustrated at playing games, "why would Alexis Radev want to involve you? Why blow up a riverboat?"

"I am speculating of course because I refused to be involved in the incident, but I think the whole palaver is a set up," Dodge thumped the desk again, "they blew up the boat to cover up the abduction and they wanted someone else in the frame. What you really need to do is speak to his boss."

"And who would that be Mr Dodge?" said Bell looking over the top rim of his glasses curiously.

"Roman Kordinski," Dodge replied very slowly pronouncing each vowel.

David Bell removed his glasses again and stood up. He walked to the end of the small interview room and leaned against the wall, "Roman Kordinski the oil magnet? Roman Kordinski the premiership football club owner? Roman Kordinski the celebrity businessman?" he asked incredulously.

"Roman Kordinski the drug baron, the sex slave trafficker, the assassin and all round mafia boss," Dodge laughed, "that's the very same man."

CHAPTER 29
Tunnel/Chen/Clarky

As Clarky and the Brigade men reached the ventilation tunnel the lights in the casino went out. Seconds later there was a deafening crashing noise as the JCB breached the walls.

"Something isn't right Dano," Clarky said grabbing his arm, "did you see the blood in the kitchen? Pinn is fucking us over."

"We haven't got time to mess about Clarky. We need to get out of here. We can sort this out when we get rid of the dibbles," Dano said, "You take half the lads that way and I'll take the other half this way. We'll meet up at the Quarterdeck tomorrow."

Clarky shook his head in frustration. He checked that the magazine of his Uzi 9mm was full and then headed off west down the tunnel. Emergency lights were fixed to the wall every hundred yards and he could see them reaching far into the distance until the curvature of the tunnel made them disappear. The tunnel was angled down about twenty degrees as it followed the descent of the traffic tunnels beneath the River Mersey.

"Glinka, have you got your hammer?" he asked one of the younger skinheads. Glinka always carried a four-pound claw hammer on his belt, which he used at every available opportunity to break things and hurt people.

"Yes, of course I have," Glinka answered. A blue tattooed Swastika became visible on his tongue when he spoke.

"Smash the lights as we pass them, we need to slow the dibbles down," ordered Clarky.

Glinka looked pleased with himself as he took the claw hammer and shattered the emergency lights. The group jogged quickly down the slope away from the casino, and it was four minutes before they heard the first concussion grenades exploding in the kitchen area. The noise of the grenades gave Clarky an idea. He stripped the electric wires from the tunnel wall and then separated a thin plastic coated length from the bundle. He placed a fragmentation grenade against the tunnel wall and stuffed it behind a metal conduit. Clarky tied the electric cable across the tunnel and attached it to the activation pin of the grenade. The other end he tied to a metal grill making a tripwire. Glinka waited until Clarky had finished and then he laughed as he smashed the light above it.

"Great stuff, we're going to blow them to bits," Glinka was laughing like a schoolboy as he ran away.

Clarky had no intentions of blowing up anybody. The grenade he had trip wired was called a sting grenade. It was based on the basic design of a military fragmentation grenade, but instead of being made of shrapnel producing metal, it was made from rubber instead. Two spheres of hard rubber encased an explosive charge, primer and detonator. The interior was filled with hundreds of small hard rubber balls. Anyone close to the device when it detonated was incapacitated by the blunt force of the projectiles, but not fatally injured. The sting in the grenade was provided by an additional payload of CS gas. The tear gas was produced by 120 grams of CS gas, which upon detonation combines with a small pyrotechnic composition that burns to generate an aerosol of CS-laden smoke. It would stop any pursuers in their tracks. The combination of blunt force trauma and choking gas would slow even the most determined enemy. To the rest of the Brigade men it looked exactly like a normal fragmentation grenade. Neil Clarke, or Clarky, was an MI6 agent working directly for Agent Garden. It was his intelligence gathering that had uncovered the information about the Saudi Princess. Agent Garden had blindsided Major Timms during their earlier video conference call with the defence minister. MI6 had been investigating the 18th Brigade and several other Nazi factions linked to the British National Party for years. They had no interest in their minor crime activities but their fascist agendas and political aspirations had to be closely monitored. Right wing political parties would only be tolerated as long as they enjoyed limited success. The skinhead organisations had been infiltrated by a myriad of law enforcement agencies. The law enforcement departments rarely shared information with one another, especially when undercover agents were involved.

Clarky needed to stop the Terrorist Task Force agents from apprehending him, without causing any fatalities, or years of undercover work would be wasted. He had suspected that Simon Pinn wasn't all that he seemed, but he couldn't expose him without compromising his own position. He checked the tension of the trip wire and then followed his men further down the ventilation shaft beneath the River Mersey.

Chen and his Task Force agents entered the main shaft from the casino and proceeded down the tunnel in pursuit of the Brigade men. Their protective boots made a crunching sound as they crushed the broken glass from the emergency lights.

"Switch to night vision and dark mag-lights," Chen ordered his team as they edged down the tunnel hugging the walls. They stayed close to the sides of the shaft and made it harder to be seen by keeping low. Dark mag-lights were fitted to the helmets of his team. They cast a light imperceptible to the human eye without infra-green vision. This stopped the enemy from seeing your torchlight, which made you a simple target. The dark mag-light improved vision up to about twenty feet without alerting the enemy. They made steady progress down the gentle slope. Chen spoke briefly to Tank over the coms-channel and ascertained that they had made no contact with the Brigade men either. He felt nervous as they progressed in formation down the shaft. Chen scanned the way ahead with a laser light looking for trip wires belonging to mines. The laser light prompted a short burst of 9mm machinegun fire fired from somewhere up ahead. The fat shells blasted chunks of concrete from the ceiling above them and he extinguished the light immediately to discourage another salvo.

"That came from a long way ahead," Chen spoke to his men, "we'll have to advance using infra-green only." The lead agent stopped and bent low to inspect the tunnel and then gave the thumbs up sign. The rear agent jogged from the back and overtook the front man, and then the rest followed in formation. Chen was following the agent in front of him when the Terrorist Task Force man stumbled over something. Chen saw that the wires from the tunnel wall had been stripped a split second before the sting grenade exploded in his face.

CHAPTER 30
Tank/Dano Tunnel

Dano reached the end of the access tunnel when he heard the grenades explode in the casino. He and his men had jogged six hundred yards up a gentle slope away from the river, and he could see Clarky and the others disappearing around the long curving bend into the distance. There was a wooden door in front of him and he grabbed the handle with a sweaty palm and twisted it. The door wouldn't budge. Dano stepped back a few yards and fired a short burst from his 9mm machinegun at the handle. The wood around the locking mechanism splintered into a hundred pieces and the metal handle was ripped from the door as it sprung open. Dano looked into the cavernous service building. The large motor room beyond was dimly lit by emergency lighting, and it appeared to be completely unoccupied. The Brigade men entered the building silently checking for any employees. The noise from the huge exhaust extraction fans was deafening. Dano noticed a bank of seven steel lockers across the room that were used to secure tunnel employee belongings while they worked.

"Barricade the door with those lockers," Dano ordered. He was acutely aware that the police would be in pursuit in a matter of minutes. The Brigade men carried the heavy lockers across the room and jammed them into the tunnel entrance. Dano opened every door as the lockers passed and removed overalls, high viz jackets and yellow safety helmets from them. He distributed them between the group of skinheads and they dressed quickly in silence.

"When we leave the building we leave one at a time and in different directions," Dano explained. The entire area surrounding the river was a series of construction sites. The City of Liverpool was granted European Capital of Culture status in 2008. The award preceded huge amounts of money being invested in the redevelopment of the city centre. New shopping malls were springing up all along the riverbank. Old derelict warehouses were being transformed into art galleries and cafe bars. From the Mersey tunnel service building to the myriad of construction sites was a few hundred yards. The brigade men would stand a good chance of escaping unnoticed if they could leave immediately and split up. The work wear would act as the perfect disguise.

Dano entered a corridor and a short distance along it he discovered a small control room that was surrounded by clear Perspex walls. Three sides of the room were dedicated to switchgear and electronic gauges. There was a single technician wearing a white overall and a yellow jacket, sat at a desk. He was blissfully unaware of the uninvited guests behind him as he listened to his MP3 player, and read the newspaper. The gauges monitored carbon monoxide levels caused by engine exhaust fumes in the road tunnels. The tunnels were over three miles long, and descended a mile beneath the River Mersey. Huge exhaust fans worked round the clock to maintain a breathable atmosphere in the tunnels. Any increase in carbon monoxide levels could render unsuspecting motorists unconscious. The lethal gas is an invisible killer and because it is denser than oxygen it lingers close to the floor, making it especially dangerous in traffic tunnels. Dano struck the technician on the base of the skull with his heavy metal gun. He collapsed in a heap on the floor beneath the desk. There was a large red switch on the right hand panel, which controlled the electricity supply to the fluorescent lights that illuminated the road tunnels and its service shafts.

"Start leaving one at a time. I'm going to give them something else to worry about," Dano ordered, "meet up at the Turf and Feather, in Locking Stumps when you get back." He flicked the switch to off, plunging the traffic tunnels into total darkness in an instant.

As the tunnels were plunged into inky blackness, the driver of a number twenty-six Arriva bus was caught completely unaware as he carried his passengers beneath the river from Liverpool to Birkenhead. He slammed his brakes on in the inky darkness but couldn't keep the bus straight. It careered across the centre island into the oncoming traffic causing a multiple pile up. The fuel tank of the bus was punctured as it hit the metal safety barrier, and diesel fuel sprayed over the road. The rider of a Honda Blackbird motorcycle couldn't focus in the gloom as the lights went out, and he ploughed into the back of the bus. The motorbike scraped along the tarmac and the exhaust pipe disintegrated into a shower of sparks which landed in the spreading fuel. The diesel ignited into a wall of flame and the number twenty-six bus started to burn. The pile up continued to grow quickly in both directions as oncoming traffic crashed into the stationary vehicles in front of them. Thick acrid smoke started to fill the tunnel as the bus tyres caught fire. Just when things couldn't possibly get any worse, Dano turned off the huge exhaust fans.

CHAPTER 31

Roman/Alexis

Alexis sat in the passenger seat of a black Volkswagen Toureg and pulled on a pair of black leather gloves. He reached into his leather jacket and removed a Colt 45 from its holster. The heavy silver pistol made famous by Clint Eastwood in his Dirty Harry movies weighed over three kilos when fully loaded. He ran his hand along the cold steel and its touch reassured him. The Colt was his favourite weapon and he had used it to kill many times before. Alexis had been born in 1968 in the Russian state of Georgia to ethnically Russian Jewish parents. His family moved to Moscow when he was three years old. Alexis was an amateur wrestler in his youth and his reputation as a fighter was fearsome, even before he had left school. He served a short prison sentence at the age of seventeen for his participation in a bar fight during which he dislocated his opponents shoulder. Once in the penal system he was introduced to the Russian Mafia, who identified him as a potential future asset. After his release he began to move up the ranks of the criminal world, selling goods on the black market. It wasn't long before he had become involved in gang activity. Alexis and his gang used forged police documents to enter people's houses and then rob them. In 1992 he was arrested on firearms, forgery and drug trafficking charges. Alexis received a fourteen-year jail sentence but was released after serving just two months of his term. He had made connections with Russian state intelligence organisations, and their organised crime partners, corruption was rife. Alexis had been nicknamed Yaponchik, which means 'little Japanese' due to his vaguely slanted eyes, and his criminal reputation had reached the ears of Roman Kordinski. Roman was a powerful businessman, and he reportedly bribed a Supreme Court judge to set aside Alexis' conviction. Their partnership in crime began upon his release.

Alexis was sent to America to set up business for Roman in the West. He arrived in the United States with the reputation as one of the fiercest criminals in Russia. He entered America on a regular business visa, which stated that he was to work in the film industry. The Russian Ministry of Internal Affairs advised the FBI that Alexis had come to manage and control Russian organised crime activities but their warning was ignored. The editor for the newspaper, Novoye Russkaye Slova wrote an article in 1994. He alleged that Roman Kordinski had left Russia because it was too dangerous for him there, since the new Muslim Chechen criminal entrepreneurs had set up business.

Alexis had been put in charge of a Russian gang on Brighton Beach, New York, which numbered around a hundred men. It became the premier crime group in Brooklyn. He systematically used violence and corruption to establish a monopoly on criminal enterprise. For four years they ran riot through New York's criminal underworld netting millions of dollars in the process. In 1998 he was arrested by the FBI and charged with the extortion of several million dollars from an investment advisory firm, which was run by two Russian Muslim business men. In June of the following year he was convicted with two co-defendants on the charge of extortion. During the trial one of his victims' fathers had been assassinated in Moscow, along with his wife and elderly mother. The murders were committed to discourage further testimony being given, and as a warning to a nervous jury.

The extortion charges collapsed, however Alexis was deported to Russia to face charges that he was responsible for all of the three murders. The jury in the murder trial found him not guilty and he was acquitted again. During the subsequent murder trial six witnesses, including three Russian policemen and a high-ranking government official, failed to appear in court. Alexis was released and joined Roman Kordinski in the United Kingdom where rebuilding had already begun.

Today Alexis was parked on an old World War 2 airbase on the outskirts of Warrington called Burtonwood. The airbase had been the home of the United States Air Force through the war and into the 1960's. In the 80's it had been closed and partially dismantled. There were still eight aircraft hangars standing on the old base. The hangars were 500yds long and twice as wide. They were shaped like huge barrels cut in half and laid on the floor. The curved buildings were designed to confuse enemy bomber pilots who were programmed to look for groups of rectangular shapes to bomb. The Ministry of Transport purchased part of the airfield, and several large hangars, which they converted into an inspection centre. Ten years on, Roman bought the site for redevelopment, and they had used it for the interrogation and disposal of troublesome employees, and rival gangsters. Alexis had been ordered to meet his boss at the derelict inspection hangar, which made alarm bells ring in his head. He had three of his most loyal men with him in the Volkswagen, and three more in a similar vehicle 100yds away. He wasn't going to take any chances.

Self-preservation was making his senses ultra-sharp, and he had noticed that his driver was sporting a new Rolex watch. He could be being paranoid, but paranoid was better than dead. Mafioso would often change allegiances for money, and he didn't want to take the chance that his man had betrayed him.

"Wait here and keep the engine running," Alexis ordered the driver, "the rest of you come with me." The driver flushed red, which made Alexis more suspicious of him. He locked eyes with the driver and the driver looked away immediately. Alexis took the big Colt from his shoulder holster and pulled the trigger. The massive 45-calibre bullet hit the driver in the side of the head above his ear, leaving a ragged hole the size of a plum. The force of the bullet smashed the Russians head against the window shattering the glass to smithereens. One of Alexis' men had exited the rear of the vehicle, on the opposite side, and was sprayed from head to toe with blood and gore. He stood frozen to the spot with brain matter running down his cheek, which he wiped off with the back of his sleeve. He looked at the sticky fluid with bulging eyes and then vomited against the side of the vehicle. Alexis had sent a powerful message to his men that betrayal was a capital offence. The men in the other vehicle heard the shot and ran toward them with their weapons drawn.

"Everything is fine," Alexis said replacing his gun into his holster, "Take the watch from his wrist and bring it with you," he ordered. A fat Russian Mafioso with a blond ponytail leaned into the Volkswagen and removed the Rolex. He then patted the dead man's jacket looking for his weapon and took a 9mm Luger from his waistband. The five men headed toward the hangar and the fat man handed the Rolex to Alexis. He studied the watch face and its gold metal strap. Alexis recognised it as a Submariner, which was the model Roman Kordinski favoured.

"Be on your guard," Alexis said to the group as they approached the hangar door, "I have got a feeling that we may be heading for a career change." He knew that things had gotten out of hand since Roman had received notice from the Kremlin that his oil business was to be renationalised. Greed was the route of all evil especially where money was concerned. Alexis didn't agree with the kidnap of the Saudi Princess. Roman had ordered the bombings of the riverboat and Piccadilly rail terminus to cast suspicion on Islamic extremists, and to increase the public mistrust of the Muslim communities. Judging from the reaction of the British public the ploy had worked. Public opinion was turning against an acceptance of integration with foreign immigrants, and Islamaphobia was spreading across the nation.

The previous year's terrorist attacks committed by Yasser Ahmed, and his Axe group had prompted a violent reaction from Britain's indigenous Christians. Mosques were burned to the ground and Muslim businesses became targets for vandalism. There had been riots in some areas with large Muslim populations. The volatile situation was compounded in January 2008 when five Muslim men were found guilty of conspiracy to murder. Imran Parvis and his co-conspirators plotted to kidnap a Muslim British soldier from the streets of Birmingham and behead him on camera. They were then to post the footage on the internet as a warning to other Muslims, who were considering a career in the British armed forces. Public reaction to the plot was one of horror and it added fuel to flames of racial hatred. The United Kingdom had not witnessed civil unrest on this scale since the race riots of the late 70's. Roman had counted on a similar response to the river bomb and the incident in Manchester, and he wasn't disappointed. The countries law enforcement agencies were swamped trying to maintain public order, which allowed organised crime families to trade unabated. Anti-immigrant political parties such as the BNP, and neo-Nazi groups like the 18th Brigade and Combat 18 were receiving a record number of new members. Alexis realised that the authorities would see through the plot eventually and would target all its resources against those truly responsible.

Maybe it was time for Alexis to become self employed. He could surround himself with a hardcore of ruthless Russian exiles, and concentrate on simple honest lawbreaking like drugs and prostitution, all this religious bull shit was getting out of hand. He was in fear of his life and his liberty, but he would meet with Roman one last time, and give him the opportunity to remain as his long term employer. There would be no discussions about severance pay or pension funds. It would be fine or he would give his resignation in the form a 45mm bullet.

They reached the massive hangar shutter door, and approached a smaller door, which was set into it. Alexis opened the metal door and stepped into the cavernous hangar. His footsteps echoed across the concrete. The hangar was dimly lit and at first he thought that it was empty. A black rent in the ground ran the length of the hangar splitting it into two halves. Alexis knew it was the old vehicle inspection pit. About two hundred yards away across the inspection pit, he could see a white transit van. The headlights flashed acknowledging their arrival.

"Spread out and hold your line on me," Alexis said quietly, "I don't want them to panic and do something rash."

"Rash, like shooting one of your own men in the face because you want his watch?" said the fat Soviet with the ponytail. Alexis stopped and glared at the man who glared back. The ponytail placed his hand inside his jacket and gripped the handle of his pistol. His fat face flushed, because he knew that now was not the time to challenge Alexis.

"The watch belongs to Roman you stupid fat fuck," Alexis hissed, "now why do think he would be wearing Roman's watch?" The man removed his hand from his pistol and his facial muscles relaxed giving him a confused expression. Alexis shrugged his shoulders and nodded toward the van. The men walked toward it in a line, conflict forgotten for now. They spread out as they walked, leaving fifty yards between them, and the next man. The Russians loyal to Alexis were big men. They wore leather coats of various styles and lengths and looked menacing as they approached the transit van, which was parked on the far side of the inspection pit. They looked like the reservoir dogs on steroids.

From the gloom at the far end of the hangar a set of headlights illuminated and a long black limousine crawled into view and parked next to the van. The doors of the van opened and three men exited from the front; four more climbed out of the back, making seven. The men took up positions along the deep inspection pit. No weapons were drawn yet but the anticipation of violence was tangible. Alexis' men stopped short of the pit leaving seventy yards between them and Roman's men.

The driver of the black limousine stepped from the vehicle and opened the rear passenger door to allow its occupants to alight. Roman Kordinski exited the limo followed by three more leather clad bodyguards who were all carrying Brugger & Thomet tactical TP 9mm machinegun pistols. That made twelve, including the driver. The machine pistols were favoured by Special Forces worldwide and are capable of firing 900, 9mm armour piercing bullets in a minute. Astonishingly they can be bought on the internet by anyone with a credit card for just $1200 via mail order. They stood menacingly along the inspection pit. Roman was wearing an expensive wool suit tailored at London's Saville Row. He didn't look like he was here for a scrap; he looked more like he was attending a board meeting. Roman stepped forward a few steps and indicated that Alexis should do the same.

"Why are you carrying all the hardware Alexis?" Roman asked smiling like a snake, "We are old friends. Don't you trust me anymore?"

Alexis looked along the inspection pit and counted twelve men including Roman and his driver. The fact that three of them were carrying Brugger and Thomet machineguns tipped the balance completely in Roman's favour.

"I would say that a man of your intelligence can work out who is carrying the hardware Roman," Alexis answered stepping forward slowly.

"Tell your men to place their weapons on the floor and we can talk," Roman said, "I need to get you out of the country quickly Alexis."

"What are you talking about? Where would I go?" Alexis asked.

"The police will be looking into my affairs very closely," Roman said, "Yuri's disappearance is no coincidence. Someone is trying to implicate me in the Saudi's kidnap. They will come for you first because of your previous record, and our history of working together. Tell your men to place their guns on the floor while we talk Alexis. I can smell the sweat of fear from our men. There is no need for bloodshed. We are on the same side, remember?"

Alexis thought about it, but he knew Roman too well. If he thought Alexis was a liability because of his intimate knowledge and involvement in Romans business, then he was already dead. He would not be dying easily, not today or any other day.

"My men will lay down their weapons when your men lay down theirs," Alexis challenged Roman.

"I am afraid that's not possible," Roman said laughing, as arrogance oozed from his every pore.

Alexis signalled his right hand toward an elevated metal walkway, which was situated above the hangar doors behind him, and a suppressed shot hissed across the cavernous airplane hangar. The limousine driver was knocked of his feet as .75mm bullet smashed into his chest. A hidden sniper that Alexis had deployed as insurance in case Roman turned up mob handed had fired the massive bullet. His instincts had proved correct. The bullet was fired from an A10 Marine Corps sniper rifle, and it made an exit wound the size of a football as it ripped his back out. His ribcage and lungs were liquidised by the power of the impact, and sprayed the bonnet of the long black limo with a crimson mush. A second shot impacted the concrete between Romans' feet as a warning, and shards of shattered stone covered Roman's pristine suit with cement dust.

Romans' men pulled their weapons from their holsters, and Alexi's men responded in kind. Both sets of men pointed weapons at each other across the dark inspection pit in a Mexican standoff. No one fired for fear of starting a firefight that couldn't be won. Roman's men had the added fear of becoming the unseen sniper's next target.

Roman raised his hands in a gesture of surrender, "Tell your sniper not to shoot Alexis, and you have made your point that we are covered by your sniper. Alexis you are a very clever man. That's why I hired you. It seems that you are holding all the aces, but our problem hasn't changed. You must understand that someone is trying to implicate us in the bombings, which puts me in a precarious position my old friend."

"You made your position very clear 'old friend', by turning up with all this firepower. I don't believe for one minute that you wanted to discuss smuggling me out of the country." Alexis said walking backwards slowly and indicating that his men do the same. Sniper or no sniper Roman and his machineguns could decimate Alexis' men in a matter of minutes. It was time to make a sharp exit.

"It would be far easier for you to throw me into the pit and dispose of me with the acid, like we have a dozen times before boss," Alexis emphasised the 's' in boss as edged closer to the door.

"Do you really think you can just walk away Alexis?" Roman Kordinski hissed aggressively. He was starting to lose his temper because he had been out witted, and was no longer in control. He looked from left to right trying to gauge how many men would die before they killed Alexis, and his blasted sniper.

Alexis watched Roman intently, and he could see that he was about to do something rash. He lifted his right hand again in a different direction, and another silenced rifle shot spat. This time the shot came from the rafters behind Roman and his men, as a second sniper took aim and fired. A bodyguard next to Roman staggered like a zombie toward the dark inspection pit, holding his machinegun in front of his body. His head had exploded beneath the colossal force of a .75 bullet, which had hit him from behind, arterial blood splatter sprayed Roman and his men. All that remained of the Russian's head was his front lower jaw, but his body continued to walk reflexively until it toppled over the edge of the oily service pit.

Roman's men froze, raising their hands in the air aware now that they were surrounded by at least two expert snipers. Roman stood as still as a statue as his face turned crimson with anger. Warm blood trickled down his neck into his crisp white collar. Alexis turned and ran toward the hangar door signalling to his snipers as he went. The A10 rifles spat their deadly load from both directions and Roman's men started to fall. Panic set in and both sides opened fire with fully automatic weapons, and the old hangar became a deafening killing zone.

CHAPTER 32

Yuri's Body/Graham Libby

Graham Libby was the Terrorist Task Force coroner. He pulled on his white coat and rubber gloves, and switched on a computer web cam. The camera was pointed at the tortured body of the Russian Yuri, who had been discovered at a bus stop in Paddington London, following an anonymous phone call. The discovery of certain evidence with the body quickly linked it to terrorist events in Chester and Manchester. Yuri's body was flown north to Liverpool where the final affront of an autopsy would be carried out.

"The subject appears to be in his late thirties or early forties. He is circumcised and has several Hebrew tattoos indicating he is of Jewish stock. The tattoos are the insignia of belonging to the Russian Mafia, and we can look at Wikipedia later to translate their exact significance." The coroner looked closer at the genital area using a pencil to lift the discoloured penis away from the charred testicles. He would have to remember not to chew the pencil later, or stir his coffee with it in an absent minded moment. It wouldn't be the first time it had happened.

"There are electric current burn-in marks on the head of the penis, and deep abrasions which appear to have been caused by some type of clamp." He lifted the scrotum with the rubber end of the pencil and studied the injuries.

"Similar abrasions are on the testis however the burn marks are more severe so I am concluding that they are burn-out marks, caused by the same electric current leaving the body." Graham Libby took a scalpel. He switched on a spotlight to improve the view of the groin area. He now had a pencil in one hand and the cutting tool in the other, which gave him the appearance of a mad drummer, or a barking professor. He moved the penis with the pencil and cut through the burn marks on the scrotum.

"The scar tissue on the interior of the scrotum is substantially thicker than it is on the surface, indicating burn-out marks from a low voltage electric current. There is heavy blood staining around the groin and inner thigh area. The amount of blood is not contusive to electric shock injury, even if sharp clamps were applied."

Graham Libby pulled down a steel spray head, which hung from the ceiling above the mortuary slab. He squeezed the handle and a gentle spray of warm water was directed on the congealed blood that clung to the corpse. He asked his assistant to help him turn the body.

"The blood has cleared revealing no lacerations to the thighs or groin area." He parted the fleshy buttocks with the pencil and winced as he saw the damage to the anal area. There were two deep tears to the rectal sphincter, which travelled several inches in each direction and appeared to continue upward into the lower intestine.

"The subject has been subjected to sustained electric shock torture. A low voltage has been used to ensure the victim doesn't die of a heart attack, but he would have endured incredible pain. The rectal area shows extensive lacerations contusive with violent anal rape probably by several perpetrators."

Graham Libby had seen every kind of victim a coroner could see. Victims of violent torture always made him feel incredibly vulnerable. The thought of being restrained and subjected to excruciating pain made him nauseous. The Jewish man on the slab bore all the marks of a gang member, and gang members lived by a violent code of ethics. It made little difference in the end though how tough they were. Everyone was made of flesh and blood that is frighteningly fragile. Devastating trauma can be caused to the human form by anything hard or sharp, fire, chemicals or electricity. The man on the slab had been subjected to a hideous ordeal before the bullet, which had killed him, finally ended his pain. It appeared to have been self inflicted although he couldn't confirm it until the tests for gunshot residue had been completed and returned. The fact that the dead man had finally ended his own torment gave Graham Libby little comfort. He took several swabs from the dead man's hands to send to ballistics. The science of ballistics identifies which gun was used to commit a specific crime. It is the oldest forensic science. It's especially used to link a firearm to the bullets they have fired. All gun barrels leave distinctive marks on their bullets, and once a firearm is found it can be identified with absolute certainty whether it is the particular gun being sought for that particular crime. Firing a bullet leaves distinctive marks on the bullets, which are caused by the rifling grooves found inside the gun barrel. Graham Libby had to apply forensic pathology to the firearm wound to distinguish whether it was definitely suicide, an accident or murder.

By studying the inlet and exit holes, he deduced the direction of the bullet. He also knew from which distance and angle the shot was fired. A bullet striking the skin at right angles makes a clean hole in the skin, which is slightly bigger than its own diameter. The skins elasticity makes it stretch in front of the bullet and then shrink as it passes, leaving a rim where the surface of the skin has been destroyed. If the bullet strikes from an angle then the entrance hole is oval shaped. Exit wounds on the other hand, show substantial tearing and puckering outward. The exit holes are usually much bigger than the entrance wound as the hot metal bullet flattens when it impacts with muscle and bone tissue. In the case of firearm suicides when a muzzle is held against the skin, a rush of compressed gas and their subsequent expansion tears the flesh into a cross shape and the wound is much wider than the bullet.

"The skin around the bullet wound to the lower jaw, beneath the chin is severely blackened. The skin inside the wound is torn into a cross shape and is also blackened, indicating suicide," Graham Libby said for the camera. He removed the latex gloves from his hands and dropped them into a medical waste bin, and then he walked to a hand sink and washed his hands for much longer than he needed to. Graham Libby glanced into a square mirror, which was fixed to the wall above the sink, and he noticed that the deep lines at the corner of his eyes were spreading. He sighed trying to expel the sick feeling in his guts but he knew that it would stay with him for a while yet.

CHAPTER 33
Chen/Mersey Tunnel

Chen was thrown backwards by the blast from the sting grenade. He felt like a sledge hammer had hit him. His battle vest had taken the brunt of the blast, and protected his vital organs from the rubber shrapnel projectiles. The night vision visor saved his face and eyes from any critical injuries, but the apparatus was hanging shattered from his face. He glanced around the service tunnel at his men. Two of them were sat on the floor nearby in a similar state of shock to him, but they didn't appear to be seriously injured. The men at the rear of the column rushed forward to the aid of their Task Force colleagues, and as they reached Chen the gas from the sting grenade hit them. One of his men removed his respirator from his utility belt and placed it over his face. It covered his eyes, nose and mouth and fed him oxygen through a valve. Chen's eyes were streaming as he was helped up to his feet. The Task Force team checked each other over for any serious injuries and made sure that everyone was protected from the tear gas.

"We need to move out," Chen said, "fire a volley down that tunnel at boot level. Let's see if they have left us any more nasty surprises." Two Task Force men opened fire and the muzzle flashes illuminated the tunnel. They emptied full magazines and the bullets ricocheted down the narrow tunnel knocking huge chunks of concrete from the walls. The tunnel remained silent.

"Did you see something then?" Chen asked the group. He shone his torch down the tunnel and dark tendrils of smoke drifted across the beam. Chen raised a finger to his lips hushing his men into silence. The dull sound of metal and glass crashing reached them.

"They're in the main traffic tunnel and there's a fire down there," Chen spoke into the coms channel, "Major we're going to follow the Brigade men into the main tunnel. There seems to be a fire there and we can hear what sounds like a car crash." The channel crackled then went silent. They were too deep beneath the river and thousands of tons of concrete too communicate with the support departments above. Chen checked his watch. The small oxygen valves in their respirators would last twenty minutes.

"We follow them for ten minutes then we will reassess our oxygen," Chen ordered and the Task Force team headed down the tunnel into the choking fumes in formation.

One hundred yards further on there was a culvert, which joined the service shaft to their right hand side. Chen held up his hand to halt the team. He held three fingers up and pointed down the culvert. A Task Force member fired three shots down the tunnel through the thickening smoke. There was no response.

"Let's move," Chen ordered. The Task Force men entered the culvert, which was pitch-dark. Twenty yards on they entered the main body of the two lane traffic tunnel. Flames danced from somewhere in the tunnel that they couldn't see. The tunnel had a bend about five hundred yards to their left, and the fire was beyond that out of their sight. The tunnel was two lanes wide and was shaped like the inside of a giant pipe. Either side of the road there was a raised walkway, which was for service crew to access the tunnel without affecting the traffic flow. Every hundred yards there was an emergency fire point, which contained a fire hose and portable extinguishers. In the event of a serious road traffic accident fire crews had no chance of bringing fire engines into the tunnel until all the traffic had been moved. Metal railings separated the raised walkway from the road.

The Task Force men looked at the bedlam in front of them and waited for Chen. Chen looked in both directions along the walkways and there was no sign of the brigade men. Cars were stopped bumper to bumper as far as the eye could see. Some had crashed into the cars in front when the lights had been turned off. The drivers whose headlights were intact once they had come to a standstill had switched them on, and dark shadows flickered across the arched ceiling. Many of the people were out of their cars helping those that had been injured, but many had already abandoned their vehicles when the smoke had started to appear, and headed back up the tunnel on foot. It was a scene of sheer chaos. The approaching sound of gunfire as the Task Force cleared their path down the tunnel had caused even more panic. There were hundreds of people wandering up the tunnel away from the fire, some of them injured, and most of them with dirty faces. Breathing normally was becoming almost impossible as the thick acrid smoke drifted up to the ceiling and then down the walls. They had no chance of identifying the Brigade men in this mayhem.

"We need to get to that fire," Chen said, "if they came this way then that's the way they would have gone." Chen was correct in his assumption. Undercover MI6 agent Neil Clarke was leading his men past the burning bus as the Task Force men had entered the culvert behind them. The bus passengers had long since run away from the crash and the ensuing fire. The unfortunate driver of the car that had collided with the bus had been trapped in his seat by the steering wheel. The fire had licked around the underside of his car for ages while concerned witnesses tried to free him from the wreck. Eventually the fire had become too intense for even the bravest Samaritans, and they had to leave the screaming driver to burn. Clarky and his men had watched fascinated as they ran past the bizarre scene.

"He's fucking toast," Glinka laughed as he stared at the burning car.

"Shut up you moron," Clarky hissed to the young skinhead. He reached into a car and took an abandoned baseball cap from the back seat and pulled it onto his shaved head. The Brigade men clicked onto what he was doing and followed suit. Some grabbed abandoned jackets and raincoats to make them look more normal. Baseball caps covered their bald heads and discarded gloves hid Swastika tattoos. They headed up the tunnel away from the fire taking as much looted clothing as they could muster.

Chen and the Task Force team arrived at the bus minutes behind the skinheads. They surveyed the carnage and they watched in horror as they saw that the driver of the burning car was still twitching in the inferno. Despite the raging flames that engulfed him his will to survive wouldn't allow him to surrender to the flames. The truth was that he was beyond saving. Chen nodded toward the car and passed his fingers across his throat. The

Task Force man closest to him understood the order, and fired four bullets into the burning man. He stopped struggling and slumped in his seat, his pain all gone.

"Grab that hose," Chen ordered and three Task Force men sprang into action.

"Jam it into the railings and point it at the bus, you two do the same with the hose on the opposite side of the road." Two more men jumped over the railings onto the roof of an abandoned car and then leaped from roof to roof across the tunnel until they reached the other side. The brass hose nozzles were jammed into the metal bars and then the water was switched on. Two powerful jets of water arced across the tunnel into the burning bus. Steam billowed upward toward the tunnels curved ceiling. The hissing noise was deafening and it echoed down the tunnel.

Chen gave thumbs up sign and the Task Force men headed up the tunnel away from the bus. Two men were on one walkway; Chen and the others were on the opposite side of the road. They made good time as they moved up the tunnel and passed the first members of the escaping public in a few minutes. Chen pointed to his eyes and then to the stragglers. The Task Force men studied them looking for anything that would identify them as 18th Brigade members.

Neil Clark and the brigade men had reached the back of the traffic jam. Cars were trapped in the tunnel by the vehicles behind them, but the last car in the line was drivable, as there was nothing behind it.

"We're splitting up here," Clarky said heading for the vehicle. He opened the passenger door and climbed across the centre console into the driver's seat. Glinka opened the rear door and attempted to climb in. He froze when Clarky shoved the cold metal barrel of his 9mm Berretta in his face.

"I said we are splitting up knobhead, now shut the door before I put a big hole in your thick head," Clarky needed to get away from the Brigade men without blowing his cover.

"Hey that's my car," said a black man, who had been standing on the walkway trying to see what was going on in the tunnel. Clarky climbed out of the seat and approached the man smiling.

"Listen I was moving it out of the way so that we can all move...." Clarky didn't finish the sentence; instead he head butted the man on the bridge of the nose. The black man collapsed to his knees, and Clarky searched his jacket pockets and found the man's car keys. With the car keys in his hand he turned back toward the car. Glinka was stood in front of the open driver's door with a .38mm Colt in one hand and his claw hammer in the other.

"I'll take them. I am a fucking moron am I?" Glinka snarled. He had never liked Clarky. There was something sneaky about him, something not quite right.

Clarky tossed the keys at him gently aiming toward the hand that held the Colt. Glinka instinctively tried to catch the car keys and only succeeded in dropping his gun. His face had a stunned expression as he watched the weapon clatter along the road. Clarky reached for his own gun and Glinka launched at him with the hammer. The steel claw glanced off his forehead cleaving a flap of skin from the bone. Blood flowed from the gash into his left eye. Clarky dipped his knees slightly and twisted his hips simultaneously making his body like a coiled spring. He thrust his right fist upward beneath Glinka's chin, straightening his knees and hips to maximise the impact. The vicious uppercut caught Glinka with his mouth open, which any boxer will tell you is 'Goodnight Vienna'. Glinka staggered backward against the car and spat three broken teeth mixed with blood and saliva onto the tarmac. He managed to compose himself and launched forward again, bringing the hammer down in a flashing arc. Clarky stepped sideways to avoid the blow and kicked Glinka in the stomach. The young skinhead bent double with the force of the kick and he gasped for breath. Clarky stamped the edge of his boot against the side of Glinka's knee dislocating the joint and ripping the tendons. Glinka fell against the car screaming in agony. The other Brigade men watched in awe as Clarky destroyed Glinka, who had a fearsome reputation as a fighter. They weren't sure what they should do, run or join in. While they watched the action deciding what to do, Chen and the Task Force men had caught up with them, and had them covered from the elevated walkways on both sides of the road.

"Drop your weapons and lie down on the floor with your hands above your heads. Do it now," Chen shouted. The Terrorist Task Force who looked like Robocop and bristled with weapons surrounded the Brigade men. The skinheads put up their hands, dropped their weapons and lay on the ground, all except for Clarky.

Clarky picked up the car keys and bolted for the abandoned vehicle. He slammed the door and put the keys into the ignition, and started the engine. The Task Force men opened fire at the tyres and they were shredded in seconds before the car had even moved. Chen fired six well aimed shots into the engine block and a plume of steam rose from the vehicle. The engine stopped and Clarky raised his hands in surrender. He placed his bleeding forehead on the steering wheel exhausted. Uniformed policemen arrived with sirens blaring and blue lights flashing.

"Cuff them and take them to the Task Force office," Chen ordered.

CHAPTER 34
Tank/Faz/Danio

Tank and Grace Farrington reached the motor room, and found the door barricaded.

"Blow it open," Faz ordered. A Task Force member approached the door and placed a disc shaped charge to the frame next to the hinges. The charges were shaped, which forces the explosion in a desired direction to maximise the destructive effect. He flicked a red button to activate the timer, which could be set to five second delays.

"Fire in the hole," the squad man shouted, and the team took cover to protect themselves from flying debris. As the dust cleared the door appeared to have remained intact despite the hinges being blown off. Tank took three big strides and smashed his huge shoulder against the weakened door. The wood splintered and cracked down the middle but only moved a few feet. He stepped back and launched his shoulder against the door a second time. This time the door disintegrated and the metal lockers behind it clattered across the motor room allowing them access. Tank kneeled and pointed his 9mm Glock into the dark building, and signalled the team to enter. The Terrorist Task Force entered the motor room hugging the walls and searching every potential hiding place, and then quickly declared the area clear.

"There is one casualty in the control room," an agent informed Tank, "he's got a nasty bang on the head, but he'll live. It looks like they've killed the power in the tunnel."

"Can you get it back on?" Tank asked.

"It's already done Tank. It was an isolation switch, which had been turned off. We should hear the motors kicking in any minute now." Sure enough a loud mechanical whirring noise began as the exhaust fans started to turn.

"Major have you picked up anything from the drones?" Tank asked over the coms channel. The unmanned helicopters were fitted with heat seeking equipment, which could locate, and track human body heat. Military drones were also armed with air cannons capable of firing fifteen hundred .75mm shells a minute. They have been used extensively in the mountains of Pakistan and Afghanistan in the hunt for Osama bin Laden. Unmanned drones are the cutting edge of military technology because they are fast, silent and have a range of devastating weaponry.

"They are showing several suspects entering a building site close to your position, but the CCTV pictures can't distinguish Brigade men from the construction workers," the Major answered, "uniform police units are moving into the area now, but there are over four hundred workmen on that site."

The City of Liverpool had been granted the status of City of Culture Capital for 2008. The title had sparked a tidal wave of building work as the city was regenerated and refurbished in anticipation of the tourists it would attract. The historic skyline now looked like a scene from H.G.Wells' War of the Worlds, as huge metal arms crisscrossed the city. Colossal cranes worked day and night building museums, art galleries and shopping malls. A two mile square area of the city centre had been bulldozed and was undergoing rebuilding work twenty four hours a day. The Brigade men had split up and with the aid of the safety gear they had dressed in, were almost impossible to distinguish from genuine construction tradesmen.

"We need to get onto that construction site and look for them up close and personal," Tank said, "we will split into four teams, one hundred yards apart, and stay in contact at all times. Major we need air support and back up from uniform units. Tell them to identify suspects but not to approach, repeat do not approach." Tanks request went over the open coms channel so that every uniformed officer in the city centre could hear it. The secret listening post at the old Newborough School programmed two unmanned drones to cover the area. They were deployed to hover unseen like huge black wasps above the unfinished buildings. Uniformed police monitored exit and entrance gates to the building sites, but the perimeters were so extensive it would be impossible to stop a determined fugitive from escaping.

Tank and Faz entered the construction site and headed toward a four storey concrete structure. It wasn't possible to identify exactly what it was destined to be, but there didn't appear to be any work taking place on it. Tank scanned the open floors of the structure and noticed a lone builder on the second floor. He spotted Tank and the other Task Force members entering the site and scurried off behind an unfinished staircase.

"I have a suspect on the second floor of the structure I am labelling now," Tank spoke into the coms channel. Tank had used lasers and the labelling system many times as a member of an international Special Forces unit, who were tasked with finding the whereabouts of the nefarious terrorist leader Yasser Ahmed, in the mountains of northern Turkey.

Labelling a site or a target was done using a laser, and had been perfected in the mountains of Afghanistan called the Tora Bora during the search for Osama bin Laden. Ground forces would aim a laser gun at a distant group of Taliban, or a suspect cave and then request air support. Minutes later quadruple vapour trails could be seen scoring the Afghan sky as American B-52 bombers approached at ten thousand feet. Suddenly huge dust plumes and boiling orange flames would erupt from the target identified by the laser, leaving nothing alive. Over a six month period Tora Bora was the most concentrated cluster bomb attack ever launched, but the elusive mastermind of 9/11 slipped the net.

Faz broke left and took up a position of cover on the ground floor of the structure, at the bottom of the staircase. Tank ran to the right and waited at the bottom of a scaffold, which was attached to the open side of the building. He lifted a canvas sheet, which covered the metal framework, and waited for the information from the drones.

"The drone is showing a single target located on the second floor, and he is positive for metallic substances," said the recon agent from the listening post.

The drone had scanned the suspect for the presence of any substance, which could be a weapon. The presence of metal indicated a gun, but it could just as easily be a drill or a spirit level. Faz used a thumbs-up sign to indicate that she was clear to proceed. Tank responded with an ok signal and started to climb up the scaffold with his gun holstered. Grace started up the stairs.

Neil Danelley, Dano, waited silently in the dark stairwell. He was holding his breath so that he could hear everything, even the lightest footstep. His hand was sweating around the handle of his 9mm Luger, and then he swapped the gun to his other hand and wiped the sweaty palm on his jeans. He studied the gun in his hand and smiled. The Luger was a German made pistol used extensively by Nazi officers in World War 2. They were standard issue for all ranks above Sergeant. Dano had bought it from a collector in Glasgow, and paid three times the firearms value. The vendor had shown Dano papers, which belonged to its original owner, who had been stationed at the Auschwitz death camp in 1943. The fact that gun had been used to kill Jews thrilled Dano and his fascist friends; he recounted the gun's history to anyone who would listen. He hadn't always been a racist, but the changing Britain he had grown up in made him into the worst kind of bigot.

His auntie had been a primary school teacher for twenty years, and she always dreamed of teaching underprivileged children in Africa. The opportunity to teach in the Sudan arose and she jumped at the chance. She settled in well at first although she never really became accustomed to the blazing heat. She decided to apply some of her most successful teaching methods to the curriculum of her new school. She first donated a teddy bear to her class of forty students, with the idea of each pupil taking it home for the night, and then writing a diary of what the teddy bear had done in class the next day. The project had worked well as it incorporates the whole class and improves both reading and writing skills. The first task was to name the bear. The children in the class chose the name Mohammed for the bear, which didn't seem to be a problem to the unsuspecting teacher, as she had twelve pupils with the same name in the class. The pupils had gone home very excited and told their parents about the new teacher and their new project. Extremist Islamic hardliners in the community became offended and complained to the police. Using the name of the great prophet of Islam was taken as an illegal insult against Islam itself, and the teacher was arrested. The incident was to cause one of the biggest political incidents ever experienced between the West and the Islamic community of North Africa. The naive schoolmistress was imprisoned in appalling conditions while radical fundamentalists took to the streets of Sudan demanding that she be beheaded for the affront to the great prophet.

The incident made Dano question his faith and more importantly the rational of other religions. It did not seem at all fair that someone wanted to cut off his aunt's head over a teddy bear. As his education progressed, and he grew older, immigration in Britain became daily news. Large sections of the country's biggest cities became ghetto's and no go areas for the indigenous white population. The borders of Europe were dismantled in 2005 and a tidal wave of Eastern European migrants swamped Britain's welfare state. The education system couldn't cope with the influx of foreign children, and the health service imploded beneath the strain of pregnant immigrants that came here specifically to give birth. The final straw was when he was sent home from school for wearing a crucifix, which his grandmother had given to him shortly before she died. The government and large blue chip companies banned the wearing of the crucifix because it caused offence to minority religions. Dano couldn't believe what was happening to his country when the government banned schools from performing children's Christmas nativity plays. The indigenous Christian population of the United Kingdom felt as if it were under siege. Centuries old traditions like Christmas and the wearing of the symbol of Christ, the crucifix, were becoming outlawed in their own country, to appease immigrant opinion. Yet Islamic extremist teachers were allowed to preach sermons of Jihad and hate openly on the streets of Britain, protected by the British police. Political correctness and the rise of radical Islam created more racists in the late 1990's, and early 21st century, than any other influence. Dano quickly became involved in far right politics and was swept into the 18th Brigade along with thousands of like-minded angry young men.

Dano leaned against the dusty wall behind him and listened intently. He heard a scuffle on the stairs below him and he jumped, someone was close by. The scaffold frame attached to the outside of the building to his right creaked beneath Tank's heavy weight, and Dano knew that he was being hunted by several foe. His Luger was loaded with eleven rounds, and that was all he had. He hadn't expected to be in a gunfight with Special Forces. He wasn't ready to die just yet either, and he realised that if he fired one bullet he was fair game to every armed officer in the country. Another scuff on the stairs made him hurry his decision making process. He had to lose the weapon or risk being shot.

"Don't shoot," Dano shouted down the stairwell, "I am throwing my gun down the stairs." He loved his Luger but he could always buy another with same sick history attached to it. He tossed the gun onto the concrete stairs and it clattered into the darkness out of site.

"Step away from the stairs and raise your hands where I can see them," Faz shouted as she climbed the steps slowly. She picked up the weapon. The command echoed across the unfinished building. Grace rounded the first landing pointing her Glock 9mm into the second floor space. There was no sign of the suspect. Tank reached the same floor and signalled to her that he couldn't see the target either with an exaggerated shake of his head. She rounded the corner and pressed her back against the wall staring into the gloom trying to make sense of the shadows, but she couldn't see who had thrown their gun away.

Dano appeared from behind a stud wall and hit Faz with a short length of three-by-two wood. The wood made a thunking sound in the empty concrete structure. She cried out and fell forward onto the dusty floor causing a cloud of cement dust to rise around her.

"Fucking hell you're a bird!" hissed Dano startled by the female cry, "and a bloody nignog as well," he snarled as he kicked her in the ribs knocking the wind from her lungs. Tank fired a warning shot above his head to stop the attack, and ran across the concrete floor quickly closing the distance between him and Grace. Dano twisted back behind the stud wall out of sight and followed it until he reached an open lift shaft, then he froze and held his breath once again.

"Are you ok Grace?" asked Tank as he approached her. She was breathing deeply trying to get her breath back, and holding her ribs where the vicious kick had landed. Tank and Grace had been an item for nearly two years now, which was completely against Task Force policy. There had been sexual chemistry between them since the first day they had met. They kept their relationship a secret but rumours about them were rife. Little glances and intimate comments overheard by nosey ears had fuelled speculation.

He touched her cheek and she opened her eyes. She seemed a little startled. There was a trickle of blood running down her dark skin just below her ear.

"Did you hear what he called me Tank?" she asked as she sat up. She was pouting in a false expression of distaste. Tank had seen that look a hundred times and he knew that she wasn't seriously hurt.

"What offended you most, the bird bit or the nignog?" asked Tank as he pulled her to her feet. He hadn't heard the term nignog since he was a child, and even then he thought it sounded like something his grandmother would drink at Christmas.

"Bird!" she said exasperated, "Now I'm angry and he's in really big trouble." Faz dusted herself down and checked that her gun was safe. Tank watched her facial expression fascinated by her dark eyes and chiselled features. She turned quickly and disappeared behind the stud wall without saying a word.

"Oh dear, she really is pissed off," Tank said to no one. He began to move in a parallel direction to her but on the other side of the partition. Tank moved quietly for a big man, and he arrived at the unfinished lift shaft completely unheard. He moved swiftly round the partition and bumped straight into Neil Danelley. Dano was as surprised as Tank which slowed his reaction for a split second. Tank smashed his forehead into Dano's face breaking his nose with the devastating force of the impact. Dano was knocked backward by the sickening blow but swung the thick piece of wood instinctively. Tank ducked beneath the blow and hit the big skinhead in the midriff with a vicious side-kick, which catapulted him through the partition wall. Chunks of plasterboard flew in all directions as the stud wall disintegrated beneath the big man. Amazingly Dano shook his head and picked himself up from the floor and faced Tank again. The two men were evenly matched for weight, and both were unusually muscular from years of pumping iron. Tank saw a flash of uncertainty in the skinhead's eyes. It was only for a second but it was definitely there. Mentally he was already beaten. Tank caught sight of a blur of movement to the man's right hand side, but unfortunately for Dano he hadn't. Faz had approached him from the side and once she was in striking distance she transferred her weight to the ball of her left foot. She began a 360' spin and raised her right leg at an increasing angle as the spin progressed. The physics behind spinning kicks means that the further the exponent spins the more devastating the impact becomes. Faz caught the skinhead in the face with the heel of her thick military boot, cracking his jaw in three places and knocking him backwards through the plaster partition again. Dano lay on his back out cold.

"I hate that phrase 'bird'," she said as she patted cement dust from her battle vest. Tank thought that he would be well advised to remember never to call her that.

CHAPTER 35

Roman/Alexis/the Airbase

Roman darted for the limousine as the hangar turned into a bloodbath. He dived into the open passenger door and slammed it closed behind him. He watched one of his bodyguards spinning violently as he was hit in the shoulder by a bullet fired by one of Alexis' men. The injured man jerked a second time reminding Roman of some teenagers he had once seen break-dancing. The man twitched robotically, and then he toppled into the oily inspection pit as a third bullet made his face disappear. A stray round struck the door and Roman backed away from the window. The limo had two and a half inch thick plasti-glass windows, which were totally bullet proof when they were intact. Any bullet damage to the material made it susceptible to any further ballistic impacts. Beneath the normal body panels were armour plates, which were initially manufactured for British Warrior tanks. The underside of the vehicle was reinforced to protect the occupants from a bomb attack. The front driver's door was flung open at the same time as the front passenger door. Two bodyguards clambered into the driver's compartment trying to escape the deadly bullets of the snipers. The window next to Roman shattered into a spider's web pattern as the sniper above the hangar door turned his attention to the limo.

"Get this fucking thing moving!" Roman shouted, moving away from the damaged window instinctively. The bodyguard in the driver's seat reached for the ignition keys and found they weren't there. He pulled down the sun visor desperate to find them, but it became obvious that the dead chauffer had them on his person. Two more high velocity bullets struck the windscreen causing web

158

patterns to appear, and long deep cracks radiated across the glass. It was holding for now but wouldn't withstand the bullets forever.

"Get the keys, what are you waiting for?" Roman hissed and banged the back of the driver's seat. A bullet hit the damaged side glass panel and a chunk the size of coin hit Roman in the cheek. He touched his finger to the wound and felt warm blood trickling down his face. The driver saw the look on Roman's face in the rear view mirror and he knew that he was probably safer outside the limo at the moment. Mikhail Lebedev had worked for Roman Kordinski for five years. Roman had selected him because of his Russian Spetsnaz training. He had spent six long years fighting the Muslim rebels in Chechnya before the Soviet dissolution began. Mikhail was Jewish and hated the Muslim insurgents with a passion. Once in the employ of Roman his hatred and talents were applied to seeking out, and assassinating Chechen gangsters that threatened Roman's business interests. He was eventually arrested for the murder of a Chechen gang leader, his wife and three children in a suburb of Moscow. Mikhail was sentenced to eighty years hard labour. He was sent to one of Russia's Stalin built gulags situated near the borders with China and Mongolia. The prison was called IK-10, which is four-hundred miles away from the nearest city Chita, three thousand seven hundred and seventy four miles east of Moscow. The journey for any prospective visitors by train from Moscow takes one hundred and six hours, and ends with a two-hundred kilometre taxi ride from the station to the prison. For the impoverished Russian public this ruled out the chance of ever receiving a visit from loved ones. The prisoners are forced to work in nearby uranium mines for twelve hours a day in sub zero temperatures, which was back breaking, and soul destroying work. The radio-active minerals from the uranium mines affect the water table that supplies the prisoner's drinking water. Life expectancy for prisoners is four years.

The chain gang, which he was part of, was involved in a bus crash. He was just eight weeks into his jail term. No one survived and most of the bodies were never recovered because of the remoteness of its position. The bodies recovered were burnt beyond all recognition, which pointed to a road accident, however there were reports locally which alleged the dead bodies recovered had gunshot wounds, but all the witnesses gradually disappeared too.

The bus crash had been caused by Roman Kordinski and his men in order to spring Mikhail from his incarceration. Mikhail owed Roman his loyalty and his life. Mikhail opened the door of the limo and darted round the bonnet to where the dead chauffer lay. He rifled his pockets desperately trying to find the keys. The jacket pocket was empty. A sniper's bullet slammed into the bumper of the vehicle just inches away from his head. Shards of plastic fender struck him in the neck, and he dived to the floor. The sniper above the hangar door had a clear shot at him unless he did something. Next to the dead chauffer was his discarded machinegun. The driver grabbed the Special Forces weapon and removed the safety. He couldn't see where the sniper was hiding but he was somewhere on the access platform above the hangar entrance. The platform was manufactured from 2mm steel plate which would stop any normal bullets however, the B&T machinegun was full of armour piercing bullets. He squeezed the trigger and the machinegun bucked in his hand as if it were trying to escape from his grasp. The volley of high powered armour piercing bullets ripped through the metal plates and blew large holes in the hangar wall above them. The bullets hit the steel with enough velocity to penetrate it, but they were severely flattened by the force of the impact. Six of the flattened projectiles entered the snipers chest, abdomen and groin areas virtually cutting him in half. He rolled over the edge of the platform, but his exposed intestines caught on a protruding steel bolt leaving yards of glistening viscera flesh hanging from the structure.

The bodyguard breathed a sigh of relief because he knew that the second sniper was behind the vehicle and couldn't see him. The gunfight seemed to have dissipated and he could no longer see Alexis and his men. The hangar door that they had entered through was flapping open in the wind. There were three bodies close to the door. One man was seriously injured and was crawling slowly toward it. He searched the chauffer's trouser pockets and found what he was looking for; all he had to do now was get back into the car alive. He took a deep breath and bolted for the open door, a shot hissed past his ear and he felt the breeze as the bullet narrowly missed him. He threw himself into the driver's compartment and breathed a massive sigh of relief as he slid into the seat. He said nothing as he inserted the keys into the ignition and started the engine. The bodyguard selected reverse gear and released the handbrake. The vehicle lurched backward at high speed, and the tyres squealed on the concrete leaving a melted rubber trail behind. The back window exploded in a shower of broken glass and Roman flung himself onto the floor of the limo. The driver turned the steering wheel violently to his right and the limo turned one hundred and eighty degrees, so that the windscreen faced the elevated sniper. He accelerated hard and the limo drove beneath the snipers position to safety. Roman sat up and patted the driver on the shoulder in congratulations.

"Alexis is a tricky man," Roman said laughing "he is very clever placing snipers in there. But he is not the only one with brains. I have a trick or two of my own, don't you worry about that."

The limo screeched out of the hangar onto the old runway system. Grass and weeds poked through the ancient concrete surface in random patterns. Roman could see Alexis and the two surviving members of his team approaching the black Volkswagen they had arrived in. They were three hundred yards away across the ancient tarmac.

Alexis stopped running when he heard the limo escaping the hangar, and he stared at the elongated vehicle as it sped away. He locked stares with Roman across the abandoned airfield. The two men glared at each other with venom in their eyes. They lived in a fickle violent world where friends became enemies and enemies died quickly.

"Get in, we need to get out of here, we can deal with Roman Kordinski another day when he least expects it," Alexis shouted to his remaining men. Alexis climbed into the passenger seat and thought it was odd that the engine hood didn't look closed properly. The driver inserted the ignition keys into the steering column. Alexis watched him turn the keys, and it was as if the world had been switched to slow motion.

"Slow down," Roman ordered. He lowered the shattered window to get a better view. He watched Alexis and his men climb into the Toureg, and laughed uncontrollably when the vehicle exploded into a massive fireball, which plumed sixty yards into the air.

CHAPTER 36

Terrorist Task Force Meeting/
1 Week later

Tank looked from the top floor window of Canning Place, which was the headquarters of the Merseyside police force, and the home of the international Terrorist Task Force. The dark waters of the river Mersey flowed passed on its journey to the Irish Sea. There was a flotilla of tall wooden sailing ships floating near the Albert Docks, with their white canvas sails billowing in the wind. Tank loosened his tie around his thick neck but still felt very uncomfortable. He picked up his suit jacket and pulled it on. The feeling of being restricted increased as the material stretched over his muscular frame. The wearing of business suits was mandatory for meetings when government ministers were attending, unless one was a serving member of the conventional armed forces, in which case military uniform was worn. Tank looked through the glass porthole in the door at the meeting room and frowned. The Admiral of the fleet stood talking to the Field Marshall of the British army, and the Wing Air Commander of the Royal Air Force. Behind them was the Minister of Defence, who was in deep conversation with Major Stanley Timms. Across the room were senior officers from MI5, MI6 and the Organised Crime Unit. Tank hated meetings with the top brass, especially the spooks of the intelligence agencies. Grace Farrington entered the office that he was in, and she joined him at the round window to inspect the gathering of Britain's military boffins.

"All we need now are the yanks and we'll have a complete set," Faz said squeezing Tanks huge bicep through his jacket sleeve.

"They're on their way up," Tank said, walking back to the window.

"What, you are kidding aren't you?" she replied, "Who are we expecting?"

"NSA, CIA and the FBI, full house I think," Tank said.

The door opened and three well groomed men in dark suits walked into the room. They inspected Tank and Faz with expert glances, recognising them as allied agents. The intelligence agencies trained operatives to assess people quickly with the briefest of glances. They were taught to scrutinise subjects in seconds without raising suspicion. Tank and Faz had been identified as members of an agency, which agency didn't really matter. One of the men at the rear of the new group nodded to Tank in recognition. Tank nodded back but remained silent while shaking hands with the American agents. Tank recognised the agent as a member of Delta Force, who had accompanied his unit in the search for Yasser Ahmed in the mountains of Pakistan. Delta Force men were often recruited into America's secret services, just as the Terrorist Task Force agents had been picked from Britain's elite fighting forces. The door to the meeting room opened and Major Timms ushered them into the inner office. Everyone took a seat around an elongated wooden table. The table had a just polished sheen to it, which only a dozen layers of lacquer can achieve. The Major cleared his throat and tapped his hand on the table to gain attention.

"I think we are all here," he began, "I would like to just start the meeting by introducing our American colleagues, who some of you may not be familiar with." The Major pointed to one of the Americans, who was blond and tanned. Freckles covered his nose and cheeks; a sign that most of his time was spent on the golf course in the sunshine.

"Gentlemen this is agent Shaw from the National Security Agency," Major Timms said.

The NSA is the American government's intelligence agency. It is responsible for the collection and analysis of foreign communications. They are experts in the fields of cryptanalysis and cryptography, which is basically code breaking and code making. The NSA has the capacity to eavesdrop every telephone call and e-mail made anywhere on the planet. The agency mission is to identify and secure military, diplomatic and all other sensitive, confidential communications made by enemy and allied governments alike. It is also the world biggest employer of mathematicians, and the owner of the largest single group of supercomputers. For many years the US government never acknowledged its existence. The NSA was referred to as 'no such agency' and also 'never say anything'. The headquarters are at Fort George, Maryland, approximately ten miles north of Washington. The electricity bill for the NSA building in 2007 was thirty one million dollars, and there are satellite photographs of the site, which show eighteen thousand parking spaces for its non-existent employees. It is the largest listening post in the world.

"This is agent Galvin of the Federal Bureau of Investigation, and agent David Grey of the CSA," the Major continued. The ex-Delta Force man nodded at the other people round the table. Tank remembered him well, as an outstanding soldier. He had obviously been drafted into the CIA, which was based at Langley, Virginia, a few miles east of Washington. A Muslim suicide bomber attacked the headquarters at Langley in 1993. Mir Aimal Kansi, a Pakistani national killed himself and two CIA agents with his improvised device. The CIA had field operatives all over the world; many were deployed as junior members of a diplomat's staff to cover their real identities. They are usually ex-Special Forces men, and are responsible for America's clandestine and covert operations. The CIA now acts upon the information gathered by the NSA, where previously the CIA gathered its own data. In the 1950's before the formation of the NSA, the CIA were also responsible for gathering vital military information. Their intelligence gathering had proved to be floored on several key occasions in modern history. On October 13th, 1950 the CIA director assured President Truman that the Chinese Army would not invade Korea. Six days later over one-million Chinese troops crossed the border. The most recent CIA gaff was the absolute certainty that Saddam Hussein was in possession of weapons of mass destruction. Years after the allied invasion of Iraq there were no such weapons found. Saddam was found hiding in a hole in the ground. Despite all the efforts of the Allied invaders no weapons of mass destruction were ever found.

The formalities over, the Major went on to outline the situation to the multi-agency gathering. A wall opposite the window had a plasma screen attached to it. Images appeared and changed as the Major talked through recent events.

"We are now certain that the River Dee attack was carried out by members of a Russian organised crime syndicate. They employed members of the 18th Brigade to snatch a Saudi national called Jeannie Kellesh. She is the daughter of a member of the Saudi royal family."

"The riverboat bomb was made to look like an extremist attack in an attempt to confuse the investigation. A second attack at the Piccadilly rail terminus was also carried out to implicate Islamic extremists as the culprits. It was actually committed to destroy all the loose ends from the kidnap plot, and to cause civil unrest against our Muslim communities."

"It appears that there was a breakdown in the relationship between the two parties involved, and the Brigade went on the rampage, targeting Russian interests across the North West. We have six members of the Brigade in custody and they are undergoing interrogation. We also have two, and I repeat, two undercover agents being debriefed." The Major looked over the top of his glasses and glared at the MI6 director, Garden. The Terrorist Task Force had been aware that an Organised Crime Unit officer was working in the Brigade, but the MI6 agency had not disclosed that it too had penetrated its ranks.

"We have two dead Russians in the strong room of the casino, both shot with 9mm bullets from a gun which we recovered from Agent Simon Pinn of the Organised Crime Unit. The same gun killed a nineteen year old member of the Brigade who was found in the walk-in refrigerator of the casino." The uniformed police superintendent in charge of the Organised Crime Unit flushed red with anger, which made Tank smirk. The police chief glared at Tank, and Grace kicked Tank's foot under the table in an attempt to avoid the obvious oncoming conflict.

"My men had that casino sealed off, and the situation was under control until Officer John Tankersley and his team turned up. Do you have evidence that officer Pinn shot these people?" the police chief spluttered. Tank shifted in his chair and loosened his tie again. He grinned at the police chief.

"We have the gun, the bullets, three dead bodies, an empty safe and your officer's prints all over the weapon. He has tested positive for gunshot residue on his hands, which proves positive that he fired that weapon. You don't have to be Sherlock Holmes to work out that your officer will be charged with murder," Tank countered. The police chief reddened again but thought better of arguing. The evidence was overwhelming, and they had expressed concerns themselves about their officer.

"We also have agent Neil Clarke in custody, who it turns out is a current employee of her Majesty's MI6. He was arrested trying to escape capture and was bloody lucky that he wasn't shot in the process," the Major looked over his spectacles again at the MI6 director who wouldn't meet his withering gaze.

"We needed to keep our agent's position in the 18th Brigade intact. He was trying not be compromised, which unfortunately did not happen. He was on the verge of communicating the contact names and details of right wing extremist leaders on the continent and across the US," the MI6 director explained and he coughed nervously, "Clarke was just one of many agents we have infiltrating these groups. He was part of an Anglo-American intelligence gathering operation."

The three Americans glanced at each other embarrassed by what the MI6 man had disclosed. The operation was clandestine which meant that it should not be discussed outside of the agencies directly involved. The Minister of Defence glared at the Americans and made a note on his pad. Protocol insisted that allied intelligence agencies must inform the host government of any covert operations on its soil. Now was not the time or the place for remonstrations but the issue would not be forgotten.

"Washington has serious concerns about right wing extremists groups in our country and abroad. They are gaining significant political ground, especially when immigration and racial integration is concerned," the NSA man explained, trying to lift the tense atmosphere. "They are receiving campaign funds running into the millions and their networks have become worldwide and well organised." Tank looked at Faz and rolled his eyes up to the ceiling, politics, politics, politics he thought.

"Back to the subject at hand gentlemen please," the Major steered the meeting back on track. There had been several serious breaches of political protocol highlighted so far, which could be dealt with by the Minister of Defence at a later date.

"The situation has gotten out of hand. We are staring at a serious international incident. The Saudis incorrectly bombed a suspected terror camp inside Syria's border. The Kuwait army are reinforcing their borders with Saudi Arabia with over two-thousand tanks, which in turn has caused the Iranians to mobilise their armoured divisions. Syria and Israel are also moving troops into stand-off positions either side of the Golan Heights. The situation is a tinderbox gentlemen, which is exactly what the Russian Jewish gangs intended to create. They have caused a significant rift between the Islamic Arabian countries in the Middle East, and domestic turmoil in our towns and cities." The Major paused to allow the significance of what he had just outlined sink in.

"Now the facts here in the UK are as follows. We have a dead Russian exile with injuries consistent with interrogation under torture. He was dumped along with audio tapes near a police station in London. The tapes hold recordings in which he accuses a high profile Russian businessman of kidnapping Jeannie Kellesh. We also recovered a mobile telephone which we can link to Roman Kordinski," the Major paused a moment because the mention of the Russian oil tycoon's name had caused a reaction from the Americans.

"We have recovered ten dead bodies from a disused airbase in Cheshire. All the men have injuries consistent with a gun battle. The men bear tattoos consistent with those found on Russian gang members, or the Organizatsiya. We haven't identified all of them, but several have Russian military records, and all of them are Jewish extraction. The land is owned by a company which is registered in the Caiman Islands, and the director is one Roman Kordinski," the Major studied the faces round the table and the Russian's name was definitely familiar to them. His instincts told him that there was some history between Kordinski and the American intelligence agencies.

"The Saudis now know that Jeannie Kellesh was not killed in the River Dee incident," the Major stood up and walked to the window. A packed Mersey passenger ferry was docking at the Pierhead and hundreds of Japanese tourists were disembarking, cameras at the ready.

"They know that she has been kidnapped, and the unprecedented spike in the cost of crude oil adds proof to the pudding. They also know that we know. The problem is that no one can actually broach the subject without endangering the girl. We think that she is in a Chechen medical facility inside Dagestan."

"Are you planning to arrest the Russian?" asked agent Shaw,

from the NSA.

Tank looked sternly at the tanned American and had to restrain himself from being abusive. "What kind of question is that? The man is responsible for two major terrorist attacks, which claimed hundreds of lives, and has sparked an international incident. Maybe we should ask him to apologise and stop being so naughty," Tank was starting to lose his temper. The Major stepped into the breach.

"We are going to arrest Roman Kordinski today. He will be taken to Belmarsh prison and held under the suspicion of terrorism act 2002, which means that we can hold him for 28 days before concrete charges need to be filed."

"I am afraid that we must object to Kordinski being arrested today or any other day Major," agent Garden of MI6 interrupted. The room was stunned into silence and the atmosphere suddenly became charged. The American agents were looking very uncomfortable every time Garden opened his mouth. He had already dropped them in it once today by exposing the covert Anglo-American intelligence mission. Tank and Grace looked at each other and a silent communication passed between them. Tank wanted to shoot Garden in the face but it probably wouldn't go down well with the Minister of Defence. The Field Marshall, Admiral of the fleet and the Wing Commander shook their heads in disbelief. They were the heads of Britain's armed forces, soldiers and fighting men. They didn't hold any respect for the intelligence agencies, especially, MI6. Major Stanley Timms removed his glasses and placed them onto the polished table top. He reached for his glass of water and sipped it. His hand was shaking slightly as he placed the glass back down, but he remained silent. Everyone looked to the MI6 director to qualify his statement, except for the American agents who were looking down to avoid eye contact with anyone. They knew that agent Garden was about to slip on a huge political banana skin.

"We have been gaining information from Kordinski for a number of years now, when I say we, I mean the joint intelligence agencies of the UK and America," he stuttered, "his connections in the Kremlin, and other influential Soviet organisations are a valuable source of intelligence."

Agent Galvin of the FBI looked up at the ceiling exasperated, and he could not believe that a spy of Garden's rank was so incompetent, not to mention forthcoming. The room stayed silent.

"The New York Police Department arrested Roman Kordinski and four of his Organizatsiya brigadiers six years ago. They were charged with racketeering, extortion, kidnap, multiple murders, and robbery with violence, I could go on all day," agent Shaw said, "Kordinski is a very rich man with power and influence in the Soviet halls of government. He made a trade with the department of justice. He attained sensitive Russian military documents and other such top secret information; in return he was given his liberty."

"He was given his liberty on the condition that he moved his business enterprises to the United Kingdom," Tank finished the sentence for him. "Her Majesty's MI6 knew all about this trade-off, and allowed him to come to Britain without letting anyone else know, because the Americans were sharing the information with them." Tank spoke slowly and stared at the MI6 man in disgust.

"The information we have received from Kordinski has been vital to our dealings with the Soviet Union. We have detailed information about their nuclear fleet," Garden tried to defend his position but the incredulous expressions around the room brought him to a stuttering halt.

"It would be highly embarrassing for both our governments if Kordinski was to be arrested. If details of our arrangement were leaked to the press then every defence lawyer in America would have a field day in the appeal courts," agent Shaw butted in, trying to assist the MI6 man. The British government would never acknowledge that such an agreement existed, but the look on the Minister of Defence's face showed his horror at the situation. He had no prior knowledge of what he had just heard from his own head of department.

"When is Kordinski being arrested Major?" the Minister asked looking at his watch. He needed to speak to the Prime Minister immediately. The political fall-out from this type of situation could be devastating to a government that won the general election on the back of a 'tough on crime' policy. The fact that MI6 had agreed to an international gangster setting up business on British soil in return for military secrets was a shocking breech of public trust.

The Major looked at his watch and then looked at Tank and smiled.

"We arrested him forty-five minutes ago," the Major said, smiling at the now purple agent Garden.

169

CHAPTER 37

International Agencies meeting cont.

"I insist that he is released immediately, Minister," Garden slammed his hand on the desk for effect. He was a very small weedy man in stature, so he felt the need to use grand gestures to make a point. Tank responded by slamming his huge fist on the table causing it to shudder violently, spilling water from the glasses on the table. Agent Garden jumped in fright on his chair, and looked at Tank with fear in his eyes.

"You are in no position to insist anything Garden, this is a Terrorist Task Force investigation and we answer directly to the Prime Minister," Tank said pointing a finger at the MI6 man, "and if you bang your hand on this table again I'll break your arm."

Garden sat back in his chair. His mouth opened as if he was about to retaliate, but the look in Tank's eye made him think better of it.

"Minister I think you should step in here," said agent Shaw, "both our governments will suffer if Kordinski speaks out about our arrangement."

The minister flicked through his papers aimlessly as he mulled over the conundrum. The intelligence agencies from both countries had shattered his confidence in their operational integrity. They had no integrity from what he had heard today. He looked at Tank across the table and imagined that he probably would break agent Garden's arm without a second thought.

"At this point in time agent Tankersley I am inclined to believe that you would indeed break the MI6, Chief of Staff's appendage, and I would jolly well recommend you for a commendation if you did," growled the Minister of Defence. He could tell that his military chiefs were speechless at the behaviour of their allies, and their own intelligence community. Tank, the Major and Grace Farrington had brought this investigation this far in a professional impartial manner. The intelligence agencies appeared to operate unilaterally, with their own agendas top of the objective list.

"Agent Garden, how long exactly have you been aware of the Kordinski affair?" the Minister asked, "was this agreement entered into by you or your predecessor?"

"Err, we were made aware of the situation from the beginning Minister, we....I mean that," Garden mumbled as the Minister interrupted him.

"Did you or your predecessor make the agreement with the American secret service agent Garden? It's a straight forward question," the Minister pushed.

"It was my decision Minister made for...." spluttered Garden.

"You're fired Garden, I will have your desk cleared and your things forwarded to you. Please leave your security pass at reception and leave the building," the Minister turned to the American agents who were sitting open mouthed.

"Roman Kordinski is the hub of a Terrorist Task Force investigation, and he will feel the full weight of the British judicial system upon him," the Minister began, but then he turned his attention again.

"Agent Garden why are you still here?" the Minster snapped at the stunned MI6 director, who was still sat in his chair. The ex-director stood up shaking, and picked up his papers. He walked toward the door, opened it and stepped into the outer office. He paused as if he were about to speak. Tank stood up and walked toward him. He placed his huge hand gently against Garden's chest and firmly pushed him through the door, and then he slammed the door shut on Garden's face and career simultaneously.

Tank took his seat at the table and nodded to the Minister, signalling him to continue.

"Roman Kordinski will be detained under the prevention of terrorism act. His role as a spy or informer will not gift him any special privileges. I will arrange a further meeting with your agency directors at a later date to discuss future protocol," the Minster was assertive in his manner and the Americans decided not to challenge his decision.

"Now if we can move on, Major Timms where do we stand

with the matter internationally?"

"The arrest of Kordinski is going to affect the Kellesh issue," the Major began, "whoever is holding the girl is going to realise that she is no longer of any value to Kordinski. Our theory is that the Russian government has given notice to all exiles, that their business interests within the Soviet Union will become state property. The sharp rise in Saudi crude oil prices could be a response to a kidnap demand. Kordinski could be trying to maximise his profits before he loses his oil revenue."

The Americans nodded in agreement with the Major's theory. The US agencies had come to a similar conclusion. The Minster coughed dryly and took a sip of water.

"What are our options to resolve the issue?" the Minister asked.

"The Russian constitution does not allow any business to be controlled from outside of the Union, if the directors are proved to be involved in criminal activity."

Tank looked at the faces round the table, and he deducted that most of the attendees had no idea where the meeting was headed. He wasn't a hundred percent sure himself. The meeting was attended by covert agencies only. The only member of any government was the British Minister of Defence, which meant that no action requiring conventional allied forces could be proposed. Whatever was coming would require covert operations by clandestine agents. Tank's sensory perception made his skin tingle with excitement, and he had a feeling that he would be at the centre of what was to come.

"I propose that we inform the Russian government that we have arrested Roman Kordinski, and that he has allegedly been passing top secret information to the Americans," the Major held up his hand to stop any objections from the American agents before he finished his sentence, "we need them to snatch his business's immediately. Without his millions he is just another criminal."

The Americans scribbled notes on their pads but they seemed to accept the story so far. Tank sat forward in anticipation of what was coming. He sensed that an opportunity to right a wrong was about to rear its head. Faz nudged his foot under the table, as she could see where this was going too. Tank looked at her and stared into her deep brown eyes. If this was headed where he thought it was, then there was no way he could take Grace with him. He loved her too much to risk losing her and it would be an extremely dangerous mission. That's why the Task Force forbade agents being in relationships with one another. Grace would expect to be number two on the list of agents selected, and she would play merry hell if she wasn't. That was one problem; the other consideration was that Faz was the best agent he had. She would go ballistic if she were excluded from an operation this big. Tank swallowed hard and waited for the Major to propose his plans to resolve the situation.

"We will then approach the Saudi Royal family, and explain the advantages of returning the price of crude oil to its lowest level possible. Any stockpiles that Kordinski has stashed will be rendered valueless, and tensions in the Middle East should be relaxed somewhat," the Major paused while people caught up mentally with his plan.

"Why would the Saudis listen to us?" asked agent Shaw.

"They wouldn't listen to you," the Major looked over his glasses at the agent, "you're American and they don't trust you." The American agents flushed red with embarrassment. This had not been a good meeting for them at all.

"They will listen to us however, especially if we return Jeannie Kellesh to them unharmed."

The room was once again stunned into silence. Tank almost cheered with enthusiasm, and he had to restrain himself again. He knew what the Major had in mind now.

"We need to send a covert operations group led by Senior Agent John Tankersley into Dagestan, via Chechnya to extract the Saudi Princess," the Major looked at every face in the room looking for agreement. His gaze was met with silent acknowledgment and nodding heads. Tank looked at Grace again and he could see the concern in her eyes. Fine lines creased the black skin on her forehead, which showed she was worried. Tank broke her intense gaze and looked directly at Major Stanley Timms. The Major and Tank had been waiting for an opportunity to enter Soviet territory with a crack team of Special Forces, with the direct backing of both American and British governments. This was their chance to do it without causing a serious political crisis. Chechnya and Dagestan were Islamic extremist strongholds, but more importantly they were the last known whereabouts of the nefarious Yasser Ahmed. The time had come to collect on a debt.

CHAPTER 38

12 Months Earlier
(Yasser Ahmed)

Yasser Ahmed had been born in Iraq and was the spiritual leader and inspiration to the Islamic Extremist group known as 'Ishmael's Axe'. The parable of Ishmael, who was descended from the line of great prophets, which included Moses, is told in the teachings of Islam. The worship of carved images or statues is forbidden in the Islamic religion. The story goes that the statues and wooden carvings of pagan gods in the temple where he lived angered the great prophet Ishmael. He placed plates of fresh fruit at the feet of the carvings as offerings to the gods they represented. That night he returned to the temple to find that his fruit had not been taken, and so having proved that the gods were false idols he smashed them up with his axe. So Yasser took the name of his organisation from the parable to represent the destruction of the enemies of Islam, as he saw them. They had once been affiliated to Osama bin Laden and his al-Qaeda movement but had split to form a splinter group under the influence of Yasser Ahmed.

Eighteen months earlier Yasser had started his 'Soft Target' campaign, which attacked famous American tourist destinations killing hundreds and wiping billions of dollars off the stock markets world-wide. His campaign had brought him to Britain where he plotted to destroy a major oil storage depot, which was foiled at the last minute. Yasser deployed a fleet of ice-cream vans and hotdog stalls, which had been converted into mobile bombs by packing them full of Semtex, to the world famous Anfield football stadium. The fixture was to attract over ninety thousand excited football fans onto the streets of Liverpool, where he had laid his deadly convoy in wait.

Yasser had a younger brother called Mustapha who was identical to him visually, but who did not share his extreme beliefs. Tank had anticipated Yasser's intentions, and employed Mustapha to help the Task Force by acting as a decoy to confuse Yasser's suicide bombers.

Tank had gathered his team around him before Mustapha arrived at the stadium, in an unmarked police car. They had identified a total of twelve ice-cream vendors working around the stadium, who could be potential suicide bombers. Four of them had men of Middle Eastern appearance working in them. In addition they had located 18 hot-dog stands dotted around the streets outside the stadium. Tank had ordered his men to commandeer the Liverpool Football Club souvenir shop for padded overcoats that would help the agents to blend into the football crowd, and hide the weapons that they carried. If the crowds of people saw a gun, panic would ensue, and the bombers would be alerted. If the bombers panicked then they may activate their devices early. Tank's plan was risky but simple.

Mustapha Ahmed was to approach the suspect vans from a reasonable distance and then signal the occupants to come to him. Once the suspects had left the vehicle they would be neutralised and the bomb squad could make the vehicle safe. It would be too risky to try and move the vans in case they had been booby trapped with motion sensors or mercury switches. Mercury being a liquid metal could conduct an electric charge to trigger a bomb. It would also move like a liquid does if the device was moved, making a circuit contact complete and triggering the booby-trap.

Grace had been in contact with the Anfield Stadium management and had indicated that there was a large security service operation in motion outside the stadium. Their cooperation would be required to make the operation run smoothly, and avoid the possible loss of life. Terrorist Task Force Agents were located inside the stadium control room monitoring the CCTV. Grace had also asked the ground staff to pipe music through the external sound system to nullify the nose of any gunfire. She had also insisted that it was turned up to full volume to make it very uncomfortable to remain close by the stadium. They could not risk the arrest of one terrorist to alert another. The music was blaring on the streets outside the ground making it very uncomfortable for sightseers to just wander aimlessly. The crowds started to drift slowly further away from the ground using the bars and shops located a safer distance from the stadium.

The crowds had thinned significantly when Mustapha arrived. The music was deafening. Tank briefed Mustapha on the plan and they approached the first target near to the Shankly Gates. The gates were a memorial to one of the clubs greatest ever managers, Bill Shankly. Mustapha stood across the street from the idle ice-cream van, which tank had picked as a potential suspect vehicle, and leaned against the wall behind him. He looked through his darkened sunglasses toward the Middle Eastern looking man who was in the vehicle. Mustapha pretended to be making a call on his cell phone when the man appeared to recognise him. He looked intently at Mustapha and half raised his hand in a gesture of acknowledgement. Mustapha waved to him in a gesture of beckoning. The Asian man hesitated briefly and then opened the passenger door and climbed out of the vehicle. He crossed the road heading toward Mustapha through the crowd.

Tank grabbed the man from behind crushing the breath from his lungs as he lifted him off his feet. He pinned both of the man's arms to his sides in the vice like grip that he held him in. Agents rushed in and fastened the terrorist's wrists and ankles together with plasticuffs. Startled members of the public who were shocked by the incident quickly moved on when Task Force ID cards were displayed. The bomb squad cordoned the van off by parking a huge truck alongside it to protect innocent passersby from any potential blast. They quickly confirmed their worst suspicions. The freezer storage space inside the van was packed with Semtex and ball bearings.

"That's one suspect down with no weapons drawn ladies and gentlemen. Target two is two hundred yards away on Brecks Road," Tank instructed his agents and Mustapha through their earpieces. He continued.

"We have just received information that an attack on Stanlow Oil Refinery has been foiled. Suspect was neutralised. He managed to release an RPG but it exploded short of his intended target. Let's get the same result here."

Tank indicated where he wanted Mustapha to go and he crossed the busy street and made himself visible to the occupant of the second vehicle. Inside the van was Ali and he stooped low to make sure that it was Yasser that he could see beckoning him out of the van. He was sure it was him but something made him suspicious. Ali took the safety catch off his Magnum .357 and pushed it into the waistband of his jeans. He opened the driver's door and stepped down from the ice-cream van. Mustapha was sweating as Ali approached him, and he did not look comfortable as the man neared him. Football fans were hampering the Task Force Agents as they tried to approach Ali without alerting him to their presence. They could not be sure if the terrorists would have the facility to remote-detonate the devices until the bomb squad had analysed the first device. Tank couldn't grab Ali and ensure that his hands had been neutralised because of the crowds in his proximity. Mustapha wiped sweat from his forehead, and his sleeve removed the make-up that was covering a deep bite mark on his cheék. He had been bitten in a fight with a Bosnian Muslim who had shot the woman he loved just days before. The Bosnian had left a deep wound in Mustapha's face that would scar for life.

Ali realised in an instant that this was not Yasser Ahmed although the likeness was uncanny. He pulled his gun from his waistband and aimed at Mustapha. Mustapha froze in fear as Ali fired three rounds at him through the crowd. The deafening music muffled the booming gunshots, and only those closest to Ali realised that shots had been fired. Mustapha felt shattered pieces of house brick scratch his face and neck as the bullets from the .357 Magnum shattered the wall behind him. Tank reached Ali and placed his Glock 9mm against the top of the shorter man's head. The gun was pointed vertically down at the floor. Tank fired twice. The 9mm bullets ripped downwards through Ali's brain and into his torso. The devastating effect of the bullets liquidised most of the Iranian's brain before he had even realised that he had been shot. His legs buckled and he crumpled to the floor. Tank had to shoot down through the terrorist's head to minimise the risk of a through and through bullet continuing on its journey into an innocent football fan.

"A second target is down. Was there any response to the gunfire from the other vehicles Grace?" Tank asked as he made his way to Mustapha through the crowd.

"Nothing at all, I don't think they heard it at all. Bomb squad have just informed us that the devices are manually activated. There is no remote detonation facility on the first device," Grace replied.

Tank reached Mustapha and he noticed how pale he looked. He was going into nervous shock.

"Are you feeling alright, there are only two more ice-cream vans that fit the profile? Can you carry on Mustapha?" Tank shook him a little trying to get a response but Mustapha was staring at the Ice-cream van.

"Look it's Pinky and Perky," Mustapha said pointing to the driver's door of the van.

"Mustapha I need you to hold it together for just a little bit longer. Don't you worry about the two little pigs right now." Tank was getting annoyed. They needed to move on quickly.

"You don't understand what I am saying to you Tank. Both vans had Pinky and Perky decals on the driver's door. It might help to narrow down the search," Mustapha shouted over the booming music from the external sound system. Tank realised what Mustapha had noticed, and he reacted immediately.

"Grace get every vendor checked for decals on the driver's door of Pinky and Perky. If the same person re-sprayed all these vans then he may have left a pattern without even realising it. Chen, you pass the information on to uniform as soon as possible please." Tank knew that Chen and the fat controller had been coordinating events and information that was coming in from units all over the city. They had deployed the relevant assets to the relevant situations, and so far they were on top.

Tank guided Mustapha toward the third target and pointed to the position that he wanted him to maintain. Mustapha looked at the ice-cream vendor and the man caught his eye. The Asian man took a double take at Mustapha and then bolted toward the back of the vehicle. Tank watched in horror as the man reached for the detonator in an attempt to blow the van, and the public around it to smithereens. For some reason the man knew that Mustapha was not Yasser straight away.

Tank closed the distance between himself and the van in a few strides. He drew the 9mm Glock simultaneously and emptied the clip of sixteen high velocity bullets through the glass, into the terrorist. The bullets smashed through the man's chest spraying blood and cartilage up the windows of the van. As he collapsed, three rounds to the neck area ripped his head from his body completely. The terrorist wouldn't get the chance to detonate his bomb.

The dead terrorist had realised that Mustapha was not Yasser Ahmed because Yasser had left the van just seconds before. Yasser Ahmed watched the action unfold from the safety of the crowds as his affiliate was gunned down inside his mobile bomb. He was fascinated as he saw his younger brother Mustapha being led away by a big man with a shaved head. Yasser backed slowly into an alleyway transfixed by his younger brother. Yasser hadn't seen him since he was a small boy. Although there was six years between them he was stunned by their resemblance to each other.

The shooting of the ice-cream vendor had been witnessed by hundreds of people and word had spread around the pubs and bars that the police had shot someone. Speculation was rife that it was a potential terrorist. Why else would the police shoot an Ice-cream man at a football game? Customers from a local pub called The Sand Dune had come out onto the street as soon as they had heard what was going on. They stood holding pint glasses on the pavement outside the pub watching the bomb squad going in and out of an Ice-cream van that was parked just a few hundred yards away. Some of the football fans were just ten feet from a hot dog stand that was on the corner of Brecks Road and Anfield Road. Speculation was rife that a terrorist had been shot. There was a nervous buzz around the stadium. No one was really sure if they themselves were in any danger.

Two fans approached the abandoned hot dog stand still holding their precious beer in their hands. There didn't appear to be anyone staffing it. One of the men lifted the lid from a stainless steel pan and looked at the hot dog sausages inside the steaming container.

"Here we are lad free hot dogs. The bloke must have fucked off somewhere. Tell the rest of the lads and I'll get some more bread rolls out of the bottom here," the drunken fans pushed and shoved each other mischievously around the hot dog stand.

One of them opened the stainless steel door beneath the stand and thought that it was odd that there were wires everywhere inside. He never thought of anything ever again. The stand exploded and the members of the Sand Dune took the full blast of the shrapnel bomb.

Tank had instinctively pushed Mustapha to the ground when

he heard the explosion and covered him with his own body. The crowds around the stadium scattered in all directions as realisation of what had happened struck home. The remnants of the bodies from the blast were strewn across the street like bloody confetti. Within seconds the immediate area was almost empty.

"Take the last target down immediately," Tank shouted across the airwaves. Three agents dressed in red Liverpool FC shirts drew weapons and surrounded the remaining van, and pumped it full of bullets. The occupant was left dangling from the serving hatch where a pool of his blood spread on the road beneath him.

The remaining hot dog stand bomb was cordoned off and a controlled explosion was carried out. It too had been left unattended and unnoticed by the huge crowds that passed unaware.

"Tank, uniform has reported two unattended Ice-cream vans next to the Anglican Cathedral. They both have the Pinky and Perky decals on the driver's door. We are evacuating the building now and beginning a search of the building. Everyone leaving the cathedral has been searched," Chen informed Tank of the breaking news.

"What time is it? Get everyone away from the building immediately. Chen if you are right about the optimum time for exploding the devices being 3pm, then we only have five minutes left." Tank realised that Chen was probably correct in his assumption.

He lifted Mustapha off the road onto his feet. The Iraqi man was badly shaken by the blast. Tank walked him toward a police transit van that was parked on the pavement nearby, 70-yards away.

Yasser watched from the safety of the alleyway as the big skinhead walked toward the van, carrying his younger brother. The police transit van had a white background with the distinctive orange stripes carried by police vehicles around the middle of it. Tank noticed that the police markings didn't look quite right. He realised that the markings were upside down. There were two parallel orange stripes on a genuine police vehicle. The thicker of the two stripes was fixed above the thinner band. This one was upside down.

The disguised police van exploded at exactly 3pm, as did the Semtex in the bell tower of the Anglican cathedral. The cathedral bell tower, weakened by the blast had disintegrated beneath the massive weight of the bells. Huge sandstone blocks weighing tons, had tumbled into the cavernous building crushing six-members of the Terrorist Bomb Squad that had not had time to escape. The skyline of Liverpool had changed forever.

Tank was blown across the street with Mustapha when the police van exploded. The two men were stunned into unconsciousness by the power of the shockwave.

Tank had woken up in intensive care at The Royal Liverpool Hospital 48-hours later. He had woken just long enough to ask Grace, who was waiting by his bedside what had happened. Then he passed out again and didn't come round for another three days. The swelling to Tank's brain caused by the concussion wave had nearly killed him. The surgeons had drilled a hole into his skull to relieve the pressure from the bleeding, and that saved his life.

Seven Terrorist Task Force members lost their lives at the Cathedral blast along with the nine football fans, near the stadium.

Mustapha had never arrived at the hospital at all. Witnesses said that he was seen being helped away from the scene by an Asian man, who looked like he was related to him.

Tank and his team returned to duty as normal, once all the scars had healed. The Terrorist Task Force tracked the alleged movements of the ghost like Yasser Ahmed across the planet. Several reports of him were received from the Philippines and Afghanistan over the following six months, but nothing concrete ever surfaced.

Eventually a report came in from an American Black operations team that specialised in rendition. These people don't officially exist of course but they specialise in counter terrorism and interrogation under torture. This process is usually carried out on foreign soil. The American people are not made aware of such procedures being utilised by their government. Countries with a broader moral outlook are used to extract information. Western populations cannot prove the use of torture if there are no western witnesses to tell the tale.

The black operations team reportedly captured Yasser Ahmed in Iraq. They interrogated him for two months in a prison in Chechnya. His heart had finally given in after eight weeks of intense torture and malnutrition. When Tank saw the autopsy pictures he recognised the bite mark on the cheek of the corpse. It wasn't Yasser that they had captured and tortured. Mustapha had denied being Yasser Ahmed right up to the point where his heart stopped beating. The wrong brother had been captured and killed. Tank felt responsible.

CHAPTER 39
Yasser Ahmed/Mustapha
(Escaping Britain)

Eighteen months ago when Yasser had watched the bogus police van explode, he had jumped at the opportunity to grab his concussed sibling. The big skinhead policeman had been stunned by the blast, and people were running in all directions away from the bomb. Yasser grabbed his brother off the street where he lay and carried him away from the scene. He had a camper van parked a half mile away from the football stadium, and some kind hearted people who heard about the terrorist explosions had helped him to carry Mustapha to the camper and lay him down on the bed. Mustapha remained unconscious for two days, drifting into consciousness for only seconds at a time. Yasser had driven north from Liverpool to the east coast port of Hull. He had used his network of sympathisers, and had arranged for the camper to be craned onto a container boat, which had an Islamic crew from the Yemen, and was headed for the Middle East. By the time Mustapha awoke, the ship was in the middle of the North Sea, and he really didn't have the heart to struggle against his older brother. Yasser was a very persuasive personality, and by the time they reached their destination Mustapha was resigned to returning home to his beloved Iraq.

They had been welcomed into their family's homes at first, especially Mustapha, who had been a small boy when he was smuggled abroad for his own safety. Following the deposal of Saddam, Iraq had turned into a boiling pot of racial, tribal unrest. Law enforcement was nonexistent and life hung in the balance. Suspicion and betrayal were insipid in the indigenous population, as Sunni's and Shia's Muslims struggled against each other for political power. Rumours became rife that legendary Mujahideen leader Yasser Ahmed had returned home. Some saw it as a sign from God that they would be delivered from allied occupation, while others saw his presence as a powerful threat to their authority, and a financially lucrative opportunity. The allies would pay handsomely to know the whereabouts of Yasser Ahmed. Yasser began to plot again and at least a dozen roadside bombs attacks against the invading forces were attributed to him. Informants had passed on information to the Americans and they began to scour the local townships for him.

Yasser became concerned for his family's safety and he left to join the Islamic struggles in Afghanistan and Chechnya. When the allies eventually got wind of his operations in Iraq he was already long gone. Weeks after Yasser's departure a neighbour of different Muslim extraction mistakenly identified Mustapha to an American black ops team, as Yasser Ahmed. He was paid the equivalent of fifteen British pounds for the information. Mustapha was snatched later the same day, and his family was taken into custody with him. They were taken to a temporary airfield where they were briefly questioned. American secret services had sent the only picture they possessed of Yasser Ahmed to the black ops team, and they were in no doubt that they had the right man.

Mustapha and his family were placed inside a huge twin bladed Chinook helicopter, which was unmarked and had a crew of foreign extraction. Once over the desert the side doors were opened and Mustapha's uncle was dragged toward the opening. The wind from the twin blades howled through the huge machine and the frightened family huddled together. The uncle was thrown from the door two thousand feet up. The foreign soldiers wore no identifying insignia on their uniforms. Mustapha pleaded with them when his Auntie was taken to the door and asked to identify Mustapha as Yasser; she refused to confirm that he was Yasser and followed her husband to her death. The process was repeated until only Mustapha was left in the helicopter sobbing for the loss of his innocent family. The memories of the screams of terror remained with him until the day he died under interrogation. Each family member denied that Mustapha was Yasser. Even though they had watched their kin thrown to their deaths they did not betray him.

CHAPTER 40

Chechnya/Yasser Ahmed

In the 16th century the powerful Islamic Ottoman Empire controlled what are now the Middle East, North Africa and Asia. Under its control the small region of Chechnya was converted to the Sunni Muslim faith. Its conversion to Islam began a long religious struggle against its Jewish and Christian neighbours, which has lasted for centuries. It is the 76th largest federal subject of Russia, located in the Northern Caucasus Mountains. It borders Stavropol Krai to the north west, the republic of Dagestan to the east and north east, Georgia to the south and the republics of Ingushetia and North Ossetia to the west. After the collapse of the Soviet Union in 1991 it declared itself a republic separate from Russia, and despite numerous Soviet invasions it remains a rogue Islamic state. The only government to recognise the existence of the republic of Chechnya is the Afghan Taliban Council, who themselves are no longer a recognised government. Hundreds of thousands of Arab Mujahideen answered the call to arms to fight against the invading Russian Christian, Zionist aggressors in both Afghanistan and Chechnya.

The Muslim defenders see the invasion of Chechnya as another attempt by the West's Christian-Jewish alliance to control Islamic oil fields. Although a relatively small country it is a major hub in the oil infrastructure of the Russian federation, and would hurt the Soviet economy if it were allowed its independence. The armed struggle by Islamic insurgents has cost the Russian armed forces over seventeen and a half thousand deaths since 1991, despite their overwhelming manpower, weaponry and air support. According to Chechen rebel leaders the Russian army has slaughtered over thirty-five thousand civilians since 1994.

Yasser Ahmed was an influential leader and inspiration to millions of would be Mujahideen fighters. He was the number one most wanted Islamic terrorist on the planet, and because of this he had travelled to the remote regions of Afghanistan, then Dagestan and Chechnya to fight the Kufur. Yasser became a religious hero within months as his exploits attacking targets in the US and UK became well known across the Soviet region. Upon his arrival Yasser began to organise the ragbag groups into effective fighting units, and advised and trained the Islamic guerrilla fighters how to manufacture 'improvised explosive devices' or roadside bombs that could penetrate Russian tank armour. From Moscow the Chechen mafia donated millions of dollars from its illegal operations across Russia, into Yasser's hidden bank accounts to finance weapons and munitions to aid the struggle for Islamic independence. Modern explosives are expensive so Yasser taught them how to use discarded ordinance or unexploded shells to manufacture 'improvised explosive devices'. They were easily made by attaching conventional military explosives, such as an artillery round, attached to a detonating mechanism. Once fabricated the devices could be customised to incorporate destructive, lethal, noxious, pyrotechnic or chemical substances to destroy or incapacitate personnel or vehicles.

Yasser also financed the purchase of four thousand RPG anti-tank weapons from Libya, which they had employed with devastating effect against low flying Soviet helicopter gunships. Rocket Propelled Grenades have been used by the Afghan Mujahideen for years in an anti-aircraft role. Helicopters are typically ambushed as they land or hover. Yasser taught the rebels to modify the grenade launchers for use against flying helicopters by adding a curved pipe to the rear of the launch tube. This addition diverted the exhaust gasses away from the user, allowing the weapon to be fired upwards at an aircraft from a prone position. This made the operator less visible prior to firing, and decreased the risk of injury from dangerous back-blast. Yasser was a veteran of Afghanistan and Iraq and he knew every guerrilla tactic in the book. The arrival of Yasser Ahmed turned the tide against the invading Soviet forces.

There was an interesting phenomenon, which became

apparent during the Islamic struggle in Chechnya, the emergence of determined female suicide bombers known as the Chechen 'Black Widows'. The use of suicide belts or, 'Shaheed belts', has been a tactic adopted by various terrorist organisations since its conception in 1991. The first documented use of this weapon was by the Tamil Tiger group in Sri Lanka who sent Thenmuli Rajaratnam, a 25-year old widow, to a government rally. She approached Rajiv Gandhi and detonated her device killing the target and herself. The suicide belts usually consist of several metal cylinders filled with explosive. The explosive is surrounded by a fragmentation jacket that produces the shrapnel, which causes most of the collateral damage. The jacket becomes a crude body-worn claymore mine. Once the vest is detonated, the explosion becomes similar to an Omni-directional shotgun blast. The most dangerous and most widely used shrapnel are steel ball bearings but many cheaper materials such as screws, nuts, bolts and barbed wire are often substituted. The bravery of the Muslim women had been used as a devastating weapon to attack Russian targets, and Yasser planned to harness their uncanny determination in a new campaign of terror, both here and in the West.

On October 5th, 2003 a Chechen Islamic separatist leader conspired with the Russian invaders to organise democratic elections within Chechnya. His cooperation with the Christian, Zionist invaders was seen as treason and a direct insult to the Muslim population. Many separatist organisations boycotted the elections, and the Muslim militia groups started a campaign of fear, threatening people to vote against the traitor. The elections were monitored by an international inspection team, who reported incidents of ballot stuffing and voter intimidation by Russian soldiers. Several separatist parties were completely excluded from entering the elections by Russian officials.

Once the votes were counted Akmad Kadyrov was entrusted as the Soviet sponsored leader despite the allegations of corruption and vote rigging. He was the wealthiest and most powerful man in the republic and he surrounded himself with mercenary bodyguards to protect him from Islamic extremists. On May 9th, 2004 at his official inauguration, he was seated on a stage inside the Grozny football stadium watching a parade go past in his honour. A Chechen woman dressed in black clothing and wearing an

Islamic headscarf or 'hijab' approached the new president carrying a bouquet of flowers. Her name was Medna Bayrakova and she was a 26-year old resident of Grozny. She had been married to her childhood sweetheart at the age of 15, which is the customary age in that region. Medna and her husband lived by strict Shari' a law, but they were soul mates and very happy. They had survived two Russian invasions since 1991, but had lost most of their families during the conflicts. Their only regret was that they had never conceived a child, and in a poor country like Chechnya medical assistance was non-existent. Her husband had naively expressed his anger in public at the cooperation that Kadyrov had given to the Russians, and he had called it religious betrayal. Several days later he had been snatched from the small blacksmith shop where he had worked since he was a child. Like thousands of others he never returned home, and had likely been tortured to death by the mercenaries. Medna was broken hearted and left destitute, because losing your husband also meant losing your livelihood. She couldn't pay her rent and was evicted within weeks of her husband's disappearance. Medna was living rough on the streets and surviving on what scraps she could beg or steal. One morning she was awoken by a Mullah from the local mosque and given hot sweet tea to drink. He fed her and gave her clean clothing and began the process of grooming her to become a Martyr. In just three days she was convinced that she could leave this life of grief and turmoil behind her, and go to a much happier place with her God, and her beloved husband. She saw the opportunity to extract revenge against Kadyrov as her ticket to heaven. The thought of eternity in heaven next to her beloved husband was far more attractive than a life of lonely destitution and poverty. Being hungry everyday soon takes its toll on the will to live.

She slipped through the passing parade and headed for the stage were her nemesis was seated. As she stepped on to the stage and approached the president she tripped. Bodyguards stopped the woman, but the president waved her through flattered by the sight of the flowers she carried as a gift. As she handed the flowers to him, she triggered a remote detonator on her Shaheed vest, and blew herself and the Muslim traitor to pieces.

CHAPTER 41

Yasser/Chechen Black Widows

Yasser sat on a boulder next to the camp fire and stared at the flames as they flickered and danced. He and several hundred Mujahideen fighters were taking cover in a network of natural caves situated high in the mountains of Chechnya. As he watched the fire glow he thought about his dead sister Yasmine and how beautiful she had been, and about his younger brother Mustapha, who had looked like his twin. Word had reached his mountain hideaway two months earlier that his family's home in Iraq was deserted. Neighbours had told his spies that 'ninja' soldiers dressed head to foot in black uniforms had taken them away in the dead of night, and that they had never been seen or heard from again. He knew that the soldiers were looking for him. Mustapha and his family would have been imprisoned and interrogated, at least that's what he hoped, but in his heart he knew that no one returned when the 'Ninja' soldiers came. The soldiers dressed in black were Special Operations men sent to assassinate him. They would have killed his family instead of him, trying to make them divulge his whereabouts.

Footsteps and hushed voices disturbed his thoughts as a group of Mujahideen fighters returned from their evening mission. The men were skinny from lack of food, and dirty from the wind borne dust that covered the mountains. They had their weapons and ammunition slung around their shoulders and the flames from the fire reflected on the dull metal. There were men sleeping around the cave floor and they sat up and moved to make space for the returning fighters. The nights were becoming cold enough for frost to form on the grey rocks. The returning Mujahideen gathered around the fire to report their mission to Yasser.

Earlier that day they had encountered a Russian patrol and become involved in a fire fight. Two of their men had been taken prisoner, and several others killed and wounded. The number of wounded was increasing every day. Most of them didn't talk much, exhausted from their journey. One of the younger men cleaned and checked a captured light machinegun while the others ate the remnants of a thin chicken stew that had been cooked several hours earlier. Yasser was still well funded despite Western governments freezing the assets they could find, but the Russians monitored food sales looking for purchases that could be used to feed large groups of enemy soldiers. They had to purchase supplies from all over the country in small batches, and bring it to the mountains where only a handful of people knew where they would be hiding on any given day. Some days supplies didn't arrive and rations were meagre. It was 3am and everyone knew that the bombing would start in about four hours, so it was time to get some sleep. The Russians knew that Yasser and his men were somewhere in this region of the mountains above Grozny, and they targeted a section every day for carpet bombing. At seven o'clock that morning the distinctive triple contrails caused by Russian bombers appeared on the horizon leaving straight white lines against the blue sky. Minutes later huge plumes of rock, flames and smoke would explode along distant ridges. Seconds after that the noise and blast wave would reach them, tugging at their clothes. The blast would cause small dust devils to form and swirl around the caves. While the men slept Yasser stared into the flames and watched his plans taking shape. He stroked the matted beard that he had grown since arriving in the mountains, because it still felt alien to him. There was no running water here to shave or bathe.

As the bombs began to fall miles away across the misty valley, the men shuffled around the cave preparing for the day's struggle against the Russian invaders. They hung ammunition belts around their necks and then wrapped thin blankets over their 'shalwar kameez' or smock tops. The straps on their Kalashnikov rifles were hitched over the shoulder, and extra bullet magazines stuffed into homemade webbing pouches. Yasser mingled with his men and patted them encouragingly, kissing some on the cheek and assuring them that their God was fighting alongside them. The men were a mixture of Iranians, Jordanians, Egyptians, Somalia's,

Iraqis, Afghans, Uzbeks, Ingushes, Dags, Kumyks and indigenous Chechens. The sky had begun to lighten and Yasser could see long files of Mujahideen marching from the caves along the ridge toward the steep, dark, forested slopes that rose in the distance to snowy peaks. To the north he could see the city of Grozny through the lifting mists, and the mountains beyond. The Mujahideen left the caves to take up their combat positions and lie in wait for unsuspecting Soviets troops to ambush.

Yasser watched them leave and then returned to the fire and sat down on the boulder again. He had a canvas bag next to him, and he picked it up and reached inside. Yasser removed a bundle of old newspapers, tattered and torn around the edges, the paper was yellowed. He was looking at the front cover of the New York Times dated three months earlier. On the cover was the black and white image of a tickertape parade in Times Square, New York. Millions of pieces of coloured confetti floated from the surrounding buildings, and in the centre of the picture was a woman riding an open top bus through crowded streets. The woman had short sculptured black hair and perfect porcelain teeth, which she was displaying with a winning smile. Her name was Hilary Rice and she had made history by becoming the first black female President of the United States. The picture had been taken when she had won the presidential by-election in the State of New York, on the way to The White House. She was pictured waving to an adoring crowd, surrounded by her election team, which consisted of thirty two people. Twenty eight of her closest associates were women, which had given Yasser his plan.

On May 12th 2003 a pro-Moscow festival was organised by Russia's President Putin as a tribute to the great Prophet Mohammed, in the town of Ilaskhan-Yurt. It was seen as a cynical attempt to quieten Islamic insurgents, and became the target of a Chechen rebel attack. Thousands of Muslim pilgrims attended the festival, which was to be addressed by the pro-Russian Chechen administrator, and senior religious figures who supported Putin's peace plan. Shakhida Baimuratova was the forty six year old mother of three missing, presumed dead sons. Her sons had been taken for questioning by the authorities six years earlier and were never heard of again. Her husband had been wrongly identified as a Chechen rebel in 1999 and shot dead in front of her in the town's local market. She arrived at the festival carrying twenty eight pounds of high explosives beneath her Muslim dress, and approached the stand where the officials were sitting. Shakhida detonated her suicide vest resulting in the deaths of 150 pilgrims. Putin was not injured but five of his bodyguards were killed, and he stated that he was concerned that there would be further attacks by a new breed of suicide bombers. He described the attacks as a frightening new form of rebel insurgency in a decade old conflict. A day after his reaction to the bombing another woman, in the usually peaceful north of the country, drove a truck packed full of explosives into a government compound killing seventy-five soldiers. Russia began taking the threat of the Black Widows seriously when the attacks were happening on an almost daily basis.

Thursday June 5th, 2003 at 7.36am, Masdika Korchnoi was waiting at a bus stop near the military air base of Mozdok, which is a major military installation in Russia's North Ossetia province. She was a 25 year old widow, and mother of two missing sons. Masdika dressed in a white overall disguised as a nurse, and waited for the bus to arrive. She was surrounded by Russian soldiers and civilian support staff when the bus arrived. The bus had slowed down to allow a car to pull away from the bus stop, and when its doors opened there was only room for a few more passengers, which did not include the would be bomber. Madika threw herself underneath the bus and detonated her device. Fifty seven people were killed and seventeen seriously injured in the blast.

Yasser knew that he could harness the hatred that these Black Widows harboured into a powerful asset. Hiding in caves and killing a handful of Russian conscript soldiers would not win Islam's Jihad. Yasser wanted to reach into his enemy's backyard again, and hit them where they were most vulnerable. Although his plan was not one hundred percent completed it was close to being put into action. He just needed a little more time to finalise details and recruit the assistance from abroad that he would require. The Russians were closing in on the Chechen rebels, and getting closer to the network of caves every day. They needed to move back across the border to Dagestan to regroup and rearm. Many of the Mujahideen needed medical attention, and there was a hospital facility forty miles across the border, which was sympathetic to the rebels cause. Yasser saw the white exhaust trail of a Russian passenger jet approaching

Grozny airport and he aimed an imaginary rifle at it and pulled the imaginary trigger smiling.

Two Russian passenger jets crashed in 2004 causing huge embarrassment to President Putin, who had gained power on a promise to eradicate Chechen violence and bring renewed security to Russia. Officials discovered the remains and DNA of two Chechen women, thought to be suicide bombers, and Black Widows. Traces of explosives were found on the remains of the two women. The loss of the two Russian passenger jets was the first successful attack on airlines by Islamic extremists since September 11th. The smaller of the two jets, a TU-134, carrying forty four people, crashed near Tula in the south of Moscow. The Chechen woman on board this plane was identified as Amanta Nagayeva. She bought her ticket just one hour before the flight took off. Two fragments of her body were found two and a half miles apart, and she was the only woman not to have her remains claimed. Nagayeva was born in 1977 near Vadeno, which was the home of Islamic Chechen warlord, Shamil Basayev, and lived in Grozny.

The larger jet exploded minutes later near the city of Rostov, killing forty six people. Experts found traces of the military explosive Hexogen in the wreckage, and on the remains of another Chechen woman called Djerbikhanova. She was originally booked on another flight but swapped it at the last minute to the evening flight, which carried more passengers. Djerbikhanova requested seat 19 f, nine rows from the tail, which is considered to be the most vulnerable part of the aircraft. Once again she was the only passenger to remain unclaimed by family. The attacks were brushed under the carpet by the Russians because of lapses in airport security, which had allowed the suicide bombers to gain passage onto the planes.

Many in the West didn't know anything about the Chechen Black Widows or the wider Islamic struggles against the Russians in Afghanistan and Chechnya. Yasser Ahmed was going to change that in dramatic fashion. The West would know and remember the Black Widows for centuries to come. He took one last look at the picture of Hilary Rice and smiled. He placed the newspaper back into his canvas bag and hitched his Kalashnikov rifle over his shoulder before heading down the rocky slopes to join the Mujahideen.

CHAPTER 42

Special Operations
Team/Tank

Tank watched a team of United States Air Force technicians dismantling four MQ-1 Predator drones. Unlike the British unmanned helicopter drones the Predators were small pilotless airplanes. Each Predator air vehicle can be disassembled into six smaller components and loaded into a container nicknamed 'the coffin'. This enables all system components and support equipment to be rapidly deployed anywhere in the world. The largest component is the ground control station which is designed to be rolled into the back of a C-130 Hercules transporter plane, and its associated twenty foot satellite dish. The drones need one hundred and fifty yards of flat ground to take off and land and are virtually silent when they are airborne.

"How good are these drones Chen?" Tank asked his colleague, who was a mine of technical information.

Chen frowned at Tank and his jaw dropped, and his mouth opened making him look a bit simple. "The MQ-1 has been used extensively in Afghanistan since about 2005," Chen began, "it has participated in more than two-hundred and fifty separate raids, engaged one-hundred and thirty two different troop divisions, fired over five-hundred Hellfire missiles, surveyed eighteen-thousand targets, escorted forty convoys and flown over two-thousand sorties for more than thirty-three thousand, eight-hundred and thirty-three hours." Chen shrugged his shoulders as if everyone should know that.

"You really are a nerd," Tank said patting Chen on the head with his big hand.

"You should read your e-mails Tank, I am just repeating

information that you have also received," Chen replied sounding offended.

"I seem to remember an al-Qaeda camp being taken out recently by one of these," Tank recalled.

"That's right," Chen perked up at the opportunity to impart more useful information, "October 30th, 2006 the CIA launched a drone to strike an alleged training camp in the Bajaur region. They had received information that al-Qaeda's second in command, Ayman al-Zawahiri was residing there. The religious school was hit by six Hellfire missiles, killing eighty-five extremists, including five senior al-Qaeda members."

"Well we will need all the back-up we can get on this trip," Tank said, "as it stands, we can afford to deploy eighty men to attack the hospital in Kizlyar, and extract the Saudi. Apache special operation attack helicopters will take us in and take out any artillery in the surrounding area, but they don't have airspace clearance to hang around. MH-53 Pave Low, long range helicopters will supply us with long wheel base armoured Land Rovers for our evac. Apart from the drone's support our exit strategy is exposed, because we're not supposed to be there, we will be on our own."

The mission was dangerous. AH-6 'little birds' helicopters would drop in a reconnaissance squad to identify where the anti-aircraft positions were located. Combined with the information from the drones, which could pick up human signatures by tracking body heat from ten-thousand feet up, a clear picture could be analysed before the main body of the attack force was inserted. AH-64D Apache gunships would then destroy armoured positions and heavy machinegun posts before quickly returning over the border before they could be detected. The Apache gunships had been crucial for destroying Iraqi tanks in the second invasion of Iraq. On March 24th, 2003 the US launched thirty-two Apache helicopters against the Iraqi Medina armoured division. The results were spectacular; seven Iraqi air defence positions were destroyed along with three long range artillery systems, five radar posts and seventy-five T-52 tanks. They virtually cleared the road to Baghdad.

"What information do we have about the minefields?" Tank asked Chen. During the siege of Kizlyar hospital Russian Spetsnaz had used cluster bombs to attack the Chechen rebels. They dispersed anti-personnel mines over a wide area to discourage enemy soldiers returning to the site. The mines varied in size and makeup. Some were metal and detectable, but others were made from wood and plastic, making them invisible to metal detectors, and stopping them from corroding so that they were active for decades.

"We know that we will need to clear paths through the minefield surrounding the facility, but the Dagestan border regions are also heavily mined and we won't be able to go anywhere quickly or quietly," Chen answered. British Special Forces had a tactical weapon called the 'Rapid Anti-Personnel Minefield Breaching System' or RAMBS 11. It is adapted from a rifle grenade and provides an effective and flexible method of clearing a safe path sixty metres wide, and a half metre deep through mined areas. The obvious problem was the noise it generated and the length of time taken. Most of the borders around the mountainous region between the southern Soviet states and the Middle Eastern countries of Turkey and Iran have areas that are mined. Afghanistan, Pakistan, Uzbekistan and Tajikistan all deploy mines on their borders. The mines are deployed by indigenous government forces trying to stop Islamic extremists groups and drug traffickers crossing into their country from the mountains.

"Let's hope that we don't need to leave in a hurry," Tank mused, "we have forty miles to cover before the helicopters can return to perform an extraction." Satellite pictures monitored troops crossing the mountains from Chechnya into Dagestan sporadically. They were usually employed to focus on the mountains further east in the search for Osama bin Laden, because they knew he was there somewhere. Information about Yasser Ahmed was sketchy and based on rumour and uncorroborated hearsay. They couldn't dedicate a satellite to the extraction mission because officially it didn't exist.

"Once we have the Saudi I doubt the rebels will pursue us," Chen said, "the number of rebels defending the facility seems to yo-yo when the Mujahideen leave Chechnya to resupply. Numbers can treble overnight because it's so close to the Dagestan border. The satellite information we have shows hundreds of Mujahideen active in the mountains above Grozny, and as long as they stay that side of the border then we should be in and out."

"When was Yasser Ahmed last seen," Tank asked, he knew the information was unreliable but any news was better than no news.

"Roughly three months ago," Chen answered frowning, "I thought Jeannie Kellesh was our objective Tank. We won't have the time or the resources to go on a witch hunt in the Chechen mountains."

"I have got a funny feeling that we might not have to look too far Chen," Tank answered, "that facility is an essential part of the Mujahideen struggle. We know its bank accounts are supplied with money made in Russia by the Chechen mafia. If Yasser Ahmed is in Chechnya then he has been to that hospital, and if he has been there recently then I'm going to find him."

Chen didn't challenge Tank because the look on his face said it all.

CHAPTER 43

Roman Kordinski/
Chester High Court

Roman was perched on a low wooden seat and handcuffed to a metal bracket, which was attached to the floor of the prison van. The prison van was white with blacked out reflective windows, which stopped the paparazzi from taking pictures of notorious criminals inside it. The prison van looked like a horse box with windows. Inside a central isle led to twelve holding cells, six on one side, and six on the other. The holding cells were three feet square and incredibly cramped, containing a narrow wooden ledge for a prisoner to perch on during the journey from prison to court, and back. Roman looked out of the mirrored window as the van slowed down to enter the access road, which led to the Chester City High Courts. He had been arrested and charged under the terrorism act, which dictated that suspects must be committed to trial by jury. Committal to trial had to be carried out in the province where the alleged crime was committed, which required a trip north to Chester.

To his left, steep stone steps descended from street level down to Chester's racecourse, which is called the Roodee. The manicured grass track was the smallest horse racetrack in the world, and is almost completely surrounded by the River Dee. Records show it as the oldest racecourse still in use in England, dating back to the early sixteenth century. Roman had enjoyed the races at Chester many times prior to his arrest, usually arriving by private helicopter as opposed to a prison van. His memory wandered back to sunny days stood in the huge white grandstand watching the well groomed thoroughbreds galloping toward the finishing post. The ancient 65-acre racecourse lies on the site of an old Roman harbour built during the Roman settlement of the city, which took place during the Dark Ages. Through the centuries the river silted up making navigation impossible. He looked to the east of the racecourse which abuts directly onto Chester's ancient city walls, which were once used to moor Roman trading vessels. He longed to be free of the handcuffs and the locked doors, barred windows and prison guards. The racecourse looked so attractive in the sunshine that he yearned for his freedom.

The prison van turned into the grounds of the court and passed beneath a grey stone arch. The historic arch was topped with a full size statue of the female warrior Boadicea, riding in her chariot behind two huge bronze horses. Armed policemen lined the courtyard awaiting Roman Kordinski's arrival. The fact that the oil tycoon was implicated in two high profile terrorist attacks made him a possible target for a vigilante attack. He also had the financial might to finance a prison break, despite the fact that his visible assets had been frozen. It was widely believed by the security services that Kordinski had millions hidden from the government's reach. The most vulnerable position that a guest of Her Majesty's Prison Service could be in, was outside the prison walls. Transporting high profile prisoners to and from court was fraught with danger, especially someone of Kordinski's means. The British prison service is armed only with batons. Armed support had to be provided by the police service to protect the convoy.

The van came to a halt and Roman heard keys unlocking the main door of the prison vehicle. The door was yanked open and bright light filled the gloom. He squinted his eyes as they became accustomed to the sunshine. The van swayed and rocked as three burly prison guards entered the vehicle.

"Stand up Boris," said the first guard trying to be offensive. Roman's face flushed with anger. If he got out of the British penal system he would make sure that the fat prison guard and his family were shot. He would make sure that his men killed him last, after making him watch his children die first. He knew that an escape attempt would be made but he didn't know when or how yet. When it did come he would remember this man's abuse.

"I said stand up Boris," the guard repeated angrily.

"You seem to be confused about my name," Roman answered still seated on the bench, "you must be thinking about when you can buy your next chocolate bar you fat bastard."

The prison guard was furious and he reached through the bars and grabbed Roman by the hair. He pulled violently ripping tufts from the scalp and hitting the Russian's head against the bars. Roman did not utter a sound. He waited for the guards grip to loosen slightly and twisted his head upward and sank his teeth into the fat guard's thumb. His movement was restricted by his handcuffs, but he had no problem biting with crushing force into the warder's digit. The guard screamed in pain and cursed through gritted teeth, but he couldn't free his hand. His colleagues tried desperately to reach the prisoner but the main isle of the vehicle was too narrow to let them pass. The stricken guard was so fat that he completely blocked the access to the prisoner's cell, and he was wedged against the bars. Roman bit harder and he felt his teeth contact bone. Blood filled his mouth and dribbled down his chin, but he wouldn't let go of the vice like grip. He bit harder still and shook his head violently, feeling a tendon snap excited him further. Roman swallowed and the coppery taste of blood filled his senses. The two free prison guards grabbed the injured man and pulled him backward trying to wrench him free from the Russian's bite. Roman felt the ligament rip as they pulled, and he bit harder still crunching through the cartilage between the knuckle of the thumb. The combined weight of the guards ripped the remaining flesh and sinew from the ruined thumb, and he bit the top two inches clean off. The screaming guard crashed backward, falling against his colleagues. He was staring wild eyed at the bloody stump where his thumb used to be. He cursed incoherently and started to blubber like a hysterical child. One of the shocked guards grabbed the injured man and dragged him from the vehicle by his feet. Armed police reacted quickly to the commotion from the prison van and they came to the aid of the guards.

"Get pressure on the wound," a police man said, "he needs a hospital immediately. Where's the thumb?" The guards ran back into the vehicle and looked into Roman's cell. They scoured the floor looking for the top of the guard's thumb, but it was nowhere to be seen. Roman Kordinski sat staring out of the cell window at the beautiful racecourse in the distance laughing like a lunatic as he swallowed the fat guard's appendage.

"Fucking hell I think he's just swallowed it," said one of the police men.

CHAPTER 44

Khava Bararayeva/
Black Widow

Khava waited in line as the long white tourist train approached the excited crowd. The train engine passed and it made a hooting sound imitating a steam train. Children whooped with delight as the carriages came to a halt allowing them to scramble aboard. The Florida sun was shining and the temperature was already heading for the 90's, even though it was only eleven o'clock in the morning. Khava climbed aboard the imitation passenger train which transported millions of tourists from their cars, to the theme parks, and back again.

"Good afternoon folks, and welcome to Disney's Animal Kingdom on this beautiful morning," said the train driver over the public address system. He was wearing white flannel pants and a bright yellow striped blazer. On his head was a red baseball cap emblazoned with the Disney logo.

"Please move all the way across the bench seats, and allow the other folks to climb aboard. Five people per bench," he continued his well rehearsed safety guidelines, "Your children must sit in between the adults and must not be seated next to the doors. Keep your hands and heads inside the vehicle at all times and please remain seated. You have joined the train at the Zebra car park folks, so don't forget where you've parked your vehicles. We will have you at Animal Kingdom in just a few minutes and I wish you all a wonderful day, because it's your day."

The train jerked as it pulled away and began the short journey to the theme park entrance. Khava didn't know why she had picked this one to visit, because they all seemed the same to her. She had driven the rental car down Buena Vista drive and passed Down

Town Disney, where four of her Mujahideen brothers had taken the lives of hundreds of Kufur (non-Muslims), two years earlier. They had disguised themselves as Disney characters and then detonated their suicide vests inside the crowded resort. The political repercussions had been colossal then, and they would be again this time. A mile further on she saw the sign for Animal Kingdom and decided that it would be her target. Animal Kingdom was the fourth theme park to be built on Lake Buena Vista, Florida. When it first opened its' gates in 1998 it became the largest Disney theme park in the world, covering over five hundred acres. Khava's dark sunglasses hid the tears that welled up in her eyes, as she stared at the thousands and thousands of cars parked as far as the eye could see. It was a national holiday and children were enjoying a week off school. Disney was a Mecca for families the world over to visit. Khava looked at the giant 'tree of life', which was situated in the centre of the theme park, its branches towered above the park in the distance. The tree was carved with the shape of hundreds of species of animals, from top to bottom. Only as you approach it can you start to distinguish the carvings from the trunk. The huge tree was once the icon of Animal Kingdom but is now dwarfed by the artificial snow topped mountain that encapsulates a rollercoaster ride called 'Expedition Everest'. Khava was amazed at the sheer scale of the theme park. She wiped a tear from her cheek and tried to be brave. The truth was that she was frightened, more frightened than she had ever been before.

Four days before she had been resolute that her destiny was to kill herself, and as many Westerners as possible, but now she wasn't so sure. Khava had been selected for this mission from a group of female volunteers, and then groomed with the details of the plan by the legendry Muslim warrior Yasser Ahmed. Yasser spent hours with her alone reciting historical events and milestones from times past. The struggle Islam had faced since its conception was now more prevalent than it had ever been. Yasser had convinced her and others that their own existence was absolutely crucial to the global status of Islam. Their actions here on earth would be rewarded tenfold when they arrived to greet their God. When the time to leave had come, Khava had been driven to Grozny airport, and sent on a flight to Moscow along with two other Chechen women. They were never introduced to each other even though they knew of the others existence. During the journey to the airport they had sat in silence, each one of them lost in their own thoughts of what was to be. At the airport they were separated and given tickets and documents that would keep them apart to protect each individual mission. Khava had never been on a plane before, now she had four flights in front of her. From Moscow she had flown to Amsterdam where she changed planes to fly to Chicago. She had been amazed at the size of Chicago airport, especially when she had to board a train to travel from one terminal to another. Khava felt lost and alone in the huge international terminus, and it was there that her doubts started to eat at her. Standing on a long moving walkway she bypassed boarding gate after boarding gate. They all looked alike, just the faces of the people waiting were different.

Khava passed a waiting area designated for an American Airlines flight to New York. The passengers were forming a line at the gate as they had been called to board. Near the back of the line was one of the women that she had travelled to Grozny airport with. One of Yasser Ahmed's Black Widows. She caught her eye as she walked and they stared at each other for a moment. Khava saw recognition in her eyes along with something else. There was a deep sadness there too. Khava recognised the emotion in her, and it was an empty desperate feeling of hopelessness. The travelator carried her away from the New York boarding gate and the moment was gone. Khava was alone again. She waited forty-five minutes in line to pass through security checks before she boarded her flight to Florida. Khava had been picked up from the airport by Yasser's affiliates and taken to a Best Western hotel in Kissimmee. There she was given the keys to a hire car, a one day Disney pass and her instructions. She had never felt so alone in her short miserable life than she did now. Not even when her husband had his throat cut in a bar in Grozny by a Russian soldier, who had made a drunken pass at Khava. Her husband had obviously sprung to her defence and paid with his life. Khava was hysterical as she watched her husband bleeding to death on the filthy wooden floor. Before he had even stopped twitching the Russian soldiers dragged Khava through a fire exit and raped her in the alleyway outside. The authorities recorded the death of her husband as a bar brawl for which no one was arrested or charged, and rape was never registered. Destitute and disgraced she became filled with a bitter hatred. Giving her life to aid in the struggle against the Christians and Jews was a natural option. They had taken everything she had ever loved from her and now was her time for revenge.

"Please leave the carriages from the right hand side folks, and check that you have taken all your belongings, especially the children with you!" the train driver interrupted her thoughts as they arrived at the gates to Animal Kingdom.

CHAPTER 45
New York

Zareta Katharina walked slowly along a promenade on the shores of the mighty Hudson River. She was heading for Battery Park where she was going to take a New York water taxi to Ellis Island, and the Statue of Liberty. Zareta had arrived in New York late the previous evening; too tired to even eat she had slept through until midday. The flights from Chechnya had taken twenty-seven hours in total, leaving her drained of energy. The connecting flights had been uneventful except for catching a fleeting glimpse of another woman from Grozny, at Chicago airport. She too was to become a Chechen Black Widow and a martyr of Islam. Zareta had thirty-six hours until she completed her mission, and she decided to spend them exploring the colossal metropolis that was New York. She had never experienced anything like it before, and she never would again.

Battery Park was vibrant when she arrived. The twenty-one acre green space is the southernmost tip of the New York, borough of Manhattan, facing the harbour. The park is named after the artillery battery that was built by the British Army to protect the city in the seventeenth century. Zareta drifted through the busy park toward the pier, which was once a fireboat station, and she sat and watched the ferries whilst drinking frothy American coffees for an hour before she boarded one herself. A medium sized latte cost more money than she had needed to feed herself for a week in Chechnya, but she had been given money to spend and she couldn't take it with her so she intended to spend it. There are no pockets in a shroud. Once onboard the ferryboat Zareta headed for the rear viewing deck. She stood there looking at the buildings in awe of the sheer scale of the city. As the ferries sail closer the Statue of Liberty the true size of Manhattan Island and its huge skyscrapers becomes apparent. The skyline is a truly amazing site to behold, especially for an untraveled eye. Zareta stared at the Chrysler building in wonder, and she thought it was difficult to believe that it was once dwarfed by the twin towers of the World Trade Centre. The sun glinted from its' glass exterior. The thought of the towers brought her back to earth with a mental bump. The true purpose of her mission returned to her and it made her stomach turn. Chechnya and the constant state of war now seemed so far away. Yasser Ahmed's well rehearsed rhetoric had cemented her resolve, but now alone in this incredible city the Jihad was no longer as crucial as it had once seemed. Doubts niggled at her faith. Two young boys chased each other around the passenger deck laughing, and they reminded her of her own lost children. As she looked at the city from the harbour there is an invisible space where the towers once stood, which is hidden by the surrounding buildings. The events of 9/11 returned to her to challenge her doubts.

Zareta felt that the decision to commit an act of terrorism had not been a simple one for her. When the Russian-Christian, Zionist invaders committed atrocities in her homeland then she felt that their attacks were wrong. The crusades had never ended. Islam was constantly under attack from Western cultures determined to annihilate the Muslim faith. 'What was the difference in that, and what she was about to do?' asked the voice in her head. Most of us would agree that terror attacks of any type are wrong; killing people, especially defenceless citizens with no political or religious inclinations is unacceptable to any human being. The problem comes when the injustices suffered by Zareta and her people are perceived to be worse than their revenge attacks. Cries for the death penalty as the ultimate deterrent in the legal system are heard more clearly by the relatives of a murdered victim, than an impartial bystander. Zareta, and Chechen women like her had been robbed of their sons, fathers and husbands for two decades. The phenomenal size and power of the Russian armed forces left Chechen Muslims with no other military options than to use ambush, guerrilla tactics and suicide bombings to force their struggle onto the world stage. If Zareta's mission was completed successfully then it would stop the Western world in its tracks. Muslim terrorists had demonstrated repeatedly that the enormously complex global transport system that we now share, which carries literally millions of people around our planet, ironically offers freelance terrorists more opportunities for sabotage abroad than at any other time in history, especially if those terrorists are prepared to commit suicide in pursuit of their goal. Zareta thought about the devastation caused by two groups of terrorists armed only with box cutter knives, who flew those planes into the twin towers. So twisted was her interpretation of Islam that their sacrifice steeled her resolve. She could not turn away from her people's struggle now, and there was nowhere else for her to turn but to her God.

Ellis Island came into view and the ferry slowed as it approached the dock to allow passengers to disembark. The Island had become a magnet for tourists who wanted to visit the museum there for nostalgia's sake. The ancestors of America's diverse population mostly entered the country through the immigration processing centre, which was based on the Island. Many of America's Italian, Jewish and Irish population would be able to trace their ancestry through Ellis Island. The engines went into reverse and the water behind the boat boiled and foamed white as the propellers thundered.

Zareta was reminded of the day her sons were killed by invading Russian soldiers. They had entered her village to look for the perpetrators of a road-side bomb attack, which had killed nine Soviet soldiers the previous day. The culprits were miles away high in the mountains near the border of Dagestan, when the soldiers arrived looking for recompense. The Chechen men from the village were lined up and questioned by the Russian officers. No one imparted any useful information to them, which frustrated them further. Zareta's teenage sons were led away from the town square, with a group of boys of a similar age, to a small stone bridge, which separated one side of the village from the other. The small bridge had room enough for one vehicle at a time to pass over it. Beneath it the River Yagi flowed through a deep gulley thirty-feet below. The water was a torrent as it passed beneath the bridge, where it entered a deep water hole becoming almost still before flowing over the next series of falls into the valley below. The deep water hole was clear, and the rocks it contained were visible beneath the surface. Despite her hysterical pleas for clemency the soldiers tossed a local boy from the bridge to entice information from the villagers. The sad truth was that the local inhabitants rarely knew anything of the whereabouts of the rebel Mujahideen. The presence of Arab Muslims amongst the Chechens fighters raised suspicion from the indigenous Muslim community and vice versa. The twelve year old plunged into the deep freezing water below the bridge and he disappeared from sight. Long seconds passed until he surfaced again, but he was face down and still. Blood coloured the water around him seeping from a deep wound on his skull, as his body headed toward the next waterfall. His clothes snagged on the sharp rocks at the edge of the pool and he remained snagged on them for a moment, before the current finally tipped his body over the edge and out of view. His mother had screamed like a banshee, and she had hammered at a Russian soldier with clenched fists only to be pistol whipped to the ground, losing two decaying teeth in the process. Her husband had long since been taken away from the village by the Russians never to return, and the rest of the villagers remained silent. They were too scared to come to her defence.

The soldiers grabbed Zareta's eldest son Akmad and they wrestled the skinny little kid toward the wall. A big Russian soldier picked him up by his ankles and dangled the terrified teenager over the opposite edge of the bridge above the raging torrent. Zareta's younger son picked up a tree branch and attacked the offending Russian with it. The branch struck the soldier in the mouth, wiping the sick smile from his face, and splitting both the top and bottom lips simultaneously. The soldier was furious and he swung the dangling boy in a vicious arc toward his younger brother. Their heads collided at speed and the force of the impact shattered the younger sibling's cheek bone. He was knocked headlong over the low wall. The soldier bellowed in rage and tossed the older boy over the bridge onto the rocks below, just yards away from where his brother had landed. Despite the thirty-foot drop onto the jagged rocks, which had twisted and cracked their bones, they managed to cling onto the rocks, and each other as the raging torrent tore at them. The water seemed desperate to drag them from the purchase that they held on the slippery rocks. The Russians laughed as the young brothers clung on for dear life, and one of them offered a bet as to which would succumb to the power of the waterfall first. Zareta jabbered uncontrollably attracting the attention of the cruel

Russian soldier, who had tossed her beloved offspring from the bridge, as if they were garbage. She screamed abuse at him as she was dragged to the edge of the wall by the Russian with the broken lips. He forced her against the stone bridge and bent her over the wall, forcing her to watch her injured children clinging to the rocks. He barked questions to her about the whereabouts of the insurgents but she did not have any answers for him. Zareta felt as if her heart would break as her youngest boy's strength failed, and the river dragged him away from the gulley and tossed him like a leaf down the rocks into the deep water beneath the bridge. The soldier laughed in her ear, and the bristles on his unshaven face scratched at her neck and cheek. She felt sick as his feted breath reached her nostrils. The world seemed to freeze and she felt like she was no longer an active participant on planet Earth. Zareta stared at her son and felt nothing but numbness inside her. She felt the material of her dress ripping but her muscles refused to respond, even when she realised his erect penis was pressed against her. Her eldest son maintained his grip on the rock while the Russian took her there, bent over the wall in front of the whole village. She felt nothing but the pain of a bereaved mother, and thankfully the ordeal didn't last long. None of the other soldiers joined in the rape, which was unusual in this war where the systematic dehumanising of the female Chechens was implemented on a daily basis. No one tried to help her because no one really could, without risking their own lives. The rape of Chechen women by Russian soldiers was a much an everyday occurrence as Chechen men disappearing. They were just casualties of war. When he had finished he zipped up his pants and pulled out his pistol. Then he shot the boy that was still clinging to the slippery rock twice, once in the shoulder, and again in the back of the head. He tumbled down the waterfall to join his dead brother in the pool below the bridge.

"All aboard ladies and gentlemen please, stand away from the guard rails. The next stop will be at Battery Park, New York City," said the voice of the ships pilot over the speaker system. The voice made her jump and brought her back to reality. Zareta had watched the foaming water at the back of the ferry for forty-minutes while she remembered that horrific day. She had completely missed the ferry stop at the Statue of Liberty, lost in her memories. Her heart felt cold and empty again. The hopelessness of a decade of war against Christians and Jews returned to her. Hilary Rice the first black female president of the United States of America was arriving in New York tomorrow. She was to address the first ever Ethnic Minority Women's Action Group at their conference, which was taking place at the world famous Madison Square Garden the next day. Zareta would be there at the conference, and she was desperate to meet the new President in person.

CHAPTER 46

Roman Kordinski/
Liverpool

Roman heard the metal panel in the cell door slide open. He felt stiff and bruised as he sat up on his cot bed. The prison guards had used Taser guns to subdue him in the van, when he had bitten the fat guard's thumb off. The weapons had been introduced to British law enforcement officers as a less than lethal option. They were used to control belligerent or potentially dangerous subjects, by hitting the prisoner with thirty thousand volts. The voltage had floored Roman rendering him unconscious. When he woke he was lying in a small cell, and was restrained with a straight jacket device. Roman looked around the cell and decided it was just a holding facility, probably situated in a police station or beneath a court room. There was no toilet, which ruled out a conventional penitentiary.

The face that appeared at the hatch was that of his solicitor. He heard angry muffled voices outside the door, and then the noise of keys being inserted into the lock. The series of metal bolts slid back into their housing noisily and the door squealed open. Two armed policemen entered the cell, and roughly pulled Roman from the cot. Armed policemen did not work in police station custody suites, he thought, it was not a good sign.

"I must insist that my client is released from that straight jacket immediately," mumbled the lawyer to the armed guards. They didn't respond to his request at all, in fact they hadn't spoken to him once since he had arrived. The lawyer, Alan Williams, had been waiting for his client at the High Court in Chester. When his client had not arrived he enquired about his whereabouts. Alan was informed that his celebrity client had bitten the thumb from a prison guard, and had been transferred to the holding suite at the

Terrorist Task Force headquarters, Canning Place, Liverpool. The fortress style building had underground access to secret government facilities miles across the city, and fortified tunnels, which led to the Crown Court building in the city centre. They were originally built to facilitate the incarceration and prosecution of Irish Republican terrorists, without fear of prison break attempts. Fears of Roman's criminal network attempting to free him had been highlighted by Major Stanley Timms. British law insisted that Kordinski must be committed to trial in the county where his crime was committed. Unless the safety of the prisoner was threatened, which the Major now insisted that it was. Having caused grievous bodily harm to a popular prison warder would make Roman a target for revenge by vigilante officers. The Major had no real concerns for the Russian's safety, but he had applied the letter of the law to ensure the Terrorist Task Force gained control of Kordinski's whereabouts. It would take an army to attempt to release him from the cells beneath Canning Place.

"I have noted your lack of response to my request, and I need both your names and ranks please, so that I can present a formal complaint," the lawyer blustered, flushing red with frustration. He looked at the policemen and realised that they had no registration numbers on their shoulder lapels. British police wear an identity number on their uniforms unique to each officer. These officers had no such identification on them, which worried Alan Williams greatly. His client was to be charged with involvement in acts of terrorism, which at first glance was incredulous. He was one of the richest oil tycoons in the world, not a terrorist. The fact that he was being held in a secret facility beneath the River Mersey by British policemen, who wore no identity marks testified to the gravity of the situation. The officers opened a door, which led into an interview room and roughly sat Roman in a plastic chair. The room held two grey plastic chairs either side of a small metal table. All the furniture was bolted to the ground. The walls were bare except for a two way mirror fitted into the left hand wall. Romans straight jacket was attached to the chair, which prevented him from rising. There was barely enough room for the four men, who occupied its space. It was a deliberate tactic by the designers to cause claustrophobia.

"I really must insist that my client is freed from these restraints officer," the lawyer tried again, "why is he being treated in this manner?" "He is innocent until proven guilty." Alan Williams had to try to defend his client, but the truth of the matter was that he was disgusted by the charges being brought against the Russian businessman. If they were proved then he would be locked up for the remainder of his life. The evidence pointed to his involvement in two of the worst terrorist incidents ever witnessed on the British mainland. That itself was bad enough, but anonymous information had been passed to Alan's office, which indicated that the motive was monetary. The fact that there was no tangible political or religious purpose seemed to make it worse.

"Your client is being held under the Terrorist Act, which means you have exactly thirty-minutes to communicate to him, starting from now. He is being restrained because he attacked an officer of Her Majesty's Prison Service, which resulted in him losing his thumb. You now have twenty-eight minutes." The guard looked at his watch.

"Well I am certainly going to require more than thirty minutes officer, whatever your name is. Also I will require privacy please," Alan Williams was at a loss with the situation. Roman Kordinski had been a golden goose of a client. His practice had literally disposed of its other clients six years ago to service Roman and his legal requirements. There had been some serious accusations against the Russian tycoon, but nothing that couldn't be made to disappear with enough money thrown at it. This was a different kettle of fish altogether. Tax evasion and accusations of mafia connections were one thing, this was another.

"This is where you will hold your communication sessions with the prisoner. We will remain present at all times, and you have twenty-six minutes remaining." The Task Force officer looked at his watch again.

Alan Williams flushed purple with anger, but there seemed little to be gained by protesting at this time. He would have to use the courtroom to air his grievances.

"Did you assault a prison guard?" Alan asked Roman in a whisper, shaking his head in disbelief. Roman eyes brightened at the memory, but only for a second. Then he seemed to withdraw again. Roman Kordinski had always been in control of his life, and the life of those around him. Incarceration was magnifying the cracks in his schizophrenic personality.

"Roman are you alright?" Alan pushed his client for a response, "I can't help you unless you talk to me, did you assault a prison officer?"

"Yes I bit the fat fucker's thumb off," Roman shrugged off his reply as if it were just par for the course, "he attacked me in the prison van, I was defending myself." Roman lowered his head to show his lawyer bloody bald patches where the guard had ripped his hair out. Alan Williams frowned at the guards and removed a small silver digital camera from his scruffy briefcase. He flicked open the lens and snapped four pictures of Roman's injuries.

"They knocked me out with Taser guns," Roman added, and he lifted his chin up from his chest to reveal a deepening blue bruise just below his neck, which disappeared beneath the straight jacket.

The lawyer snapped three more pictures of the electric shock injuries and tutted audibly for the policemen's benefit. Taser is a trademark name, and is an acronym for 'Thomas A. Swift's Electric Rifle', named after it's science fiction teenage inventor. They were still controversial experimental law enforcement weapons because of the injuries and deaths they had caused.

"I want it noted that I am formally complaining about my client's injuries, reasonable force has not been applied in this case," Alan Williams said for the benefit of whoever was behind the two way mirror. It would not be the first time a dead cert guilty client had walked free from a courtroom because of a technicality. Alan had to try to find every chink in the police evidence. The problem was that the evidence looked solid. Failure to apply proper policy and procedure was the only weakness that Alan could see at the moment.

"What's happening to my business outside," Roman asked, "when will you get me out of here?" Roman stared at an enlarged mole on his lawyer's forehead as if he had never noticed it before. He studied it with a vacant look in his eyes.

"There have been some serious issues with your Russian portfolio of business interests, but you should be more concerned with getting out of here right now," Alan Williams replied.

"What issues?" Roman snapped back at his lawyer, trying to stand up but forgetting that he was restrained. He looked down at the straight jacket as if it just suddenly appeared, with a look of concerned surprise on his face.

"We don't have much time Roman, and we need to go through the rebuttal evidence before your committal hearing," Alan said matter of factly, trying to avoid the issue of Roman's Soviet interests. There was something very different about his client's behaviour, he couldn't put his finger on what it was, just something missing.

"I asked you, what issues?" Roman leaned forward as far as the straight jacket would allow him to move, and snarled the words toward his lawyer emphasising each syllable, making his accent more pronounced.

"Because you have been incarcerated there seems to be an issue with your legal right to operate businesses within Russian borders," Alan answered rubbing his hand through his thinning hair.

"What are you saying Alan. Spell it out, what issues?" Roman stared at his council with angry eyes. They were cold eyes like a shark has.

"The Russian government has confiscated your companies and has taken over the running of them," his lawyer blurted out, as if saying it quickly wouldn't sound as bad.

"What did you say?" Roman was not used to being so helpless. His liberty had been taken, now it sounded like his main income stream had been terminated irreparably.

"You heard what I said Roman, look it's more important that we get you out of the legal system so that we can appeal their decisions. We cannot do anything whilst you are behind bars," Alan raised his voice a little trying to gain control of the situation.

"Shut up you fucking idiot, which business have they confiscated?" Roman jerked violently in his seat, but the straps held him. The lawyer looked briefly at one of the policemen but they stared uninterested at the wall beyond. Alan was becoming concerned that Roman might snap his restraints, but the nonchalant expressions on the armed policemen reassured him that he was safe.

"I said which businesses have they confiscated?" This time Roman was screaming. Spittle flew from his teeth, and dribbled down his chin as he began to fight against the restraints more vigorously.

"Calm down Roman," his lawyer said in a hushed voice, but he was beginning to see the man behind the celebrity mask. The man behind the smiles and press shoots was very frightening indeed, and the more Alan could see the more he believed his client was indeed guilty.

"Answer the fucking question, you useless piece of shit," Roman gritted his teeth together and hissed the question. "Which business have they confiscated?" he screamed. The Russian's face was purple from excursion, and the veins in his neck and temples were pumped up to busting point. Alan was past the point of being offended by Roman, as he often lost his temper and became rude to his employees.

"All of them Roman," the lawyer sat back in his chair, shocked and afraid at the mental state that his celebrity client was displaying. "The Russian government have seized all your businesses that are within the Soviet Union. They have also frozen your assets and bank accounts."

"The bastards can't do that, stop them," Roman was almost hysterical now and a long globule of saliva dribbled from his chin. His head was shaking from side to side in denial of the facts. "That's what I pay you for useless prick, stop them. Sell my oil reserves. That's what you must do. Sell my oil reserves before they seize them, cash them in immediately."

"The Saudi's have slashed the price of a barrel of crude to the lowest level for decades Roman. The OPEC countries and Russia have followed their lead. Your reserves aren't worth a penny," Alan Williams had tried to consolidate Roman's assets prior to this meeting, but it seemed that invisible hands were pulling important strings in the world of politics and espionage. It was as if an international conspiracy was manipulating the financial markets to destroy Roman's criminal empire. He was literally penniless apart from secret stashes of money and investments, which only Roman would know about.

"What, the Saudi's have done what, I'll fucking kill her. That's it, the Saudi bitch is dead," Roman started rocking in his chair violently. Alan Williams sat open mouthed at the implication of what Roman's ranting had pointed to. The two policemen looked toward the mirror in unison, clinically aware of the strength of the damming evidence they had just witnessed.

"Roman be quiet!" Alan Williams regained his composure and tried to stop his client from putting any more nails in his own coffin.

"I won't be silenced, that Saudi bitch is as good as dead! They have double crossed the wrong man! Those fucking Arabs have crossed the wrong man!" Roman screamed a tirade of Russian swearwords. He looked like he was about to go into a seizure when the door opened and Major Stanley Timms entered the room. Behind him was Graham Libby, who was the Task Force pathologist and all round medical expert.

"I think that your client needs sedating," said Graham Libby to Alan Williams. He placed a gentle hand on the lawyer's shoulder sympathetically. The lawyer just nodded completely lost for words. He had never seen anyone having a psychotic episode before. He didn't think that too much damage had been done legally because the implication of the killing of a Saudi girl was purely coincidental evidence. His client's mental state would be taken into account too, he thought, when Roman shouted again.

"That Muslim bitch Kellesh is dead, she's fucking dead!" He was still screaming her name when they injected him with a strong sedative, by which time Alan Williams was being escorted from the custody suite into the long subterranean corridor, which led to an adjoining court room. He would have no choice but to change his client's plea to not guilty on the grounds of insanity. Alan Williams thought that a trial would be a long drawn out process, at the end of which there was only one outcome. What Alan didn't know was that he would never see Roman Kordinski alive again.

CHAPTER 47

Yasser Ahmed/ Kizlyar

Yasser and his men were resting deep inside a cave, high in the mountains above Grozny, Chechnya. Russian bombers were carpet bombing the ridge directly above them, in a vain attempt to kill the Mujahideen fighters that plagued their operations on the ground. The mountain shook violently and the constant deafening explosions made their ears ring. Incredibly the majority of the rebel fighters still managed to catch some sleep. The atmosphere in the cave was almost cosy. A fire burned in the centre of the floor space, and its orange glow flickered on the stone walls, making hypnotic shadows dance. As the men dozed a symphony of snoring and farting echoed softly from the vaulted rock ceiling. The lack of running water and appalling food hygiene caused an almost constant state of gastric poisoning amongst the Mujahideen. Wind was one of the unfortunate side effects that they all had to tolerate. It was definitely time for them to cross the border into Dagestan. Once today's bombing ceased Yasser would lead the bulk of his fighting force 40 miles to Kizlyar, a small town just across the border. The small town was capable of resupplying the rebels and its' hospital could treat the injured Mujahideen. In Kizlyar they could eat fresh food, and bathe, luxuries not readily available to guerrilla fighters. It was also the current abode of the Saudi Princess Jeannie Kellesh, who had been in a drug induced coma state for two weeks and three days since her capture.

A lone fighter entered the cave, having made his way up the mountain trying to avoid the rock falls created by the Russian bombs. He was wearing Western trousers and a pair of battered Nike training shoes. On his head he wore a loose scarf, which looped, beneath his chin and round his neck, which was known locally as Lungees. A Kalashnikov hung from his right shoulder, and a canvas bag hung from his left. He spotted Yasser in the glow of the fire and carefully stepped over the sleeping Mujahideen fighters to reach him. He opened his canvas bag and handed Yasser a bundle of recent newspapers, which he had purchased at Grozny Airport two days earlier. Yasser nodded his thanks and kissed the man once on each cheek.

"Shukraan, As-Salaam alaykum," Yasser said greeting the man, thank you, greetings and may peace be with you, was the rough translation.

"Our sisters have reached their destinations, and have all been contacted by our friends abroad," the man informed Yasser whilst bowing his head to pay homage to his leader.

"You have done well brother," Yasser replied. He filled a bowl with watery chicken stew, making sure that he found plenty of white meat. He handed the bowl of food to the man. Being handed food by a superior is considered a great honour in the Arab world. The man sat and ate his prize noisily. Yasser scanned the newspapers looking for information from abroad. The Chicago Tribune reported that Yasser Ahmed had been spotted in Syria, and was the potential target of the Israeli Special Forces, Mossad, who were allegedly hot on his tail, which made him chuckle to himself. The Israeli special operations division is called the Metsada, and is involved in assassination, paramilitary operations, sabotage and psychological warfare. Reported sightings of himself always amused him, but the piece went on to report the more serious assassination of a legendary Muslim fighter in Damascus. Convicted murderer and terrorist Mohammed Ali Hammadi was a key member of the military wing of the Palestinian political group Hezbollah. He was the ringleader of the hijacking of TWA flight 847 in 1985, during which American diver Robert Stetham was executed and thrown onto the tarmac runway at Beirut Airport, in front of the world's media . Through the 1980's, long before the names of Osama bin Laden and al Qaeda were known, Hammadi was the most wanted terrorist on the planet. On 13th February 2008 his car exploded in the Syrian capital, Damascus, killing him instantly. Israeli's Mossad and America's CIA were blamed for the assassination. Half the world celebrated the death of a murdering terrorist, whilst the other half mourned the death of a legendary freedom fighter.

Yasser whispered silent prayers for the soul of his dead Mujahideen brother. He also prayed to his God for luck and support, the strength to fight on against the Christians and Jews. Yasser knew that the forces of Israel, Britain, and America would pursue him forever as they had perused Hammadi. There would be no court or court-martials, just the violent death and ensuing peace that a car bomb or bullet brings to its target.

Yasser read on with dismay, an article written from an interview with Sayyed Imam al-Sharif, who was one of the al-Qaeda's most senior theologians. Speaking from his prison cell in Saudi Arabia he was calling for his followers to end their violent Jihad against Christians and Jews. He was quoted as saying that the 9/11 attacks were a catastrophe for all Muslims, and that Osama bin Laden had betrayed the Taliban leader Mullah Omar in Afghanistan. The lapsed Jihadist called for the formation of a special Muslim court to try bin Laden and his deputy Ayman al-Zawahiri for their crimes against Islam. Yasser was aware that the popularity of bin Laden was waning, but he also wandered what tortures Imam al-Sharif had endured in his Saudi prison cell to have such a dramatic change in conviction.

Osama bin Laden and his deputy al-Zawahiri were blamed by many conservative Muslims for the American invasion of Afghanistan, and the defeat of the Taliban. They were also blamed for the insurgency that raged in the north of Pakistan and Kashmir.

On the 26th December 2007 former Pakistani Prime Minister Benazir Bhutto was assassinated in a suicide attack. She had just addressed an election rally in Rawalpindi when an al-Qaeda gunman shot her in the neck, before exploding his suicide bomb, killing himself and 20 of her supporters. Several al-Qaeda web sites claimed responsibility for the murder of what they called, 'America's most precious asset'. The pro-Western Bhutto had vowed to rid her beloved Pakistan from Islamic extremists, if she gained power in the upcoming elections. The Islamic struggle was gaining momentum across the globe. Yasser was going to up the ante and make sure that Islam was protected from the Christian, Jewish aggressors.

A two week old copy of the New York Times had front page coverage of the upcoming visit of the new President of the United

States of America. Hilary Rice was going to address a women's conference in Madison Square Garden. Much excitement was attached to the President's visit, and Yasser smiled. He wandered what the headlines would read the day after her visit. He would enjoy reading them. The schedule they had received from their affiliates in New York was still intact, and the plan was running like clockwork. Yasser remembered the world-wide furore following his 'Soft Target' campaign and he knew this new wave would dwarf that in comparison. The current plan was to activate the Disney cell three days before the President visited New York. Hilary Rice had won the Presidency, on a tough on terrorism ticket. Yasser was counting on her stoic response to the imminent bombing, including not changing her schedule. Displaying a stern unaffected exterior to terror attacks weakened their effect, and strengthened the American people's resolve. Yasser hoped that her bravery would cost her dearly. Everything seemed to be going to plan until he read the headlines of London based newspaper, the Guardian.

Prominent Russian Jewish oil tycoon, Roman Kordinski, had been arrested and charged with offences under the terrorism act. The article gave a brief summary of the facts that had been released to the press, which did not allude to any kidnap plot. The reasons behind the bombings appeared to be racially motivated, in that they had been orchestrated to cause racial violence, between immigrant Muslims and the wider Indigenous British public. The ensuing civil unrest, which included riots, racially motivated vigilante attacks on people and property, were a welcome distraction. The law enforcement agencies were so focused on the bombs and the aftermath that organised crime families were given free rein to operate unchallenged. It was alleged that several huge consignments of drugs had been smuggled into the country during the nationwide unrest, which had followed the bombs. The price of heroin and cocaine had dropped to its lowest level for decades, indicating that massive shipments had arrived under the radar, whilst the law enforcement agencies were busy addressing internal issues.

The story was like waving a red flag to a bull. Yasser had Roman Kordinski on his hit list a decade ago, when he was still Moscow's leading Mafioso. He epitomised everything Yasser was fighting against. Decadence, greed and the exploitation of Islamic nations by Western Christians and Jews, were the root cause of his struggle.

Since the early Crusaders arrived in Jerusalem they had done nothing but exploit the region for financial gain, controlling trade routes and looting religious treasures. Then came the discovery of oil, God's gift to the Arabs. Chechnya could never be recognised as an independent country by Russia because of rich oil reserves. Decades of war between the Muslim countries of Iraq and Iran were caused by the oil rich region of southern Iran called Khuzestan. Both regimes claimed sovereignty over the region because of the oil reserves beneath its sand. Saddam Husain's invasion of Kuwait was fuelled by his desire to capture and control its rich oil fields. Iraq was virtually bankrupt following years of armed struggle with Iran, so Saddam targeted Kuwait as a new income stream. China and Britain's contributions to the corrupt government of Sudan runs into billions of dollars every year, because it has huge oil reserves beneath its' deserts. America's repeated incursions into South America, Grenada and conflict with Venezuela are all oil related. The war for the Falkland Islands between Britain and the Argentine Junta are ultimately because of the potential oil reserves close to its shores. The small islands are situated thousands of miles away from Britain in the Southern Atlantic Ocean, yet they still claim sovereignty over them. Would any one bother if they were just volcanic rocks in the middle of an ocean on the other side of the world? Yasser didn't think that they would.

Roman Kordinski was being held in the English city, Liverpool. Yasser had been there before during the 'Soft Target' campaign. He lost his sister there, when she was mistakenly shot by British Special Forces. She had been wearing a crash helmet and the snipers thought she was Yasser. There was still a score to be settled in Liverpool and Yasser had just the plan to send a little message. If Kordinski was being tried there, then he would be in one place every day for months. His only protection would be British police, who would be concentrating on foiling any escape attempt. There was an 'Axe' cell already in Britain, because he had originally planned to target London, using a Chechen Black Widow. His plan had just changed.

The Russian aerial bombing subsided outside, and Yasser knew that it would be followed up with ground troops looking for evidence of successfully killing Mujahideen. The Russian troops would be here in a couple of hours. There was enough time to set a dozen booby traps around the cave areas, and remove all evidence of them ever being used by rebel forces.

"Wake up my Muslim brothers," Yasser shouted standing up and clapping his hands to rouse his men, "we leave for Kizlyar in an hour."

CHAPTER 48

Kizlyar/Tank/ Special Forces

Two dust covered Mujahideen characters approached a road block, which was two-hundred yards away from the hospital facility in Kizlyar. They were wearing local dress, and looked like they had spent weeks in the mountains, unfed and unwashed. They wore Lungees scarves around their heads and tucked them around the neck area. On their heads they had Pakols, which was a type of turban, and long baggy Chapans, which were long cotton coats that were covered in dust and dirt. The guard at the road block eyed them suspiciously as they approached. The rebel on the left had black shiny skin, similar to natives of Sudan or North Africa. His teeth were blackened with decay, and he was leaning heavily on an improvised wooden crutch, limping badly. There was a blood stained field dressing wrapped around one foot. The other had slanted eyes and olive skin, indicating that he was of Tajikistan or Far Eastern origin. He carried his companion's weight on the opposite side of where the crutch was. The guard looked at his face beneath the Lungees and cringed. The man with the slanted eyes wore a patch over one of them. His forehead and cheek were badly burned and blistered, the skin was hanging in flaps, and the injury ran down the neck beneath his clothing. The guard recoiled at the sight of the wound and allowed them to pass through to the hospital.

"Ahlan Wa Sahlan," said the guard welcoming them, "keep to the left to avoid the mines." The road beyond was little more than a dirt track pitted with bomb craters.

"Ahlan Wa Sahlan Beekum," said the fighter with the eye patch, and the black skinned man just nodded his head in acknowledgment. The cratered road turned to the left through scrubland, which was pitted like the surface of the moon. Shell holes of every conceivable size could be seen stretching into the distance. The hospital facility came into view and it looked starkly out of place in this landscape. It was a modern style two storey building fabricated from a metal framework, which was filled in with breeze block. The roof was long and low with just the slightest slant to it, and made from a corrugated metal sheet design. The left hand side of the building was still under construction. It looked like it had been an afterthought.

The injured men hobbled through the entrance into the building. The reception area was chaotic and smelled of disinfectant and vomit. Injured fighters were strewn all over the large entrance hall and staff in once white overalls rushed about prioritising the casualties. There was a wide open area past the reception, which held a modern cafeteria type facility. There looked to be about forty seats there, which were all full of Mujahideen sitting in groups, drinking hot sweet tea and eating luxury items like chocolate bars, and pieces of fruit. Rifles and machineguns were discarded to lean against walls and pieces of furniture. The two new arrivals went unnoticed as they headed to the left, through swinging fire doors, and into the unoccupied sterile corridor beyond. They continued along the corridor quickly. The black skinned man's limp was suddenly much improved, and the two moved much quicker. At the end of the corridor was a deserted nurse's station, and behind that was an empty office. The nurse's station looked like a long reception desk, but there were no telephones or clipboards to be seen anywhere. There was a film of pinkish dust that covered the surfaces, which was in fact saw dust. The part of the hospital they had entered had only recently been built and had never been occupied or utilised yet. Half seemed to be completed and other sections were still under construction, but there didn't seem to be any particular pattern to the building progress. They stood in the empty office and crossed to the window. The floor was still just a concrete base and the walls were yet to be plastered.

Grace Farrington put down her fake crutch and removed a small transmitter from her dirty clothing. Chen lifted the eye patch from his face and placed a thin wire antenna to the window ledge. Chen's blistered scar was a compound called Collodion which is widely used in the film industry to create horrific looking burn injuries. Nightmare on Elm Street's Freddie Kruger was the result of its stunning effects.

"Pilgrim one, we are in the building," Grace said into the transmitter, "the hospital has around seventy unexpected guests. There is at least a battalion of Mujahideen in the casualty area."

"Roger that Pilgrim one," Tank replied from an armoured Land Rover one mile away, "do you think you can extract the target without being identified Faz?"

"That depends on the condition of our patient when we find her," Faz replied, "we will progress to stage two and establish coms shortly."

The two Task Force agents replaced their disguises and headed back into the empty corridor to find Jeannie Kellesh. They had argued black was blue with Tank and Major Stanley Timms about their plan. Faz and Chen were correct when they said that they were the only ones who could walk into the facility undetected, with the help of some special effects. A full frontal attack was out of the question, without endangering the target's life and losing men. Tank was furious and tried to scupper the plan at every opportunity, but the more he tried the more determined Grace became, and it did make perfect sense. Inserting two of the best special ops agents in the world into the hospital facility to provide reconnaissance, and possibly extract the girl without firing a shot was an opportunity not to be missed. Major Timms noted the over protective response from Tank, and decided that the issue of his alleged personal relationship with Grace must be dealt with following the mission. One of them would have to leave the Terrorist Task Force.

Faz and Chen limped through a series of unfinished corridors that they had studied from stolen plans prior to the incursion, which had been provided by MI6. Anything in the former Soviet Union could be purchased for the right price. They reached a door with a round glass porthole fitted to it, and they peered into the corridor beyond. Medical staff buzzed around a modern hospital ward, which was decked out with hi-tech fixtures and fittings. The staff wore clean starched uniforms, which were very different from the employees at the front of the building.

"Pilgrim one, we are in the private sector of the building," Faz whispered into the coms. "There is no sign of our patient yet."

"Roger that, Pilgrim one, have you found access to the first floor yet? It should be directly to your left," Tank replied through their ear pieces. He was following their progress via minute trackers fitted into their shoes and clothing.

Faz nudged Chen toward a stairwell on their left and they limped toward the doorway maintaining their disguise. The doorway had no frame fitted to it yet, and a strip of yellow tape formed a cross to prevent anyone entering. The stairwell on the plans had not been built yet. There was just an open concrete shaft.

"Pilgrim one, there is no access to the primary stairwell," Faz whispered into the coms, "it hasn't been built yet, we need an alternative route Tank." Her request was answered by static in her ear. The seconds dragged while they waited for a response.

"Pilgrim one, there should be a lift fifty yards down the corridor to your right," Tanks voice crackled, "the only other stairwells are in the occupied sectors of the hospital."

"That leads us back to the reception area. The corridors there are full of gurneys carrying wounded rebels," answered Chen, "that's a negative Tank it's too dangerous." Chen tapped Faz and nodded his head back toward the way they came. They limped quickly back toward the deserted nurses station. Chen pointed to a newly built cleaner's cupboard. The door was wedged open with a half used bag of cement, and inside leaning against the wall was a double step ladder. Within thirty seconds they were climbing up the empty shaft toward the first floor. Grace reached the next level first, and she reached behind her to pull Chen up into the empty first floor corridor. The corridor mimicked the one beneath it so they were just yards from a set of double doors containing the same round glass windows as the ground floor had. There was a ward along a corridor but it was completely empty. At the far end of the corridor stood a solitary guard next to a door, which looked like it led to a single room, or side ward. His gun was not a Russian made Kalashnikov. It was an Israeli made Uzi 9mm.

"Bingo Pilgrim one, we've located our patient," whispered Grace. "We'll establish her condition."

"Roger that Pilgrim one, what's the security like?" Tank answered anxiously. He was answered with two static clicks, which indicated that a verbal response wasn't possible. Faz and Chen were already moving into the private sector of the hospital.

CHAPTER 49

Khava Bararayeva/
Animal Kingdom

Khava stood patiently in line waiting for the security check at the gate to the largest Disney theme park in the world. She had a rubber new born baby doll strapped to her chest in a baby harness. The dummies are so realistic that it's almost impossible to distinguish them from the real thing. The Disney security guard cooed at the rubber child and commented on how beautiful it looked, after distinguishing what sex it was. That always seems to be the first question. What is it, a boy or a girl? Then it becomes he or she, and they are always beautiful. Has anyone ever been told their baby is odd looking? Or does anyone say how come the baby is not the same colour as your husband? New born babies bring out the innocence within us all, and that was exactly what Yasser Ahmed was counting on. The security guard checked Khava's bag, but found only baby milk and spare nappies amongst the usual necessaries carried by parents the world over.

Khava breathed a sigh of relief as she passed through the gate into the park. A wooden sign post stood in the centre of a tarmac area. To the right hand side was a mobility station, which rented electric scooters to less able people, to help them navigate around the huge theme park. That was what the scooters were for in theory. In truth the majority of its customers were fat people, who really needed the exercise, but couldn't be bothered walking in the heat. It often left the real less able people waiting ages for scooters to be returned. Khava thought that the large number of overweight people was just another example of Western decadence, as she watched them queue for the electric carts. Straight ahead of her was a section of dense tropical trees dissected by a wide pathway. She headed up the path into the trees. To the left were beautiful grey Macaw parrots perched in the trees. Kava stopped and stared at them open mouthed. She read the sign again and couldn't understand why anyone would call them grey, because they were the most stunning parrots she had ever seen. They were the only parrots she had ever seen more to the point. Someone stood close to her and asked her what sex the baby was, prompting her to move away quickly. Khava could see the exit out of the trees up ahead, when she was struck by a powerful odour. To her right hand side was a rock pool, which acted as a barrier to prevent four pot bellied pigs from escaping into the general population of Animal Kingdom. The four fat pigs snuffled around their enclosure in what looked like a six inch layer of their own excrement. The smell knocked her sick and she gagged at the thought of eating pork. Christians ate it every morning, she thought, some of them will not eat it tomorrow morning, that's for sure.

As she left the wooded area she crossed an ornately carved bridge that spanned a man made canal. A mock steamboat was passing beneath her, occupied by the whole Disney clan playing musical instruments, conducted by the famous Mouse himself. Children pointed excitedly at the costume band and stood in awe of their first sighting of Mickey and his pals. Khava saw the sign for a roller coaster ride called Expedition Everest, which towered above the theme park across an artificial lake. The colossal imitation mountain stood three hundred feet high, and could be seen from miles around. A long rollercoaster appeared from a dark aperture at the top of the mountain and then roared down a terrifyingly steep slope before disappearing into the mountain again. She could hear the terrified screams of the ride's passengers echoing across the lake. It seemed the obvious place to explode her bomb.

Khava walked into the ladies restrooms and opened the door to a baby change cubical. She pulled the baby unit from the wall and placed her bag on it. After unzipping her carrier bag she removed three bottles of prepared baby milk, and then twisted off the teats. The bottles did contain milk, but it was added to a water gel explosive called Tovex. The majority of commercial blasting agents used for mining or demolition are now saturated aqueous solutions. It is the rapid displacement of solid explosive substances such as Semtex or dynamite, which has led to the banning of liquids being taken onboard commercial airlines. Water gel explosives can simply be poured into the bomb casing, and hey presto, you have complete devastation.

On August 11TH 2006, British counter terrorist agencies discovered the worst terrorist plot ever encountered in the United Kingdom. The suspected plot involved targeting multiple aeroplanes simultaneously, using water gel explosives. Had the plot not been discovered it would have led to the most catastrophic loss of innocent civilian lives since the 9/11 attacks in New York. It is believed that al-Qaeda operatives planned to smuggle water gel explosives onto passenger aircraft using sports drink bottles. The foiled plan involved the terrorists dyeing the liquid explosive red to match the sports drink inside, and then sealing the top half of the bottle, so that on close inspection the bottles would appear to be unopened. The bottom half of the bottle would have water gel explosives injected into them. A detonator could be made by something as innocent as a camera flash or a mobile phone. Their plan was to explode the bombs while the planes were airborne over densely populated areas. England was immediately placed on red alert and airport security became chaotic as hand luggage was banned from all passenger aircraft. The investigation led to the arrest of twenty-four suspected terrorists, but it also highlighted the global shift to the use of liquid gel explosives.

Khava twisted the head from the rubber doll, which was still strapped to her chest in her harness. She poured the liquid explosive Tovex from the baby bottles into the body cavity of the doll, and then she placed the empty bottles back in her bag. Gently she placed the head back on the rubber baby. Khava crossed the cubicle to the toilet, where she lifted the lid from the cistern. Taped inside the cistern was a plastic bag, which she removed. The bag had been left by an accomplice, who was probably an employee at the park. She dried it and then placed it back onto the baby change unit. She ripped open the bag and spread the contents out. There were six bags of twenty-five cents coins, or quarters, each bag containing twenty dollars worth of metal coins. That made a total of four-hundred and eighty shiny pieces of shrapnel, which she poured into the doll to mix with the liquid explosives. She caught her reflection in the mirror and froze. Khava was amazed how old her reflection had become since losing her husband. The fine laughter lines around her blue eyes that her husband had found so attractive were now deep wrinkles. Dark circles curved under her eyes, and her face looked gaunt and grey. Her forehead was creased with deep lines, which furrowed when she frowned. She frowned a lot and rarely laughed nowadays.

"I look like a woman who is damned," she whispered quietly to her reflection in the mirror. Modern Islamic terrorists are shaped by the world around them. They are not born terrorists. A hopeless feeling of injustice seeps into them over a period of time. If you then add the introduction or reinforcement of an ideology into the process, then people can be groomed and moulded into suicide bombers. The individuals feel that they can then overcome any feelings of wrong doing. The taking of innocent lives becomes the righting of a wrong and nothing more. Poverty and deprivation, combined with constant military invasion and injustice create real life Chechen Black Widows like Khava every day. For Khava it was time to leave this world and its constant pain behind.

'The bad things she had seen were carved into every line on her face' she thought as she turned from the mirror and opened the door.

As Khava left the restroom the heat of the Florida sun struck her, like walking into a brick wall. The rubber baby had become very heavy now that it was filled with its deadly cargo. She passed a theatre called Bug's Life and walked toward Dinoland, on her way to Expedition Everest. Khava jumped out of her skin when she felt a hand on her arm and she froze.

"Sorry if I startled you ma'am but you seem to have left your bag in the ladies room," said a Mexican lady, who was pushing a stroller. She handed the bag that contained the empty milk bottles and diapers to Khava, but Khava was still a little shocked. She just looked at the Mexican lady blankly, and she started to shake.

"Your bag, I think that this is your bag," the lady repeated smiling, "how old is your baby? Is it a boy or a girl?"

"Oh thank you," Khava composed herself, "it's a boy. I mean he is a boy." Khava grabbed the bag smiling and tucked it under her arm. She nodded twice and walked off quickly into Dinoland.

The Mexican woman pulled her husband's arm to attract his attention.

"Did you see that baby? Its head was twisted the wrong way, I don't even think that was a baby. We need to tell the police," she ranted as the scenario dawned on her. Why would anyone have an imitation baby? It looked real except its head was at an impossible angle. Her husband didn't have a clue what she was ranting about as she stormed off pushing the stroller through the crowds, looking for a policeman.

There were no policemen in Disney but she saw a female security guard and her heart sank. The woman was dressed in a green safari uniform, which included a khaki safari hat with corks dangling from it. Donald Duck was emblazoned on the front of her hat. The female officer looked like she ate the Grand Slam breakfast at Denny's diner every day, followed by pancakes and syrup, then lunch. She was sweating as she waddled through the crowd holding a large coke.

"Officer there is a suspicious lady in the park. She has a rubber baby. At least I think its rubber. It could have been plastic, but anyways the head is twisted. That's how I know it wasn't a genuine baby. Don't you think that's weird? I mean who has a rubber baby unless there's going to be trouble? You have to stop her at least," the Mexican woman blurted out. The officer took a long sip on her coke and looked at the woman.

"Could you say all that again for me one more time, but real slow so that I can understand," she said, knowing that today was going to be one of those days, rubber baby indeed.

Khava crossed the bridge over the lake that took her to the entrance gate for Expedition Everest. There was a sign, which explained that no food or drink was allowed, and also no children. Khava stopped in her tracks. The rollercoaster thundered out of the mountain above her. Its arrival was announced by the screams of its passengers. What next? Her thoughts were interrupted by a commotion on the bridge. Khava watched an overweight woman wearing a cork hat trying to run over the bridge. She was running alongside a Mexican woman who was pushing her stroller at thirty-miles an hour whilst pointing toward Khava. The woman in the cork hat looked like some kind of Disney policewoman. She had a themed uniform to blend in with the atmosphere, but Disney didn't make guns and the policewoman had hers drawn. Khava turned to look for an escape, but she could see men in uniforms running through the crowds from the other direction toward her. They too had their guns drawn. Bystanders watched open mouthed as the scene developed. No one was sure whether or not this was real or just another Disney show time performed by actors.

"Don't move lady, put your hands up where I can see them," the female officer shouted. She was out of breath and really wanted her coke back, but she had dropped it when she realised the potential gravity of the situation. Khava turned slowly in a circle and assessed her options. The crowds had now parted around her leaving her exposed and isolated. The majority of the tourists were now running away from the scene in a panic. Memories of the Down Town Disney bombings the year before were still raw in people's minds. Khava put her hand into her right hand pocket and removed a disposable camera. There was a thin wire filament running form the flash bulb into the body of the rubber baby bomb. A voice came from behind her demanding that she remain still but she ignored, and she started to edge slowly toward a group of tourists who were trapped in the queuing system that fed the rollercoaster.

"Drop it now, you have three seconds," another group of officers had cleared their way through the crowds, and she was now surrounded. She edged closer to the panicking tourists and they began to climb the barriers that penned them in. Chaos broke out as normal everyday people started to panic. Self preservation took over, and men trampled on women and children to escape. One man pulled another from the railings to speed his own escape, and the fallen man was swallowed beneath the panicked crowds and crushed to death.

Khava felt an explosion of pain and blinding white light as a high velocity bullet smashed through her skull, and liquefied her brain. The momentary pain was indescribable, and the shock stunned her body into inactivity. She knew that all she needed to do was press the flash button and her mission was completed. She could join her beloved husband in heaven, and never be hungry again. For a moment her motor neurons reconnected, and she felt a twitch in her fingers. It wasn't enough to detonate her bomb though, and the second, third and fourth high velocity bullets ripped what was left of her head from her shoulders. Her headless body slumped to its knees on the ground and remained in a bizarre kneeling position, with her hands around the rubber baby. She was still there when the bomb squad arrived forty-minutes later.

CHAPTER 50

Kizlyar/Mujahideen 'vs. Terrorist Task Force

Grace and Chen limped down the corridor toward the mercenary soldier, who was guarding the room that they wanted to enter. The mercenary stood straight and lifted his Uzi 9mm machinegun as soon as the two Mujahideen entered the corridor. This part of the hospital was designated to predominantly Russian cliental, exuberant prices were paid to treat patients, mostly gangland shootings or the odd plastic surgery procedure. The Mujahideen and local Dagestan casualties were treated on the lower floors for a few shekels. The rebels came to the hospital to have their wounded treated and to eat and rest. The nearby village helped them to rearm and resupply.

Many of them brewed a noxious substance, which they drank to relax. It was opiate based and could have a hallucinatory effect if drunk to excess. The mercenary thought these two men that were approaching him had had too much to drink, and had wandered into the private sector by mistake. He knew that a number of Mujahideen fighters had arrived earlier that day under the cover of darkness. They always brought trouble with them.

Grace pushed Chen gently away from her, and leaned her weight against the wall as if she were resting her injury a moment. The mercenary walked toward them curious as to what they were doing. Suddenly she hurled the crutch like a javelin, which struck the guard in the middle of his forehead knocking him over backward. Chen pounced on him like a cat and dropped his knee across the man's throat smashing his larynx. There was a brief gurgling sound from his throat then he was still. They picked him up by his legs, and dragged him into the first floor cleaner's cupboard. They

233

bundled him and closed the door to hide the body. Faz tucked the Uzi into her waistband. They rushed to the doorway and peered inside. The man in the bed had had facial surgery recently, and lay unconscious attached to a drip feed. There was no sign of Jeannie Kellesh. Faz nodded to Chen and they moved as one down the corridor to the next room, which was empty. There was a double doorway leading into the next sector and Chen peeped through it. Two more mercenaries stood guard either side of a door, on the right hand side of the passageway.

Faz pointed her index finger at the man on the left and then ran it across her throat in a slow slashing motion. The covert military language for I'll kill the one on the left, you kill the other. She counted her fingers down in front of Chen's face, three, two, one and they moved swiftly and silently. They pushed through the doors with Special Forces Glock pistols drawn. They were fitted with a three inch noise suppressor to the business end of the barrel, which quelled the sound of a high velocity round being fired. Faz's gun spat three times, chest, chest and head. It's called triple tap shooting and absolutely guarantees that your target will not get up and shoot back at you. Chen's target collapsed in a heap next to the other mercenary with identical bullet holes in him.

A quick glance through the door revealed the Saudi Princess. She was sedated and attached to a methadone drip. They dragged the dead soldiers into her room and stuffed their bodies behind the bed curtain, out of sight. Chen grabbed a towel from a white porcelain sink and mopped up the smeared blood trail with it.

"Pilgrim one, we have located our patient," whispered Faz into the coms, "she is heavily sedated and will need assistance during evac." It was the worst possible scenario because they couldn't take her out undetected. Faz looked out of the first floor window, which was situated at the rear of the hospital facility, over what looked like a lunar landscape. The land to the rear was heavily cratered with shell holes, and scattered with razor wire at irregular intervals.

"Pilgrim one, we need a pathway made directly beneath this room for approximately four-hundred yards in a westerly direction," said Faz, "I can see the road at the top of the next ridge. If you clear the minefield and position an evac helicopter on that ridge we can get her out of here. You will have to keep our rebel friends busy at the front though."

"Roger that Pilgrim one, take cover," Tanks voice sounded more guttural than usual, adrenalin was thickening the saliva in his throat, "attack will be launched on my mark, three, two, one." An almighty explosion rocked the building and Faz dived for cover. Chen had the Saudi safely against the wall below the window. The explosion was a Hellfire missile fired from a circling unmanned drone, which destroyed the reception area of the facility and thirty of the Mujahideen that had occupied it were blown to pieces. Two more explosions rocked the building as heavy machinegun posts close to the hospital were destroyed by the drone. Faz heard the unmistakable rotor blades of an American Apache gunship approaching from the back of the hospital close to where they were. Two air cannon machineguns, which were attached beneath the Apache's chassis roared into life. They sounded like two Harley Davidson motorbike engines as they unleashed an avalanche of red hot high velocity 50 calibre bullets. The expert pilot combined with an expert gunner raked the minefield behind the hospital creating a safe pathway across the wilderness. Huge plumes of dirt and dust exploded into the air as the machinegun bullets detonated buried ordinance. The hospital's windows blew out, showering Faz and the Saudi girl with splintered shards of glass.

The whooshing sound of air to ground rockets indicated to Faz that someone had foolishly started firing back at the Apache gunship. The gunship responded and half a dozen colossal explosions could be heard to the east of the hospital, where the road block had been situated. She glanced out over the window ledge and saw a smouldering crater where the checkpoint had once stood.

"Pilgrim one, it's time to go," Tanks voice boomed over the coms. They could hear machinegun fire in the background as if Tank's position was taking fire.

"Roger that, Pilgrim one," Faz said as she headed for the window. She removed a synthetic knotted rope from her webbing and wrapped it beneath the Saudi's armpits. Chen lifted her legs over the window ledge and they quickly lowered her to the dusty ground beneath them. She hit the floor with a bump and folded into an awkward position, but at least she was free. Chen and Faz vaulted the window and rested their weight on a narrow ledge just below the opening. They were perched twenty feet above the ground, too far to jump without sustaining an injury. Machinegun bullets smashed into the breeze block walls close to Chen, shattering the block into dust and splinters of concrete. A two inch shard stuck into his cheek and he cried out as it chipped the bone beneath, but he clung onto the ledge.

"Pilgrim one, we are taking machinegun fire," Faz screamed into the coms, their position was desperately exposed without support. The gun fire was coming from a machinegun nest, which was well hidden from view beneath a copse of trees. The nest was dug into the scorched earth, but Faz could see the dull metal of the huge 50 calibre barrel finding its bead on them. The machinegun nest opened fire and three rounds ripped into the ledge they were clinging to. Suddenly the machinegun nest erupted in a boiling plume of flame that climbed skywards before folding in on itself to form a huge mushroom cloud of flame. The Apache helicopter that had fired the Napalm missile roared overhead at low altitude, it almost seemed close enough to touch. The pilot banked the aircraft and hovered in the air for a moment, and he waved a thumbs-up sign to them. Faz and Chen dropped from the ledge to the ground and grabbed the girl. They had to cover four-hundred yards to make it to the ridge.

Tank opened the door to the armoured Land Rover that he was in, and dived out. They were taking heavy machinegun fire from a ridge two-hundred yards to his right. The wheels of the vehicle had become trapped in the shifting sand dunes that blow across the border regions. They were sitting ducks for the machinegun team. There was a Task Force man firing a turret mounted 50 calibre machinegun at the ridge, but the insurgents were too well dug in. Tank sprinted behind a rock outcrop, keeping low and moving quickly for a big man. Air support was tied up providing cover at the hospital, and he had to sort this problem out on his own. The Land Rover was a sitting duck. His other units all seemed to be in similar positions taking heavy incoming fire all along the ridgeline. Tank circled the rocks and flanked the machine gunners. He could see three men. One was firing the 50 calibre, while one loaded the bullet belt into it to stop it from jamming. The other was the spotter using binoculars to locate targets. Tank carried a 40mm, M16 machinegun, which was fitted with the M203 grenade launcher beneath the main barrel. He chambered a grenade and fired, aiming for the middle man who was loading the bullets into the troublesome machinegun. The grenade left the rifle with a whooshing sound and landed right on target. The three rebels had heard the grenade launching, and turned in fear to look behind them. Three sets of terrified eyes looked into Tank's for just a second before the grenade exploded. Before the dirt had settled Tank emptied a magazine of thirty bullets into the dead men, just to make sure. The directional effect of rifle grenade's shrapnel was erratic, and many a soldier had been killed because his targets had survived the blast and returned fire. Best to be sure, kill them twice, that was Tank's motto.

He ran to the ridge and waved to the driver of the Land Rover. The men exited the vehicle and pushed it clear of the sand. They drove up the ridge and picked up Tank. He was sweating and covered in sand. He grabbed a metal flask of water and gulped greedily.

"Let's move out," said Tank over the coms.

Up until ten minutes ago you would have been forgiven for thinking today would be a normal day at the office. The early morning ride across the mountains had been tranquil enough. The Baby Bird helicopters had taken Grace and Chen ahead as the reconnaissance team. Tank and the others had driven slowly across the border in the Land Rovers bringing the main strike force with them. The air had been filled with dust, which seeped into the vehicles through every aperture. Within minutes of being in the country the dust had invaded your nose, mouth, underwear and socks. The vehicles were cramped to make room for extra ammunition and water, but Tank already wished that they had brought more. They weren't expecting to encounter such aggressive resistance this soon in the operation. They had ten vehicles carrying eight men apiece. Four of the vehicles had turret mounted 50 calibre heavy machineguns, which could bring down aircraft, and destroy enemy armoured vehicles. At the top of the ridge Tank signalled the Land Rover to stop. He counted only nine vehicles, so one was missing.

"Beagle one, sound off all Beagles," Tank ordered over the radio, "request a drone on a search mission, we are one vehicle down."

The Land Rovers cleared the tree line onto the ridge, one at a time.

"Beagle two, clear. Beagle three, clear." The other platoons sounded off in numerical order. All except Beagle eight, that had been positioned nearest to the town, about half a mile west of the hospital.

"Pilgrim father here, the drone can't find any trace of Beagle eight," came the voice from mission control, "its trackers can't be found." Each vehicle was fitted with a chip so that mission control could locate them at all times in case someone became separated from the main battle group.

Tank was becoming worried when his thoughts were interrupted by a rocket propelled grenade exploding underneath Beagle six, one-hundred yards to his left. Two more exploded close to the vehicles along the ridge and at least a dozen AK-47's and Kalashnikovs opened fire on their position. The convoy was exposed and coming under increasingly heavy fire.

"Pilgrim one, I think they know that we are here," Tank boomed jumping from the vehicle, "evasive action and full assault."

The Land Rovers deployed their men and spun their wheels in tight circles heading back into the cover of the tree line. The 50 calibre machine gunners opened fire and layed down a deadly covering fire. Empty brass cartridges showered the dusty earth as the Task Force returned fire. Tank approached the Land Rover that had been hit by the RPG and discovered its occupants returning fire from behind the cover of the machine. One man lay prone being attended to by a medic, and he was holding a bloody swab to his abdomen. As Tank approached the medic shook his head and removed the swab to reveal the wound. Intestines were clearly visible and he was bleeding profusely.

"We need to get him to that evac helicopter or he'll not make it," the medic said.

"Roger that, Pilgrim one, we need air support east of the hospital. We have one more passenger for that evac," Tank ordered, "All units prepare to follow my spearhead. I repeat, follow Beagle one."

Suddenly over the coms came an Arabic voice, and then what sounded like a reply in the same guttural dialect. Tank looked to his Lieutenant and they exchanged concerned glances. Someone had captured one of their coms units.

"I guess we know what's happened to Beagle eight," the young officer said, "poor bastards." Tank nodded as the Apache gunship roared overhead. It hovered above their position and its weapons carriage thundered into life. Hellfire missiles screamed across the sky heading toward enemy positions unseen from the ground. Air cannons pounded out thousands of rounds every minute, stripping the trees and vegetation from the earth like a huge invisible strimming machine. Tank pointed an empty hand forward and his Land Rover jerked toward the evac point, followed in an arrow formation by the other Task Force units.

CHAPTER 51
Roman Kordinski/RIP

Roman's case had been adjourned while psychiatric reports were compiled. He had been diagnosed as a recessed paranoid schizophrenic. He was capable of blending into society normally until emotional pressure was applied, and then the repressed violence surfaced. This type of personality is completely driven by whatever motivates them, and they would focus obsessively on achieving their goals, to the extent that nothing else had a value, including human life. Roman had mentally imploded, losing his businesses, his riches and his football team, which had been put into administration when his bank accounts were frozen. He just couldn't cope mentally. He sacked his long time legal advisor Alan Williams in favour of a Jewish firm. He also refused to communicate in English with the police or legal representatives from the courts. Translators were being brought to assist, but he had already attacked two of them because they had not translated what he had said exactly.

Now he was sat at the back of a special high court in Liverpool enclosed in a bullet proof compartment. The protective prison dock was made of thick clear plate-glass, which is used to glaze limousines. The agency that had been tasked with helping him was struggling to find translators who were willing to work with Kordinski.

Natasha Rasht had been sent to try to get near Roman to assess the chances of sending an assassin to kill him. She was a Muslim from Kosovo. Kosovo was a satellite state of Serbia, which in turn was part of the old Soviet Union. The Serbians were Christians, while the Kosovan people were Islamic. After the breakdown of the Soviet Union in 1991 Kosovo declared its independence several times from Serbia. Each time Serbia responded by invading Kosovo and enforcing rule upon them. Ethnic cleansing and the wholesale slaughter of Muslims was commonplace. The United Nations eventually intervened by providing a protective umbrella using American and British Air Forces. The air cover attacked Serbian ground forces repeatedly until they withdrew its soldiers from the tiny country. Natasha had been a small child orphaned by the war and given refuge in Britain. She grew up in foster homes, a foreign orphan in a foreign land. Her hatred of Christians festered over the years. When she left the social service system things became worse. She had failed miserably at school and had no qualifications. She couldn't find a job and soon realised that the only skill she had was attracting men. Her new found occupation was well paid, although not the most hygienic career. She became involved in a Chechen prostitute ring and finally felt part of a family. They were subversive, and sent finance for the Muslim rebels at home to purchase arms with. There were several Chechens being hidden amongst them who were called sleeper cells. Suicide bombers just waiting for the order to strike. Natasha wasn't one of them though, she had no intentions of killing herself, but she was more than willing to use her sexuality to gather information that aided the global Jihad. She had acquired a press pass by giving its previous owner a blow job, which gave her access to the courtroom, where she had spent two days thinking of ways to reach Roman behind his bulletproof screen. The only other people inside the dock were two burly armed policemen, and his interpreter, when they turned up. The courtroom door opened and in rushed a young woman, who was very red faced and flustered. The young woman was a part time interpreter sent by an agency, in the employee of Roman Kordinski. Natasha recognised her but she couldn't place where she had seen her before. The interpreter removed her jacket as she was ushered into the plasti-glass dock and Natasha saw the blue insignia on the pocket of her white blouse. It was the 'Golden Arches', the most recognised brand in the world. The interpreter worked full-time for McDonalds Restaurants as a shift manager. That's where Natasha had seen her before, and it was the opportunity that she had been looking for.

Christina Renilsonski was a Polish immigrant. She had travelled to the Uk when the European Union had dismantled

Britain's borders, along with a tidal wave of Eastern European migrants. Christina settled in Liverpool and began her search for work. Her first two weeks were bitterly disappointing, as she was refused work at every place that she asked. Every day she bought the city's daily newspaper, the Liverpool Echo, and every day she trawled through the situations vacancies section. Every day she received the same disappointing response, and she was beginning to wonder if the long journey west had been the right move. After a particularly gruelling day job hunting around the city, in freezing rain and high winds, she walked into the city centre McDonalds on Lord Street. It is situated just a few yards from the road that the Beatles made famous, Mathew Street. She ordered a hot cup of tea to warm her weary bones, while she dried off. The restaurant was bright and warm. The atmosphere was vibrant and exciting as tourists and locals came and went through the busy doors. Large murals of local historic tourist attractions adorned the walls, which gave the store a strong identity. It was proud to be part of the city in which it traded. Christina watched the staff working on the front counter and was amazed by the synchronicity of the operation, as the service team worked in unison to serve hundreds of hungry customers every hour. The staff seemed to be having such fun. It made Christina feel all the more isolated.

As Christina was finishing her tea a hostess approached her dressed in a red waistcoat, and carrying a tray.

"Would you like a top up dear?" said the smiling hostess whose badge introduced her as Rita. "You look soaked through, you poor thing." Surprised and impressed by the kindness she had been shown, Cristina struck up a conversation with the hostess. She was told that there were several vacancies available in the restaurant and a week later she started her first shift as a McDonalds' employee. Christina worked all the overtime that she could. She was amazed at the structured training that everyone was given, and within three months she was qualified to work on every station in the restaurant. McDonalds is a company that returns whatever is put into it tenfold, and Christina learned quickly. Within twelve months she had completed health and safety training, food hygiene programmes and management training courses. She spent the next six months learning to be a shift manager. A month after that was the proudest day of her life when she opened the restaurant's doors with her shift running manager's keys. Managing her first day shift she had to fire up and calibrate all the major pieces of equipment used in the preparation of food. She checked the use by dates of every item of stock, and checked that all the cooking and refrigeration temperatures were correct. There are a myriad of regimented systems applied to every restaurant that operated under the Golden Arches brand. That was the secret to the food giant's success, motivated staff with enthusiasm and passion. Christina positioned all her staff, checked that the trading tills all had the right money in them, and then she proudly opened the doors to her hungry public. All this was achievable at the dizzy age of nineteen. Christina loved her job and had a great relationship with her regular customers. It was whilst chatting to one regular customer one morning that she was offered extra part time work acting as an interpreter. Polish was her first language but she was also fluent in Russian. Her grandmother had been Russian and spoke to her in Russian from an early age. She worked regularly for the agency as migrant numbers were steadily rising. The need for interpreters grew accordingly, and the money was a welcome supplement to her income.

The job of translating for a Russian criminal at the Crown Court was offered to her at short notice, but because it's situated just a hundred yards from the restaurant, she agreed, finished her breakfast shift at McDonalds, and headed to the court with her coat on over her work uniform. Christina was five minutes late when she rushed into the courtroom.

The morning session was dull as the opposing barristers argued legal technicalities to and fro. Christina translated the narrative into Russian for her client, who appeared to be disinterested to say the least. He also seemed to be following proceedings himself anyway, which confused her. At lunch time the prison guards led Roman Kordinski downstairs to his holding cell and unlocked the plasti-glass dock to allow Christina to leave. She headed for the square outside and grabbed a coffee from a kiosk there. She sat down at a small table and lit a cigarette. Christina smiled at a face that was vaguely familiar to her. The woman returned her smile and walked toward her table. Christina noticed her press pass, and remembered her from the courtroom gallery.

"Hi there, you're from McDonalds aren't you?" the woman

smiled and took a seat opposite Christina.

"Yes I am," Christina answered recognising that her accent wasn't local to Liverpool or England. The two women got chatting about their various adventures arriving in the UK, and how they were enjoying their new home. Natasha obviously lied through her pearly white teeth as she gained Christina's trust. The hour adjournment flew by as the women chatted beneath the stony faced statue of Queen Victoria, which dominated the square outside the Crown Court. They finished another cigarette each and then headed back into the courtroom.

As they approached the courtroom doors Natasha grabbed Christina's elbow.

"Listen we should meet up for a glass of wine after the session this afternoon," Natasha said smiling.

"Definitely, I'd like that," answered Christina, opening the courtroom doors. The guards were leading Roman up the steep steps from the cells below. They spotted Christina and opened the side panel of the plasti-glass dock to allow her entry to her seat.

"Look, I think this afternoon will be a long session, take this I'll get another one. You can't leave the dock once you're in," said Natasha handing Christina a bottle of red Gatorade.

"Thanks, that's a great idea," said Christina as she entered the dock. The guards locked the bulletproof panel behind her. She took her seat next to Roman Kordinski, between two armed guards in the transparent plasti-glass cubicle. Christina took her coat off and noticed her new friend Natasha had left the courtroom already, which she thought was odd. Maybe she had gone to replace the drink that she had thoughtfully given to her. Never mind, she would see her later. She picked up her drink bottle and thought she could feel a minute vibration for just a millisecond, before the liquid gel explosive inside it detonated. The two guards, Christina and Roman Kordinski died instantly. The armoured plasti-glass cubicle remained intact which concentrated the blast-wave inside, it looked like someone had put a giant frog in a massive liquidiser and then switched it on.

CHAPTER 52

Yasser Ahmed/ Kizlyar

Yasser had been returning from the small town centre of Kizlyar when he spotted the Land Rover in the trees. There had been a glint of sunshine reflecting off metal or glass in the distance that caught his attention. Whatever it was, it shouldn't be there. He and a small group of Mujahideen had been buying munitions and other supplies. Arranging drinking water and a sustainable food supply for the coming weeks in the mountains was difficult. The bulk of his force had remained nearby the hospital. The hospital was heavily guarded and his men could relax safely. The Land Rover that he had spotted was unmarked, and the soldiers inside were wearing non-descript uniforms without any identifying insignia. Yasser knew that they weren't Russian troops for certain. Their weapons were too modern. Yasser and his men took cover behind a low stonewall and watched the soldiers through binoculars. Yasser whispered an order to a lieutenant and he scurried off toward the village. Five minutes later he returned with three young boys, who looked about seven or eight. The boys were spoken to sternly and they nodded their dirty faces in agreement. They were even more compliant when Yasser broke a chocolate bar and shared it amongst them.

The three amigos skipped along the dusty dirt road toward the foreign soldiers, who were still sat unaware in their vehicle. The chattering boys were only spotted by the soldiers when they were yards away, and they weren't deemed a serious threat. It was only when the first boy threw a primed hand grenade into the open window that the soldiers realised that they had been duped, and by then it was too late.

Yasser and his men picked through the wreckage of the Land Rover. One of the soldiers was still alive, and despite shooting him five times in the legs he wouldn't divulge his mission before he died from shock. Yasser knew they were Special Forces, there were not even wristwatches to indicate their origin. They carried nothing that would divulge their nationality. Beneath the rear wheel arch Yasser found the vehicle identification tracking device and he smashed it with a rock. They removed their weapons and the radio coms unit, and headed overland toward the hospital facility. Yasser knew there would be more soldiers, although he couldn't really understand how they knew that he was here. That's the only reason anyone would send special forces into Dagestan, to capture or kill Yasser Ahmed, he thought.

As they neared the minefields the sound of a fierce fire-fight reached them. Heavy machinegun fire and loud explosions retorted across the hills in the distance. Yasser scanned the ridgeline in the distance through his binoculars, and he saw the familiar shape of unmanned drones above Kizlyar. The huge wasp like shape of an Apache helicopter gunship appeared into view with its guns blazing. Whoever they were looking for they had sent a formidable force to find them. He signalled his men and they moved forward carefully picking their way through the minefield. Yasser's guide skipped over the ground with a confident gait, because he had travelled this path many times before. They reached the top of a low hilly knoll and watched the battle raging below them, lying in the dirt on their bellies. A convoy of armoured Land Rovers was speeding across the dusty hills toward a road that ran along a rocky ridgeline. Roof mounted 50calibre heavy machineguns were tearing up Mujahideen positions all along the ridge. An Apache gunship was wreaking havoc firing its deadly payload with frightening accuracy. The Mujahideen were being blown to pieces.

Yasser turned the glasses toward the hospital building and saw two Mujahideen carrying a casualty across a shell hole ridden plateau. He focused the glasses and gritted his teeth in anger as he realised that the men weren't all that they first appeared to be. The casualty was a woman of Middle Eastern appearance, and it dawned on him that she was the focus of this incursion. The Land Rovers reached the road and parked in a circular formation. They continued laying down covering fire with the 50 calibres. The soldiers inside the Land Rovers exited the vehicles and adopted positions of safety to fire from, to protect Faz and Chen as they approached the evac site. There was little resistance left. The Apache flew low over the ridgeline and landed in the centre of the Land Rovers, and the side door was slid open. Two Special Forces men carried their injured colleague and placed him on a stretcher inside the helicopter. They ducked low beneath the rotor blades as they returned to their vehicle.

Yasser scanned the Land Rovers and stopped suddenly on the lead vehicle. Stood by the passenger door holding an M16 on his hip was the big agent that he had seen with his brother Mustapha. He had seen them near the Anfield football stadium in Liverpool. Yasser thought he had been killed in a bomb blast, but he was obviously alive and well. He stared at the bald agent and saw the look of concern on his face. The bald man was looking worriedly toward the two disguised men, who were carrying the girl, and shouting encouragement to them as they neared the Land Rovers. Yasser focused again on the trio in the minefield. The black skinned man was a woman. He could see that clearly now. Her attractive chiselled features were exposed as the downdraft from the rotor blades blew her headscarf from her face. Three agents broke cover and grabbed Jeannie Kellesh. They rushed her into the waiting helicopter were she was taken by aircrew and laid in a canvas gurney. Grace Farrington ran toward Tank's position, where she crouched down next to him against the Land Rover. Tank squeezed her arm tightly and they exchanged a glance, which communicated their affectionate concern for each other in the face of danger. Chen scurried next to them and nodded at Tank. Tank nodded back to him and smiled. They had done well so far, they had the girl. Even though they had lost men they had removed several dozen extremists from circulation. As Tank was assessing their situation he saw a muzzle flash from a knoll in the distance. A second later Grace Farrington was slammed into the Land Rover's door by a high velocity bullet which hit her in the chest.

CHAPTER 53

New York/
Zareta Katharina

Madison Square Garden, 2008, is the third incarnation of the world famous sporting venue. Situated above the Penn Street railway station in the centre of Manhattan, it's the ideal venue for a large political rally. Political rallies don't get any bigger than when the President of the United States of America is attending. She had the remarkable role of being the first female president, and the first black president combined. If she had been gay too, then all the bases would have been covered. Hilary Rice had achieved the top job in American politics by appealing to the electorate's desire for change. The majority of her voters were America's female population, and a large percentage of the country's black vote.

Today Hilary Rice had a dilemma. She was the key speaker at a woman's rally, which was attended predominantly by ethnic minorities. The problem was that a foiled attack on Florida's Disney parks had raised security status to critical. The successful assassination of a Jewish Russian exile that was in the custody of, and under the protection of the British Counter Terrorist Agencies, underlined the seriousness of the situation. It appeared that liquid explosive had been used in both bombs. There was no way to stop all liquids coming into proximity with the president. It was also widely believed that the attackers were of Chechen origin, and female. The general consensus of opinion was that the attacks were of the genre favoured by Yasser Ahmed and his 'Ishmael's Axe' group.

The president could not abort the conference speech as too many sections of the community would be offended, or made to feel isolated. She most definitely could not take the risk of becoming Yasser Ahmed's sitting duck either. Video presentation teams were brought in and a ten minute film was produced. The President narrated the film which incorporated successful women in America's industries with, community, business and judicial role models. The short film was designed to be a shot in the arm for the audience. A heart thumping sound track was added, and fireworks would be arranged as a finale to the film. The plan was to stamp the president's presence on the memories of everyone that attended, without her actually saying a word. The key to the plan was deploying the president's stand in look-alike. With everyone focused on the big screen the stunt double would be not be scrutinised by the audience. Stunt doubles had been used throughout history to keep important leaders safe from assassination attempts. Churchill, General Montgomery and Adolf Hitler himself all used look-alikes several times through the Second World War. More recently Saddam Husain used several doubles to ease his paranoia. Sometimes it was because an assassination attempt was imminent, but the plan was not known. Other times it was used to flush out co-conspirators from within their own ranks.

While Hilary Rice made her movie and prepped her look-alike, Zareta was making preparations of her own in a motel room. She had been given money and detailed plans to follow. She had begun by going to a supermarket and buying a roll of polythene ice-cube bags, and some duct tape. Zareta filled the ice-cube bags with Tovex liquid gel explosive, and then taped it around her breasts and back. Beneath her clothing the lethal polythene roll felt like fat. If she was to be frisked then nothing untoward would be suspected. She wore a bright red ornate silk robe and head scarf to match, which was the traditional formal attire of Indian Hindu women. Zareta painted a red spot on her forehead and glued a tiny diamante stud into the centre of it to finish the disguise. She felt nothing as she prepared herself. Zareta had long since lost her self esteem, and everyone she loved was dead, stolen from her. Her heart was numb, cold and cruel. Any compassion that she had was ripped from when she watched her sons murdered. Now all she wanted was to join them, and this last act of destruction was her passport to everlasting peace.

Zareta placed a mobile phone into her purse, placed a silk shawl around her shoulders and stepped out of her hotel. The hotel was called the Penn Towers, and was across the street from the station that shared its name. Taxis and limousines lined the street dropping off their passengers. The steps, which led into the Madison Square Garden, were fifty yards away, and were awash with women from every continent. There was a heavy uniformed police presence all around the building. National dress and formal costumes were the order of the day and every effort had been given to this prestigious occasion by its attendees. Zareta saw the women arriving, all excited and chattering to each other. She recognised several women wearing the traditional dress of her country, and it saddened her. She felt incredibly alone as she pulled her shawl tightly around her. The wind chilled her to the bone as she stepped into the road. Tyres squealed and a car horn blared making her jump backward in fright. The car stopped just inches short of Zareta, and the driver opened his window and hurled abuse at her. Zareta stared at the driver blankly before setting off again on unsteady legs. As she passed the bonnet of the car confused and frightened she stepped blindly into the next lane. Traffic screamed to a halt again as another car stopped just short of hitting her. Zareta realised that she was getting the jitters. She was walking aimlessly to her death, but she was putting her plan in jeopardy. She had to get a grip, but her mind felt like it had turned to fudge. She couldn't think straight because she was so scared.

A traffic cop noticed the commotion and walked toward the stationary cars.

"Are you ok lady?" the cop asked brashly, "do you have a death wish or something? The pedestrian crossing is just ten yards away for cripes sake."

He approached the vacant Asian woman and grabbed her roughly by the arm, trying to guide her back to the pavement. A symphony of different car horns blared again as drivers lost their patience with the woman. The policeman held up his hand to the angry drivers as he pushed Zareta back toward the hotel side of the road. She allowed herself to be pushed by the lawman, and it took her back to that day on the bridge when she had lost her sons and her dignity. Zareta had had enough. She couldn't go on any more. She felt like she was walking through treacle. The policeman leaned close to her face and she smelt stale cigarettes and whisky. Although she saw his lips move she couldn't understand what he was saying. He sneered at her with a twisted smile, and Zareta looked into his soul as she triggered her bomb, ending her sadness forever.

CHAPTER 54

Grace Farrington/Tank

Tank opened his mouth in a silent scream as Grace was blown off her feet by the bullet that smashed into her chest. Her battle vest took much of the impact and spread the shockwave through its specially designed material. The bullet was an armour piercing 76mm round and it compromised the vest, and had penetrated her chest just above the left breast. The bullet had been flattened as it impacted with the battle vest, making the wound beneath it wider and more ragged. Dark blood poured from the wound, which indicated that the spleen had been ruptured. Chen quickly pulled a field dressing from Tank's webbing and applied pressure to the wound. Faz's eyes were wide open in shock. A second bullet ripped through her right bicep muscle and pinged off the Land Rover door. The ricochet looped high in air before dropping onto Tank's leg. The sight of the flattened slug covered in Grace's blood and tissue shocked him into action. Grace's eyes started to glaze over and her dark pupils were dilating.

"Stay with me Grace," he said as he picked her up in his big arms and sprinted to the Apache. The medics jumped from the departing helicopter and went to work on her wounds while Tank held her. They took her from him and put her into the aircraft. Tank watched through tears as the rotor blades increased their speed and the Apache climbed steeply hundreds of feet every second, taking his Grace with them.

"Put everything we have onto that hill," Tank ordered with a venom in his voice that defied question, "Pilgrim one where is the drone? Put everything it has got onto the knoll 300 yards due east of the evac zone."

The truck mounted 50 calibres turned their deadly barrage onto the knoll, and the first two foot of rock and soil was blown to dust and smithereens in seconds. The drone flew over their position and two Napalm filled Hellfire missiles screamed from beneath its wings. The knoll turned into a plume of boiling flames, which tumbled and rolled upward to form a familiar mushroom cloud.

"Pilgrim one the drone is picking up four fugitives one hundred yards from the knoll, seeking permission to engage," said the voice from mission control. They were here to extract Jeannie Kellesh by any means necessary. Enemy soldiers taking flight were not legitimate targets.

"Negative pilgrim one," Tank replied, "they're mine."

Tank climbed into the Land Rover, and his men did likewise in silence. The sight of Grace Farrington taking two hits had knocked the stuffing out of every soldier there. The Land Rover wheels span in the dust as the driver gave it full torque, and it lurched toward the escaping Mujahideen.

"Pilgrim one, the other side of the knoll is charted as minefields Tank," said the static voice from mission control. Tank didn't reply. The driver of the vehicle glanced at Tank momentarily, but he chose not to comment. Tank chambered a new clip into his M16 and filled the grenade slide. Chen and the men in the rear were doing similar in silence.

"How long have we got that drone for?" Tank asked Chen. He looked at a radio control panel fixed to the rear bulkhead of the vehicle.

"Ten minutes at the most," Chen replied. The drone was running low on fuel and at 15 million dollars apiece it needed to return safely. They rounded the knoll and Tank sighted the men running across barren brush land. There was very little cover, and although it was some distance from the hospital, bomb craters pockmarked the area. The men seemed to be following a narrow trail through the mined scrubland. From their elevated position Tank and his men could see the route that had been carved through the scrub clearly. To stray from the path would be fatal. Tank chambered a grenade and fired. The grenade whooshed over the heads of the escaping men and exploded fifty yards in front of them, on the path. The men crouched to take cover, and they turned to see where their attackers were firing from. Tank raised his binoculars and looked directly into the dusty face of Yasser Ahmed. The veins in his temple filled to bursting point and the muscles in his jaw twitched visibly. Yasser and his men stood and scrambled forward again, running for their lives. Tank pointed both fingers along the line of vehicles and then made looping signs with his hands. He had communicated that his men should fire in front of them. Grenades whizzed skyward and 50 calibres raked the wilderness in front of the escaping men. Without deliberating the four men ran in separate directions, leaving the safe path through the minefield.

Anti-personnel mines fall into two categories, blast mines and shrapnel mines. The majority are called bounding Omni-directional mines. Usually about the size of a shoe polish tin they are triggered by the weight of its victim standing on it. Once triggered a small charge ignites a propellant, which launches the mine upward to around waist height, where it explodes causing the maximum damage to whoever is in the shrapnel range. Blast mines are different in that they remain beneath the earth when they explode, and rely on a directed shaped charge causing horrific injuries to one combatant.

Yasser's guide stumbled through the scrub terrified by the barrage that had been laid down in front of them. Sweat trickled into his eyes stinging them and blurring his vision. He wiped his sweaty brow and tripped over a tree root. He fell headlong onto the dirt jarring his elbows painfully as he landed. He tried to stand up. The last thing he heard was the click whir sound of a fragmentation mine. The small metal disc jumped out of the ground and exploded next to his face.

One of Yasser's men saw and heard the explosion and froze, frightened by the sight of the guide's sticky end. He held his hands above his head in surrender. Tank saw the man gesturing that he was surrendering and he looked at him through the binoculars. It wasn't Yasser Ahmed. Tank fired half a dozen bullets around the feet of the stationary man, forcing him to take flight again. He made it exactly twelve feet before he detonated a blast mine, which tore both his legs off at the knees. His screams could be heard a long way off as he rolled in agony in the dirt. He rolled over a second mine, which launched his shattered body twenty-foot into the air, and silenced him permanently.

Yasser was close behind, but to the right of the remaining rebel, when he appeared to complete an involuntary cartwheel in the air. The blast wave hit Yasser and knocked him from his feet into the dust. Tank held his hand in the air and the barrage ceased. Only Yasser remained alive in the killing field. He picked himself up slowly and dusted the dirt from his face and mouth. Tank focused on him through the binoculars. It was Yasser, no doubt about it. He appeared to be smiling. Yasser removed a 9mm Luger from his belt, and chambered a round. Tank dropped to his knees and raised the M16 to his shoulder in what seemed like slow motion. Yasser raised the pistol toward his own head. If this was where it was going to end then it would be by his own hand, not that of the Kufur. Tank steadied the M16 and took aim. The Luger arced passed Yasser's shoulder and the barrel twisted toward his temple. Yasser closed his eyes as Tank fired.

CHAPTER 55

Terrorist Task Force/Liverpool
(Six months later)

Grace Farrington hadn't opened her eyes since she was placed on the Apache helicopter. The surgeons had removed what was left of her spleen, which left her susceptible to infections. The shattered bones in her arm and chest had knitted together months ago, and would cause no more problems if she ever regained consciousness. She had lost a chunk of bicep muscle, but even that had healed well enough. The problems were internal. Her kidneys were weak from blood infections, and despite all the drugs and treatment she was still in a coma. Tank visited her every day before and after work. He talked to her for hours on end about work and life in general, but he mostly talked to her about what they would do together when she woke up. He had never said I love you enough when she was awake, and now he couldn't stop saying it. His heart felt heavy with regret for the things they hadn't done yet. In the back of his mind he suspected that his one true soul mate was gone forever.

"I won't ask you to marry me," he had whispered to her with a tear in his eye one day, "because then you'll never wake up! And I want you to wake Grace, wake up and talk to me babe."

He missed her and wished that he had never agreed to the mission. She probably would have shot him if he had protested anyway, but he felt responsible.

The Saudi girl Jeannie Kellesh had been returned to her family, which eased tensions in the Middle East. They had lost good men in the process, and Grace Farrington was very poorly. She was critically ill in fact, and the longer she stayed unconscious the less chance she had of making it without incurring permanent brain damage. Tank knew in his heart of hearts that a full recovery was unlikely if she lived at all. Whether she lived or died was in the lap of the gods and only time would tell.

CHAPTER 56

Yasser Ahmed

The American government had legal claim to Yasser Ahmed despite the fact that it was British Special Forces that had captured him. They still had first claim on him for his planning and execution of the first Soft Target campaign. In the minefield at Kizlyar, Tank had put three rounds into his arm and shoulder, stopping his suicide attempt. He had been flown to a military hospital in Istanbul, and handed over to the Americans. Tank sat next to him on his stretcher all the way through the flight. Every time Yasser looked like he was about to pass out or drift to sleep Tank punched him in the wounded arm. Eventually the medical staff attended to him, doing their best to patch him up. There had been extensive damage to his upper arm and shoulder, and despite several attempts to knit the bones with metal pins there seemed to be little improvement. Not long afterward Tank was informed that Yasser had contracted gangrene in his wounds, which resulted in the amputation of his arm at the shoulder.

From there, the art of extraordinary rendition had been applied to its extreme by his American captors. Yasser was processed for six months into what was called his debrief. Bad luck or good fortune brought him to be held for a time at a political prison in the north of Chechnya. He was in the same cell that his unfortunate younger brother had occupied before his death. Yasser had been there for days before he had noticed the scratching in the plaster on the wall. The names of dozens of poor souls were carved at various angles around the dark dank cell, some carved, and some smeared in excrement or blood. There was a circular deep stinking hole cut into the floor in one corner of the room, which ran into an open sewer. The waste and excrement of a hundred prisoners flowed through his cell on its way to a cess pit beyond the thick walls of the medieval prison. He spent his waking hours being tortured by methods he had never dreamed of in his worst nightmares. His sleeping hours were spent dwelling on the pain his amputated arm still caused him and the myriad of new injuries that they added to every day.

One morning daylight entered through a small barred window, which was set high in the wall of his cell. They usually came for him soon after but today they hadn't come at all. The dull light illuminated the inside of his cell, and for the first time he read the desperate graffiti on the walls. There were several different languages, some he understood and some he didn't. He focused on two words and a name written in Arabic. He couldn't turn his gaze away from it, as hot stinging tears ran down his cheeks.

BAKRAH AK'E
Mustapha Ahmed

In English it read I HATE MY BROTHER. By Mustapha Ahmed, it appeared to have been written smeared with his own blood.

EPILOGUE

Five years on/Liverpool

Dave Simmons was drunk and broke. He had spent most of life the same way, but he was approaching rock bottom. Simms had once owned a share in a busy wine bar in the Preston area, which suited his drinking habits, until his unscrupulous partner had screwed him. Left bankrupt and destitute Simmons soon found that his friends weren't his friends at all; they had just been hangers on. The fat happy faces that crowded around him when he was buying a round of drinks were gone. In the space of six months he lost his business, his wife and children and his pride. Since then he had drifted from crap job to crap job, crap relationship to crap relationship. The few good people he ever met soon tired of his self loathing alcoholism. Simmons sought solace in the bottom of a cider bottle.

Dave Simmons staggered toward a large brick building that was undergoing renovations. He was near the River Mersey and the building looked like one of the old motor housings that used to hold the exhaust fans that serviced the traffic tunnels. The wind was howling and rain was driving horizontally into his stubbly face. He pulled his coat tighter to keep out the wind, and noticed the vomit down the front of it. Things were getting desperate, because he couldn't remember being sick at all. Simmons climbed over the hoardings to escape the rain, and found himself in what must have once been the control room. He pushed the broken door closed trying to keep the wind out and looked for somewhere cosy to sleep. To the left was a narrow access tunnel. He headed for the tunnel, thinking that he could sleep there out of sight of any patrolling security guards. Fifty yards down the tunnel he found an equipment cupboard, which was covered in dust, and opened the door. The door creaked as he pulled it, and inside covered in cobwebs was a fire blanket, and he shook it before wrapping it round his shivering body. He stared past the cobwebs into the dark and saw there was a holdall in the corner. He pulled it free of the dust and spider webs. He opened the zip and stared inside. His eyes widened at the contents of the bag. Inside covered in dust was exactly three hundred thousand reasons why his life had just got better.

Authors' Note;

All the places in the story are real, but there may be some artistic license applied to make them fit the plot. Any similarities to any persons not already in the public domain are purely coincidence. All the events in this story took place at different times in different countries, but are real. Every organisation in the story actually exists, although some have been called something different.

Authors' thanks;

First and foremost thank you to my beautiful wife Ruth for the faith and support you have shown throughout both Soft Target projects. Without your endless love and encouragement neither book would have come to fruition. If I were to write love stories instead of thrillers then they would all be about you x.

To my family

Mum Jean, brothers Stanley-Timothy and Graham-Congelous (he doesn't like being called that, but it's his name!!) All my big sisters, Pamela, Libby, Kath, Jeanette (not sure who my favourite is, so they are in age order!!) My brother-in-law Alan who is guinea pig number one. Thank you for your support and daft e-mails, I love you all very much.

To my friends everywhere who have supported me by buying the book and not saying it was crap, and who kept me laughing in the pub and keep telling me to get a proper job.

To my mate Bobby for not getting arrested during your awful leaflet distribution, and your help and support at book signings! Ta, mate.

Thanks to everyone at Radio Merseyside, Wire FM, Radio Manchester, The Manchester Evening News, The Liverpool Echo, The Warrington Guardian, The Holyhead and Anglesey Mail, The St. Helens Reporter, and Limited Edition Magazine, for your support.

Thanks to FBB Commandant Chris Barker, and his storm troopers Mike Stout and John Platt enough said.